LOCAL
GIRL
MISSING

BOOKS BY LISA REGAN

LOCAL GIRL MISSING

LISA REGAN

bookouture

Published by Bookouture in 2022

An imprint of Storyfire Ltd.
Carmelite House
50 Victoria Embankment
London EC4Y 0DZ

www.bookouture.com

Copyright © Lisa Regan, 2022

Lisa Regan has asserted her right to be identified
as the author of this work.

All rights reserved. No part of this publication may be reproduced, stored in
any retrieval system, or transmitted, in any form or by any means, electronic,
mechanical, photocopying, recording or otherwise, without the prior written
permission of the publishers.

ISBN: 978-1-80314-540-2
eBook ISBN: 978-1-80314-539-6

This book is a work of fiction. Names, characters, businesses, organizations,
places and events other than those clearly in the public domain, are either
the product of the author's imagination or are used fictitiously. Any
resemblance to actual persons, living or dead, events or locales is entirely
coincidental.

For Jessie Botterill, who makes all things possible

CHAPTER 1

She is eight years old the first time she hears all the different ways bones can break. Some crack. Some crunch like gravel underfoot. Some even pop. She hears other sounds that day, too. She only went into the garage to see if her dad had fixed the flat tire on her bike, like he promised. He makes lots of promises, but he doesn't always keep them. Usually, Mom ends up doing whatever it is he promised to do, apologizing for him the entire time. This was an important promise, though, and he said it three times on three different occasions.

"Yes, I'll fix your bike. I promise."

But when she gets to the garage, she doesn't see her dad. Instead, there is a group of men. Some of them she recognizes although she doesn't know their names. Others she has never seen. They're gathered around something on the floor. At first, her heart lifts with excitement. Her bike! They've come to help her dad fix the tire. A promise kept. Maybe he waited so long to fix it because he needed help.

When she hears someone cry out in agony, she realizes that she's wrong. Looking to the right of the men, she sees her bike leaning against the garage wall, its front tire still deflated. For a moment she is confused. Then she hears another sound. A moist *thwap* followed by a noise like her water gun makes when she sprays it upward and arcs the water across the wall. After that comes a gurgling.

Inside her chest, something pinches. It feels funny when she breathes.

The men haven't seen her yet, and she is afraid of what will happen if they do. The door back to the house seems miles away and yet, she can't go forward. The men are talking now, their postures loosening, and she's afraid they'll turn around and see her. Without thought, her feet carry her into a corner of the garage opposite her bike. She finds a hiding place behind a snowblower and folds herself down into the smallest shape her body can make. She concentrates on the pinching feeling inside her body and the way her breath seems to hitch and catch when she tries to take in air.

That's when the sound of bones breaking starts.

It feels like days before it stops; before the men disperse. She can't feel her legs or the cold concrete beneath them. In fact, everything feels numb, like it's a dream. She wonders if it is a dream when one of the men appears, looking down at her, his big bushy eyebrows knit with concern. She's not even scared when he reaches down and lifts her from her hiding place. She recognizes him as one of her dad's good friends. She doesn't know his real name. Her dad calls him Mug. She knows it's a nickname because she once asked her mom why Dad's friend was named after a cup. "It's a nickname, Pea. Kind of like how I call you Pea because you're a Sweet Pea."

"Did you see that, sweetheart?" Mug asks softly, quietly.

Pea doesn't answer. She doesn't want to talk about *that*. She just wants her bike fixed. She just wants to go back inside to her toys and forget the garage even exists.

He carries her like her dad used to carry her when she was just a toddler, with a forearm tucked under her upper thighs like a bar. Back in the house, everything is silent and sunny and warm. He sets her down on the couch, careful with her like she's made of glass.

"Listen, sweetheart," he says. "How about we don't talk to your parents about that, okay? They've got a lot on their minds, and they'll be upset if they knew you saw that."

Pea nods because she doesn't even want to think about *that*. Not ever. As far as she's concerned, *that* never happened.

"Good girl," says Mug and pats her on the head.

CHAPTER 2

Josie's hands ached from gripping the steering wheel so hard. The fog ahead was an impenetrable mist, swallowing everything around them. A glance at the speedometer told her they were only traveling about fifteen miles an hour. At this rate, it would take them hours to cross the remaining five miles to their house. Weak daylight fought its way through the thick gray haze all around them. Maybe the fog would burn off by then. The digital display on her console reminded her it was almost seven thirty in the morning. Her eyes felt dry and gritty. She and her husband, Noah, had been traveling for over twelve hours, and they were both exhausted.

From the passenger's seat, Noah grumbled, "We should have stayed in St. Thomas another day."

"And risk getting stuck there in the middle of a hurricane?" Josie said. "No thank you."

"Being trapped in a hotel room together wouldn't be so bad," he replied.

Josie felt his warm palm on her thigh and smiled, thinking of the week they'd just spent in a beachfront resort.

The thought of all those hours spent naked, just the two of them, the entire world a distant memory, brought a happy flush to her cheeks. Eighteen months after their wedding they had finally made it to St. Thomas for a proper honeymoon. They both worked for the Denton Police Department, Josie as a detective and Noah as a lieutenant. Denton was a small but bustling city nestled among the mountains of Central Pennsylvania. Although the main area of the city lay in a valley, much of the rest of it was spread out among winding mountain roads like the one they were on now.

They had arrived by plane in Philadelphia two hours ago after several delayed flights. They had almost made it home via the interstate before encountering a series of accidents caused by the dense fog. It had been Josie's idea to get off the highway and take the backroads into Denton. She knew them intimately, but still, the fog posed a bigger challenge than either of them had anticipated.

Noah squeezed her thigh. "Just pull over. We'll wait for it to burn off. That's the safest option. Plus, I can think of at least one thing we could do in this car to pass the time."

Josie smiled, seriously considering taking him up on his offer. Their jobs kept them busy and exhausted. Sometimes the brutality of the things they saw each day was too much for either of them to bear. Many days, it was all they could do just to survive. The week away had done wonders for them. She had never felt so connected to him, and the electricity between them was more palpable than it had been when they'd first started dating. As exhausted as she was, every cell in her body yearned to get lost in his touch.

As if reading her mind, he added, "Just to be absolutely clear, I was talking about sleep."

She gave him a brief glance, noting his devilish grin, and laughed. "I bet I could change your mind."

"Bring it on," he said.

But even pulling over was dicey, given that they could only see two feet ahead of them, and the fact that this particular road dipped and climbed the side of a large mountain. There were ridges she dared not risk getting too close to. Josie checked her mental map of the area, considering how many miles they'd been on this particular road. If her calculations were correct, they were close to a wide, grassy area to their right where they could safely pull off for an hour or two.

"I might be able to pull over up here," Josie began, but then a sound pierced the dense vapor all around them.

"Did you hear that?" asked Noah, rolling his window down.

"It sounded like a scream," Josie said. She punched a button on the console, turning off the low hum of the heater. The car continued rolling forward. She kept her eyes ahead but strained to listen.

Another shriek sounded, closer. Then a figure streaked through the fog in front of the car. All Josie could make out was a lithe frame, a flash of white clothing, and long, dark hair. She slammed on the brakes, but there was no need. The figure was gone. The mist devoured everything.

Noah put his hand on the dash. "What the hell was that?"

"I think it was a girl," said Josie.

They listened for a beat, but no more sounds came.

"Pull over," Noah told her. "Anywhere."

The car lurched forward a few more feet and Josie carefully guided it onto the gravel shoulder of the road, praying there was enough room for them and no drop-off. Noah said, "Leave the four-way blinkers on so we don't lose the car in this crap."

They got out of the vehicle, turning slowly in each direction, trying to see something, anything.

The world was eerily silent. It was as if the fog had muted everything. The weak beginnings of daylight barely penetrated it. Josie couldn't even hear birdsong. Noah pointed to their left. "She went that way."

They walked across the road, Josie in the lead. "Hello?" she called out.

On the opposite side of the road, they were met with several thick tree trunks. "This is forest," Josie said. "It goes for miles until it comes out by the old textile mill near Denton East High."

They took a few more steps into the trees, both of them calling out for the girl.

No answer.

Josie turned back toward the road. She could just make out the blinking yellow glow of their car's hazard lights across the road. "The real question is, what was she running from?"

Noah turned away from the trees, walking back toward their car. Josie followed. Beyond their vehicle was a slight dip in the terrain. A large grassy area sprawled before another treeline. She and Noah picked their way across the dewy grass, still only able to see a few feet in front of them.

The faint sound of music floated through the air. As they continued on, Josie made out some of the words from a newly released song by a debut teen artist called Vyla Grace. It was popular and had become ubiquitous, played on the radio and television. Josie knew the words without ever having tried to learn them.

Stay or die, tell the lie. You don't love me.

"This way," Noah said. He took her hand and pulled her along, changing direction to follow the music.

> *Keep me here. You don't care. You don't*
> *love me.*

The low thrum of a car engine became audible. Someone had pulled over—or had they crashed?

Something crunched beneath Josie's foot. Then slipped. Only Noah's hand kept her upright. When she regained her balance, she looked down to see she'd slipped on a make-up compact. Its mirror was cracked, and broken chunks of the ivory powder spilled into the grass. They kept going, following a trail of items: a blue-handled hairbrush with thick brown hairs tangled in its teeth; a tube of pink lip gloss; a cell phone lying face down, its thick pink rubber cover in the shape of a bottle. The words "Boys' Tears" stretched across its label.

The music grew louder.

> *I'll tell your lie, tell your lie until I die from*
> *your savage heart. You don't love me.*

Then came the sound of grunting, rustling. Noah opened his mouth to call out, but Josie squeezed his hand, indicating for him to remain silent. She zeroed in on the sound, to their right. Pointing in that direction, she motioned for Noah to follow her through the fog. As the noises became clearer—the song, the car engine, and what sounded like a struggle—Josie's heart did a double tap.

In the distance, red brake lights glowed through the hazy mist. Beyond them, Josie first saw two feet, clad in a pair of pink-checkered sneakers. The markings of their soles identified them as a brand popular among high school students. Blue jeans.

Then the full tableau came into view.

The girl lay on her back. A man in a light gray suit straddled her, his hands wrapped around her throat. "Where is it?" he snarled. "Where the hell is it?"

"Hey!" Josie shouted, tearing her hand from Noah's. She lunged toward the man, throwing her entire body into him. Together, they tumbled away from the girl. Landing on her back, Josie felt the dew soak through her T-shirt and wet her hair. The man's weight was heavy on top of her, his labored breath hot against her ear. She was vaguely aware of Noah's voice calling her name. Using her hips, she bucked the man off. He didn't fight her, instead rolling to the side and climbing to his feet. He staggered away from her.

"Stop!" Josie called, springing up. Out of instinct, her right hand reached for her pistol, but it wasn't there. She wasn't on duty. She was returning from her damn honeymoon.

The man froze. He looked over his shoulder at her. Mist swirled around him but only a few feet away, his face was clearly visible. Late thirties, early forties, Josie estimated. Dark hair in disarray. Stubble along his jaw. Brown eyes wild with panic. Droplets of blood stood out against the white of his shirt.

"Denton Police," Josie said. "Stop right there."

His skin turned bloodless. Horror crept into his expression, his eyes going wide. Then he turned and ran.

CHAPTER 3

From her periphery, Josie saw Noah drop to his knees beside the girl. Ahead, the mist threatened to swallow the man's form entirely. Josie ran after him, trying to keep him in view. He flew away from the road and into the woods, Josie on his heels. She lost sight of him as they entered the forest, but his labored breath and the sounds of twigs snapping beneath his feet kept her on his trail. The air was thick and damp. Within seconds, Josie was wet, her sweat mingling with the moisture in the air.

"Stop!" she called after him.

He was obscured by the fog, but Josie knew she was closing in on him because she could hear him straining to breathe. His footsteps grew heavier. A slight incline in the terrain slowed him down, allowing her to get close enough to see him again. The gray of his suit blended well with the gray morning haze, but his dark hair was easy to spot.

"Stop!"

He looked over his shoulder, as if startled by her proximity, but he didn't slow down. Instead, his arms pumped harder, the flaps of his jacket fluttering at his sides. Around them, the trees thinned out, giving way to large boulders. Checking her mental map of the area, Josie realized they were coming up on a ridge that overlooked Roaring Creek. It was a large, wide creek that cut a path through the mountains and emptied out near Denton's East Bridge. The fall from their current elevation would be dangerous except that all the creeks in and around the city were high and swollen with the recent onslaught of early-October rain.

"There's a cliff ahead of you," Josie yelled. "You have to stop. You'll fall!"

She saw hesitation in his gait. He stumbled, his dress shoes sliding in the mud and undergrowth. Then he continued on, climbing up onto a large boulder. He stopped, teetering on its edge. Josie wondered if he could see the creek below or if the drop-off revealed nothing but gray, just like everything else around them. She dared not get closer to him. If she startled him, he could plunge over the edge. Instead, she stopped at the base of the boulder and waited for him to regain his balance. The steady roar of the creek reached her ears. He looked back at her.

Sweat beaded along his hairline and upper lip. Beneath dark stubble, his face was ghost-white. His hands trembled at his sides. Only one emotion flashed in his dark eyes: fear. He turned back to the abyss.

Josie said, "Whatever is going on, you don't have to run. I just want to talk to you. That's all."

No response.

She went on, "I'll make this easy. We don't even have to talk about whatever happened back there or why you're running. Let's just start with names. Mine is Josie. What's yours?"

He gave her a quick glance over his shoulder but didn't answer.

"Okay," she said. "You don't even have to tell me your name. We don't have to talk at all if you don't want to, but why don't you just come down from there? It's a long drop-off into Roaring Creek. You could get hurt if you fall."

His words were so quiet, she almost didn't hear them. "I'm not going to fall. I'm going to jump."

"I don't recommend that either," Josie said. "You don't have to do this. Whatever is happening in your life, we can talk about it. Figure out what we can do to get you some help."

"No one can help me," he told her. His upper body leaned forward.

Josie took a step closer, trying to get within grasp of him. "You don't know that," she said. "You can't know that until you try to get help. Listen, right now, all I'm asking is for you to get down from the rock. That's it."

Without looking at her, he asked, "Will it kill me? The jump?"

She hesitated. The truth was that she didn't know. It depended on how high the water was, how rough, the way he hit the surface, where in the creek he entered, whether or not there was debris, and how well he could swim.

"I'll take the chance," he said, and jumped.

Josie lunged forward, throwing her upper body across the top of the boulder, both hands reaching for any part of him or his clothing she could grasp. The fabric of his pants brushed her fingers, and then he was gone.

His fall was soundless. Huffing and shaken, she climbed to the top of the boulder and looked below, where there was nothing apart from heavy gray fog.

CHAPTER 4

The sun had come up and it made a valiant attempt to penetrate the fog, but Josie still needed the PhoneFinder app on her phone to get back to where she'd left Noah. Before he came into view, she heard music playing from the car they'd discovered earlier. This time it was a ballad, its rich notes wending through the trees.

> *I'll love you in every lifetime.*
> *Forever doesn't stand a chance.*

Just as she'd left him, Noah knelt beside the girl, except now he was performing CPR. Josie broke into a jog, dodging more items in the grass: a tube of mascara, a set of keys, a phone charger, and a pack of gum. Noah bent to the girl's mouth, tilting her chin into position and blowing air into her lungs. Two breaths. Then he placed his hands, one on top of the other, on the girl's chest and began compressions. Sweat plastered his white T-shirt to his body and soaked his sandy hair. Josie dropped down next to him and nudged him aside so she could take over. Noah didn't protest. Instead, he fell backward, exhausted. As Josie put her own mouth to the girl's cold lips, he took out his phone.

"Oh God," he said. "It's been almost twenty minutes."

She started her own compressions, counting them off in her head while Noah dialed police dispatch on his phone, giving their approximate location and a brief rundown of the situation.

After breathing into the girl's lungs once more, Josie said, "I didn't see the other girl. The suspect jumped into Roaring Creek. We need searchers."

Noah repeated her request as Josie carried on with compressions. Droplets of sweat slid off her nose and fell onto the girl's dark T-shirt. She had no idea how many minutes went by before Noah took over again. The muscles in her arms and shoulders burned. Still, the cold from the girl's body seemed to cling to Josie's palms. She was already dead, and given how long they had been administering CPR with no response, Josie did not think they were going to get her back.

"Noah," she said, touching his shoulder. "She's gone."

He shrugged her off, giving two more rescue breaths before resuming compressions. "Can't stop."

Josie watched him, noting the way his jaw was locked, his brow furrowed. She knew he was reliving a similar scenario, over four years earlier, when they had found his mother in her garden, unresponsive. He had frozen then, and Josie had tried to bring her back but couldn't. She knew that his paralysis in that moment was something he had always regretted. Today, he wasn't going to stop until the EMTs arrived.

Josie waited until his fatigued muscles forced him to

slow down and then she pushed him out of the way. "Let me have a turn."

Together, they kept working, even as the girl grew colder beneath their ministrations. Sunlight burned through the fog around them, evaporating much of it by the time the ambulance and patrol cars arrived. The first EMT to approach was Sawyer Hayes. Although not blood-related, he and Josie had shared a grandmother. Their relationship was not without its problems, but when their eyes locked, he seemed to understand the situation. He glanced at the girl's face and then back at Josie, giving her a nod. He got down next to Noah and muscled him aside. His partner rushed over, the two of them assessing her while Josie and Noah stepped back, taking a moment to catch their breath.

For the first time, Josie took a close look at the girl. She was curvy with long, dark hair, now matted with grass and dirt. She had high cheekbones, a narrow nose and thin lips. Even at this time of the morning, Josie could see that she wore heavy make-up over her olive skin, including false eyelashes. A tiny diamond stud sparkled on the left side of her nose. In spite of all of that, lying before them she looked young, her skin supple, unlined, and unmarred. Across her black crop top, the word LOVE was emblazoned in sparkly letters.

Sawyer looked over. "It's been over thirty minutes, according to what Fraley told dispatch. She's gone."

Josie thought of the man with his hands wrapped around her throat. "I'm going to call Dr. Feist and the ERT."

"I'll do it," said Noah, phone in hand. He walked away from the scene.

Two uniformed officers approached. Josie gave them a rundown of all that had happened and instructed them to secure the scene and send the other responding units into the forest to search for the man and the other girl they had seen. As they dispersed, Sawyer said, "Is that music I hear?"

"Yeah," said Josie. "It's coming from the car."

For the first time since they'd pulled over, Josie had a chance to take in their surroundings and everything they hadn't been able to see in the thick of the fog. She circled the sedan, noting its distance from the road and the fact that both front doors were flung open. There was no damage to the body of the car, so they had likely pulled over just like Josie and Noah had. The grass on the driver's side had drag marks that led to where the dead girl now rested. All around her lay the items Josie had nearly tripped over. Near the back tire of the car was a large brown purse, dumped upside down. Next to it was a pink backpack, clothing spilled from inside it—a pair of black jeans and a white shirt. On the passenger's side was more detritus. Another purse, this one smaller and black, lay discarded, its zipper torn half off its closure. Scattered around it was a small bottle of ibuprofen, a maxi pad, a pen, a small wallet, and a cell phone, this one with a plain purple cover. Then came a duffel bag, on its side, clothing yanked from within it, tossed into the grass. Josie noted another pair of black jeans and a white shirt together with what looked like cotton pajamas.

"Dr. Feist and the ERT are on their way," Noah said, returning to her side. "I also called Gretchen since this is more than just a car accident. What've we got?"

Josie was relieved to see that some of the tension had left his face. His eyes were sharp, his focus in the present.

"Two girls, from what I can tell," she said. "I think they pulled over. I don't know if the man was in the car with them or not—"

"He wasn't," said Noah. "There's another car, up ahead,

pulled over onto the shoulder. One of the patrol guys is running its plate right now to see who it belongs to. They'll run the tag for this vehicle as well."

"Great," said Josie. "So maybe the guy was following them. They pulled over, he passed them and pulled over as well."

"They wouldn't have seen him approaching in the fog," said Noah.

"He walked right up to their car. It looks as though the driver was dragged out of the vehicle."

Josie's breath caught as she peered deeper into the passenger's side of the car. "Noah, look."

Without touching the vehicle, he leaned closer. Across the tan-colored dash was a spray of blood, droplets too numerous to count. On the seat itself were two large drops of blood, now drying to a burnished brown.

"He attacked the passenger, too," Noah said. "But she got away from him."

"I haven't seen any weapons," Josie said. "He didn't appear to have any when I got close enough to talk with him."

Noah pointed to the dash. "Look at the pattern. He probably smashed her head into the dash and broke her nose. Broken noses can bleed a lot."

"Let's hope that's all he did to her. Both their purses were dumped," Josie pointed out. "He was looking for something. Noah, the other girl is still out there, and she's injured."

"I'll call in more searchers," Noah said, phone already in hand. "We should see if we can get an ID on her."

Josie was loath to disturb the scene any more than they already had by traipsing through it but with another teen out in the woods scared and alone, she needed more information sooner rather than later. She went over to the ambulance and asked them for a pair of latex gloves. Normally, when they were on shift, she and Noah carried them. But technically, they were still on vacation.

Sawyer handed her a pair of gloves and she snapped them on. She found one wallet on the driver's side of the car. She took a photo of its location to document precisely where it was before she disturbed it. Then she picked it up. "Dina Hale," Josie read from the girl's driver's license. "Eighteen years old. Lived in Denton."

Noah hung up his phone and pocketed it. Over her shoulder, he studied the driver's license photo. In it, the girl's hair was brushed and glossy. Her smile was wide, one of her top front teeth just a hair crooked, but not detracting from her radiance at all. "That's definitely the driver."

Josie held up the license so Noah could snap a picture with his phone. Then she placed it back on the ground so that the Evidence Response Team could collect and process it. It took some searching on the other side of the vehicle, but they found the other girl's wallet, documenting its position before picking it up.

"Alison Mills," Josie said. "Also from Denton. Seventeen years old."

Alison's hair was a lighter brown than Dina's, and curly. Whereas Dina's skin was olive, Alison's was pale and freckled. In her driver's license photo, she gave a nervous smile, as though she was perplexed that she'd managed to get a license in the first place. If Josie had to guess based on their driver's license photos, Dina was probably the more confident and outgoing of the two girls. Sadness crept into Josie's heart. Had they been best friends? It was just one of many questions they had for Alison.

First, they had to find her.

Noah snapped a photo of her license and Josie put it back in its place. "We've got time before Dr. Feist and the ERT get here to process everything," she said. "Gretchen is on her way. The scene is secure. Let's go join the search for Alison Mills."

CHAPTER 5

Josie shared the photo of Alison Mills' driver's license with her colleagues. Then she and Noah joined the search teams in the woods across the road from where Dina's body lay. The sunlight cut through what was left of the fog, warming the day and giving them a clear view of the forest. There was no way of knowing precisely which way the girl had run. Josie and Noah only knew she was on the opposite side of the road to the ridge that dropped off into Roaring Creek. If she ran in a straight line from the point they had last seen her and kept going in that direction, eventually she would end up in East Denton, near the abandoned textile mill. If she continued through the woods, she would reach the stacks, an area behind Denton East High School where several large slabs of stone had pancaked on top of one another, forming flat rocky outcroppings where the students often hung out to smoke, drink, and do other questionable things. Or she could veer away from the mill and find the road that ran parallel to the mill and Denton East High and into Central Denton. But trekking through the woods could be disorienting. Everything looked similar, and Josie knew that in this part of the forest that surrounded Denton, there were few, if any, natural landmarks. She could be running in circles.

As Josie, Noah, and the rest of the searchers trudged through the trees, they called out her name. Maybe she had gotten tired and stopped running. Maybe she had decided to try to return to the vehicle. After all, her phone had been left at the scene. She had no way of knowing that Josie and Noah had stopped or that they were with the Denton Police Department. Some strange man had emerged from the fog on a winding mountain road and attacked her and her friend. She was injured and bleeding. Panicked.

Hours passed. The sun rose higher in the sky. Although the temperature dropped precipitously at night, the mid-October days in Denton had been trending warmer with each year. Josie and Noah were soaked through with perspiration and starving by the time they gave up and returned to the scene. Other searchers had found fresh droplets of blood, but not Alison. As they tromped back to where they had left their vehicle, Josie saw Gretchen standing on the side of the road, scribbling on her trusty notepad. In her mid-forties, Gretchen was easily the most experienced on their investigative team. Before joining the Denton PD, she'd been a homicide detective for the City of Philadelphia for fifteen years.

Beside her, a uniformed officer stood as sentry, eyeing every vehicle that slowed as it passed the scene and waving them on their way. Gretchen looked up as they approached and shook her head. She tucked her pen behind her ear. "I thought the two of you were under strict instructions from Chief Chitwood that there was to be no working on your honeymoon. By my calculations, this is the last day of your honeymoon."

Noah laughed. "I told Josie we should have stayed an extra day."

Josie wiped sweat from her brow with the back of one hand. "Now I'm thinking getting stuck in a hurricane wouldn't have been so bad. What've you got?"

Gretchen reached up to her short, spiked gray-brown hair, snagging her reading glasses and sliding them on. She flipped a page in her notebook. "Dina Hale's body has been transported to the morgue. The car she was driving is registered to a man named Guy Hale, same address as Dina. Likely her father, given their age difference. The ERT is finishing up here. They will be impounding both vehicles. I'll keep the search teams out looking for Alison Mills. She takes priority. We've also got searchers out looking for your male assailant. I've got teams going up and down Roaring Creek and to the river looking for him."

Noah swiped a hand through his wet hair. "Did you get an ID on him?"

Gretchen nodded. "We believe the man you two saw was forty-year-old Elliott Calvert. From Denton. That is his car. I pulled up a copy of his driver's license on the Mobile Data Terminal. You can confirm if he's the man you saw." She reached into the back pocket of her jeans for her cell phone, resting it on top of her notebook. After swiping a few times, she turned the screen so that Josie and Noah could see the photo from Elliott Calvert's license.

Noah shook his head. "I didn't get a good enough look at his face."

"That's him," said Josie. "I'm certain."

"Does he have a record?" asked Noah.

"No," said Gretchen. "A few traffic violations, that's it. I did a little searching while I was waiting for the ERT to process the scene. He's got social media accounts that he hardly uses, but I was able to glean that he works for the Stamoran Firm. Architecture. Also, he's married, and it appears that he and his wife have just had a baby."

Josie shook her head. "I can't even imagine having to tell his wife what happened today."

Noah said, "What is a forty-year-old married father of a newborn doing attacking two teenage girls all the way out here? What was he looking for?"

Gretchen said, "We'll get to the bottom of it. Like I said, we've got units out looking for this guy. Right now, we need to prioritize Alison Mills, particularly if she is injured. Someone's got to go over to her house and talk with her parents. So far, we've kept this entire incident pretty quiet, but word will get around that police are searching for people. I don't want them finding out from social media or the press that their daughter is missing. Hopefully we'll find her before that happens, but her parents should know what's going on. I am going to need your help on this. Mettner and Amber are away this weekend. They won't be back till Monday."

Detective Finn Mettner was the fourth member of their investigative team as well as the youngest. He'd been brought up through the Denton PD ranks and promoted to Detective by their current Chief of Police, Bob Chitwood. Amber Watts was his girlfriend as well as the Denton PD's press liaison.

"We'll talk to her family," said Josie.

"Perfect," Gretchen replied. Over her reading glasses, she looked them up and down. Then she sniffed the air and wrinkled her nose. "Maybe take a shower and get a change of clothes first."

Josie glanced down at her dirt- and sweat-stained clothes, then over at Noah, who didn't look much better. "Sure," she said. "No problem."

CHAPTER 6

Josie and Noah dragged their luggage into their house. Instinctually, Josie listened for the tip-tap of their Boston terrier, Trout's, feet along the hardwood floors. Expecting to see him barreling toward them like he always did when they came home, she felt a momentary burst of excitement send her heartbeat ticking upward, but then she remembered that they'd left him with their friend, Misty DeRossi and her son, Harris, for the week.

Noah paused inside the door and smiled. "It's weird, right? No Trout."

Josie smiled. "He's probably getting so spoiled by Misty and Harris he won't even want to come home with us." Even Misty and Harris's chiweiner dog, Pepper, loved Trout.

Noah lifted both their suitcases and started up the steps. "That's the truth."

Josie followed. "But we're still going to get him tonight. I can't wait to see him."

"Me too," Noah said over his shoulder. "As wonderful

as it was being able to sleep right next to my wife for a week. You know, instead of a farting dog."

Twenty minutes later, they were both showered and dressed in fresh pairs of slacks and their Denton PD polo shirts. They retrieved their pistols and police credentials from a lockbox they kept hidden in the house. In the kitchen, Josie opened the fridge, expecting to find a foul smell and a bunch of expired products. Instead, there was a large Tupperware container with a note on it. Josie recognized Misty's handwriting.

I know neither of you ~~can~~ will want to cook when you get back, so here is a casserole. A few minutes in the microwave should do it. P.S. Trout said he wants to live with us permanently. Just kidding. He misses you. A little. Can't wait to see you lovebirds. Enjoy! M.

Josie laughed as she popped the container into their microwave.

"What is it?" asked Noah.

She handed him the note. He read it while the food heated up. As a delicious smell emanated from the microwave, he said, "I don't even care that she implied that neither of us can cook."

Years ago, after Josie separated from her first husband, the late Ray Quinn, Misty had dated him. Their son, Harris, was born after Ray's death, and what had started as Josie helping out with Harris blossomed into one of the most important relationships of both Josie's and Noah's lives. For most of her life, Josie didn't have close female friends—she'd barely had friends—but Misty had changed all that. She'd made Josie a better person, and Josie couldn't imagine her life without Misty. Her support over the years was so valuable and in many ways, helped Josie and Noah to cope with the pressures of the job. This thought brought Josie's mind back to the scene they'd happened on that morning. Again, she wondered how close Dina and Alison had been. Had it been a superficial relationship, or were they best friends? Regardless, with Dina's death, lives were shattered. Dina's family would never be the same. Even Alison would never be the same after this morning's events. Josie could not imagine how frightened the girl must have been at that moment—on the run, alone, injured, and knowing that her friend had also been attacked.

Josie barely tasted Misty's concoction although she was grateful for it. Neither she nor Noah had eaten in hours, and they would need fuel for what was to come. In the car, Josie checked her phone. "No updates from Gretchen," she said. "She had units search the old textile mill, but they turned up nothing. Where could this girl have gone?"

"I don't know," said Noah as he punched Alison Mills' address into the GPS. "She must have made it out of the woods. With all those people out there searching for so many hours it seems like she would have been found by now. I'm surprised they didn't turn anything up at the mill."

Josie pulled out of their driveway. "Which means she made it to the other side of the woods, to the high school, maybe—that's where the searchers are headed next—or possibly beyond to a populated area. Except no one would know to look for her or to call the police if they saw her."

As they drove through Denton, Noah pointed out, "But she was attacked. She's injured—even if she's only got a broken nose, she might still be dizzy, disoriented, frightened. Why wouldn't she flag down the first person she saw and ask them to call the police for her?"

"Because she could be lying injured somewhere, unconscious or incapacitated. If you're right and he slammed her head into the dash, she could also be concussed," Josie pointed out, willing to give the girl the benefit of the doubt.

"If she were that badly injured, we would have found her in the forest long before she reached the city."

"Not necessarily," said Josie. "Remember the time that gentleman with dementia escaped from the Alzheimer's unit at Rockview?"

Josie wove through the streets of Central Denton, laid out in grid fashion, toward North Denton, which was much more sparsely populated.

Noah let out a sigh. "I forgot about that. There were thirty of us out looking for him."

"And we all walked right past where he was, didn't we?" Josie said. "Because somehow he'd gotten himself beneath the brush and fallen asleep. No one thought he would walk into it. You'd walk around thick brush, wouldn't you?"

"Not if you've got dementia, apparently," Noah noted. "The dogs found him in minutes. We need dogs looking for Alison Mills. I'll text Gretchen." He took out his phone. "Tell her to request an assist from the sheriff's K-9 unit for Alison."

Noah's fingers tapped against his phone screen. Josie kept her focus on driving. Around them, greenery filled out more of the space between houses. Wide residential streets with sidewalks gave way to narrow mountain roads hemmed in by thin, dirt shoulders, much like the road they'd found the girls on that morning on the easternmost side of Denton.

"This is it," Josie said, slowing beside a bright red mailbox.

She pulled into a long driveway that wound its way up a hill to where the Mills' squat, tan two-story home sat among the trees. There were no vehicles in the driveway, and the doors to the attached garage were closed. Still, Josie and Noah parked and walked up to the front door. Noah rang the doorbell. A couple of minutes passed. He rang again. Finally, Josie heard footsteps on the other side of the door. Then it swung open. A woman in her late forties stood before them. Josie immediately saw the resemblance to Alison—the curly brown hair, pale skin, and freckles smattered across her face. She was taller than Josie and wore a yellow, loose-fitting V-neck blouse over jeans. No shoes. Her toenails were painted blue.

"Mrs. Mills?" asked Josie.

"Yes, I'm Marlene Mills. I— What is this about?"

"Are you Alison Mills' mother?"

Confusion creased her face. Josie watched as she looked back and forth between them, taking in the Denton Police Department name and badge embroidered on the left breast of their shirts as well as their holstered pistols, eyes growing wider by the second. In a high-pitched voice, Marlene said, "What's going on? What's going on here? Where is Alison?"

Noah said, "Mrs. Mills, my name is Lieutenant—"

She cut him off, her voice at a full scream now. "Where is my Alison? What happened to her? Please. Just tell me. Is she dead?"

CHAPTER 7

Josie stepped forward and grasped Marlene's upper arms before she collapsed. Noah quickly positioned himself on the woman's right side, slipping an arm around her waist. They held her upright while Josie spoke calmly into her left ear. "Mrs. Mills, we need you to calm down. We need to talk to you about Alison. It's very important."

Tears gleamed in her eyes as she turned to search Josie's face. "Tell me the truth. Is she dead? Please, just tell me the truth. No one sends police to your door to talk about your child unless the news is—oh God. Just tell me."

Noah said, "We do not believe Alison is dead."

She froze for a moment, head swiveling to stare at him. "What does that mean? You don't *believe* she is dead? Tell me!"

In their arms, she began to flail, getting her footing again. They released her. Josie said, "Mrs. Mills, I promise that we will explain everything, but we need you to calm down. Can we come inside so we can sit down?"

Marlene's body trembled. She took a moment to study them, her eyes glassy with tears. She nodded and led them inside to a large, airy living room decorated in varying shades of gray, from the walls to the sectional with its accent pillows and rumpled blanket. On its edge, Josie saw the words "The Mills Family" embroidered in white. The end tables held several framed photographs of Alison and one of Alison with her mother and a man Josie guessed was her father.

"Is Alison's father here?" Josie asked.

Marlene collapsed into a corner of the sectional, shaking her head. She waved toward the space next to her, indicating Josie and Noah should sit down. "He's in Hong Kong, of all places. For work. Oh my God. I should call him, shouldn't I? What time is it there? I guess it doesn't matter, does it? He deserves to know what's going on."

Her eyes searched the room, landing on the coffee table where a cell phone rested among a host of other items: two remote controls, a magazine, a stack of mail and a box of tissues. Josie grabbed the phone and handed it to her.

Noah said, "Mrs. Mills, we really need to speak with you first."

Marlene dropped the phone into her lap. Her hands fluttered around her face, now flushed a rosy pink. "I'm sorry. I'm sorry. I'm a mess. You have to understand, with everything we went through with Alison, even though it's behind us, I'm always waiting, you know? Waiting for the other shoe to drop, as they say."

Josie made a mental note to circle back to this statement later and find out what they'd gone through with Alison that had put Marlene so on edge. "Mrs. Mills, at approximately seven thirty this morning, Lieutenant Fraley and I were returning from an out-of-town trip. We were driving on Widow's Ridge Road. It was foggy enough that we couldn't see more than a foot or two in front of our vehicle. We saw a figure run across the road, and we decided to pull over to see if someone needed assistance. When we got out of our car, we saw that another vehicle had also pulled over. That vehicle is registered to Guy Hale."

"Dina's dad," Marlene said. "Dina always drove them. Alison doesn't have her own car. Were they in an accident? Where are they? Oh, my God. They're at the hospital, aren't they? I have to get over there. I need to find my purse—"

Noah held up a hand to silence her. "Please, Mrs. Mills. Let us finish."

Josie continued, "We do not believe it was an accident. By all appearances, they pulled over, likely due to the fog. When we approached the car, we saw a man who appeared to be attacking Dina. We believe that Alison ran away from the scene and that she was the figure we saw crossing the road."

Marlene shook her head back and forth. "An attack? I don't understand. No, no. Why would someone attack a couple of teenage girls? This makes no sense. Where did Alison go? Is she okay?"

"We haven't been able to locate her," Noah said. "That's why we're here."

"Oh," said Marlene. She picked up her phone again. "I'll just call her. I'll call her and tell her to come home. Or I'll go get her, because she doesn't have a car. Of course. I can't ask her to just come home. What's she going to do, walk?" A peel of nervous, high-pitched laughter escaped her throat.

Josie reached over and put a hand on Marlene's forearm. "Mrs. Mills, she left her phone at the scene."

"What? No. No. She wouldn't do that. You don't understand these kids today. Their phones are like the air they breathe. She would never leave it behind."

Josie said, "We took it into evidence."

"Mrs. Mills," Noah began. "There's something else. We believe that Alison might have been injured in some sort of altercation with this man."

Both Marlene's hands pressed into the center of her chest. "Oh my God, no. What happened? What do you mean, you believe she was injured? Why won't you just tell me what's going on?" Her voice had risen to a shout.

They were trying to tell her what was going on, but it was proving very difficult to keep her focused. Gently, Josie said, "What's going on is that Alison ran away from the attacker, into the woods. We've had teams out searching for her since this happened. We have not located her yet, but we will do everything we can to find her, Mrs. Mills. That is a promise."

"What about the injury? What happened to her?"

"We're not sure," Josie answered. "We did find blood at the scene. Based on its location in the passenger's side front of the vehicle, we're theorizing that it belongs to Alison."

Beneath her hands, Marlene's chest heaved. Her face lost all its color. Josie was afraid she was going to pass out. Noah stood up and knelt at her feet. "Mrs. Mills, I know this is scary, but we're doing everything we can to find your daughter. Now, I need you to take some deep breaths. Can you do that for me?"

She shook her head violently but met his eyes. He nodded and put a hand to his own chest, making exaggerated movements as he breathed in and out slowly. "Keep your eyes on me," he told her. "That's good. In and out. Nice and slow."

After a couple of minutes, Marlene began to mirror

Noah's deep breathing. Some of the color returned to her face. Josie walked to the back of the house and found the kitchen. There were clean glasses on a drainboard. She filled one up with tap water and returned to the living room, handing it to Marlene.

She took a few sips and then handed it to Noah, who put it on the coffee table. "I'm so sorry," she breathed.

"No apologies," Josie said. "We understand that this is terrifying and that's why we want to find Alison as soon as possible."

"And for that," Noah said, his gentle smile still in place as he perched on the edge of the coffee table facing Marlene, "we need your help."

She sucked in a few more breaths, picked up her phone, dropped it again, and said, "That's everything you know? The girls were driving, they pulled over, they were attacked by some man, and Alison was bleeding and then she ran away? Do you think she was shot? Stabbed? Is she laying in a ditch somewhere, dying?"

Josie said, "It did not appear that any weapons were involved. She may have hit her face on the dash and broken her nose. There was not enough blood to suggest that her life was in danger from bleeding out."

Noah added, "Detective Quinn and I were out with the search teams this morning. Some additional blood was found, but it was only a few drops."

"That's a good thing, right?" Marlene said hopefully.

"We believe so," said Josie.

"What about Dina? Is Dina okay? Oh God, I should probably call her dad." She picked up her phone again.

Josie met Noah's eyes. They couldn't tell her that Dina Hale was dead before the family had been notified. Not to mention that it would cause her to become even more upset.

Noah said, "Someone from our team will speak with Dina's dad. For now, we really need to ask you some questions."

Josie let out a slow breath of relief when Marlene dropped her phone and looked back at Noah, too distracted and overwhelmed to realize he hadn't answered her question about whether or not Dina was all right. "Questions? What questions?"

CHAPTER 8

"Let's start with this morning," Josie instructed. "When was the last time you saw Alison?"

"Oh, not this morning," said Marlene. "She slept over at Dina's house last night. They work together. That's how they met—through work."

"Where do they work?" Noah asked.

"The Eudora Hotel. My friend, Sadie, is a housekeeper there. Last year she told me that the events department was looking for teenage girls to work as part of the catering team during special events. They only work on weekends for a few hours. Basically, they walk around carrying trays of food or drink and offer them to guests. Sometimes they serve food and clear dirty dishes. Whatever the catering department needs. They do weddings, parties, workshops, conferences, all kinds of corporate events. Anything that has to be catered. It's easy money. Lots of times they get really good tips, too."

Josie said, "Did they work last night?"

"Yes. Some corporate party. Those usually run late, and I know they had a brunch for some local nonprofit organization this morning, so Alison decided just to stay over at Dina's house. Dina was supposed to drop her off here after work today. Oh my God." Again, she pressed both hands into her chest.

Before hysteria claimed her, Noah asked, "When was the last time you heard from Alison by phone?"

Marlene picked up her phone but didn't look at it. "Last night. Around midnight. She texted me to say that she was safely at Dina's and—" Here, she faltered, her breath coming faster. Punching a passcode into her phone, she swiped a few times and then turned the screen toward Josie and then Noah.

Made it to Dina's ok. Long night but big tips. Night, Mom. Love you lots and lots.

Moneybag emojis followed the word "tips" and several heart and kiss emojis followed the end of the message. Then, after the hearts, was a Ferris wheel emoji.

Josie asked, "What's the Ferris wheel for?"

Marlene turned the screen back so she could look at the message. She gave a little laugh. "It's silly. Alison and I—we have this... I don't know what you'd call it. A game? A tradition? But when we text one another we always add at least one emoji that is completely unrelated to what we were texting about. I know it's really stupid, but we have great fun with it. Look, I texted her back with a fork emoji." Again, she turned the screen to them, scrolling up so they could see her reply.

Glad to hear it. Night. Love you tons. See you tomorrow.

Marlene had ended the message with three hearts and a fork.

Josie smiled. "Sweet."

"It started by accident," Marlene explained. "I was accidentally adding random emojis to my texts when I first got this phone. Now it's a thing."

"Do you know what time they were supposed to be at the hotel this morning?" asked Noah.

"I'm not sure. I know it was early. Even though it's a brunch event, all the girls have to come in early to help set up."

"No one from the Eudora called you when Alison didn't arrive for work today?" asked Josie.

"No, but they wouldn't. I mean, yes, I'm her emergency contact, obviously, but she's almost eighteen. They would call her directly if she didn't show up to work. Dina, too. They might have called both of them. I don't know."

Noah said, "As Detective Quinn indicated earlier, we took Alison's phone into evidence. Is her phone under your name since she is still a minor?"

"Yes," answered Marlene. "We have a family plan."

"May we have permission to examine the contents of her phone, Mrs. Mills? Before we return it to you?"

With wide eyes, she looked back and forth between them again. "Examine the contents?"

Josie said, "Given that the girls were attacked this morning, it's standard procedure to make sure that no one was harassing either of them in the days or weeks leading to today's incident. One of the ways we do that is by looking at their phones and checking any messages or social media platforms for the last several weeks. Do you know of anyone who might have been bothering either one of the girls recently?"

Marlene shook her head slowly. "No. I don't. I'm sure that Alison would have told me. I know everyone says that about their kids—*oh, they tell me everything. I know everything they're doing on and offline and who they're talking to and what about*—when usually it's total crap, but Alison is really good about it. I don't want her to have secrets from us. We have always told her that if she gets into some kind of trouble, we want her first thought to be, 'I better call Mom and Dad for help' and not, 'I have to hide this from Mom and Dad.' But anyway, if you want to look at her phone, please, go ahead."

"Thank you," said Josie. "How about Dina? Did Alison mention whether or not Dina was having trouble with anyone?"

Another slow shake of her head. "No. Nothing."

"Were Alison and Dina close?" asked Josie.

"Yes. They hit it off right away when they met last year at the hotel. They don't go to the same high school, but they were seeing one another almost every weekend at work so they kind of became best friends. Alison has lots of other friends, but if I had to choose her closest friend, it's probably Dina."

Noah said, "Have either Alison or Dina ever gotten into trouble either at school or with the law?"

Josie knew they could easily check this once they were back at the stationhouse, but it was always instructive to know how much parents knew and how involved they were in their children's lives. Sometimes a parent told the police their kid was a perfect angel and it turned out that same kid had been getting into trouble at school for weeks or more; or that the kid had been cited for something and the parents weren't even aware of it. Other times, parents knew exactly what their children and their children's friends were doing.

Marlene said, "Not Alison, but I know Dina has had some issues with shoplifting in the past. Alison told me about it."

"What about drug use?" asked Josie.

Marlene pursed her lips for a moment and then let out a long breath. "If Alison has done drugs, she hasn't told me. I suspect that she and Dina have smoked pot at least once, but I could never prove it. I've given Alison the talk many times. The one time I thought she'd been smoking pot, I really lit into her about drugs and alcohol but she denied, denied, denied. If she's done any drugs since then, I haven't been able to tell and I haven't found anything in this house to make me suspect so. Neither has my husband, and he's talked with her about the evils of drugs and alcohol too."

"You said your husband is in Hong Kong," said Noah. "How long has he been there?"

At the mention of her husband, Marlene looked down at her phone. Its screen was black. Her thumb hovered over its surface but she didn't bring it to life. "About two months now. He works for a huge company that sells and installs solar power systems all over the world. Unfortunately, the project he's on now requires him to be in the Hong Kong office. He used to have his own business doing residential solar power systems and then, well, there were some problems. A lot of problems. Then the whole thing with Alison. We're still paying off her medical bills from before."

"What kinds of problems did your husband have with his business?" asked Noah.

Marlene clasped the phone between her palms. Her body rocked forward and back, the motion slow and rhythmic like a metronome of anxiety. "His business partner, Billy, died. They were best friends since childhood. Did everything together. The business was finally starting to show some growth and then they got into this terrible car accident. The police found Clint at fault." She looked at her feet, shaking her head. "He's never forgiven himself. He never will. They were going to do an estimate and then afterward they were supposed to go out to dinner. Clint was driving. Alison was in the car. Clint, um, he was distracted. On the phone with a client. He didn't have that hands-free thing, so he was holding his phone. This tractor trailer in front of him lost one of its tires—you know how they burn up and disintegrate and fly all over the road? Clint avoided most of it, but he was trying to get out of the way of a pretty big piece when he lost control of the car. Went off the highway, flipped the car. It was terrible. Anyway, he wasn't the same after that. Not after losing Billy. Plus, Alison got hurt. She actually broke her hip and they had to put in a couple of pins. Then the area where they'd placed sutures got infected, but we didn't realize it right away because she had this massive cast on. She was septic. We almost lost her. They had to go back in a few times just to operate on the wound. She was in the hospital on and off for months with different surgeries. I mean, the hospital was our second home! Then there was the physical therapy and follow-up visits. We went broke."

"I'm sorry to hear that," Josie said. "Earlier, when you said 'everything Alison went through,' were you referring to the accident and medical issues?"

Marlene nodded. "Yes."

"Is she still suffering from those injuries in any way?"

"No, no. That was three years ago, but I still worry so much about her. That's why I kind of lost it when you got here. I know she's recovered from that, but you know how life is." Her body stilled and she lifted her hands, palms facing upward. The phone dropped into her lap again.

"While you're busy worrying about one thing, something totally different comes along and clobbers you! Like this. All this time, I've been worried about her breaking her hip again or doing something that would cause damage to it, and I never for one second thought she would be missing or get attacked!"

"We don't have a lot of information yet," Noah told her. "But we're going to be looking closely at the man we found at the scene. We have reason to believe he targeted Dina and Alison."

Marlene picked up her phone once more, but her body remained still. "Targeted them? How?"

"We're not sure," said Josie. "But it was very foggy. Early in the morning. He had driven past them, pulled over, got out, and then approached their car. We believe he was looking for something."

"Like what? What could two teenage girls have that a grown man would be looking for?" Marlene asked incredulously.

"We're not sure," said Noah.

"Maybe it's a case of mistaken identity," Marlene suggested.

"That's certainly possible," Josie agreed. "We don't know all the facts yet. Does the name Elliott Calvert sound familiar to you?"

Marlene shook her head.

Josie nodded to Noah who took out his phone and pulled up the driver's license photo of Elliott Calvert. He showed it to Marlene, but her gaze remained blank. "I've never seen him before in my life."

"Are you absolutely certain?" asked Josie. "Take a moment to think about it. Is it possible that he frequents the same establishments your family does? Could he be a coworker? Of Alison's? Yours? Your husband's?"

"I don't think so. I don't recognize him. He's definitely not a coworker of mine. I can't speak for Alison. I suppose it's possible that he works with my husband, although why would he be attacking our daughter?"

Noah pointed to the phone in Marlene's lap. "Mrs. Mills, I think now would be a good time to call your husband. Once you speak with him, we can text him this photo and maybe he can tell us if he recognizes Elliott Calvert."

"Okay, yes," she said, seeming relieved to have something to do. Some concrete action to take. "After that, will you take me to where you saw her? Where it happened?"

Noah said, "There's nothing there now, Mrs. Mills. The vehicles have been impounded. All personal effects have been taken into evidence. The searchers are probably still staged there, but—"

"Please," she begged, voice cracking. "Please. I need to see it."

"Of course," said Josie. "In fact, we've asked for an assist from the sheriff's K-9 unit. Sometimes dogs can find people faster than people can. It would help if you could give us a personal item of Alison's that would still have her scent on it."

"There's a sweatshirt she wears around the house," Marlene said. "I'm always begging her to wash it but she rarely does."

"That would be perfect," said Josie. "We'll wait here while you contact your husband and get the sweatshirt. Then we'll take you over to where we found the girls."

CHAPTER 9

Police cars lined the shoulders of Widow's Ridge Road where Josie and Noah had discovered Elliott Calvert attacking Dina Hale. Now, several hours later, the sun shone brightly overhead in a pristine blue sky. Soft, warm breezes sighed through the trees. Birds chirped happily, flitting from branch to branch. The day seemed entirely too cheerful to hold the horrible thing that had unfolded on the shoulder of the road that morning. Marlene sat in the back seat of their car, her cell phone clutched in one hand and Alison's black, hooded sweatshirt in the other. She had been mostly silent since they left her home. Every so often, Josie glanced at her in the rear-view mirror. She looked perpetually stunned.

As Josie tried to find a spot for their vehicle among all the others, Noah asked Marlene, "What did Mr. Mills say?"

"What? Oh. He's going to get on the first flight back. Although I'm not sure if he can get a direct flight on such short notice. That would be over eighteen hours anyway, and direct flights don't fly into Philadelphia so he'd have to land at JFK, which would mean hours of driving to get here..."

Noah said, "What about Elliott Calvert? Does your husband know him? Did he recognize the photo?"

"No, he didn't," Marlene answered. "We have no idea who this man was or why he would attack the girls. Maybe you should ask Dina or her parents—"

Before Marlene could ask about Dina's condition again, Josie blurted out, "Here's a spot!"

She found an opening among the line of cars and wedged their vehicle into it. Ahead, she saw the crime scene tape still tied to trees along the shoulder of the road. As they got out and walked toward the cordoned-off area, Josie noted that everything had been cleaned up. The cars were gone, as were the personal effects that had been scattered all over the shoulder. Gretchen stood practically where they'd left her, scribbling furiously into her notebook while she pinched her cell phone between her ear and her shoulder.

"Still here?" Noah said as they approached.

Gretchen held up her pen in a gesture that indicated that they should give her a minute. Marlene hugged Alison's sweatshirt to her chest and looked around the empty clearing behind the tape. "This is where it happened?"

"Yes," Josie said. She pointed out approximately where each vehicle had been and the direction Alison had gone.

Marlene turned in a slow circle, taking in all the police cars. "All these people are looking for my Alison?"

"Yes," Josie said. "Although at this point it is possible she made it all the way to the city."

Marlene took her phone out from the folds of the sweatshirt and checked the screen. "If she made it to the city then why hasn't she flagged someone down and asked to use their phone? She should have called 911, or asked someone else to do it. Or she could have called me. She knows my number, even without looking at her phone. I taught it to her when she was four by using a song."

Marlene began to hum her telephone number to the tune of a familiar nursery rhyme. She stopped abruptly when Gretchen walked over and extended a hand. "Detective Gretchen Palmer. You must be Mrs. Mills. I'm very sorry that we have to meet under these circumstances. I assume my colleagues have brought you up to speed."

Marlene nodded and held out the sweatshirt to Gretchen. "That's for the dogs."

Gretchen took it and thanked her. "The sheriff's ETA is about twenty minutes. That's why I'm still here. As you can see, both vehicles have been impounded. The scene has been processed. I can probably take this tape down now."

As she talked, Marlene walked off, wandering up and down the length of the crime scene tape, running her fingers across it. She stared at the empty area beyond it, as if searching for something. Her daughter? An explanation? Both?

Josie lowered her voice, "She doesn't know that Dina is dead."

"Good," said Gretchen. "I'm going to need you two to notify Dina's family next."

"No updates on Alison or Calvert?" asked Noah.

Gretchen said, "Searchers found what they believe is Calvert's cell phone a few miles down the creek, just before it opens into the river. It was wedged between two rocks on the riverbank."

"That could be anyone's phone, don't you think?" Noah said.

Gretchen shrugged. "It could be, but a few feet from it

they also found a cufflink with the initials *EC* on it. I'm thinking the phone is very likely Calvert's. We'll get a warrant for it. Also, someone is going to have to pay his wife a visit to let her know what's happening and find out what she knows, if anything, about why this guy attacked these kids."

"We can do that after we talk with Dina's family," Josie said.

"Great," said Gretchen. She motioned toward Marlene. "What did you get from her?"

Josie and Noah recapped their conversation with Marlene. Gretchen nodded along as they spoke, scrawling in her notebook. "She had no idea what these girls were into or what they had that this man might be looking for?"

"None," Noah said. "Maybe we'll have better luck with Dina's parents."

Marlene returned, looking every bit as shell-shocked as she had in the car. "Mrs. Mills," said Gretchen. "As I just indicated, we've got a K-9 unit on its way to help with the search for Alison. We're wondering if the reason that she hasn't asked someone to call you or 911, if she made it into the city, is because she's scared. It would certainly be understandable, given what she went through this morning."

Marlene nodded.

Gretchen said, "Your daughter, how is she under stress? Is she able to stay calm? Does she become hysterical? Shut down?"

Marlene bit her lower lip. "Alison is just a kid. The only real stress she's ever been under was after the accident when she was in the hospital all those months."

"That certainly qualifies as great stress, Mrs. Mills," Gretchen pointed out. "How did she respond?"

"The shutting-down thing," Marlene answered. "I

mean, she hates needles. Always cried for those. But everything else, she just went silent. It was hard to draw her out. Why are you asking me this?"

Gretchen smiled. "I'm just trying to get a feel for how she might have responded earlier today. If she was frightened enough and not thinking clearly, maybe instead of flagging someone down for help, she decided to hide. It stands to reason that she might not be comfortable approaching a stranger after she'd just been attacked by one."

Relief loosened the lines on Marlene's face. "Oh yes. You're right. That makes sense. Where do you think she is?"

Josie said, "We were hoping you could tell us. Is there somewhere she might go that is maybe closer to Denton East High School than your home? Somewhere she might feel comfortable hiding out until she composes herself?"

"You mean, like a friend's house?" Marlene asked.

Josie didn't mention that had Alison gone to a friend's house, she would expect that the friend would let Alison call either the police or her mother or call on Alison's behalf. "Yes," Josie said. "Or anywhere that she might think to hide?"

"No. I don't know."

Gretchen said, "That's okay. It was worth asking. Mrs. Mills, thank you so much for helping us. There are two more things I need to ask of you."

Earnestly, Marlene said, "Yes, yes. Anything."

"I need you to go home—Detective Quinn and Lieutenant Fraley will drive you—in case Alison finds her way there. The second thing is that once you are there, I need you to make a list of all her friends and their numbers for us. In fact, if you're feeling up to it and you want to do even more, you could call everyone on that list and ask if they've seen her and if not, ask them to call you or us if they do."

"I can do that," Marlene said. "I can definitely do that. I'll start right away."

Noah began walking her back toward their car. Josie looked at Gretchen. "If Elliott Calvert walked out of Roaring Creek near the city and Alison Mills made it into the city as well, what are the odds that they'll run into one another?"

Gretchen said, "They went in opposite directions."

"Yeah, but assuming they both made it to downtown Denton, they wouldn't have been very far apart once they made it there. She got away the first time, but if there's a second time—"

Gretchen cut her off. "I'm going to do everything I can to make sure there is no second time. I'm going to be on these searches while you guys make the rounds talking to families. I want to find this girl alive."

CHAPTER 10

The Hales lived in a townhouse near the edge of town, in a development that sat three to four miles uphill from where Josie and Noah had found Elliott Calvert attacking Dina. Each home was identical. Only the house numbers, vehicles in the driveways, and any touches the individual owners chose to put on the exteriors distinguished them from one another in appearance. In the driveway of the Hale residence sat a sporty, cherry-red Toyota sedan. Josie and Noah edged around it and rang the doorbell.

They heard a woman's voice before the door swung open. "...you forget your key again? You really need to be more responsible. You're lucky, I'm about to leave for—"

Her words halted when she opened the door to see Josie and Noah standing there. Taking them in, much the way Marlene Mills had, her arm fell to her side and she muttered, "Shit."

This woman was the polar opposite of Marlene Mills. She wore torn jeans, heavy black boots and a tight-fitting black shirt that showed her ample cleavage. Her hair was dyed a deep purple, and she had a nose ring, and tattoos covering both her arms. Josie estimated her to be in her late thirties, early forties.

"Are you Mrs. Hale?" Josie tried. "Dina's mother?"

She mumbled another expletive. Then she said, "Yes, I'm her mother. Britta Hale. I'm guessing by the looks on your faces that you need to come in."

"I'm afraid so," Noah told her. He held out his credentials. Josie did the same. "I'm Lieutenant Noah Fraley of the Denton PD. This is my colleague, Detective Josie Quinn."

She barely glanced at their police credentials before stepping back and gesturing for them to enter. The Hale home was far smaller than the Mills', and although the walls and furniture were a generic tan color, the rest of the decor struck Josie as New Age. There was a painting on the living room wall of a figure on a blue background, outlined in white light, seated in a lotus position with its chakras glowing from crown to sacrum. On the coffee table, a teal-colored plate held a number of crystals. On a bookshelf in the corner, Josie noted several books. Half the titles had to do with tattoo art and the others had to do with spirituality. On one shelf sat a wooden incense holder with a half-burned incense stick protruding from it. Above that was a photo of Britta, Dina, and a man Josie assumed was Guy at Disney World, smiling in front of Cinderella's castle. Dina looked considerably younger.

Neither Josie nor Noah sat down, and Britta didn't offer them seats. Instead, she stood across the room from them and folded her arms over her chest, regarding them warily.

Noah cleared his throat. "Is Mr. Hale here?"

"Um, no," Britta said, her voice catching. "He's at work. He owns Razor tattoo parlor in town. Do I—do I need to call him?"

Josie could see that her tough façade was cracking.

Given what Marlene had said—that Dina had gotten in trouble before for shoplifting and possibly some drug offenses—it was likely that Britta initially assumed they were there for something minor. But with each second that passed, Josie knew her mind was cycling through other possibilities, worse possibilities.

Josie was a firm believer in ripping off the bandage when giving bad news. Waiting or leading up to it didn't make it any easier to hear. "Mrs. Hale," she said. "You are going to need to call your husband. I'm very sorry to inform you that your daughter, Dina, was killed this morning."

The moment hung between them, as if it took several seconds for Josie's words to travel across the room, land, and be absorbed. Britta let out a small gasp. Then she closed her eyes and swayed on her feet. Noah moved toward her in case she fainted but before he reached her, her eyes snapped open and she put up a hand to stop him.

Josie said, "We can call your husband for you, if you'd like."

Britta shook her head. "No. I'll do it."

Her body listed to the side, and she fell onto the nearest chair. She pulled a cell phone from inside her bra. After a few swipes, scrolls, and taps, she held it to her ear. Josie didn't hear Guy Hale's voice on the other end but Britta said, "You need to come home right now. No. No questions. Just come home. Right now."

She hung up and tossed her phone onto the coffee table. Squeezing both palms between her knees, she rocked forward, body trembling. Her hair slid down, covering both sides of her face. A tattoo of a blue butterfly spread its wings across the back of her neck. Her cries were silent, and Josie felt a stab of recognition in her own soul. She had cried tears like these. The kind where the hurt was so big and so unimaginable, so against reality as you knew it, that you couldn't draw enough air to make sounds. Josie wanted to walk over and gather Britta in her arms, but at the same time, the last thing she wanted to do was overstep. Everyone reacted to grief differently. Some people didn't want to be touched at all, especially by a stranger. Besides, Josie had to maintain her professionalism.

After several minutes, Britta looked up at them, wiping tears away with the heels of her hands.

Noah said, "Mrs. Hale, we'll step outside until your husband arrives. Give you some privacy."

They started walking toward the door but Britta said, "Stop! Please. Please stay."

Turning back, Josie said, "Of course."

This time, Britta waved at the couch across from her, indicating for them to sit down. They stared at one another for a long, awkward moment. Britta sniffed. "I want to ask questions, but I'll wait till Guy gets here. It shouldn't be long."

Another fifteen minutes passed. Then they heard the peel of tires against asphalt. Outside, a car door slammed. Feet pounded up the front steps. The front door burst open. "Brit! Brit!"

Guy pulled up short when he looked to his left and saw them all seated. He had long brown hair pulled back into a ponytail, deep-set brown eyes, and a goatee. Like his wife, his arms were covered in tattoos. A leather vest covered a white T-shirt that announced: *Razor Tattoo Shop.*

"Mr. Hale," Josie said.

He registered his wife's tears, then the two detectives seated on the couch. "Oh no," he said. "No. No. Where's Dina?"

Josie and Noah stood, ready to present their credentials and introduce themselves, but Britta said, "She's dead."

He stared at her, all the color draining from his face. His knees slammed against the floor. Britta slid out of her chair and crawled to him. Together, they wept. Josie and Noah waited until they were able to compose themselves. Finally, they stood on shaky legs. Britta sat back in the chair. Guy perched on the arm, his arm around his wife's shoulders. "Tell us," he said.

Josie and Noah described what they had seen and experienced that morning.

"Wait," Guy said. "You're saying some guy saw the girls sitting on the side of the road in the fog and decided to just walk up to their car and attack them?"

"We believe he was looking for something," Josie explained. "He very likely targeted the girls."

"He doesn't live near here," Noah said. "But he was on the road at the same time as Dina and Alison, very early in the morning. There's a good chance he was here, watching them, and that he followed them and saw an opportunity. It could be random. We don't have enough information yet to make that determination but because he was looking for something, we're assessing that he targeted the girls."

Guy and Britta looked at one another but neither spoke.

Josie said, "The man I saw—his name is Elliott Calvert. Does that sound familiar to either of you?"

"No," Guy said. Looking down at Britta, he asked, "Could he be one of the guys from the bar?"

"I don't know," she said. To Josie and Noah, she added, "I work at the Atlas Taproom. We have lots of patrons in and out. It's a popular spot. Do you have a picture of him?"

Noah brought up Elliott Calvert's driver's license photo and showed them. Both their faces remained blank. Finally,

Britta said, "Never saw him. I'm good with faces. Have to be, in my line of work. You recognize him? Has he ever come into your shop?"

Guy shook his head. "Never seen him."

Josie said, "Well, half the police force is looking for him right now. The other half is looking for Alison. We won't stop until we find him."

Britta sniffled again. "What about Dina? Where is she now?"

"At the morgue," said Noah. "We'll give you the medical examiner's details so that you can contact her to find out when Dina's body will be released."

A sob ripped from Britta's frame, rocking her body. Guy slid both arms around her, whispering inaudibly into her hair while he swayed back and forth with her.

Josie stood up. "Mr. and Mrs. Hale, we do have several more questions for you, but we can come back another time. Or you can come to the police station when you're ready. Whatever is convenient for you."

Noah scribbled Dr. Feist's name and phone number on the back of one of his cards and handed it to Guy. Then he followed Josie to the door.

Britta called out, "Wait. Please. I don't—your questions, will they help you figure out why this happened to our little girl?"

Josie turned back to her. "Yes, they will, but Mrs. Hale, you absolutely do not have to speak with us right now."

"I want to. I want to talk now. I want you to find this Calvert guy and put him away for life. I want to know why he did this to my Dina. Please. Stay."

Josie and Noah looked back and forth between the parents. Josie could see them shoring themselves up in the way they stiffened their postures, straightened their spines, and jutted their chins forward. They were being strong for Dina, and it broke Josie's heart.

"Okay," she said, returning to the couch with Noah by her side. "But the moment you're ready to stop, you say the word, and we'll leave you be."

"What do you need to know?" Britta asked, wiping tears from her cheeks.

"Let's start with last night. Marlene Mills said that Alison was here for a sleepover," said Noah.

Britta looked up at Guy. He nodded. "Yeah, they were. Brit was at work."

"I go in around four or five in the afternoon, but I don't get home until four a.m. most times. Everyone's asleep. I came home last night and crashed. Dina started locking her bedroom door years ago so I stopped looking in on her when I got home."

Guy said, "I was here. They came home from work after eleven. Exhausted. It was a corporate party. They had to be back at work early this morning. Dina and Alison both know that Alison is welcome here anytime. They were hungry. Dina asked me to make them grilled cheese. Even though she's eighteen, I did it. I saw how tired they were, and Dina did that pouty lip thing—" He stopped abruptly, gasping, his breath frozen.

Britta stroked his arm. In a raspy voice, she said, "Dina's been pouting at him since she was two years old. It gets him every time."

Guy licked his dry lips and tried again. "They went to bed. I didn't hear them get up but when I woke at nine, they were gone."

"Did either of you hear from Dina after they left the house?" Josie asked.

Both shook their heads. Britta said, "No, but that's not

unusual. She's eighteen now. About to graduate from high school. We've been giving her as much independence as possible. She usually doesn't check in with us unless she needs something."

"Dina's phone was found at the scene," Josie said. "Is that phone in her name or is she on your plan?"

"Ours," said Guy.

"In that case," Josie said, "may we have your permission to examine its contents before we return it to you?"

Guy shrugged. He looked down at his wife, who also shrugged. "Sure," she said. "I guess. What do you think you'll find?"

"We're not sure," said Josie. "But if there is anything on it that connects her to Calvert in any way, we need to know."

"Had Dina been having any problems with anyone in the last few days or weeks?" said Noah.

"Not that we know of," Guy answered, swiping a hand over his goatee. He looked to Britta for confirmation, and she nodded.

"Was Dina dating anyone, or seeing anyone casually?" asked Noah.

Both parents shook their heads. Britta said, "No. If she was, she never talked about it to us."

"Would you say that Alison is her best friend?" asked Josie.

"Yeah," Britta said. "Now she is, and we're pretty happy that they met."

Guy added, "Alison is a good kid and a good influence on Dina."

Britta looked at her lap. "Before she met Alison she was hanging around with kids from her high school."

"A bunch of burn-outs," Guy complained. "All they did

was sit around and do drugs. Shoplift. Dina got into trouble a bunch of times. It was rough for a while there. Her grades were in the crapper. But she turned it around. Then she got the job at the hotel, started making decent money, for a teenager. Met Alison."

"Dina hasn't been in trouble for at least a year," Britta said. "Maybe longer."

Guy looked down at his wife, again tugging at his goatee. Josie felt her phone vibrate in her pocket, but she ignored it.

"Would it be possible for the two of you to make a list of all of her friends, past and present, for us?" asked Noah.

"We can," said Britta. "But we don't have numbers. Her phone is probably the best source for that."

"If Dina was having problems with someone, would she tell you?" asked Josie.

Britta sighed. "I don't know. It's not that she wouldn't trust us but that we're all so busy, and with me and Guy working nights mostly—I mean, he's home by eight or nine at least but I'm gone most of the time that Dina is home, unfortunately. I don't know, I—" She broke off and covered her mouth with her fist. Guy rubbed her back.

Josie waited a beat and then asked, "Is there anything you can think of that Dina or Alison might have had that someone would want? Something that might be valuable to another person?"

Both parents shook their heads. Britta said, "I won't lie to you. Dina used to experiment with drugs. She had a pretty bad weed problem, and I know she was getting it from somewhere. I think she might have tried other stuff, but that's just my suspicion. We never caught her. I truly thought she was done with that for the last year, but maybe she wasn't? Maybe she had drugs?"

"No," Guy said, his hand back at his chin. "She didn't. I, uh, checked her room a couple of weeks ago."

Britta's head reared back. She pulled away from Guy. "What? Why? You never mentioned it."

His palm wandered upward and covered his mouth for just a second before moving back down to his facial hair, fidgeting with it. By now Josie was certain that it was a nervous tell. Guy Hale was hiding something. He avoided his wife's eyes. "It was nothing really. She seemed extra tired to me. I asked her if she was using anything, and she swore she wasn't. We had a little fight over it, and she told me to search her room. I was so mad at her that I did. She was telling the truth. There was nothing there."

Britta's jaw was set. Angrily, she looked away from her husband. Josie knew that if Dina had been in possession of drugs, they could certainly have been in her car or her purse —both of which the Denton PD now had. Elliott Calvert had run the moment Josie and Noah showed up. Whatever he'd been looking for, he hadn't found it. Besides, Dina would have had to have her hands on a significant amount of drugs in order for someone to kill her over them. With a teen who had used drugs regularly in the past, it wasn't out of the question to follow that avenue of inquiry—whether or not drugs had played a part in the morning's events—but to Josie, something just didn't add up. Either there was something Guy Hale wasn't telling them or they needed to know more about Elliott Calvert. Or both.

Noah said, "You've got my card. If you think of anything else, please call. Also, contact Dr. Feist as soon as possible. We're very sorry for your loss."

They left the parents sitting in the chair, this time with some space between them. Josie met Guy's eyes as they left, pinning him with a stare. He couldn't hold her gaze.

Josie and Noah walked to their vehicle in silence. Josie stood beside the driver's door and took her phone out. There was a message from Gretchen.

Dogs are out looking for Alison. No developments. We still have a missing teen and a missing suspect. Can you head to Calvert's next?

From across the car's roof, Noah said, "You think that dad is hiding something?"

"Sure do," she replied, tapping back the word "yes" to Gretchen.

Noah looked back toward the house and mumbled, "Maybe we'll find out what it is."

Josie heard a door slam and then saw Guy running down the driveway. "Wait!" he said.

"Mr. Hale?" Josie said, pocketing her phone. "Is there something else?"

He nodded and glanced back at his house. The door remained closed. Stepping closer to their car, he lowered his voice. "My wife doesn't know this. I didn't tell her because... well, I didn't want her to worry."

"What is it?" asked Noah.

"A couple of weeks ago, I came home from work—Britta was at the bar and Dina was at the movies with Alison—and our entire house was turned upside down."

Josie took a step closer to him. "What do you mean, upside down?"

"Like in the movies," he said. "Like someone came in and ransacked it, searching for something. The books from the bookshelves were on the floor. The couch cushions were out of their covers, tossed all over. Every kitchen drawer was dumped.

The same in the whole house. Closets. Our bedrooms. I was standing there with my jaw on the ground when Dina came home. I guess I thought the same thing that Britta thought: maybe she was back to doing drugs and hanging out with lowlifes. The 'friends' she had back then were not the types I would trust with anything. A few times they stole money from us. I always got it back. Well, Dina always got it back."

"You never called the police?" asked Josie.

He shook his head. "It was twenty dollars here or there. The most they ever took was sixty bucks. I told Dina to tell them they could give it back and we would be square or if they didn't give it back, I was calling the police. I always got the money. They weren't allowed over here ever again, though."

Noah said, "Was anything missing this time?"

Guy glanced up at the front door again to make sure his wife wasn't there. Then he shook his head slowly. "No. That's the weird thing. Dina and I checked for valuables first. Everything was still there. I have a safe under our bed. Just a small portable one, nothing crazy. I keep about two grand in there in case of emergencies. Someone had pried it open but left the money in there. All of Britta and Dina's jewelry was still there. Everything."

Josie and Noah exchanged a curious look. Josie asked, "You didn't call the police?"

He shrugged. "And say what? Someone broke in and made a mess? You know, they didn't even break in. One of the kitchen windows out back was open. Whoever did it just popped the screen off and climbed in. Besides the safe, the only thing that was even broken was a single dinner plate. The real pain in the ass was cleaning everything up. Took us hours."

"What did Dina have to say about this incident?" asked Noah.

"I'm ashamed to say it but I blamed her old friends right away. I yelled. Said some pretty shitty things to her. Accused her of being back on drugs, messing around with people she shouldn't. She swore up and down that it wasn't true. What I said in there was right—I accused her, she denied it, and I did search her room. Her room, her car, her purse. Everything. There was nothing. She swore she knew nothing about it. I believed her. I figured maybe it was just a case of mistaken identity, like they got the wrong house."

"Do you still have the safe?" asked Noah.

Guy checked his front door again. Still no Britta. "It was destroyed. I had to throw it away. Why? You think you could get prints or something?"

Noah said, "The odds are very, very slim but it might have been worth a try. If you can think of any other item they might have touched where their prints might still be present, we could check. But we'd need elimination prints from you and your wife."

They'd need them from Dina as well, Josie thought, but Dr. Feist could take them. She wasn't about to bring that up to a grieving father.

Guy said, "My wife—I—I don't want to scare her... but I guess the worst has already happened, so..."

Noah said, "If you can find something, put it in a paper bag—not plastic—and bring it to the station. We'll have our forensic officers take care of it. If we find anything, we can let you know."

Josie glanced up at the front of the house. "You don't have any home surveillance cameras? Ring? Wyse? Nest?"

Guy shook his head. He gestured around them, to the other houses. "Look at this place. It's nice, right? We never have any trouble here. Sometimes the neighbor's kids play baseball out in the street in the summertime. They'll break a window. Their parents pay for it. That's it. We moved to this development because of how safe it is here."

Josie knew he was right. There were certain developments in Denton, especially on the outer edges of the city, whose crime rates were zero. This was one of them.

Noah extended a hand and Guy shook it. "Thank you for telling us. If we have any follow-up questions, we'll be in touch."

Guy stood in his driveway, hands in his jeans pockets, and watched them go.

As they drove away, Noah said, "This is getting stranger by the hour. Where to next?"

"Elliott Calvert's house."

CHAPTER 11

She is ten the first time she throws a punch. Not because she wants to but because Mug says everyone should know how to throw a punch, even little girls. "Especially little girls," he says. Pea isn't sure what he means by this. At school, it's always the boys who are fighting. Pushing each other into walls and desks, knocking over Mrs. Rex's school supply organizer. One time, a kid named Timmy Tralies pushed another boy's head right into the chalkboard. Really hard. Pea didn't like the sound it made at all. For a split second, she was frozen, pushed back in time to the garage— to *that thing* that never happened that she never saw.

But the girls at school didn't fight. The worst thing girls did was freeze each other out. "Social exclusion," Pea's mother called it. Her dad said it was "little bitches being little bitches," which made Pea laugh until her mother gave her The Glare. She stopped laughing, but when her mom left the room and her dad winked and made a goofy face, she laughed a little more.

"Are you listening to me, sweetheart?" Mug tousles her hair. "Pay attention. This is important."

She comes back to herself. They are in the family room and the big television is playing a news story about a boy who got beat up by a bunch of other boys after school, which reminds her of the day in the garage. Mug is there because he is waiting for her dad. They are going somewhere together. They are always going places together.

Pushing away more memories of *that*, Pea mutters, "Why do people hurt other people?"

Mug says, "Sometimes you have to hurt people."

"Mom says you never have to hurt anyone," Pea insists.

Her dad would have spent the next hour making fun of that. He hates her mom's "weak philosophies." But Mug simply says, "You have to hurt someone if they try to hurt you. Sometimes you have to hurt them before they can hurt you. Like if you know they're coming."

Pea doesn't understand but she doesn't want to talk about hurting people anymore.

Mug says, "Come on, I'll show you how to fight."

He makes Pea stand in a wide stance, body turned slightly ("never let 'em at your center"), both arms up ("keep 'em up at all times") and hands fisted ("thumb on the outside, always on the outside. Tuck it in.") Mug is on his knees which brings him face-level with her. He holds up two meaty hands, palms facing her. They're rough and calloused with dirt caked in the fine creases. "Come on, sweetheart, hit me as hard as you can. Right here. Right in the middle of my palms."

Pea throws a few half-hearted punches. Then she says, "I don't want to do this anymore."

She sees genuine sympathy in his eyes. "Sweetheart," he says. "No one wants to fight, but sometimes you have to handle your business. Now try again."

CHAPTER 12

The Calverts lived in West Denton. It was another fairly safe area of the city. The homes were upscale but not super wealthy. Josie knew from a prior case that most of the families in this area worked white-collar jobs. Many of the mothers stayed home while their children were young, leaving the fathers to handle the income. The Calvert home was an elegant two-story Tudor with carefully tended flower beds running the length of the front of the house. Fall blooms strained to stay upright above the garden's mulch, making their last hurrahs before the cold weather set in. Josie and Noah parked on the street and walked up the driveway. Josie rang the doorbell. A moment later, a tall, lithe woman with her black hair piled high on her head in a messy bun answered the door. She wore a white tank top with orange stains dotting the front and a pink pair of sweatpants. Pink, fuzzy slippers completed the ensemble. On her hip was a rosy-cheeked infant in a onesie, with a pink bib around her neck. Both onesie and bib had matching orange stains on them. What little blonde hair she had was tied in a pink ribbon on top of her downy head.

"Can I help you?" asked the woman.

Josie and Noah held out their credentials. Josie said, "I'm Detective Josie Quinn and this is my colleague, Lieutenant Noah Fraley. We're looking for Elliott Calvert."

She studied their IDs with one delicate eyebrow raised. "You're looking for Elliott? Whatever for?"

Noah asked, "Are you his wife?"

"Tori," she said, shifting the baby on her hip. Uninterested in Josie or Noah, the baby put her fingers into her mouth, gathering up a great deal of drool. With that same hand, she tried to reach her mother's bun. Tori gently pushed her hand down. A string of spit caught on Tori's hair and stretched from her head to the baby's mouth.

Josie wondered why it hadn't yet occurred to her that Elliott might not be okay. Marlene Mills had had an immediate and visceral reaction to the very sight of Josie and Noah. Britta Hale had become shaken within moments of their arrival, even before they delivered the shattering news. Tori seemed perfectly relaxed.

"Mrs. Calvert," said Josie. "May we come in?"

The baby made a loud noise in her throat and then, as if delighted by it, she giggled. Tori laughed. "I'm sorry," she said. Her tone remained completely calm and reasonable when she asked, "Don't you guys need, like, a warrant or something to come into people's houses for no reason? This is weird, right? If you're looking for Elliott, he's at work. I'll give you the address if you tell me what this is all about. He is my husband, after all."

Noah said, "We don't need a warrant to speak with people, Mrs. Calvert. Your husband is not at work. We're trying to locate him."

The baby tried again to touch Tori's bun, this time snagging a piece of long hair and unraveling it from its place.

Clutching it, she stuffed the end of it into her mouth. Tori didn't stop her. For the first time since she opened the door, concern blanketed her face. "Locate him? What do you mean?"

Josie said, "Mrs. Calvert, at approximately seven this morning, my colleague and I were traveling on Widow's Ridge Road. It was foggy. We were attempting to pull over. We came upon your husband attacking a teenage girl on the shoulder of the road."

Tori stared at them for a long moment, several emotions trying themselves on her face: bewilderment, skepticism, fear, confusion, shock, and then incredulity. She laughed. The baby laughed in response, waving the slimy strand of hair clutched in her tiny hand through the air, as if in victory. "Now I know you have the wrong person," said Tori. "That's absurd. My husband would never do something like that. Also, as I said, he's been at work all day."

They said nothing.

Rolling her eyes, she shifted the baby again and turned away from them. "Fine. I'll just call him and you'll see."

Josie and Noah stood in the doorway and watched as she disappeared down a hallway into what was presumably her kitchen. She returned with a cell phone pressed to her ear. The baby saw it and tried to grab it, but Tori managed to keep it out of reach. A long minute ticked past. Tori pulled the phone away and looked at it as if it had betrayed her in some way. "He's not answering. I'll just—I'll call his office."

Bouncing the baby gently on her hip, she awkwardly found the number and pressed call. Another minute ticked past. She shook her head. "That was his direct line. I'll just call the receptionist. She might still be there. They don't usually work Saturdays, but things have been crazy there lately." Again, she found a number and called it. "Hi, Steph? This is Tori Calvert. Is my husband in his office? Could you put me through to him, please?"

A silence. Tori's brow knit. "What about this morning? Was he there? Did you see him at all today?"

The baby lunged for the phone and Tori lost her grip. Josie surged through the door and grabbed for the infant, catching her just as she fell through Tori's arms. The baby seemed to think it was a game and, delighted, she squealed. Josie held her close and bounced her. Tori barely noticed, too intent on whatever the receptionist was saying. "That's impossible," she told her. "He said he was going to work. He's been working like crazy lately. He kept saying he was behind on the Locke Heights account."

Josie was close enough now to make out the faint words coming through the line. "I'm sorry, Mrs. Calvert, he was not here today."

Tori didn't bother with a goodbye. She simply punched the End Call icon and dropped her phone onto a nearby foyer table. She looked around as if she had no idea where she was, not even registering that Josie now had her baby.

Noah stepped inside. "Mrs. Calvert," he tried again. "May we please come in and ask you some questions?"

Tori continued looking around the foyer with its polished hardwood floors, large faux potted plants, and ornately carved heavy wooden chairs with matching tables as if she didn't recognize it. Finally, she threw her arms into the air and let them fall back to her sides. "Fine," she said. "Sure, I guess. Come into the kitchen."

They followed her toward the back of the house, emerging into a kitchen that had been modernized in white and chrome, the only trace of its Tudor style the thick wooden beams running the length of the ceiling. A high chair sat at the table, a kitchen chair facing it. On its tray was a cup filled with orange mush and a baby spoon. Josie remembered when Misty's son, Harris, was a baby. Given the chair, the baby food, and the weight and appearance of the baby in her arms, Josie estimated the Calverts' daughter to be about five months old. She pointed to the cup on the high chair tray and said, "Sweet potatoes?"

Tori was still gazing at their surroundings, oblivious to them. "What?"

Josie stepped directly in front of Tori and said, "Your daughter was eating sweet potatoes?"

Tori blinked, seeming to come back to herself. Tears glistened in her eyes. For the first time she noticed her daughter in Josie's arms. Smiling, she thanked Josie and took the baby, strapping her back into the high chair. "She loves sweet potatoes," Tori whispered. "But I think she loves getting them everywhere but her mouth more."

The baby slapped both hands on the tray, making a "dadadada" sound and then screeching a laugh. She reached for the cup and spoon, but Tori got there first, snatching them up and then spoon-feeding a bite into the baby's mouth. Tori said, "Please, sit down."

They each took a seat at the table. Noah said, "She's a very happy baby."

Tori smiled wanly. "She is, isn't she? I think we were very lucky. Teething is no picnic, but my mother says that's normal."

"Five months old?" asked Josie.

Tori looked surprised but nodded. "Yes, next week she will be five months. Her name is Amalise."

"That's a lovely name," Josie said.

"It was the only one we could agree on," Tori mumbled. With the next spoonful, Amalise smacked her lips and then made a long "buhbuhbuh" sound, spraying herself, her chair and her mother with sweet potatoes. More giggles.

Tori got up and went to the sink, grabbing a handful of paper towels and running them under the faucet. "Are you sure you have the right man?" she asked.

Josie said, "I am sure, yes."

Tori returned to her seat and wiped Amalise's face with the towels. The baby struggled, turning her head back and forth to avoid the towel. When Tori finished, she resumed the feeding. "Where is my husband?" she asked, resignation heavy in her voice.

Josie said, "We don't know. When we saw him, he ran from us. I pursued him into the woods. He jumped off a cliff into Roaring Creek. Searchers found what we believe is his phone and one of his cufflinks on the bank of the creek a few miles away, so we do believe he survived the jump and is likely on foot."

Tori met Josie's eyes. Horrified, she said, "He jumped?"

"I'm afraid so," Josie replied.

"Did he—did he say anything?"

Amalise leaned over the side of her chair, holding a slime-covered hand out to Josie, who pretended to take and eat some of the sweet potatoes, much to the baby's delight. "He asked me if the jump would kill him. Before I could respond, he said he would take the chance. Then he jumped."

Tori scraped the last of the sweet potatoes out of the cup and fed them to Amalise, who, instead of swallowing, put both hands into her mouth and then squished the orange mush between her fingers.

"I'm sorry," Tori said. "I just—I'm just having a very hard time understanding what's happening here. Can you tell me again exactly what happened? I mean, how do you know this was really my husband? What would he be doing up on Widow's Ridge Road, first of all, and what would he want with two teenage girls?"

"We're trying to figure that out," Noah said.

Together, they took her through the morning's events again. Josie concluded by saying, "The car that was pulled over near the girls' vehicle was a Nissan Altima, registered to your husband at this address."

Tori blinked back tears. She watched Amalise smear the sweet potatoes in her hair but didn't stop her. She sat that way for what felt like several minutes. Noah stood and retrieved a fresh clump of wet paper towels. He gently wiped Amalise's face and hands, and then tried to get what he could out of her hair. Blinking back into the present, Tori said, "Thank you. I'm sorry. I'm a little shell-shocked, to be honest. This is coming out of nowhere. Elliott is not the kind of person who would ever do something like this. I'm just trying to figure out what the hell is going on."

"We understand," said Josie. "We're trying to figure out what happened and why ourselves."

"Are the girls okay? You said there were two of them."

"Yes," Noah replied. "Two of them. One of them is deceased and the other is injured and missing."

Tears spilled down her pale cheeks. "Oh my God. This is so hard to believe. You think my husband killed one of these girls?"

Josie said, "We would like to talk to him about what happened. Mrs. Calvert, when was the last time you saw your husband?"

Tori used the wet towels bunched in her hands to dab at her eyes but only succeeded in getting sweet potato on her cheek. She didn't seem to care. "Late last night. He got in around one a.m. I was angry. We had a fight. It woke

Amalise. He went into her nursery to comfort her and then he ended up falling asleep in the rocking chair beside her crib. I knew he was leaving super early to go into the office today because he told me while we were fighting. He knows better than to wake me if I'm asleep now—I get so little sleep as it is with the baby. So he must have got up, got dressed, and left. Amalise woke me at seven. I heard her on the monitor."

Noah asked, "What were you fighting about?"

Tori waved the clump of towels in the air. "The baby, what else? Do either of you have kids?"

"No," they answered in unison.

"Let me tell you, it's not what it's cracked up to be. Don't get me wrong, I love this baby and I would die for her. I would do anything for her. She is my life now. But this is a lot of work and not much sleep."

Josie almost said, "I remember," but stopped herself. She had helped Misty with Harris during his infancy. Although she didn't have a child of her own, she had seen first-hand how exhausting it was for her friend. Josie, Noah, and Ray's mom had done everything they could to support Misty, during the first year especially. Instead, Josie said, "I'm sure it's exhausting, and with your husband working a lot, it must make it so much harder."

Tori nodded. Amalise batted a palm against her mouth, making more noises that delighted her. "It is so much harder. I don't have a support system here. We're both transplants. We lived in New York City before this. His family is still there. Mine lives even farther away in upstate New York. My mom has come down a few times to help, especially in the beginning. I had a C-section and it took weeks for me to be able to handle Amalise alone. Still, even with her help now and then, it's just not enough, and most of the time, when Elliott is home, he spends ten minutes with her and then he's watching television or on his phone. It's been very stressful, and we've been fighting a lot."

"You two met in New York City?" prompted Josie.

Tori laughed. "Sort of. We both lived there but we met on a dating app. Fast-forward six years, and here I am."

She looked lovingly at Amalise, but Josie saw deep sadness behind her eyes. She wondered what Tori had left behind. "Did you move here for work?" she asked.

Tori sighed, shoulders slumped. "For Elliott's work. He's an architect. Some guy he knew back in college opened a firm here ages ago. After we got married, he offered Elliott a position. It seemed ideal. I was a ballerina with the Allard ballet company in New York City. I could have kept dancing for a few more years but Elliott convinced me to retire early so we could start a family. It seemed like the perfect scenario. I was all in and so was he, I thought, until the baby came. I guess it was not what either of us expected. Not that I regret it." She reached forward and tickled Amalise's chubby belly, eliciting a happy shriek of laughter. In spite of herself, Tori laughed as well. "Now I have this little lovebug. I wouldn't give her up for anything in the world."

Noah said, "Other than being a new dad, was your husband under any stress of any kind?"

Tori shrugged. "He's been working on some big project at work for months. So much overtime. He didn't seem particularly stressed about it, but he was hardly ever home. The Locke Heights account. That's all he's talked about for months and months. I feel like our lives revolve around it. I can't wait till that's done and we can—" She stopped herself, eyes widening as she realized that the Locke Heights account didn't matter anymore. "You're going to arrest him, aren't you?" she whispered.

"I'm afraid so," Josie said. "Yes."

Noah asked, "I'd like to show you photos of the two girls who were at the scene today to see if you recognize them. Would that be okay?"

Tori nodded.

Noah pulled up Dina and Alison's driver's license photos on his phone and came around the table to show Tori. She swiped back and forth between them several times but shook her head. "I've never seen them before. If I have, I don't remember."

Josie said, "When we arrived on scene, he was saying 'where is it?' to one of the girls. Do you know what he might have meant by that?"

Confused, Tori said, "Where is what?"

Noah replied, "We believe he was looking for something and whatever it was, he seemed to think the girls had it. Do you know what he could have been looking for?"

Amalise kept her eyes on her mother, trying out a new sound. "Mamamama."

Tori said, "I really don't, and again, I just can't believe you've got the right person. My husband may not have been holding up his end as a new dad, but what you're telling me today? It's completely and utterly out of character for him. He's a sweet, charming man. A kind man. I've never seen even a shred of evidence that he could ever be violent to anyone."

Josie asked, "Does your husband take any medication?"

Tori shook her head again. "He takes Prilosec for heartburn. That's it."

"Illegal drugs?" asked Noah.

"No. Not Elliott."

"Has he ever used illegal drugs, to your knowledge?" asked Josie.

"No. Not that I am aware of. If he did before we met, he never told me about it and no one in his family or his circle of friends mentioned anything either."

"What about alcohol?" asked Noah. "Does he drink?"

Amalise banged both palms against the high chair, as if she were growing impatient now that the sweet potatoes were no longer forthcoming. Tori answered, "A beer now and then. That's it. Usually on the weekends if he's watching a game or something. He watches a lot of sports. When we used to go out—before I got pregnant—he would drink more but it was never an issue."

Josie said, "Mrs. Calvert, can you think of any reason at all that your husband would attack two teenage girls?"

"No. I really can't."

Noah asked, "Does your husband own any firearms?"

"A gun? Elliott? No."

"As far as we know, your husband is on the run," Noah said. "Can you think of any place he might go if he was trying to elude law enforcement? Any place he might hide?"

Amalise clapped her hands again, switching back to "dadadada" sounds.

Tori said, "No. I honestly can't. His office, maybe? That's the only other place he goes besides here. We haven't had a chance to make friends here, so I don't know where he would go if he was trying to hide."

Noah asked, "Do you or your husband own any other properties besides this home?"

"No," said Tori. "This is it."

Josie thought of asking about the Calverts' cell phone plan but cell phones weren't considered marital property, even if they were attached to the same account, which meant that Tori couldn't give them permission to peruse her husband's phone. It would be easier and quicker to simply get a warrant for the contents of Elliott's phone.

Josie and Noah stood and thanked her for her time. "If your husband comes home or contacts you," Josie added, "please call 911 right away. Or contact me." She handed Tori a business card.

Noah said, "You might also consider going to stay with your mother until we figure out what's going on here."

Tori looked up from Josie's card, shock evident on her face. "You think Elliott would hurt me? Is that why you're saying that?"

Josie answered, "We don't know, but based on his behavior today, we do have concerns for the safety of you and Amalise. It's not a requirement, just a suggestion, that you might be safer out of town, at least for a few days."

"No." Tori shook her head once more. "No. Elliott would never hurt me or Amalise. Never."

"Fair enough," Josie said. "But we would still like for you to call us if you see or hear from him."

CHAPTER 13

It was late, and according to Gretchen, no progress in the searches for Alison Mills or Elliott Calvert had been made. Chief Chitwood had instructed her to go home and get some rest while he supervised the search teams through the night. He also insisted that Josie and Noah—who weren't even due back to work until the next day—go home for the night. As much as Josie wanted to keep going and keep working, she knew the Chief had a point. They'd need rest and food to keep going.

She and Noah went to Misty's house to pick up Trout. Josie was somewhat relieved to find that Misty's note had indeed been a joke and that Trout did, in fact, want to come home with them. The moment Josie and Noah walked through Misty's door, Trout came running into the foyer. They both dropped to their knees to greet him. He was ecstatic to see them, his little butt wiggling at warp speed as he jumped up to lick their faces, making small high-pitched noises of excitement. Misty's chiweiner dog, Pepper, joined him. It took several minutes for the two dogs to calm down.

Soon Harris joined them, his six-year-old body a blur as

he came barreling down the hall and into Josie's arms. "You're back! You're back!" he cried. Josie squeezed him hard and buried her face into his hair, inhaling the scents of watermelon shampoo and grape juice. He wore PAW Patrol pajamas and held a dinosaur action figure in one hand. Looking at his thick blond hair and bright blue eyes, the resemblance to her late husband Ray nearly took her breath away. The older he got, more and more moments like these caught Josie off guard. Misty stood in the kitchen doorway, a towel in her hands, smiling.

"You guys caught a bad one, didn't you?" she said.

Josie stood up. "On our way home, no less. I'm sorry we're so late. We did thoroughly enjoy the meal you left for us, though."

"Yeah," Noah said, still on his knees. "That was very thoughtful."

Harris jumped onto Noah's back, and they proceeded to wrestle around on the foyer floor. It was their new thing. Conflicted, Trout skittered back and forth between them and Josie, unsure what to do. Finally, he barked at Noah and Harris.

Misty said, "Boys, stop. Come on into the kitchen. Let's eat."

Josie's stomach growled as she followed Misty, Trout bumping her leg as he went with her. Glancing behind her, she saw Noah, now standing, with Harris on his back, spinning in a circle. Harris's giggles filled the entire downstairs.

The house was a point of pride with Misty. It was a large Victorian home in one of Denton's historic districts, and Misty had always kept it furnished with lavish antique furniture, some of it from the actual Victorian period. It had always looked like something out of a magazine. Then came Harris. Since his birth, much of the Victorian decor had been replaced with more practical items which had, as expected, become stained or scuffed by the resident toddler.

The kitchen was redolent with the smells of a roast. No matter when she and Noah visited, Misty always had something cooking. Josie wasn't sure how she did it, being a single mom with a full-time job. Noah walked into the room, now dangling Harris by his ankles.

Josie said, "Please, stop. It makes me so nervous when you do that."

"Oh, he's fine," Noah and Misty said in unison.

Expertly, Noah flipped him upright and onto his feet. Harris immediately clung to Noah's thigh and tried climbing up his body. "It's fun, JoJo."

Josie shook her head. Of the three of them, she was the most anxious when it came to Harris's safety. Even more so than his mother, who was inclined to give him more freedom, independence, and room to play.

Moments later they were all seated around Misty's table eating dinner while Trout lay beneath the table, his warm little body sprawled across Josie's feet. Misty asked them about their honeymoon and then the topic of conversation moved on to Harris's sixth birthday, which they'd commemorated the month before with a small gathering of adults and a cake. Harris had wanted a party with all of his friends from school, but Misty had explained that his school friends already had birthday parties booked every weekend and so she'd had to postpone Harris's until mid-October.

"I want a bouncy house," Harris proclaimed. "A big one with a slide."

Noah laughed. "That sounds like fun. Can I go on it?"

Harris eyed him. "I don't know. You're pretty big. Mom, can we get one that's big enough to hold Uncle Noah?"

Misty shook her head. "I didn't say yes to the bouncy house, Harris."

"Because of the yard?"

Josie said, "What's wrong with the yard?"

Misty sighed. "It's not big enough for the bouncy house he has in mind, although I can afford to rent one for the kids. I suspect he's already told everyone he's going to have one."

She looked at her son, one brow kinked in an exaggerated way. He giggled but admitted nothing. Misty continued, "I mean, they'd probably be occupied for hours with it, but it's too big for our yard."

"Put it in ours," said Josie. She glanced at Noah. His mouth was full of food but he nodded emphatically.

Misty laughed. "I can't have my six-year-old's birthday party at your house. Are you crazy?"

"Why not?" said Noah. "We've got plenty of room. Besides, you just watched our 'kid' for a week."

"You guys have a kid?" asked Harris.

"He means Trout," Josie said.

Harris giggled. "He's not your kid! Although you guys kind of treat him like he is."

This time, Misty giggled. "He's not wrong."

Noah shook his head. "I'm not even sorry. Look, have the party at our place. Get the bouncy house."

Josie added, "And make sure it can hold a grown man, would you?"

Harris stood up on his chair and pumped both fists into the air. "This is going to be the best birthday party ever!"

Josie held Trout in her lap as Noah drove them home. They took him for a walk, and he kept glancing back at them every few feet, as if he was afraid they would disappear any moment. At home, they finally slid into bed, and Josie sighed with pleasure to be back in her own home and reunited with Trout. The meal with Harris and Misty had left her feeling a contented warmth, and as she drifted off to sleep, guilt pricked at her for feeling so happy when the Hale family was utterly destroyed, Tori and Amalise Calvert's world was turned on its head, and the Mills family's own happiness and security hung in the balance.

"Stop," Noah said softly from his side of the bed.

Trout, who had been at their feet, crept up slowly between their bodies.

"Stop what?" asked Josie.

"Feeling bad about feeling happy," he said.

They'd been together for five years, married for just over one year and Josie still couldn't figure out how he was able to read her mind and more importantly, her emotions. She didn't even understand them herself sometimes. "I can't help it," she said.

"Try," Noah answered gently.

Josie felt him reach across Trout's back and touch her arm, running his fingers lightly up and down from her shoulder to her wrist. The effect was soothing.

"We see every day how hard happiness is to come by," he added. "How it can be shattered and sucked away in a matter of seconds."

"Yes," Josie agreed. "That's why it feels wrong to enjoy it."

"What you're feeling right now?" Noah answered. "The Hales would kill to have that. They'd probably give up everything to feel the kind of peace that you and I feel now. You know I'm right. That's how I felt when my mom died."

"And that's how I felt when my grandmother died,"

Josie whispered. "Sometimes, when I miss her the most, I still feel like I would do anything to feel a little bit of peace or joy."

"You're feeling it now," Noah pointed out. "You felt it while we were away."

Josie caught his hand in hers as it moved to her wrist. Squeezing, she said, "A lot of that joy had to do with you, in particular that thing you do with your—"

"Josie," he cut her off, laughing softly. "You know what I mean. I'm just saying it's okay for us to be happy."

She wanted to believe him.

CHAPTER 14

Josie woke before dawn, chest heaving as she gulped in air. Vestiges of her dreams slipped just out of reach as she blinked her eyes open. She knew her mind had been busy while she rested—so busy that her body had been tricked into believing it was exerting itself. Awake, she couldn't recall the exact events of her dreams, only that she was running through the woods. She wasn't running from someone; she was searching for someone. It made sense, given the case they'd stumbled onto the day before. Beside her, both Noah and Trout snored. Her digital clock read 4:30 a.m. She tried to slow her pounding heart, putting both hands on her stomach and focusing on her breath. Her therapist had given her a host of different breathing exercises for various occasions. She still wasn't convinced any of them worked, but she kept doing them. Maybe one day she would notice a difference. As her body calmed, she waited for sleep to return. Wished for it.

But her mind kept going back to Elliott Calvert.

I'm not going to fall. I'm going to jump.

Whatever he'd been looking for had made him

desperate enough to attack two teenage girls and yet, standing on the precipice of Roaring Creek, he didn't care at all whether he lived or died. He was afraid, that much was obvious, but he was also desperate. What made a man so desperate that he would lose all control and regard for his own life?

More practically, where the hell was he?

Josie turned over and retrieved her cell phone from the nightstand, checking for any text messages from the Chief or anyone in the department. There was nothing. She texted the Chief:

Any progress on the searches?

His answer came back within a minute.

No. Go back to sleep.

Josie ignored his instructions.

Send me the location of where his phone and cufflink were found.

The clock on her phone ticked from one minute to the next. She could practically hear the Chief grumbling from wherever he was in Denton at that moment. After six minutes, a photo of a map with an arrow pointing to a place in the center of it appeared in the message thread. Then the words:

I mean it, Quinn. Go back to sleep.

Josie sat up, swinging her legs over the side of the bed.

From behind her came Noah's sleep-muffled voice. "What are you doing?"

She used her thumb and index finger on the screen to zoom in on the location where Elliott Calvert's personal items had been found. Josie had grown up in Denton, and other than when she went to college, had always lived there. She was more intimately familiar with it than most people on the police force.

"Josie," said Noah, his voice more alert.

Calvert had emerged from Roaring Creek almost two miles from where he had jumped into it. He had also gotten out on the side of the creek that led away from the city. The area was heavily wooded, and the terrain was difficult. Back when Josie was on patrol, two teenagers had been hunting out there. One of them fell and broke his leg. The other went for help. When he finally found a road and flagged someone down for help, three hours had already passed. When police responded, they realized they couldn't get any vehicles back to where the injured boy remained. They had tried getting close with ATVs but ultimately, Josie and another officer had carried him out on foot using a backboard. It wasn't the last time they'd had to do that near that location. It was a well-used deer-hunting spot.

"Josie," Noah repeated.

Trout snored on, oblivious.

"I know where Calvert is," she said.

A groan sounded from Noah's side of the bed. "Is there any way that you can text the location to the Chief and let him take care of it?"

"The Chief can't travel through that part of the woods on foot. His leg still bothers him."

Noah touched her hip, his palm warm and heavy,

comforting. "No, but he's got plenty of patrol officers at his disposal who can walk through those woods."

Josie waggled her phone in his direction so he could see the map. "It's not exactly easy to explain. There aren't landmarks, but I know what I'm looking for."

She felt the bed shift, heard Trout groan in protest at being disturbed, and then Noah's lips were on her neck. They traveled up to her ear, planting light kisses. Then he whispered, "Fine. Let's get dressed."

Dawn was breaking by the time Josie, Noah, the Chief and two uniformed officers gathered on the side of the road closest to where Elliott Calvert had gotten out of Roaring Creek. There was some fog but not nearly as much as the day before. Visibility wouldn't be an issue. Radios squawked as they checked them to make sure they all worked. Chief Chitwood stood along the narrow shoulder of the road. Two cars rolled down toward the city. He waved for them to keep going. One driver stopped, rolling his window down to ask the Chief questions. Josie couldn't hear any of their conversation, only the Chief's raised voice, responding with annoyance. His thin arms flapped in the air, gesticulating for the driver to move along. When he turned back to face them, Josie could see his pale, acne-pitted face was flushed.

"Busybodies," the Chief muttered, joining their circle. He patted down a loose strand of white hair floating over his balding pate. "I'm going to stay right here while you guys search."

One of the uniformed officers, Brennan, said, "We already searched this area. Calvert's not here."

The Chief said, "Quinn thinks he's still here. Hiding in a deer blind."

Brennan scoffed. "You think we didn't check for deer blinds?"

His partner, an officer named Daugherty, added, "Detectives, this isn't our first outdoor search."

Josie nodded. "Of course it's not. I wasn't suggesting that. How many blinds did you find?"

They stared at her. Daugherty said, "There weren't any deer blinds. We found two tree stands. That was it."

Brennan added, "How would we know if there was a deer blind out here anyway? It's not like there's some registry. Anyone can put one up as long as they have permission from the property owner. There could be none or there could be a dozen."

Daugherty said, "If there were a dozen we definitely would have seen them."

Brennan's eyes darted toward him.

Daugherty rolled his eyes. "They're freestanding. You can't miss them."

"That's not true," said Josie. "Not all of them are free-standing." She took out her phone and pulled up the screen-shot of the map that the Chief had sent her. "This land, from Roaring Creek to this road where we're standing, belongs to Al Funk."

More blank stares. Josie went on, "He's in his eighties now. Lives at Rockview."

"The nursing home?" asked Brennan.

"Yes," said Josie. "My grandmother, when she was alive, knew him. Introduced us. He's owned this land for over fifty years. He's hunted it. So have his kids, his grandkids and great-grandkids. He's even allowed extended family and friends to hunt here."

"So what?" said Daugherty. "We told you, all we found were two tree stands. Both empty. No blinds."

A pair of headlights cut through the early-morning light. A car lumbered up the narrow road, slowing as it came to them. The Chief waved it along.

Josie shook her head. "Mr. Funk has a deer blind. It's large and well disguised, especially during this time of the year when everything is green. His family still uses it. They leave supplies up there year-round. If Elliott Calvert found it—and judging by the fact that he hasn't been found anywhere else, it seems he did—he would have been able to hide for some time. Mr. Funk's grandson used to keep a steel ammo can up there with granola bars and bottled water. Calvert's probably waiting for the searches to die down and the sun to come up so he can come out. Then he'll disappear."

"How do you know this?" Daugherty said, a note of accusation in his voice.

"Because it's so high up that there have been accidents. One of Funk's great-grandsons fell out of it and broke a leg a few years back."

"If we didn't find it when we were searching," said Brennan, "how did Calvert find it?"

Josie said, "Mr. Funk told me that he installed a piece of bright orange climbing rope that hangs from the blind so it's easier to locate and so you can pull yourself up inside. If you didn't see the rope during your search, then Calvert probably pulled it up when he got into the blind."

The Chief said, "You two about done questioning Detective Quinn? This Calvert guy attacked two teenage girls. That makes him a danger to my city. If he's out here hiding in some deer blind, I want him found. Now."

They looked everywhere but at Josie and nodded. Noah said, "Let's go. We'll spread out to cover as much of the forest here as we can."

As they moved into the woods, Josie said, "Mr. Funk built it himself. It's in the center of three trees. Two hickory trees and a catalpa."

"It's custom-made?" asked Brennan.

"Right," Josie replied. "With wood. It's nestled among the trees, and spray-painted to blend in. There's also a lot of foliage surrounding the trees that makes the ladder difficult to find, which is why the climbing rope was helpful. If I'm right, and Calvert pulled the rope up so that it's no longer visible, then you'll have to look very carefully."

They spread apart but still within sight of one another. Moving slowly, they picked through the increasingly thick undergrowth, climbing over tree roots and large rocks as they went. The only sounds were their footsteps and the birds chirping and singing as they flitted from tree to tree. A slight chill hung in the crisp air, evaporating as the sun fought through the canopy of foliage overhead. Josie stayed a few feet ahead of Noah and the others, doing her best to lead the way to the blind from memory. The forested areas in and around Denton were filled with various rock formations. Most were well known to locals, but the one Josie was looking for that marked the area just before the Funk blind was small and obscure. She only knew it because she and Mr. Funk had discussed it when they'd met at Rockview. When she'd asked him how he found the area in which he'd built the blind each time he went hunting, he'd told her he searched for a small, rounded boulder with what looked like a cat's ear jutting from the top of it.

It didn't take long to find the cat's ear rock. Still, sweat pooled at the base of Josie's spine and left a cool film over the bare skin of her arms. She looked behind her to see Noah and the two uniformed officers trudging along. "It's just up here," she told them.

Noah picked up his pace, but the others remained unimpressed, not even looking up from their paths.

Just as Josie remembered, about four feet beyond the cat's ear formation was one of the three tree trunks that held Mr. Funk's blind—the thick, gnarled trunk of the catalpa. She stopped when she came to it, face turned toward the treetop. Up high among its leafy branches, a small part of one of the blind's walls was visible. Painted in a green camouflage pattern, it blended in so well that Josie second-guessed herself. Kudzu crept up one side of the tree, spreading along some of its branches like coiled veins. A tangle of its vines hung down like a curtain. Josie pushed it aside and stepped past it. She noted the other two trees, and now that she was in the center of them, she saw the base of the blind squarely overhead.

Noah's face appeared in the opening she'd just stepped through. "This is it," he said. "You were right. I don't see any orange rope anywhere. Where is the ladder?"

Josie pointed to one of the hickory trees where the ladder had been made using two-by-fours that were also painted a camouflage pattern and drilled into the trunk.

Noah's eyes followed the ladder rungs up to the blind. "That's really steep."

"And high," said Brennan as he and Daugherty stepped beneath the blind. "How do you even get into the blind from the top of that tree?"

Josie said, "There's a two-foot by three-foot platform outside the blind door. You stand on that."

"A blind with a front porch?" said Daugherty.

"Sort of," said Josie.

"It's basically a treehouse," Brennan remarked.

A creak sounded overhead. They all looked up.

Noah said, "He's up there. Let's get into position."

They walked out from under the blind and surrounded the trees. Josie found a place where she could see part of the platform that led to the blind's door. Noah was several feet away. He met her eyes. "No chance Mr. Funk or anyone in his family left a loaded firearm up there, right?"

Josie shook her head. "No. They're too careful for that."

He nodded. Then he cupped his hands around his mouth and called out, "Elliott Calvert! This the Denton Police. Please vacate the deer blind."

There was no sound or movement overhead. Noah yelled out again. They waited. After the third time, Brennan said, "You sure he's up there?"

Josie hollered, "Mr. Calvert. This is Detective Josie Quinn of the Denton Police Department. We met yesterday. Please come out."

There was another creak. Josie thought she saw the blind door swing open, but the tree branches with their thick leaves made it difficult to tell. "Mr. Calvert?" she called.

Footsteps tapped and then branches shook. Josie kept her eyes on the platform, waiting for any glimpse of Calvert.

Brennan called, "Sir. Come down here now. You need to come with us."

What happened next took seconds, but in Josie's mind each event stretched into a slow-motion montage. A hand thrust out from the branches obscuring the platform. Noah yelled, "Josie, watch out!" Following the hand, Elliott Calvert's face poked from the edge of the platform. Her brain struggled to process what she was seeing as the rest of his body flew into the air, arms and legs flailing. His entire form rushed at her, a blur of limbs. Noah's body slammed into hers so hard, all of her breath was forced from her lungs. The left side of her body hit the dirt of the forest floor. Her body had no feeling. There was no air. No thought. Only Noah's face floating over her. Concern filled his eyes. Josie was aware that he was touching her face, but she felt nothing. Then came bellows, low and guttural, the sounds of agony.

"Josie, try to catch your breath." Noah's words finally broke through.

Finally, her airway opened, and she sucked in as much air as she could get. Noah brought her to a sitting position, and she looked around to see where the cries were coming from. Noah said, "It's Calvert."

Three feet away, Calvert lay on the ground, writhing, holding one of his arms to his chest. His face went from ashen to a sickening green. Brennan and Daugherty stood over him, watching as he rolled onto his side and vomited.

Noah pulled Josie to her feet. "He jumped. He would have landed on you."

"Thanks," she breathed, brushing off her jeans.

Dry heaves rocked Calvert's body. Drawing closer, Josie saw fresh blood seeping from between the fingers of his right hand where it held his left wrist.

Daugherty said, "I think he broke something. He went down pretty hard."

"It's a long fall," said Brennan.

"Not a fall," Noah corrected. "A jump."

Josie stood and brushed herself off, ignoring the pain stinging the left side of her body. She walked over and knelt beside Calvert. Fishing a pair of latex gloves from her pocket, she snapped them on and put a hand on his shoulder. "Mr. Calvert. Let me see your arm."

Breathing through gritted teeth, he squeezed his eyes closed and slowly rolled onto his back. As his right hand loosened its grip, his body started trembling. Josie said,

"He's going into shock. Radio the Chief. We need an ambulance."

Brennan began speaking into his radio.

Noah said, "No ambulance is getting back here. We'll have to carry him out."

Calvert's eyes sprang open. "No. No. No."

Gently, Josie pushed his right hand aside so she could take the full measure of the damage he had done to his left arm.

"Oh God," said Brennan.

Josie steeled herself, willing her face to remain impassive as she saw the jagged piece of bone that had punched through the skin of Calvert's forearm, covered in blood. Behind her, Daugherty retched.

Josie folded Calvert's fingers back around the open wound, careful to avoid the protruding bone, keeping gentle pressure on it. Blood oozed around his grip. She turned and shouted over Daugherty's gagging noises. "Daugherty, run back out to the vehicles and get a first aid kit from your cruiser. Bring it back. As fast as you can."

He stood upright, a string of saliva hanging from his chin.

"Right now," Josie said. "Run."

Wiping his face with the back of his hand, he took off in a jog, heading back toward the road.

Noah shook his head. "We have to minimize any kind of jostling."

Josie used her free hand to touch Calvert's forehead. Even through her glove, she could feel how cold and clammy his skin had become. Her fingers moved to the side of his throat. His pulse galloped beneath her touch.

Noah added, "We may have to walk him out of here."

"I don't think that's gonna happen," said Brennan.

Josie said, "We have to get him out of here sooner rather than later. We can't wait here for the hours it could take to get equipment out here. Brennan, while we're waiting for that first aid kit, go find me a stick about the length of your forearm, the wider the better. Noah, give me your jacket."

He sensed her plan without being told. Pulling his jacket off, he began fashioning a sling out of it. Brennan ran off in search of a stick. Calvert's howls of pain receded to grunts and whimpers. Minutes later, Daugherty returned with the first aid kit. "Chief said the ambulance will be waiting when we get back."

With Noah's help, Josie wrapped the wound in sterile gauze. They used rolls of it to pack the area around the bone in order to pad it from any potential contact with anything. When Brennan returned with the stick, they taped it to Calvert's forearm, immobilizing it as best they could. Brennan helped Josie sit Calvert upright, and Noah slipped his head through the tied arms of the jacket. Tears streamed down Calvert's face as Josie helped Noah secure his broken arm inside the makeshift sling. Together, they pulled him to standing and Noah tucked himself under Calvert's good arm, holding him up as they lurched through the woods. Brennan and Daugherty followed.

The four of them took turns as Calvert's crutch, guiding him through the trees. Twice he fell, his wobbly knees giving out. Miraculously, they caught him before his injured arm made contact with anything. Three times he was beset by dry heaves. Sweat poured off him in rivulets, down the sides of his face and the bridge of his nose. The only sounds were his labored breath, his occasional cries of pain, and the birds singing high above in the trees.

It felt like hours before they reached the road. As the Chief had promised, an ambulance waited, doors open.

Sawyer and another paramedic rushed over as soon as they spotted the officers emerging from the woods with Calvert. Sawyer and his colleague got him into the back of the ambulance and began assessing him, calling out findings and instructions to one another. On the gurney, Calvert looked small, almost frail. It was hard to imagine this was the same man who had viciously attacked two teenage girls the day before.

Josie stood at the doors to the ambulance. "I'm going to call your wife, Mr. Calvert," she said.

His eyes found hers and grew wide. "No, don't call her. Don't call my wife. Whatever you do, don't call her."

Sawyer stepped toward Josie and grabbed the handles of the doors. "We have to get him to Denton Memorial now. He's going to need surgery."

Josie nodded. As Sawyer pulled the doors closed, Elliott continued to yell, "Don't call my wife. Whatever you do, don't call my wife. It's not safe. Please."

CHAPTER 15

Josie found the creamers at the back of a table hidden in a dark corner of the hospital cafeteria. She set two steaming paper cups of coffee onto the table's sticky surface and began emptying the creamers into them. Apparently sugar, or even stirrers, was too much to ask. With a sigh, she fitted lids onto the cups and carried them through a maze of hallways until she found the emergency department. She and Noah had followed the ambulance over to the hospital while the Chief went back to the stationhouse. By the time Calvert was brought into the hospital, he had calmed considerably, but he still looked as though he might pass out from pain at any moment. After Josie read him his rights and advised that he was under arrest for assaulting Dina Hale, he was whisked away to the radiology department within moments. Josie had gone in search of coffee while they waited for news.

Noah leaned against the counter of the nurses' station, thumbs tapping away at his phone screen. Josie put a cup of coffee in front of him. "No sugar," she said.

"That's fine." He put the phone down on the counter

and picked up the coffee, peeling back the tab and taking a sip. With a grimace, he stared at the cup. "I have a feeling I'm going to regret this later."

"Same," Josie said, taking three sizable gulps of a substance so acidic and stringent, it barely passed for coffee.

"You think they left cleaning solution in the coffeemaker?" Noah asked.

She shook her head. "Could be. Did you talk to the attending physician?"

"Yeah. Calvert's going right up to surgery. Since he is officially in our custody, the Chief is going to send a uniformed officer over to guard him until he's well enough to leave the hospital. Oh, and I called Calvert's wife."

"How did she take it?" Josie asked.

He shrugged. "As well as can be expected."

"How much did you tell her?"

"I told her everything."

She put her coffee cup down next to him and met his eyes. "Including the fact that the last thing he said in the ambulance before they brought him here was not to call Tori because 'it's not safe?'"

"I did."

Josie sighed. She couldn't help picturing sweet, smiling Amalise. "Did you happen to suggest that she take the baby and leave town for a while?"

Noah picked up his own coffee cup, took a sip, and wrinkled his nose. "She said the same thing she said yesterday. Elliott would never hurt her or the baby."

"Which means there's someone else involved in whatever it is that's going on here," Josie said. "Whatever prompted Elliott to attack Alison and Dina."

"Then we'll need to find out who," Noah said. "We'll hit this investigation hard today and see what we can turn up. Alison Mills is still out there. Whatever she knows could blow this whole thing wide open. If we find any reason to believe that Tori and the baby are in immediate danger, then we have a much more serious conversation with her. That's all we can do."

Josie let out another sigh, finished her own coffee, and looked around. The ER was fairly busy for a Sunday morning. Nurses and doctors bustled about, going from room to room, from curtain to curtain. Various alarms and call bells beeped and chimed throughout the space. Family members drifted in and out, searching for their loved ones. "Calvert will be in surgery for hours," she said.

"Even after he wakes up from surgery, he might not talk with us," Noah said.

"True," Josie agreed. "But we've got a lot of ground to cover in this investigation. We're already here. Why don't we go downstairs and see if Dr. Feist has finished with Dina Hale's autopsy."

CHAPTER 16

The Denton city morgue was located in the basement of Denton Memorial Hospital. Emerging from an elevator, Josie and Noah made their way down a hall punctuated by abandoned rooms. Grime filmed the white walls, turning them gray. Their feet tapped against yellowed floor tiles now beginning to crack with age. Josie smelled the morgue before they reached it—the odor of human decomposition mixing with a host of chemicals that did little to mask the sickening scent of death. Dr. Feist presided over a large exam room and her private office. Josie and Noah found her in the exam room, wearing navy-blue scrubs, her silver-blonde hair tucked up beneath a skull cap. She stood at one of the long stainless-steel tables that ran the length of the wall at the back of the room, tapping away on a laptop. She looked up as they walked in and then went back to typing.

"I was going to call one of you soon," she said. "You beat me to it."

On one of the tables a figure lay, shrouded by a white sheet.

"We were already here," Josie said. "We thought we'd check in with you."

Dr. Feist lifted a hand from the keyboard and motioned to the body. "I spoke with her parents yesterday afternoon. Heartbreaking."

"It is," Josie said softly.

Dr. Feist stopped typing and turned toward them, a tight smile on her face. "They're all heartbreaking in this line of work."

Josie and Noah walked over to the body. "What can you tell us about Dina Hale?"

Dr. Feist joined them. "She was a well-nourished, well-developed eighteen-year-old Caucasian female. No significant medical history." She walked over and carefully folded the sheet down to Dina's shoulders. The girl's eyes were closed, her face almost peaceful. Dr. Feist pointed to her throat. "I found patterned bruising around her neck and throat."

Josie leaned over so she could see the faint marks shaped like fingertips scattered across Dina's skin.

Dr. Feist went on. "She also had petechiae in her eyes, indicating that she was deprived of oxygen before her death."

"Not surprising," said Noah. "We caught the perpetrator in the act. Cause of death is strangulation?"

Dr. Feist nodded. "Indeed. He strangled her with such force that he fractured her hyoid bone."

Josie knew from previous cases that the hyoid was the horseshoe-shaped bone in the throat, just below the mandible. It provided attachments for the tongue, which sat above it, and the larynx which was below it. She also knew that the hyoid was fractured in only about one third of strangulation cases. It took a great deal of force to break it.

"Well," said Josie. "We're going to need to update our arrest warrant with a charge of homicide."

Noah said, "Is there anything else?"

"I didn't find any sign of sexual assault, if that's what you're wondering," said Dr. Feist. "But there is something else. Something concerning."

She moved to Dina's right side and lifted the sheet, tucking it against Dina's body so that just her forearm and hand were showing. Lifting the hand, she pointed to Dina's fingers. Two of her fingers and her thumb bore the remnants of broken acrylic nails. Her other two fingernails had thick clumps of nail glue on top. It looked as though she had tried to file the jagged edges away. The tips of all five digits were red and slightly swollen.

Noah said, "Do you think she broke her nails when she was struggling with Calvert?"

"There were no nails at the scene," Josie said.

Dr. Feist said, "Come closer. It's not the broken nails that concern me."

Josie said, "What are we looking at?"

Dr. Feist held Dina's fingertips up so that Josie and Noah could peer more closely at them. In addition to the redness and swelling, Josie noted what looked like tiny punctures in the tops of her nailbeds. She looked up to see Dr. Feist's lips tightly pursed.

Noah said, "Doc, this is one of those things you can't tell us precisely, right? In the event you have to testify to anything, you have to be certain, medically."

Dr. Feist nodded and tucked Dina's arm back beneath the sheet.

Noah folded his arms over his chest. "Tell us what these injuries are consistent with, then."

A shadow crossed Dr. Feist's face and she grimaced as

she looked down at Dina. "The injuries under her nails are consistent with someone stabbing beneath her nails with something."

Josie said, "Stabbing with what?"

"A needle, perhaps? These are punctures."

Noah said, "You think someone stuck needles under her nails?"

"Yes," said Dr. Feist. "I also think she was denailed. She's missing two nails on this hand and one on the other."

"You're saying someone pulled her nails off?" Noah clarified.

"I can't testify to that specifically, I—"

He held up a hand to silence her. "I'm not asking what's going into your report. I'm asking what you think. Anya Feist. It's just you, me, and Josie here. We need to know what we're dealing with."

Dr. Feist looked again at Dina Hale's face. With a heavy sigh, she said, "I think this girl might have been tortured. Denailing and the insertion of needles under the nails are forms of torture that go back to medieval times. Maybe even further than that."

"Tortured?" said Josie. "She's a high school student."

"I'm telling you what I think. These injuries are consistent with torture."

"Nothing else?" said Noah.

Dr. Feist threw her hands in the air and let them fall back to her sides. "If there was something else, I would have led with that. Listen, it's not my job to tell you why a high school student would be tortured this way. That's for you to figure out. I can only tell you what I found and, off the record, what I think, which is what you asked for."

Noah said, "There are no marks on her body other than the ones Calvert left when he strangled her?"

"None," said Dr. Feist.

Josie said, "Maybe that was the point."

Both of them turned to look at her. "The injuries to her nails aren't that visible. If you weren't looking too closely, you wouldn't even notice. Maybe you'd notice her nails are in bad shape, but plenty of women have had bad experiences with acrylic nails. You wouldn't necessarily think someone had tortured her."

Noah looked at Dina's hand again. "Whoever did this to her didn't want it to look obvious. But why?"

Josie said, "Because they need something from her. If they didn't, they would have killed her."

"Do you think Calvert did this to her?" Noah asked Dr. Feist.

"If he did, he didn't do it yesterday. These are consistent with injuries that might have occurred about three to five days ago."

Josie said, "That doesn't rule out Calvert."

"You think that guy did something like this?" Noah said.

"I think there's a whole lot we don't know yet."

CHAPTER 17

Josie cracked open the car window, sucking in the fresh air while Noah drove them back to the stationhouse. She was certain the unpleasant odor of the morgue still clung to her hair and clothes. Or maybe it was just the stinking rot of a case that had endless questions and no answers. Denton's police station came into view, a towering three-story gray stone building with a bell tower on its east side that more closely resembled a castle than a police station. It had been Denton's town hall until it was converted to police head-quarters over seventy years ago. It remained on the historic register which meant few modernizations could be made to it, but Josie still loved it. Just the sight of it filled her with a strange sort of peace.

They parked in the municipal lot at the rear of the building. Josie was glad to see that the door to the ground-floor entrance was not crowded with press. Remarkably, the public hadn't yet caught wind of anything that had happened on Widow's Ridge Road. It was likely owing to the remote location. Regardless, Josie was relieved. She and Noah climbed the stairs to the second-floor great room. It was a large open area filled with desks, filing cabinets, a printer that was potentially older than Josie herself, and a television affixed to the wall, which was almost always turned off. Only the investigative team—Josie, Noah, Gretchen, and Finn Mettner—and the press liaison, Amber, had permanent desks. The others were used as needed by the uniformed officers for paperwork or phone calls. The Chief's office was along one of the walls.

Josie was surprised to see the door open. The Chief's voice carried from inside. "I don't give a rat's ass if you're on the city council or if you're the king of your own damn country. I'm not here for any grandstanding BS. This is my budget. You think I don't know how to do a budget? I told the mayor and I'll tell you and anyone else over there that we need a K-9 unit. You know how many times a year we have to call the Sheriff to borrow theirs? You think this department doesn't reimburse them for that? I need one dog, one officer and training. It's worth it, and if you don't believe me—" His tirade cut off abruptly. When he spoke again, his voice sounded strange and uncertain, the bluster and indignation gone. "Oh, yeah. Yeah. I guess so. Sure. Anytime, then. Stop in and we'll talk. If you think you can get the rest of the council on board, then I welcome it. Yep. Sure thing. Bye."

Josie tapped against the open door, surprised once more when the Chief looked up and smiled. On the street, and even on the phone with a city council member, he was still his old self, barking orders and acting generally annoyed with everything and everyone, but lately, at the station-house, particularly when it was only him and Josie, he was almost pleasant.

"Pierce Fuller," the Chief muttered. "City council. You know him?"

Josie shook her head.

The Chief scowled at the phone on his desk as if it were Pierce Fuller. "He thinks he can get me the K-9 unit I want. Guess we'll see if he's the real deal or if he's just another bullshitter like the rest of those damn politicians."

For four and a half years, Chief Chitwood had been abrasive, thorny, and gruff. The team joked often about his surly demeanor. But when Josie's grandmother lay dying the year before, he had shown her unexpected kindness. Then a murder case earlier that year had forced him to open up to Josie and the team. Josie had learned everything there was to know about Bob Chitwood, and almost all of it was tragic. He had every right to be miserable.

"Anyway," the Chief added, "get in here, Quinn. You get anything out of Calvert?"

"No," she answered. "He was still in surgery when we left the hospital."

"Too bad." Another bright smile. "You'll talk to him after he's out. Get something from him then."

It had been five months since Josie and her team solved the case that had destroyed the Chief's family twenty-five years earlier and consumed the better part of his lifetime. Five months since the Chief had almost died helping Josie close that case. Six months since Josie and the team had stumbled onto Daisy Sims, a sixteen-year-old girl who turned out to be the Chief's much younger half-sister. A sibling no one had known about, not even the man who fathered her. After Josie had the DNA run twice to confirm their relationship, the Chief quickly gained custody of Daisy. The two had spent the last few months getting to know one another and processing their unusual, almost improbable biological connection as well as all the astonishing and heartbreaking facts that the case had brought to light.

And yet, after all the trauma, Josie had never seen him like this.

She was still staring at his grin, the light in his eyes. "Quinn!" he repeated. "Get in here!"

The Chief was happy.

Josie walked over to his desk and handed him a paper cup of coffee from Komorrah's Koffee. "The Red Eye," she mumbled.

He thanked her and took it, sipping slowly and then letting out a long moan of pleasure. "Perfect," he told her, the smile still on his face.

Who was this man?

"Chief. About Dina Hale—"

"You talked with Dr. Feist? Is the autopsy complete?"

"Yes, there were some unusual findings."

"Sit. Where's Fraley?" Instead of waiting for her to answer, he hollered, "Fraley, get your ass in here!" at the top of his lungs. The volume was typical, but the annoyance wasn't there. When Noah didn't instantly appear in the doorway, the Chief stood and walked out to the great room.

Josie sat in one of the vinyl guest chairs that faced his desk. Glancing around the room, she realized that the Chief had finally put up some personal touches. For years, mementos and accolades from his many years in law enforcement gathered dust in cardboard boxes along the floor behind his desk. Now the boxes were gone. On the walls hung certificates of commendation, letters of appreciation, service awards, and framed photos of the Chief together with task forces he'd served on. On his desk now sat a trifold picture frame. From where she sat, Josie could only see the back of it, but she estimated that it probably only allowed for four-by-six-inch photos.

From the door she could hear Noah and the Chief talking but couldn't make out the content of the conversation. Slowly, she leaned forward, trying to get a glimpse of what was in the photo frames. A tap on her shoulder made her jump right out of her seat. The Chief strode past her, laughing. "Don't try to be sneaky, Quinn," he told her.

Rounding the desk, he turned the frame toward her so she could view it. She recognized a sister he had lost decades ago and a photo of him and Daisy that she had taken herself the day he got custody. The team had taken them out to dinner to celebrate. It was the first photo of them ever taken. The Chief tapped the last photo, which was of a woman Josie didn't recognize, an older picture. "That's my mom," he said.

Noah had a stack of paper in his arms. Lowering himself into the chair next to Josie, he handed her half. Then he looked over to the small desk and office chair the Chief had installed in the corner which currently held two paperback books, a sketchpad, and a bin of pencils. "Where's Daisy?" Noah asked.

The Chief had been bringing her to work with him often as he wasn't ready to leave her alone after all she had been through. Amber and Mettner would take her with them when the Chief was working long hours and she got bored. Josie and Noah as well as Gretchen, whose adult daughter, Paula, lived with her, pitched in too.

"She spent the night at Gretchen and Paula's," he told them. "I didn't want her up all night with me, sitting here while I drove all over this damn city, although I suspect that she probably stayed up all night anyway bingeing *Ted Lasso* for the tenth time."

"Hard not to binge that one repeatedly," said Josie. "What've you got? Anything on Alison Mills yet?"

The Chief sat in his chair, leaning back until it creaked in protest. He rubbed a hand over his thinning hair, sending strands floating. For the first time, he looked exhausted. "Before we get into that, tell me about Dina Hale's autopsy."

Josie and Noah relayed Dr. Feist's findings. The Chief's face was impassive as he listened. There was a beat of silence when they finished talking. Then he said, "Tortured? Well, that certainly adds a different element to this case. Were there any other marks on her body?"

"No," said Josie. "You're thinking of branding, aren't you?"

The Chief nodded. "Not all human traffickers brand their victims, but many do. If Dina Hale got caught up in some kind of human-trafficking ring, it would explain a lot. I'm not sure it would explain Elliott Calvert, but it would explain a lot of other things. Denailing would make a point to her without damaging her appearance or rendering her unable to do whatever they were forcing her to do. Although," he pointed to the stacks of paper in their hands, "the phone records don't show any evidence that she was involved with human traffickers. Neither do her social media accounts. We'll get to those in a bit. What we really need to do is find Alison Mills as quickly as possible. Unfortunately, we've got nothing in that regard. All I can tell you is that Alison Mills definitely made it into town. The dogs followed her scent to Denton East High School, across the main road that runs up near the school and then into the woods there. Made it about twenty or thirty feet into the trees there and lost her."

"Those dogs don't lose a scent without reason," Josie

said. "Could be the wind, but usually it's when someone gets into a vehicle. She would have been close enough to the road to turn back but if she got into a vehicle with someone, wouldn't they have been concerned by how she looked? Assuming, as we have been, that she's covered in blood from some sort of injury? Or that, at the very least, her face shows trauma? Even if someone picked her up and chose to ignore all that and just drop her off where she asked, why didn't she ask to go home or come here?"

"Who would have picked her up?" asked Noah. "A stranger driving past? She couldn't have called anyone. She left her phone at the scene. Unless she borrowed someone's phone and used it to call a different person to come get her. Or she had the helpful stranger take her somewhere we don't know about. In which case, what the hell is she running from?"

"Someone who tortures teenage girls?" Josie suggested.

The Chief said, "Either of you think Calvert could have done that?"

Josie looked over at Noah, who shifted in his chair. She knew he was thinking the same thing as her.

The Chief said, "What is it?"

"On the surface, Calvert doesn't seem like the type. He's a new father with a successful and busy career. What could he possibly be involved in that would require him to torture teenage girls?"

"He killed one, Quinn," said the Chief.

"Right. That's why I said on the surface. We don't know much about him except the superficial things. I don't think we can determine whether or not he tried to denail Dina without gathering a lot more information. I also don't think we can or should rule him out."

"Although," Noah pointed out, "if we could find Alison

Mills, she might be able to tell us exactly who did that to Dina. They were best friends."

Josie said, "If the dogs tracked Alison into those woods, she either turned back and got into a car with someone or she made it through to the other side, which comes out into a residential area. People might have doorbell cameras. There could be footage of her in that neighborhood."

The Chief held up a hand. "There was, and I checked it. She wasn't on it, but it's possible she simply avoided it— on purpose or by coincidence, we don't know. There are a lot of blind spots in that neighborhood. Only about a quarter of residents have those cameras."

Noah said, "She would have been covered in blood. Did you canvass to see if anyone saw someone meeting her description who was bleeding?"

"Of course I did," the Chief said. "One lady thought she saw a girl fitting Alison's description running in the direction of Central Denton yesterday around five thirty in the afternoon."

Josie felt a stab of relief. If Alison Mills was running— even if she was running away from something or someone— she was still alive. Or she had been as of five thirty yesterday afternoon.

"I let the dogs go," the Chief said. "First thing this morning I sent fresh units out to canvass in the direction she ran. Still waiting to hear. But guess who showed up here at the crack of dawn for an update?"

"Marlene Mills," Josie said. She couldn't imagine the night Marlene had had—not knowing where Alison was or if she was okay. Her husband on the other side of the world. Josie felt an ache for the woman. Limbo was a horrible place to be. "That means Alison definitely didn't go home."

The Chief nodded. "Mrs. Mills called all of Alison's

friends last night. None of them had heard from her. She asked each of them to call her immediately if they saw or heard from Alison but as of this morning, none had."

"Did her husband get a flight back?" asked Josie.

"He's on standby," the Chief said.

Josie grimaced. In some ways, what Clint Mills was going through right now was probably worse than what Marlene was dealing with. He was stuck half a world away without even a firm date or time for returning to his family. He'd be on one or more planes for hours, and that time would probably be spent wondering and worrying whereas Marlene was only moments away, available to hear all developments as they arose. She could even join the search if she wanted. She could call friends. Do anything to stay busy. Clint would be stuck in a metal tube in the sky with nothing but recycled air and his own thoughts for fifteen or more hours.

"I know," said the Chief, noting her expression. "It's rough. Another reason why I want to find this kid yesterday. It shouldn't be this hard. She's a seventeen-year-old, not a seasoned CIA agent, for Pete's sake. Where the hell did she go? She had to spend the night somewhere."

Noah said, "She was attacked. She's scared. She didn't actually see us or know who we were. All she did was run in front of our car. For all she knew, we were with Calvert. Maybe she is too scared to come out."

"Or maybe someone else who was with Calvert found her and took her," Josie suggested. "If there is someone else involved, someone willing to torture teenage girls, maybe Alison is too scared to come to the police or even her own mother."

The Chief sighed. "I'm going to call Marlene Mills. We need to go to the press with this immediately. I can't crap around with this. I need that girl found. If we get her mom to go on television and appeal for Alison to come home, tell her it's safe, maybe she'll turn up. If that doesn't work then we need to consider Quinn's theory that someone is holding her against her will. We lost one teenage girl yesterday. I am not telling Marlene Mills we lost her daughter as well. You got that?"

Josie and Noah nodded. Tapping a finger against the stack of pages Noah had handed her, Josie said, "How about these records? Anything useful here? Whose phone records are we talking about?"

"Dina Hale's, Alison Mills', and Elliott Calvert's," answered the Chief. "I had Hummel use the GrayKey to get everything since we had permission from the girls' mothers and a warrant for Calvert's phone. I printed them out. You're gonna want to look at those right away, Detectives."

CHAPTER 18

Josie's coffee was lukewarm by the time she and Noah returned to their desks and began spreading out the phone records, dividing them into piles according to owner. She downed it anyway, wishing she had bought two of them. Noah held his coffee cup out to her from across the desks. "Here," he said. "Just finish mine. Gretchen's due in any minute. I'm sure she'll have a fresh round for all of us."

She mouthed, *I love you*, and gulped down his coffee as well.

The Chief followed them out of his office, arms crossed over his chest, bouncing on his heels in anticipation of what they were about to read. He sidled up to Noah and reached for the pile of Alison Mills' records. Flipping through some of the pages, he said, "Let's start with social media. Calvert's only got Facebook and Twitter. He doesn't appear to use either very much. The girls have every platform you can imagine. They're very active, but I didn't see anything that's germane to our investigation."

Noah said, "Not even on Snapchat or Instagram? Seems

like more and more teenagers use those to message one another."

"Yeah," said Josie. "The last few cases we had involving high school students, all the incriminating stuff was on those two apps."

The Chief shook his head. "First place I checked. Nothing incriminating. Nothing that seems even remotely related to what we're dealing with in this case. Let's move on to the GPS we pulled from their phones. All of them had it turned on and this information goes back at least a year. They've all got different cell phone carriers, and each carrier retains GPS data on the phone for a different time period, provided that the phone's owner doesn't delete it. Calvert's goes back a year. Dina Hale and Alison Mills' GPS history goes back about eighteen months. For our immediate purposes, I'm looking at the last six months. Here's what you need to know." He turned to a page on which he had highlighted several entries in yellow. "These are all the places that Alison Mills has been in the last six months that match up with where Dina Hale was at those exact times."

Josie took the pages from him and studied the list going back two weeks. Dina's house. Alison's house. A Starbucks. A clothing store. Another clothing store. The Eudora Hotel. Other entries had been highlighted in blue. "What are these?"

The Chief pulled a sheaf of paper from the Elliott Calvert pile and flipped through the pages until he found a list that was highlighted in the same color. "Those are all the places that Alison Mills, Dina Hale, and Elliott Calvert have all been in the last six months at the same time."

Josie looked up from the list the Chief was holding out and met his eyes. "The same time? There are several highlighted places here." She counted them off. Noah took the Calvert list from the Chief and moved around to Josie's desk. They held the lists side by side.

Noah read off the itemized locations. "The Eudora Hotel. The Eudora Hotel. Hotel, hotel. Then Dina's house. Dina's house. Alison's house. Dina's house again—this was the morning he attacked them."

"He definitely followed them from Dina's house," Josie said. "The question is, did they all know one another? If so, how? If they didn't know one another, does that mean he was stalking them? If so, why?"

"That's what you two need to find out," said the Chief.

Josie said, "The girls worked at the hotel, and from these non-highlighted entries, it looks like Elliott Calvert frequented the hotel even when they weren't there. He was a regular." She flipped another page. "At least for the last five months."

"He may not have been at the hotel because of them," Noah said, "but we know that at some point, he began following these girls. That he may have even tortured Dina and that he was looking for something. What the hell could it be?"

Josie said, "We can ask him about it when he's out of surgery, assuming he'll agree to talk to us, which I don't think is going to happen. We could also try asking his wife about that, but I'm guessing she won't know. I think we should focus on Calvert's boss and coworkers today and talk with anyone and everyone we find at the hotel about him and the girls. The Eudora has a pretty popular bar and restaurant on its first floor. Even people who aren't staying at the hotel use it."

"Bastian's," Noah said. "Yeah. That's where all the

swanky, hoity-toity people hang out. Like the mayor and city councilors."

The Chief nodded. "I've had to have many a lunch there with the mayor. They make a damn good filet mignon."

"If Dina and Alison worked in the catering and events department, and Elliott frequented the restaurant, it's possible that's how they came into contact with him," Josie said. "Maybe they took something from him."

"Like what?" Noah asked. "What would be worth torturing someone over? Killing someone?"

She sighed and threw the pages back onto her desk. "I don't know."

The Chief picked up a packet from Dina's pile and turned to her GPS report. "It could be drugs," he suggested. "Dina visited the East Bridge twice in the last two weeks."

There were two bridges in Denton. The South Bridge and the East Bridge. The South Bridge was small and little used, leading out of Denton into the rolling farmland of Lenore County. The East Bridge was more centrally located inside the city, larger, and the hub of the city's drug activity. The police department had long ago given up on clearing it out since its residents always returned, instead trying to keep the crime at a minimum.

Josie held out a hand and the Chief passed her the report. Disappointment was a stone in her stomach. Dina's parents had seemed so convinced that she had truly stopped using drugs. Even after someone ransacked their house, Guy Hale seemed unwilling to entertain the idea that Dina was back into them. He'd believed his daughter. But maybe she had been done with them.

People in Denton only went to the East Bridge for two reasons: to buy drugs or to sell them. Was it naïve to think that Dina had gotten her hands on some drugs—possibly from Elliott Calvert—and tried to sell them or otherwise get rid of them?

"Toxicology will tell us if Dina was using," Josie said. "Although it will take months. Her parents seemed to think she was truly done with all that. Her father searched her room recently and found nothing."

Noah said, "Maybe he found nothing because the person who ransacked it took them."

Josie nodded. "Could be. But if Elliott Calvert had drugs in his possession and somehow Dina ended up with them—whether she decided to take them to the East Bridge to unload them or not—what kind of quantity or volume are we talking about here? What would be enough that he would be willing to torture Dina and then follow her and Alison and attack them for? Also, we have the date of the day that the Hale's home was ransacked. Was Elliott Calvert there that day?"

Noah looked down at the GPS report from Calvert's phone which was still in his hands. "No, he wasn't."

Josie felt a chill drill down her spine. "Which means that someone else got into the house and ransacked it. That someone else could also be the person who tortured Dina."

The Chief said, "Maybe an East Bridger."

The stairwell door whooshed open, and Gretchen entered, carrying a cardboard tray full of Komorrah's Koffee cups. Behind her, Daisy carried a paper bag, also from Komorrah's. Josie smelled the pastries before Daisy reached the desks.

"You are goddesses," Josie told them. "Actual goddesses."

Gretchen set the cup-holder down on her desk and began handing out coffees. "You're just saying that because the amount of work we've got ahead of us seems insurmountable."

Noah said, "It does, that's true."

Josie added, "But you're still goddesses."

Daisy stood awkwardly beside Gretchen with the bag in her hands, as if waiting for instructions. Her flaxen blonde hair fell to her shoulders. It looked freshly styled. Her blue jeans looked new, hugging her slender frame, and over a fitted black shirt she wore a Portland State University hoodie that looked a size too large for her. Josie said, "Did Paula take you shopping?"

Daisy smiled shyly and nodded. She looked down at the sweatshirt. "But I borrowed her hoodie. I just like it. I want to go to college one day, too."

The Chief smiled and walked over to take the bag of pastries from Daisy's hands. "You will."

"You look great," Josie told her.

Until the Chief took custody of her, Daisy had lived an unusual and sometimes sheltered life. At sixteen she was more mature than most teens in some ways but still very childlike in others. The Chief had agonized over whether to keep her home-schooled or send her to high school with other kids. Daisy, however, craved social interaction. The occasional awkwardness her upbringing had saddled her with didn't bother her at all. She just wanted to be in the world. A therapist had recommended a small private high school in Denton, and she seemed to be doing well there.

The Chief said, "Daisy, don't you have a science test tomorrow you need to study for? I brought your school backpack. It's in my office."

Daisy looked disappointed but trudged off to the Chief's office, leaving the door ajar.

Gretchen looked around at the piles of paper all over the desks. "Bring me up to speed."

Josie, Noah, and the Chief recapped everything they had already discussed that morning. Gretchen moved around the desks, looking at the GPS reports as she was informed of their contents. She said, "What about texts and photos? Are there any texts between either girl and Calvert? Or both of them and Calvert?"

The Chief shook his head. "No. Other than the GPS coordinates, there is no evidence from their phones that they were in contact. They're not connected to him via social media either. There are some text exchanges between Dina and Alison that are worth looking into."

Josie sifted through Alison's pile and found the printout of text messages. Gretchen and Noah flanked her, reading along as she turned the pages. There were weeks of messages, most of them about coordinating how to get back and forth to work; figuring out where and when to meet to go shopping or to the movies; complaining about things that happened at work. Alison complained about her dad having to go to Hong Kong, lamenting that he might be there for several more months. She didn't want him to miss her high school graduation. She felt she was to blame for his having to take the job overseas because her medical bills were still so high.

Several text exchanges mentioned a guy named Max who Dina was obviously infatuated with. In a text message from three weeks ago, Dina had sent a photo to Alison along with several crying face emojis. She had typed:

This can't be happening? Is he serious?

The photo was clearly taken from afar and without the

consent of its subjects. Josie recognized the high-backed blue stools with their scalloped upholstery characteristic of the bar inside Bastian's restaurant at the Eudora Hotel. In the evenings, the bar was lit in a cool blue glow while the dining area was dimly lit with golden droplights over each table. In the photo, a man and a woman—a young woman— sat on barstools facing one another. The woman had her right elbow propped on the edge of the bar, her left hand in her lap. Her head rested in her right hand. Josie noted her clothes—fitted black pants, practical black shoes, and white polo shirt. She was likely part of the hotel staff. Her brown hair was pulled behind her head in a tight bun. It was difficult to see her expression as the photo showed her in profile, but she did not seem to be smiling. The man, on the other hand, wore a conspiratorial grin. He was dressed in a charcoal suit dark enough to match his thick, wavy black hair which he wore slicked back away from his face. He leaned in toward the woman, one of his hands lingering on her knee.

"Maybe this is Max," said Josie.

Over her shoulder, Noah said, "That looks almost intimate."

"From these text messages, it looks like Dina had it bad for Max," said Gretchen. "He's someone we need to speak with."

Noah stabbed a finger at the bottom of the page, where Alison had replied to the photo and text.

I told you he is a total player. He was just leading you on. He's not worth it. He doesn't even deserve you anyway.

She had added a gif of a young woman, full of attitude,

shaking her head with the words "you deserve better" beneath her.

Dina had sent back five crying face emojis and ten broken-heart emojis. Then she had written:

But her???

Alison texted back:

D, he flirts with everyone. Literally everyone. He is not worth it. Plus, he's our boss, which is just yuck.

Dina had responded with a gif of a woman looking very serious and saying: "But I want him. I want him. Bad."

Alison had replied with a gif of a woman rolling her eyes.

That was the end of that exchange. There were more texts discussing mundane things like scheduling and shopping. Then there was a more alarming conversation from two days ago.

Dina: *We need to talk.*

Alison: *I know. I'm really worried about you.*

Dina: *Did you check on that thing I asked about?*

Alison: *Yes. There is nothing there. Nothing. Are you sure that's what all this is about?*

Dina: *I don't know. They never said for sure. But if I don't find whatever it is they want, they're going to kill me. I'm really scared.*

Alison: *Me too. I don't know how to help. Maybe we should tell my mom.*

Dina: *OMG no. No parents!*

Alison: *We might have to call the police.*

Dina: *NO. NO POLICE.*

Alison: *Then what do we do?*

Dina: *IDK. Can you sleep over at my house tomorrow night? After work? We can talk then.*

Alison: *Sure.*

"What the hell did these kids get into?" Gretchen muttered.

"And who is 'they?'" asked Josie.

"There's no way to know just from these texts," said Noah. "We need to get out on the street and start talking to more people."

"We need to find Alison Mills," said Gretchen. "I'll get back on the search today if you two want to follow up on the hotel leads—in particular their coworkers and boss, who, according to these text messages, is this Max person Dina was into."

Josie plopped into her chair. She pulled up the internet browser on her computer and went to the Eudora Hotel's website. Within seconds, she found the name of the catering and events manager. "Max Combs."

It took a moment for her to search the databases at her disposal, but she matched the photo that Dina had texted to

Alison with the driver's license picture for a Max Combs living in Denton, Pennsylvania, age thirty-two. "This is the guy," she said.

From behind her, both Noah and Gretchen made noises of agreement. Then Noah said, "See if he's got a criminal record."

"Already on it," said Josie, clicking away. "Nothing. Speeding violations, parking tickets. That's it."

Gretchen said, "You guys talk to him when you go to the hotel. I can go back to the area Alison was last seen and canvass. Show her photo. If I can get a lead on her, I'll start pulling surveillance footage from doorbell cameras or the security systems from local businesses and see if I can follow her that way."

"I also want to talk to Elliott Calvert's boss and any coworkers we can get in touch with," said Josie. She found a number for the firm that employed Elliott Calvert. After a quick call, she had an appointment with his boss later that day.

The stairway door whooshed open. They all turned to find a tall man dressed in a dark suit sail through the door. Josie knew immediately by the wide, practiced smile he gave them that he was a politician. He swept toward them, opening his arms as if he were greeting old friends. A thick lock of his salt-and-pepper hair fell into his eye, and he sent it back into place with a small flick of his head.

The Chief stepped between him and them, arms folded across his narrow chest, a glare of death on his face. "Can I help you?"

The man stopped, but his camera-ready smile remained in place. He glanced behind the Chief at the rest of them, giving a conspiratorial nod, like they were in on some joke with him. "Pierce Fuller," he said. "We just talked not too long ago. I was hoping to talk to you about that K-9 unit."

The Chief's rigid posture didn't relax. "How'd you get up here?"

"Your desk sergeant let me up. I told him you said to stop in anytime." He craned his neck to look past the Chief. "You did mean anytime, didn't you? Or was that just, what did you call it? 'Grandstanding B.S.?'"

A long moment of awkward silence ensued. Finally, the Chief said, "I'm no bullshitter, Fuller. Go back downstairs and wait in the conference room. Our desk sergeant will show you to it."

Fuller's smile never cracked. Again, he tried peering around the Chief. "I can wait here. Looks like there's some pretty exciting stuff going on. If you don't mind, I'd love to listen in. Get a feel for when a K-9 unit would be useful on cases."

The Chief clapped a hand onto Fuller's shoulder and spun him back toward the door. "I do mind, Fuller. This is an active investigation and unless you've been out in the muck and mud with my officers then you don't get to listen in. I'll see you downstairs in ten minutes."

Fuller didn't object, throwing one last smile over his shoulder at the rest of them, along with a good-natured shrug that seemed to say, "I tried."

Once the door closed, the Chief huffed. "Can you believe these damn politicians? Like I'm just sitting around waiting for him to show up. Like I don't have anything better to do."

Gretchen said, "Chief, you might want to try being a little nicer to him. We could really use that K-9 unit."

The Chief glared at her. "I don't need to be nice to him.

Nice has nothing to do with it. This department will save money in the long run by having its own dog!"

Noah laughed. "I think Palmer is saying that if this guy is trying to help you then as inconvenient as his visit is, it might go more smoothly if you're... pleasant."

Josie said, "Kind of like you are to us lately." She gave a little nod in the direction of his office where Daisy peeked out.

The Chief smiled at her and waved her back into the office. "Fine, fine," he said. "Pleasant. All right. I'll do my best. Now listen, there's one more thing, Detectives."

He circled the desks until he came to Noah's seat and pointed to the pile of records from Elliott Calvert's phone. "Mr. Calvert's text messages were clean. Wife, boss, parents, old friends and colleagues in New York. Almost everything about the new baby. Photos back and forth. Promises to get together soon. Scheduling work meetings. Wife wanting to know when he's coming home."

"What about calls?" asked Josie.

"Same," said the Chief. "Except for one number which he called sixteen times in the last four months." He rattled off the number. "It's a disconnected cell phone number. A burner. That's all I could get so far."

Gretchen gestured for him to hand her the report with the number highlighted on it. "I can work on this," she said. "See if I can run it down."

Noah asked, "What about Alison and Dina? Did they ever call that number? Or any unusual numbers? Any red flags on their call lists?"

The Chief shook his head. "No, but there's one more thing you all need to see from Calvert's phone. He didn't have many photos on his phone but the ones he had were either work-related or of his baby. A couple of his wife but mostly his newborn. But..." He riffled through another set of pages until he came up with a packet of color photographs. He handed them across the desk and Josie took them.

Noah and Gretchen crowded in as she looked through them. A small spiral of nausea shot up from Josie's stomach as she thought of Tori Calvert, home with baby Amalise, exhausted, overwhelmed, and utterly devoted to the life she and Elliott had created.

There were a total of seven photos.

"These were in his camera roll?" Gretchen said.

"No," the Chief replied. "It's an app that looks like a timer but actually stores photos you don't want anyone to see."

Each photo showed a woman's partially naked body. Her olive skin was supple and unblemished. In some she lay on a bed among rumpled sheets, only her bare back and the curve of her breast visible. Other photos showed her sitting on the edge of the bed, showing her only from the waist down, wearing a lacy thong. In another, she lay flat on her back, her navel, thong, and upper thighs visible. A dark constellation of freckles in the shape of an S undulated from the left side of her navel to the edge of the thong. On her upper right thigh was a mole. None of the pictures showed her face or even her hair. Even the surroundings were generic. Only one photo panned out from her form far enough that a slice of the wall behind her was visible. Cream with eggshell-colored wainscoting, a piece of which had been gouged out, revealing splintered wood.

"That's definitely not his wife," said Josie. "Tori had a C-section."

"Could it be Dina?" asked Noah. "The skin tone is similar."

Josie studied the photos for a moment longer. "Maybe.

Gretchen, can you call Dr. Feist to see if Dina has any distinguishing features we can match up? Maybe the freckles?"

"Of course," Gretchen said.

The Chief said, "I already checked Dina's social media photos to see if she had posted pictures of herself in a bikini or crop top. Anything that would show her abdomen. She didn't post anything like that, so we can't rule her out based on social media photos."

Gretchen asked, "But why would Calvert have half-naked photos of Dina on his phone? Dina was crazy about this Max guy."

"True," agreed Noah. "But we can't rule anything out yet."

Josie said, "We need a lot more information. Let's get going. We'll start at the East Bridge. Then we'll talk with Calvert's boss and head to the hotel after that."

CHAPTER 19

She is twelve the first time she handles a gun. By now, she gravitates toward Mug. Even though her mother says that men calling women and girls "sweetheart" is dismissive and overly familiar, not to mention demeaning, the truth is that Pea loves it when Mug calls her sweetheart. It doesn't feel dismissive, overly familiar, or demeaning to Pea. Also, she doesn't understand why her mother can call her Sweet Pea, but men shouldn't call her sweetheart. Her mom tried to explain the difference, but Pea got bored and tuned her out.

She doesn't care what her mom says. The word "sweetheart" has become like a magic incantation. It's usually followed by some lesson that Mug thinks she needs to learn —like when he taught her to throw a punch. At the time, she thought it was so stupid and useless, but then she started to "develop", as her mom called it. Her body started doing things she didn't want or understand. Suddenly there was soft flesh where before she had only had bony angles and flat planes. She needed a bra and newer, larger under-wear. Most of all, she didn't like the way boys—and even men—looked at her sometimes.

Pea didn't know what the looks meant, but she finally understood there was a connection between those looks and Mug's assertion that everyone should know how to throw a punch—especially little girls. Now when Mug shows up at the house, Pea makes sure to hover. When he talks, she listens.

And when he bleeds, she gets him a towel.

"What happened?" she asks, trying to push down the panic rising in her chest.

Mug stands at their kitchen sink, holding his left hand under the running faucet. Blood pours from a gash in his palm and mixes with the water as it circles the drain. A half-eaten bowl of cereal stands in the basin and flecks of his blood dot the white milk.

"I was... working," Mug says. "Just working. I cut myself. I was supposed to meet your dad here. We gotta talk about a job. I thought it would be fine so I didn't bother going home first or to the hospital for stitches." He gives a nervous laugh. The kind he usually only gives when Pea's mother is around. "Who has time for that, right?"

"Dad isn't home yet," Pea says. "And Mom just left for some kind of meeting, or something. What should I do?"

"You got a first aid kit?"

Pea doesn't waste time answering. Instead, she races upstairs and into the bathroom. She finds some Band-Aids, some Neosporin, a roll of paper tape, but no first aid kit. She goes into her parents' bedroom and searches their closet. At the bottom of her dad's closet, next to a pair of his dress shoes, she finds a green box with a red cross painted on it along with the words: *First Aid*. Relieved, she picks it up and races back to the kitchen. Mug has turned the water off and now he holds a wad of paper towels in his palm, fingers squeezing it like a ball. Using his other hand and his teeth, he ties a kitchen towel around it.

"Bring that over here," he tells her.

When she opens the first aid kit, there is no gauze or bandages or ointments. Instead, there is a gun.

"Hmmph," says Mug.

Together, they stare at it. It is small and sleek with a handle—later, Mug will tell her it's called the "grip"—that has the same engraving on each side. A skeletal face that somehow looks womanly. Long hair flows from her scalp. One bony hand holds a scythe which stretches over her head. Her mouth is stretched wide open in either a scream or a laugh, Pea can't tell.

"You get this from your dad's room?" asks Mug.

She nods.

With his good hand, Mug picks up the gun by its grip, holding the barrel away from her. He turns it over. On this side of the grip, Pea notices that the lady reaper is missing a tooth where the surface of the grip has been damaged, dented in and scratched. Mug says, "You ever hold one of these, sweetheart?"

"No. I don't—I can't—"

He smiles. "It's okay. You have to learn sooner or later."

"I don't think that's right," says Pea. "I don't think you have to learn—"

Mug pulls at the top of the gun, revealing an opening, which he peers through to the front of the barrel. The top, which he later tells her is called the slide, snaps back into place with a sharp clack. He holds it out, the grip facing her. The lady reaper grins at Pea. "It's not loaded," he says. "Chamber's empty."

When she doesn't take it, he says, "Go on."

It feels both heavier and lighter than she expects. It is at once more and less frightening than she thought it would be. She wants to give it back, but she already knows that Mug won't let her until he's taught her what he thinks she should know.

"What do I do with it?" she asks.

CHAPTER 20

The smell of rubber burning invaded Josie's nostrils, coating the back of her throat. From where she and Noah stood on the road leading to the East Bridge, they could see a thin spiral of black smoke rise into the air. Taking a few steps down the embankment leading under the bridge, Josie saw that two people were burning a tire on the riverbank.

"Should we call the fire department?" Noah asked as they picked their way down toward the river's edge. A cool breeze stirred Josie's ponytail. The day had been exceptionally warm for mid-October and the light wind whipping off the river's surface felt good, in spite of the acrid scents it brought with it.

"Not yet," Josie said. "It's close enough to the water and far enough away from anything flammable that it shouldn't damage anything. If we call the fire department now, they'll scatter and we won't get any answers."

For as long as Josie could remember, even before she became a police officer, the East Bridge had been a gathering spot for drug dealers and users as well as a significant portion of the city's homeless population. The long-term presence of people on the riverbank had choked off any vegetation, leaving only rocks and mud. Under the bridge were a number of tents and other temporary structures made from cardboard, plastic, and anything the occupants could find to create shelter. The police department had long ago given up expelling the people who congregated under the East Bridge. Now it was just a matter of keeping them safe. Still, no one who lived under or frequented the East Bridge trusted police.

As soon as Josie and Noah stepped off the craggy incline and onto the rocky bank, people who had been loitering retreated to their makeshift dwellings. Only the two men burning the tire stayed in place, eyeing Josie and Noah with wide, glassy eyes. One of them held a stick, using it to poke the tire remnants. Josie felt her heart give a little double tap as they approached the men. The one without the stick was jittery, hopping from one foot to the other and scratching at scabs on his bare arms. They showed them both Dina Hale's and Elliott Calvert's photos but neither recognized them or if they did, they wouldn't say so.

Josie and Noah turned next to the tattered shelters beneath the bridge, approaching them one by one, calling out or knocking gently on the feeble enclosures. Many would not come out to talk with them. "We're not here to arrest anyone or give anyone any trouble," they told the East Bridge residents again and again. "We just want to know if you've seen this girl or this man in the last two weeks."

Although Calvert's GPS coordinates hadn't put him at the East Bridge, they'd decided to show his photo on the off chance he had been smart enough to go there without bringing his phone.

No one recognized Dina Hale or Elliott Calvert. If they did, they wouldn't admit to it.

Josie and Noah made their way back to the riverbank. The tire still burned, although the smoke had lessened. The jittery man tossed rocks into the river while his friend poked half-heartedly at what was left of the tire.

"Look," Noah said. He pointed down the riverbank, past the two men, to where a lone figure sat on top of a flat rock that extended halfway into the current.

Josie recognized him immediately. A knot formed in her stomach. She'd been to the East Bridge several times in the last couple of years on various investigations, but she hadn't seen him there for a long time. She had wondered if he was dead or in prison—maybe in some other jurisdiction—but she hadn't bothered to check. She didn't want to know. She didn't want Larry Ezekiel Fox, or "Needle" as she had always referred to him in her own mind, to take up any space in her head. Not anymore.

"We don't have to talk to him," Noah said. "I doubt he'll be any more forthcoming than anyone else down here."

Josie squinted against the sun and used a hand to shade her eyes, watching as Needle laid on his back, sunning on the rock like a lizard. A heaviness crept across her shoulders. "He'll tell me," she said with a sigh. "If he knows anything, he'll tell me."

Her sneakers squished in the mud as she made her way over to him with Noah in tow. Flat on the rock, Needle was almost face-level with her when he turned his head to meet her eyes.

He was in his late sixties, a lifelong drug dealer and user, usually homeless. He looked the same now as he had looked the last time she saw him two years earlier. In fact, he didn't look much different than he had when she was a kid. His hair was still long and stringy, gray but yellowing at the ends. What Josie could see of his thin face beneath his long white-yellow beard was lined and caked with dirt. Sunken pale gray eyes peered at her, the glint of recognition like a spark behind an otherwise vacant façade. He was as thin as ever and still wore a faded, threadbare olive-green jacket over a grime-covered white T-shirt. Josie had to wonder whether the green jacket was older than her or if he had had several during his life. Brown boots held together by worn duct tape sat on the rock beside his bare feet.

"JoJo," he said, sitting upright and turning to face her. When he crossed his legs, knobby knees poked from tears in his jeans.

Josie fought off a wave of nausea at the odor emanating from him. Or maybe it was simply being so close to what he represented from her past. "Zeke," she said, surprised at the steadiness in her voice. She was the only one who had ever called him Needle and that had only ever been in her own head. Only Noah knew about the nickname. As an infant, Josie had been kidnapped. Her abductor, Lila Jensen, had set her family home on fire, leading everyone to believe that Josie had perished when really, Lila had brought her to Denton and passed her off as the child of her former boyfriend, Eli Matson. Having no reason to believe that Josie wasn't his, Eli had gladly taken on the role of father. He'd loved Josie fiercely. That love had enraged Lila and led to Eli's death. Alone with Lila, Josie had endured years of abuse and horror. Among other things, Lila had been a habitual drug user. As a child, Josie knew Zeke, or "Needle," as the man who brought her mother needles.

Noah touched the small of Josie's back. It was a slight motion, out of Needle's view, meant to remind her to speak but also to comfort her. Josie straightened her spine and forced a small smile. "I need to ask you some questions."

Zeke patted the pockets of his jacket until he came up

with a half-crushed pack of cigarettes "You always got questions. Only time I see you is when you got questions."

Josie had to clamp her mouth shut to keep the words from pouring out. *Did you really think we would be friends? Did you expect that I would be making social calls to you after everything you did—and didn't do?*

Needle had stood by year after year while Lila abused Josie. He had witnessed it on many occasions, and although once or twice he'd made half-hearted attempts to get Lila to stop, mostly, he'd allowed it to go on.

Josie quieted the thoughts racing through her mind. Through gritted teeth, she said, "That's my job, Zeke. To ask questions."

He shrugged and shook out a cigarette. Placing it between his lips, he bobbed his head in Noah's direction. "Your friend got questions, too?"

Noah remained silent. Josie said, "We're not here for you, Zeke. I just need information."

Needle fished a lighter from inside one of his boots and lit the cigarette. Inhaling, he nodded. On an exhale of thick smoke, he said, "Better that you travel with a friend, JoJo. 'Specially down here. Wouldn't want nothing to happen to you."

Josie felt her temper flare, searing from her stomach right up to her throat, leaving a foul taste on her tongue. There was the part of her that wanted to punch his face in for all the times he'd let Lila hurt her—badly—and yet, she could never forget the time Needle had saved her from a scheme Lila had devised that was so evil, it likely would have ruined Josie for life. Whenever she saw him, she felt his hand on her eleven-year-old head, heard his words, the words that had saved her from a fate worse than death as far as she was concerned: "Go on outside and play now."

That day, he had taken all of Lila's rage. There was only one other time he'd ever stopped Lila. The night of the knife.

Unconsciously, the fingers of Josie's right hand traced the long scar that ran from her right ear down along her jawline to beneath her chin. So many stitches, and yet, it could have been so much worse.

Still, she hated Needle.

Josie's hands shook as she took out her phone to pull up Dina Hale's picture.

"I've got the photo," Noah said quickly, stepping closer to Needle and taking out his own phone. He tapped his passcode in at lightning speed, his fingers steady and confident. Relieved, Josie dropped her phone into her pocket and watched as Noah showed Needle Dina's driver's license photo. "Have you seen this girl down here in the last couple of weeks?"

Needle stared at the phone screen, unblinking. He took a few more puffs on his cigarette. Then he cupped his hands around his face and leaned into the screen to get a better look. "She in trouble?"

"She's dead," Josie said. "We already know she was here. We've got the GPS from her phone placing her here twelve days ago and seven days ago."

Needle lifted his head and took the cigarette out of his mouth. "You got all kinds of fancy police stuff now, dontcha, JoJo. Guess you're doing a good job."

She never understood what he expected from her. Did he really want to chat? Discuss her career? Was he going to act like he was proud of her, or something equally as disingenuous? She didn't think she could tolerate it.

Noah said, "Do you remember seeing her here on either of those dates?"

Needle glanced at Josie for a moment, his pale eyes assessing. Then he looked back at Noah. "Yeah, I saw her. She was trying to get rid of something."

"Like what?" asked Noah.

Needle took another long drag of his cigarette, turning his head so he didn't blow the smoke directly into their faces. "What do you think?"

Josie rolled her eyes. "I'm not going to arrest you, Zeke. I don't care if you bought or sold drugs to this girl. I already know you didn't kill her. Right now, I just need to know what drugs she had and what she said."

He finished his cigarette and flicked it into the river. "Didn't sell her nothing. She didn't want nothing. She had oxy."

"OxyContin?" Josie clarified.

He nodded. "Quite a bit of it, too. 'Bout ninety pills. Brand name, even."

"In a prescription bottle?" Josie asked.

"Nah. Just in a baggie. Like a sandwich bag."

Josie made some calculations in her head. The street value of OxyContin usually started at twenty dollars per pill. Brand name made it more valuable. She'd seen it sell for as much as eighty dollars a pill and as little as forty. Even on the low end, if the brand-name oxy could be sold for forty dollars a pill and Dina had ninety of them, that was a street value of $3,600.

Needle added, "She said she found it and needed to get rid of it. I told her I didn't have that kind of money to be buying that stuff."

Noah said, "What did she do?"

Needle laughed. "She went all around trying to get someone else here to buy it. It was getting embarrassing.

Finally, I told her I'd take it, but I couldn't pay her. If she wanted money, she had to come back after I sold all of it."

"Did you?" asked Josie.

"Don't remember."

"Okay," Josie said. "She came back a week ago. Was that to pick something up?"

He shook his head. "I thought so but no. She said to forget the whole thing. She just wanted to make sure that I got rid of all of it. Then she told me to forget I ever saw her."

Noah raised a brow. "Seriously, Zeke. We just need information. Did you give her anything when she came back?"

Needle spread his palms in front of him. "I'm telling you the truth. Listen, I know JoJo's a real cop, all right? I know she won't hesitate to arrest me if she gets something on me. I also know she ain't got nothing on me right now. But that don't matter, 'cause I always tell JoJo the truth, and the truth is what I just said. That girl came back and told me to forget the whole thing. Keep everything. She didn't want to be... what did she say?" He trailed off, blinking as he thought about it. Another cigarette slid from the crushed pack and went to his lips. As he lit it, he said, "I remember. She said she didn't want to be 'associated' with it." The cigarette bobbed in his lips as he chuckled. "'Associated.' That's one I hadn't heard before."

"Did she say where she got the drugs?" Josie asked.

"Said she found them. Wouldn't say where. I asked, did she steal them 'cause I didn't want to get into the middle of something. She swore up and down they were found, and she just wanted to get rid of them. That's all I know."

Noah pulled up a photo of Elliott Calvert and showed it to Needle. "You ever see this guy down here?"

Needle exhaled a puff of smoke and shook his head. "Never saw him."

Josie stared at him for a long moment, long enough to decide he really was telling the truth. Still, she couldn't bring herself to thank him. She said, "I'll see you around, Zeke."

As she and Noah turned to walk away from him, he called out, "Jojo."

She looked back, expecting him to ask for money which he sometimes did when she had reason to speak with him. Instead, he said, "Those drugs get that girl killed?"

Josie said, "I don't know."

CHAPTER 21

Josie had driven past the four-story Stamoran building dozens of times in the past several years, never giving much thought to what sort of business was inside. The words Stamoran Firm had always sounded like a law practice. Now she knew it was the architectural firm that had employed Elliott Calvert, the building, with its rusticated red brick, arched windows, and parapet along its top floor made a lot more sense. It was located in the central-most business district of the city, where the streets were laid out in grid fashion. She and Noah parked a block away and walked toward the front doors.

Noah said, "We're back to drugs. Dina 'finds' some OxyContin. She feels she needs to get rid of the pills so she takes them to the East Bridge, but whoever they belonged to wanted them back."

Josie frowned. "Maybe. But I'm not sure she'd be tortured over a few thousand dollars of oxy."

"We've had murders over less than that," Noah pointed out. "Maybe it was a dealer she took the drugs from and they were trying to make a point."

"Maybe. But where does Elliott Calvert come in?"

"He could be involved in some kind of drug trade. Or maybe he had a bad habit that no one knew about. Maybe Dina took his drugs, his fix, and he lost it. We're talking about a guy who killed a seventeen-year-old girl in broad daylight. How stable can he be? We know they were at the hotel at the same time on at least eleven occasions prior to yesterday's incident."

Josie said, "Elliott Calvert stalked and attacked two teenage girls. He murdered Dina Hale. He managed to carry on a fairly normal quiet life before that. I don't think this was about a few thousand dollars' worth of oxy. There's something more going on here. Drugs may also be involved, but my instinct is that we haven't scratched the surface of what's really going on here, especially given the torture element."

At the entrance to the Stamoran building was a glass door with a directory beside it. Each floor held a different business, with the Stamoran Firm taking up the ground floor. Josie tried the door but it was locked, so she pressed the appropriate button. Beyond the glass door she spied a large open lobby area with an empty reception desk, several benches, potted plants and a bank of elevators. Although Cornell Stamoran had promised to meet them there at four, Josie didn't see him or anyone else inside—at least not in the lobby.

They waited a few more minutes. Noah tried the bell again with no success, so Josie took out her phone to call him.

From behind them came a male voice. "Detectives! Sorry I'm late."

They turned to see Cornell Stamoran striding down the street. He was tall, easily six foot four, and thin with a shaved head and a neatly groomed goatee. Behind his glasses, brown eyes beamed. He extended a hand to both of them before using a key to let them all inside. He walked with purpose through the lobby, past the reception desk and into a suite marked

THE STAMORAN FIRM

Another, smaller reception area held a desk and several tall tables, each one boasting a model of a building. Josie guessed they were projects that Stamoran had completed. Glass walls separated the area from a large room with a long, white conference table in the center. Surrounding it were a half-dozen offices, their walls made of glass.

"Total transparency," said Cornell, watching as Josie turned in a circle, studying the surroundings. "We can all see one another. We can all see what's going on in the central meeting area. I think it helps with office culture."

Josie wasn't sure how being under a microscope all day helped with office culture other than preventing inter-office affairs, but she could see there would be no opportunity for anyone to loaf around. Each office held a desk with a couple of guest chairs as well as a large drafting table. Each one also had large, freestanding corkboards where plans and blue-prints were pinned up. A few offices had what looked like 3D printers.

Cornell pointed to a much larger room near the back of the suite that had a long table with stools tucked under it. All around it were shelves holding samples of various items: bricks, wood, siding, flooring, paint swatches. "That's our materials library," he told them. "Everyone has access to it."

"Which office is Elliott Calvert's?" asked Noah.

Cornell pointed to the first office to their left. It was

almost identical to all the others save for a large potted plant. "Do you need to look around? I'm not sure if I'm legally allowed to let you. I tried calling Elliott, by the way. I hope you don't mind. You called and said you needed to meet and that it was concerning him. I thought it only fair to give him a heads-up. He didn't answer. Didn't call me back either."

Josie took a few steps closer to the office, peering inside. A framed photo of Tori balancing a bright-eyed Amalise on one knee sat on the desk. Josie suppressed a sigh. Turning back to Cornell, she said, "He doesn't have his phone."

For the first time, Cornell seemed unsure of himself. A shadow passed over his face. "Oh my God. He's not dead, is he?"

Noah said, "No."

Cornell let out a breath of relief. "Thank God. Well, what is this about?"

Before either of them could speak, a *ding* sounded throughout the suite, like a single church bell. Cornell looked toward the reception area. Josie and Noah followed his gaze where a blonde woman in jeans and a long-sleeved black shirt had just entered. A purse hung from her shoulder. She left it at the desk and joined them in the conference room, arms crossed over her chest.

Cornell said, "This is Steph Ulmer. She's our receptionist. I thought you might like to speak with her. She probably knows more about what happens here than I do." He gave a good-natured laugh, but Steph didn't seem to find it very funny.

Her frown stayed in place as introductions were made and as she studied Josie and Noah's credentials. "What do you need to know?" she asked them pointedly.

Cornell said, "I was just getting to that."

Josie leaned her hip against the conference table. "Yesterday morning, Mr. Calvert followed two teenage girls by car. When they pulled over due to the fog, he got out of his car, approached theirs, and attacked them both. One of those girls died from her injuries."

Steph's frown morphed into a look of shock. Nervous laughter bubbled from Cornell's throat. "Okay, okay," he said. "I'm sorry to tell you this, but you've got the wrong guy. I don't know how you got Elliott's name, but I can tell you that he wouldn't do anything like that. It's crazy. You're saying—I mean, you're talking about... you said she 'died from her injuries?' That's murder, isn't it?"

Neither Josie nor Noah spoke.

The laugh lines around Cornell's eyes loosened but his face remained paralyzed in an expression that was half horror and half disbelief. He said, "I'm terribly sorry to hear that, but I can assure you, the man you're looking for is not Elliott."

Josie said, "It was him."

Steph said, "How can you be sure?"

Noah took out his phone and brought up Elliott's driver's license photo, showing it to each of them. The last vestiges of Cornell's smile disappeared. "I don't understand," he said.

"Neither do we," said Josie. "That's why we're here. We already talked with his wife."

"Tori?" Cornell said. "Oh God. You told Tori this? How is she doing? She probably thinks this is some kind of sick joke, too."

"That's why she called yesterday, isn't it?" Steph said.

Josie and Noah didn't answer but Cornell gave her a questioning look. Lifting a hand to push a strand of her hair behind one ear, she shrugged. "Tori called for him. She thought he was here."

Noah said, "Mrs. Calvert took the news as well as could be expected, and yes, it was a shock to her, too."

Cornell arched a brow. "But you're sure? I mean, so you've got his driver's license photo. How do you know it was really him? Maybe someone framed him. Maybe the other girl is lying. The other one is still alive, right?"

Josie said, "Yes, as far as we know. But Mr. Stamoran, I'm the one who saw Elliott, at the scene, in the act. In addition, he left behind his car—a Nissan Altima—registered to him, and his phone. Today, we located him hiding in the woods and took him into custody."

Steph's mouth hung open. Hugging herself more tightly, she said, "You mean you arrested him? Is he in jail?"

"The hospital," said Noah. "But yes, we've arrested him."

Cornell's skin was ashen. He took a seat at the table. "I don't understand. You're saying Elliott went... crazy? Like, he snapped?"

"We don't know," said Noah. "We're trying to figure that out."

Steph glanced toward his office and back at them. "Is he —is he okay?"

"He will be," said Josie. "When was the last time either of you had any contact with him?"

Cornell said, "Friday. End of the work day. He was there in his office." He gestured toward Elliott's glass cubicle. "I popped in. We chatted about the Monarch Ridge project. I told him to have a good weekend and I left."

"Who else was here?" asked Josie.

"I was," said Steph, raising one hand. "I left soon after that."

"How did Elliott seem that day?" asked Noah.

Steph said, "Distracted."

Cornell said, "Fine."

The two of them looked at one another. With a nervous smile, Cornell said, "Like I told you, Steph has her finger on the pulse of this place better than anyone."

"Because I'm here so much," she said, plastering a fake smile across her face. "Even on my day off."

Her pointed remark didn't register with Cornell at all.

Josie said, "Why do you say he was distracted?"

"Because he was supposed to be working on the Monarch Ridge project, preparing some permit requests for me to send out before I left for the day, but he didn't. He kept checking his phone. Going outside and coming back in. I asked him if something was wrong and he said no."

"What time did you leave?" asked Noah.

"Seven," Steph said. "Elliott left at six forty-five. I closed and locked up for the day."

"You were here yesterday," Josie said. "Do you normally work Saturdays?"

"Every other weekend."

"Had you expected Elliott in at all yesterday?" asked Noah.

Both Steph and Cornell shook their heads.

"How well do you two know Elliott?" asked Josie.

Steph shrugged. "Not well. He's a nice guy—I mean, I thought he was—but we don't talk much and when we do, it's work-related."

Noah said, "You must take calls for him. Messages? Help with his schedule?"

She nodded. "I coordinate appointments and meetings for all the architects. I keep their calendars and take calls for them. I also do a lot of their busy work, like making sure the permit requests for certain projects are in on time, remind them of project deadlines, that sort of thing."

Seeing where he was going with the line of questioning, Josie asked, "Has Tori Calvert ever called you before looking for her husband?"

"Sure, sometimes. If she can't get him on his cell phone. He's usually just in a meeting though."

Josie said, "Has Elliott ever asked you to lie to his wife about where he is?"

Cornell said, "What?"

Steph shifted her feet and looked away.

Josie and Noah waited in silence.

Cornell reached out and tapped Steph's shoulder. "Steph. Elliott asked you to lie to Tori?"

Looking at her boss, Steph said, "I didn't do it. I told him that was not part of my job. It shouldn't be part of anyone's job."

The corners of Cornell's mouth turned down. His eyes filled with sympathy. "You should have told me, Steph. That's unacceptable. I wouldn't ever want you put in a position like that. I'm sorry."

"When was this?" asked Josie.

Steph sighed. The fingers of one hand reached up and fidgeted with a strand of hair. "Like, four or five months ago. I don't know where he was going. It was around dinner time. Everyone was here. We were all working late at that time. Lots of projects with big deadlines looming. He went to leave and he said, 'If Tori calls, can you tell her I'm busy with a client?' and I asked him where he was going. He said he'd rather not say but could I just give Tori the 'standard line' that he was with a client. When he said 'standard line' I was like, 'Oh, you're asking me to lie to her.' He got very uncomfortable and that's when I told him that was not my job."

"How did he react?" asked Noah.

"He was embarrassed. He apologized, and then he left."

Cornell looked dumbfounded. Josie said, "How about you, Mr. Stamoran? How well do you know Elliott?"

He shook his head, gazing into Elliott's empty office. "Not at all, apparently. Jeez. This is really..." He drifted off. Josie and Noah waited for him to collect himself. Finally, he looked back at them. "I mean, not that well. Listen, I had no idea he had asked Steph to lie to his wife about where he went. We're not buddies. I knew him from college. We had a few classes together, but we weren't friends, even then. Since he moved here, we sometimes socialize outside of work but usually only when it relates to work. Like if we take clients out for dinner."

Noah asked, "Have you ever taken clients to Bastian's inside the Eudora?"

"No. We don't usually go there. There are a couple of spots we take clients. The Lotus Lounge and Cadeau. The atmosphere is just a little more relaxed. More fun."

Noah looked back at Steph. "Did you ever socialize with Elliott outside of work?"

She gave a short laugh. "No. Like I said, we didn't even talk that much."

Turning her attention back to Cornell, Josie asked, "Did you hire Elliott?"

"Yeah. This is my firm. He interviewed really well. He seemed motivated, eager to move here from the city, which is not always the case. He's really talented. Has some good experience under his belt. He's one of the best and most reliable guys I've got. Man, I can't believe this."

Noah asked, "How had he been acting the last couple of

weeks? Had either of you noticed anything different? Besides him being distracted? Any other changes in his behavior?"

"Not that I remember," Steph offered.

Cornell shook his head slowly. "No, no. Not really. I mean, I guess Steph is right that he seemed a bit distracted. Since she mentioned it, he was forgetting things. Nothing essential, but little things. There were a couple of emails he forgot to send, some calls to clients he hadn't returned. But he's got a new baby at home, and I know it's been stressful. Amalise is teething and Elliott and Tori haven't been getting much sleep. I just put it down to that. I told him after Amalise was born to take a couple of weeks off, but he wouldn't."

"Is that because of the Locke Heights account?" asked Josie.

Cornell looked puzzled. "Locke Heights?"

Noah said, "Tori said that he's been working on it for months. Lots and lots of overtime. She said he has been pretty stressed out about it."

Nervous laughter erupted from Cornell's throat. "We closed the Locke Heights account three months ago."

Josie said, "You're saying that Elliott hadn't been working late nights and early mornings on that account?"

"Not recently," said Cornell.

"What was he working on?" asked Noah.

Cornell looked at Steph. She rattled off the names of two accounts. "Plus the Monarch Ridge project," Cornell added.

"Are any of those projects ones that would require him to be here a lot more than normal? After regular working hours?" Josie asked.

"Not at this stage, no," Cornell answered.

Josie said, "Are either of you aware of Elliott Calvert ever using drugs?"

Steph shook her head.

Cornell looked as though she had slapped him. "Drugs? You mean in this office? Of course not. I mean, look around." He waved a hand in the air. "Like I said, total transparency. If he had been using drugs, no one here ever saw it or suspected it."

Noah said, "Have either of you ever seen Elliott with a woman who was not his wife?"

Cornell grimaced. He glanced at Steph. She said, "I never saw him with anyone, but after he asked me to lie, I was pretty sure he was having an affair. I mean, why else would you act like that?"

Cornell said, "I can't believe he would have an affair. Have you seen Tori? You know she used to be a ballerina? Why would he do that to her?"

Josie said, "That's not something we can comment on, but we still need to know if you ever saw him with a woman who was not Tori. Someone he seemed to be close to or intimate with."

Cornell shook his head again. "No, no. Of course not."

Steph lifted her chin at the glass walls all around them and added, "I only ever saw him in this office and obviously, if he was having an affair, this isn't the place to hide it."

Noah said, "We know that he frequented Bastian's at the Eudora Hotel. Were either of you aware of that?"

Steph said, "I never scheduled any meetings there for him."

"No. I wasn't," said Cornell. "But like I said, we're not friends. I knew him in college. Now he's an employee of mine. Plus, I mean, apparently he's some kind of violent psycho."

"Did you ever join him at Bastian's?" asked Josie.

"No."

Noah took out his phone once more and pulled up the photo of Dina Hale. "Have either of you ever seen this girl before?"

Both Steph and Cornell studied it, faces blank. "No," said Steph. "I don't recognize her."

"Me either," said Cornell. "Is she—is she one of the girls he... attacked?"

"Yes," said Josie.

Noah showed them Alison's photo. "How about her?"

More blank stares. Neither recognized Alison Mills.

Josie said, "We appreciate your time, Ms. Ulmer, Mr. Stamoran." She handed each of them a business card. "In the meantime, if you think of anything that you believe is important, please call right away."

CHAPTER 22

Josie's phone buzzed in her jacket pocket as she and Noah stepped inside the Eudora Hotel's cavernous lobby. She took out her phone and checked her messages. Gretchen. She hadn't yet tracked down the owner of the mystery number that Elliott Calvert had called sixteen times, but the search was still on. In the meantime, she had drawn up a new arrest warrant for Calvert for the murder of Dina Hale. She had taken it to the hospital, but he was still in surgery. The uniformed officer would serve it on him as soon as he was out of recovery and lucid enough to understand. Tori had been at the hospital, baby on her hip, so Gretchen had delivered the news of the homicide charge. She had taken it stoically. Josie wondered if Tori Calvert was in shock or maybe the homicide charge on top of what she had learned yesterday was simply too much for her to process. Regardless, Josie's heart ached for her.

Gretchen also reported that both Elliott Calvert's and Dina Hale's vehicles had been processed. Nothing of note had been found. The Chief had contacted Marlene Mills. They were about to give a press conference. Gretchen was off to continue the search for Alison. Pocketing her phone, Josie hurried to catch up to Noah, who was already halfway to the front desk. Her feet sank into the thick emerald-green carpet. All around them, patrons sat on antique furniture, chatting quietly, their conversations muffled by the classical music piped into the room. The Eudora Hotel was as old as Denton itself. At twelve stories high, it took up half a city block. Like the police station, it too, was on the historic register. Josie had to admit that the hotel was gorgeous both outside, with its ornate brickwork, and inside, with its marble columns, coffered ceilings and crystal chandeliers.

At the counter, Josie and Noah flashed their credentials and asked to speak with the manager. Five minutes later, they were seated in a swanky office just off the lobby staring at the hotel manager. His nameplate read: John W. Brown. He was relatively new to the Eudora. The last manager had detested any police presence of any kind and done every-thing and anything in his power to frustrate any inquiries they made during investigations. Mr. Brown had made their jobs a lot easier in the last couple of years on the rare occa-sions they needed information from the hotel to aid in an investigation.

Behind his desk, Brown leaned back in his chair and smoothed his red tie. "What can I do for you, Detectives?"

"We'd like to speak to Max Combs," Josie said. "The head of your catering and events department."

Brown frowned, the crow's feet gathering at the corners of his eyes. "Has Max done something?"

Noah said, "Not that we're aware of. We need to speak with him about two employees on the catering and events staff."

"Three, actually," Josie said. She took out her phone and pulled up the photo of Max with the girl at the bar that

Dina had taken and texted to Alison. "Do you know this girl?"

Brown leaned forward, picking up a pair of reading glasses from his desk and sliding them on. He studied the photo for a few seconds and said, "No. She is wearing what staff are required to wear, but I do not recognize her. However, Max has his own staff. I'm not personally aware of all of them."

Noah asked, "You don't approve his hires?"

"Nothing below management level, no," said Brown. "The catering and events staff is typically made up of young people. It's not a career ambition. The turnover is high. Most stay for six months, maybe a year, but then when they get tired of working every weekend, they move on to something else. I've left that department in Max's capable hands. Since I put him in charge, we haven't had a single weekend without a number of lucrative events booked."

"He's good at his job," Josie said.

Brown nodded.

Noah said, "Is he here?"

"I'm afraid not. He was due in an hour ago, but he hasn't arrived."

"Is that typical?" asked Josie.

Brown sighed and waved a hand in the air. "Max is certainly not known for his punctuality, but he's always here when the clients arrive and as I said, he brings in a lot of business, so I often overlook his tardiness."

"Is there someone who is in charge when Max isn't in?" Josie asked. "A second-in-command, if you will?"

A look of distaste flashed across Brown's face. It was so fast, Josie nearly missed it. He immediately covered it with a tight-lipped smile. "Yes, that would be Felicia Koslow. She is the immediate supervisor of the catering and events staff."

Noah said, "If you wouldn't mind, we'd like to talk to her and anyone on the catering staff who is present."

Again, Brown's lips turned downward. "If you're going to be moving about the hotel, asking questions and detaining our staff, I would prefer to know what this is about."

Josie said, "We're looking for a missing girl, Alison Mills. She is employed on the catering and events staff. We want to speak with anyone who knows her to determine if they can help us locate her or give us any other information relevant to the case."

"Oh." Brown nodded. "I'm so sorry to hear that. Of course. You may speak with anyone you'd like on our staff. I would only ask that you try to finish before eight p.m. That's when our largest evening event begins, and I would prefer our guests not be distracted or dismayed by the presence of police."

"Fair enough," said Josie. "One other thing." She pulled up a driver's license photo of Elliott Calvert on her phone and showed Brown. "Do you recognize this man?"

"I'm afraid not. Should I?"

Noah said, "We know that he was here at the Eudora several times in the last five months. His phone's GPS confirms it."

Josie added, "He had some contact with Alison Mills before she went missing. We are looking into all of his recent activity including what he was doing here."

Brown's eyes widened. "Has he done something with the young lady?"

"He didn't abduct her, if that's what you're asking," Noah said. "But he did attack her friend, who was also on the catering staff here. Dina Hale. Unfortunately, she died from her injuries. Alison got away. We need to get her safely home."

Brown was silent for a moment, taking this in. A long finger tapped against the mouse of his laptop, bringing the screen to life. "This is terribly tragic. I'm sorry to hear about Miss Hale and Miss Mills. I can assure you I will do everything in my power to help. If you tell me that man's name, I can look him up. I'd like to make my staff aware of this issue so that if he returns, everyone knows to call 911."

"That won't be necessary," Josie said. "He is in custody. But it would be very helpful if you could look him up." She gave him Elliott Calvert's name, spelling it out while Brown typed it into his hotel database. He typed, tapped against the mouse, and typed again. With another frown, he said, "I'm afraid he's never been a client here."

Noah asked, "You mean he's never reserved a room here."

"Correct." He turned his laptop around to face them so that they could see the database where he'd entered Calvert's name and the small box at the bottom of the screen that said: *No results.*

"What about the bar? The restaurant?" Noah said.

Brown looked up from his computer. "I'm afraid we have no way of knowing who frequents Bastian's, Lieutenant. We don't take names. People are free to come and go as they please."

Josie said, "But you take reservations during busy times, don't you?"

Brown raised a finger in the air. "You are right about that. That is a different database. If you'll give me a moment." He picked up his phone, punched in an extension and waited. Josie heard a woman's voice on the other end. Quietly,

Brown gave her Calvert's name and asked her to check for a history of reservations. A few minutes later, he hung up. "I'm afraid he's never reserved a table in our restaurant."

Noah said, "He could have used a credit card to pay at the bar or restaurant. We know he was here. His phone's GPS puts him here."

Brown rested his elbows on the desk and steepled his fingers beneath his chin. "He very well could, but I do not have access to credit card records of our patrons. For that, I believe I would need a warrant."

"We'll get you one," said Josie. "But as Lieutenant Fraley said, we already know he was here. We're less interested in proving it and more interested in finding out who he was with while he was here."

Brown stared at her, silent, waiting.

She added, "You've got security footage in the lobby and all common areas including the entrance to the restaurant. If we give you a list of the dates and times that Mr. Calvert was here, you could pull the footage."

"Our footage only goes back one month. Any further than that and we only keep footage of incidents that require us to write up reports—if someone falls or if there is an altercation. We keep that footage for one year in case litigation arises."

Josie took out her phone and checked the list of dates and times Calvert had been at the hotel. She rattled them off.

Brown hesitated, pursing his lips and tapping his fingertips together. Josie wondered if he would ask for a warrant. It was within his rights, and for all Josie and Noah knew, there might be some kind of internal hotel policy that required one. Instead, Brown opted to get them out of there as quickly as possible. "If you email me your list, Detective,

I can pull the footage from all of those dates and times while you speak to my catering and events staff." Pointing to the clock above on the wall to Josie's left, he said, "Although I understand you have a very important investigation to conduct, I am charged with the smooth operation of this hotel. Our guests have come to expect a certain standard of luxury when they come to the Eudora, whether they're here for a stay or simply to enjoy the cuisine or some drinks at Bastian's."

Noah said, "Police officers skulking around asking questions doesn't fit that standard."

His tone was sarcastic, but Brown chose to take it seriously. With a strained smile, he said, "I'm so glad you understand. I'll show you to the ballrooms and then I'll have this footage for you just as quickly as I can. I'll see to it personally."

CHAPTER 23

Back in the lobby, more patrons poured in, most heading for the elevators that led to the upper floors. Others, dressed in more formal eveningwear, headed toward the restaurant. No one noticed Josie and Noah walking behind Brown. He led them to a wide hallway off the lobby. Several free-standing signs announced:

VONDRAK WEDDING RECEPTION, BALLROOM A

and:

WOMEN'S CLUB AWARDS BANQUET, BALLROOM B.

Before they reached either ballroom, Brown stopped in front of two double doors with a sign affixed to them marked:

CATERING STAFF ONLY.

From his jacket pocket, Brown produced a card which

he discreetly swiped through a mechanism next to the door handles. A click sounded and he pushed through the doors.

More carpeted hallway. More doors. A break room. A locker room. At Josie's request, Brown unlocked both Dina Hale's and Alison Mills' lockers, but both were empty save for some old make-up products. Next they passed an office with a sign on the door announcing:

MAX COMBS, DIRECTOR OF CATERING AND EVENTS.

The door was closed. No light came from beneath it. After that was a large room that held shelves filled with toilet paper, paper towels, trash bags, disinfectant, and other supplies. A stout woman with gray-brown hair pushed a cart piled high with cleaning items out into the hallway. She wore a pair of tight-fitting black slacks and a white polo shirt with "Eudora" embroidered in dark green on its left breast. "Mr. Brown," she said with a curt nod as they approached. She glanced at Josie and Noah but kept going, maneuvering her cart past them.

"Sadie," said Mr. Brown.

She stopped and turned, giving Brown a forced smile. "Is there something I can help you with? One of the guests from the brunch service this morning vomited on the carpet in Ballroom A, and I really need to get it cleaned up as soon as possible. And yes, someone should have done it this morning, but they did not, so now I have to do it." She checked her wrist, which held a Fitbit that displayed the time. "And I don't have much time before they start setting up for the awards banquet this evening."

Brown returned a tight smile. "I do appreciate your diligence, Sadie. Have you seen Max today?"

A sigh. "No, but it's not my job to keep track of his comings and goings."

For the first time, her eyes drifted toward Josie and Noah. Her fake smile loosened and then failed altogether. "Is—is everything okay?"

Brown lowered his voice as workers from the catering and kitchen staff bustled past them. "I'm afraid not. There was some incident with two of the catering staff yesterday. Off the premises, but still, the police are conducting an investigation."

Josie stepped forward and held out her credentials, but Sadie didn't look at them. Instead, her gaze fixed intently on Josie's face. "I know who you are," she said. "You're that famous detective. The one with the famous twin sister. She's got that show—*Unsolved Crimes*."

"You're right," said Josie. "Miss...?"

"Bacarra. Sadie Bacarra."

"You're friends with Marlene Mills," said Noah, coming closer.

Sadie blinked. Worry pooled in her eyes. "Yes. Marlene and I have been friends for ages. We attended Wolfson Elementary together as kids. That was before my parents moved us to Philadelphia. We always kept in touch and when I moved back here as an adult, we became even closer. Why would you ask that? Is she okay? Wait." She glanced at Mr. Brown. "You said something happened with two people on catering. Do you mean Alison? Alison Mills?"

"Please, Sadie," said Mr. Brown. "Lower your voice."

Josie didn't tell him there was little point in her lowering her voice. Their aim was to interview everyone there. Soon, the entire staff would know what was going on.

Sadie made a fist and pressed it into her mouth. After

several seconds, she removed it and whispered, "Is Alison okay? Please tell me she's okay. Marlene would just die if something happened to Alison. It's bad enough Clint is in Hong Kong for God knows how long."

Josie said, "I'm afraid Alison is missing. We're searching for her."

Mr. Brown interjected, "If you have things well in hand here, I'll go retrieve the items we discussed earlier."

"Thank you," said Josie.

Sadie said, "Items? What items? What's going on?"

But Mr. Brown was already pushing his way through the staff doors to return to his office. Noah said, "Mr. Brown is helping us with our investigation."

"Into Alison being missing? You think she came here? Or did she go missing from here?"

"No," Josie said. "She didn't go missing from here. She and her friend, Dina Hale, were driving down Widow's Ridge Road yesterday morning. They pulled over to avoid driving in the fog, and there was some kind of incident. Dina was killed and Alison fled the scene."

Sadie's face paled. "Did you say *killed*? Incident? What kind of incident? Oh my God. Marlene didn't call me. Why didn't she call me? Is Alison hurt? Do you think she's still alive? Should I help with the search?"

Noah said, "Right now you can help by answering our questions."

Sadie fanned herself with one hand and paced back and forth the length of her cart. "Of course, of course."

Josie said, "You knew Alison well, I assume?"

Sadie nodded.

"What about Dina?"

"You mean the other girl? Alison's friend? I've seen her here, of course. I've seen her with Alison at their house many times. I know who you're talking about. I know who she is—but I don't know her. I'm not sure we've ever spoken beyond saying hello."

"When was the last time you spoke to Alison?" asked Josie.

Sadie looked up at the ceiling, eyes squinting as she considered it. "Friday evening, I think. I saw her right in this hallway, but just in passing. She was in a rush and so was I. Fridays are busy. The whole weekend is busy."

Noah took out his phone and pulled up a photo of Elliott Calvert. He showed it to her. "Do you recognize this man?"

Sadie stared at the phone. "He looks familiar. Maybe I've seen him here? So many people come and go, it's hard to keep track. I may have seen him before, but I don't know who he is. Who is he?"

Instead of answering, Noah swiped to the photo of Max and the mystery girl at the bar that Dina had been so upset over. "How about this girl? Do you know her?"

"Oh yeah. She works here. She's on the catering staff with Alison. I think her name is Gia or something like that."

"Do you know her?" Josie asked. "Personally?"

Sadie shook her head. "No, but honestly, I don't know most of the catering staff, which is pretty large. Most of them are young kids anyway, like Alison. They're not interested in making friends with some middle-aged lady. Not that there's a lot of time for that around here. Like I said, we stay busy. Felicia would definitely know her. She's younger. She's also their supervisor—although, if you ask me, she's more interested in being friends with these kids than supervising."

Ignoring the dig, Noah said, "Marlene told us that you got Alison the job here."

"Yeah," Sadie replied. "I knew Max was looking for staff and Alison was looking for work. I didn't get her the job, though. I just got her an interview."

"Do you know Max well?" asked Josie.

Sadie snorted. "Everyone knows Max well. He's a hopeless flirt. He's full-time, obviously, and so am I, so yeah, we talk sometimes."

Noah said, "Does Max have a relationship with anyone on the catering staff?"

"Right now? I don't know," said Sadie. "I think maybe him and Felicia have a thing. Or at least, they did. You'll have to ask her."

"What about with any other staff members?" Josie asked.

Sadie shrugged. "I don't know. I'm sure he has at some point. Like I said, he's a flirt. Plus he's young and handsome. I've seen the way some of the girls get starry-eyed over him. I've told him more than once to steer clear of anyone younger than him. A lot of these girls are still in high school. I told him if he has to stick his pen in the company ink, stick with Felicia. She's almost thirty. Much more appropriate."

Josie asked, "Has he ever pursued any of the younger girls?"

"I hope not," said Sadie. "I've seen him flirt but nothing more than that. Then again, it's not like Max and I are besties—that's what the kids call it these days—we work together. I have no idea what he does when he leaves here."

"Do you know whether or not he had some kind of relationship with Dina Hale?" asked Noah.

"I don't know. Then again, if I had known something like that, I would have told him off. She's entirely too young."

"What about Gia?" asked Josie.

Sadie shook her head. "I don't think so, but I really wouldn't know. Maybe she's older than the other girls. It's hard to tell, but in my mind, she'd still be too young for Max."

"Do you know where we could find her?" asked Noah.

Sadie motioned behind them to the long hallway. "Probably in the kitchen or one of the ballrooms, getting things prepped for tonight, if she's on for tonight. I don't know. Listen, I really need to get to work, and then I need to call Marlene."

Josie gave her a business card and thanked her for her time before she and Noah continued deeper into the staff areas. They passed another room which held cooking supplies and implements. Then came a massive kitchen, abuzz with activity. Workers in white aprons and chef's coats stood at numerous stations, preparing food for that evening's event. Pots and pans clanged. Knives chopped, tapping against cutting boards with precision. Instructions were shouted across the room. Billows of cold air floated from the doorway of a walk-in freezer, swirling along the floor. Steam rose from large pots of boiling water and soup on industrial-sized stovetops.

Near the back of the kitchen stood a tall, thin woman dressed in a chic fitted green pantsuit with short, ruffled sleeves. Her blonde hair was parted so that all of it hung down the left side of her face. The right side of her skull had been shaved to the quick. A series of tiny gold hoops sparkled from her ear. As they drew closer, Josie counted eight of them. Behind her ear a phoenix rose, extending its fiery wings along her neck and the side of her throat, tattooed in a deep orange that contrasted with her pale skin. Her attention was focused on a clipboard in her hands. They were a few feet from her when she looked up, noticing them for the first time. Eyes wide, she waved the clipboard, as if to ward them off. "I'm sorry but you cannot be back here. I don't know who let you in but this is—"

Noah said, "Mr. Brown let us in."

Josie held out her credentials. "We're with the Denton PD. Are you Felicia Koslow?"

Ignoring Josie's question, she said, "I don't think this is appropriate. You're coming to my place of employment? What did you say to Brown?"

Josie and Noah exchanged a curious glance. Noah said, "Are you Felicia Koslow?"

Thrusting her chin out, she said, "I don't have to tell you."

Josie said, "Why do you think we're here?"

"I'm not going to say. I don't have to talk to you at all. I can—I'll call my lawyer if you don't leave right now."

CHAPTER 24

With a sigh, Josie said, "There's no need for that—although we're not leaving. Mr. Brown has given us permission to question the staff. You don't have to talk to us but we will need to speak with someone in charge of the catering and events staff so we can coordinate our interviews. Maybe you can tell us where Felicia Koslow is—unless Max Combs has shown up?" She looked around. "Regardless, it would probably be best to gather everyone first and give them the news while they're all together."

Narrowing her eyes, the woman said, "What news?"

Noah said, "Yesterday, Dina Hale—an employee here—was murdered. Her friend, Alison Mills—also an employee—is missing. We need to speak to everyone here about Dina and Alison. Routine questions."

She made a high-pitched noise deep in her throat. The clipboard flew up, the top of it covering the lower half of her face. Her words were muffled. "Dina and Alison?"

"I'm afraid so," Josie replied. "Now, please. If you can direct us to Miss Koslow or—"

The clipboard came down, revealing a trembling lower

lip. "I'm Felicia. I'm so sorry. I didn't know. I—" She palmed her forehead, groaning loudly. Josie thought she heard Felicia mumble the word "idiot." Returning her focus back to them, she said, "You probably think I'm some kind of criminal, right? The way I acted. Oh my God. It's not that. It's just that I had this ex in Philly who used to deal drugs. The cops there thought I was part of it. I didn't even know, but they were always harassing me. I just thought—I'm so sorry. Dina is really dead?"

Noah said, "We're very sorry but yes, she is."

Felicia walked in a small circle, tapping the clipboard against her chin. When she stopped and looked at them, Josie saw tears leaking from the corners of her eyes. She used a knuckle to wipe them away. Sucking in a breath, she said, "I'm fine. I'm fine. I have to be strong. This is devastating. I just can't believe it. God, what happened?"

Josie and Noah gave her the scant details they were able to share. For a long moment, she remained silent, staring down at the floor. They waited for more questions, but none came. Finally, Josie said, "Felicia, before we speak with the rest of the staff, we need to ask you some questions."

When she didn't answer, Noah said, "Miss Koslow?"

Shaking herself from her thoughts, she looked up at them once more. "Of course, of course."

"When was the last time you spoke with Max Combs?" asked Josie.

"Oh, uh, Friday. I was off yesterday so I didn't see him." She produced a phone from a slim pocket of her pants and checked the time. "He really should be here by now, but it's not unlike him to be late."

Josie said, "When was the last time you spoke with Dina or Alison?"

"Last weekend."

"How well do you know them?"

Felicia blew out a breath. "Pretty well, I think. These kids we have working for us, most of them are teenage girls. I try to maintain a good relationship with all of them. I make sure they know when they start that they can come to me with anything. Most of them do. They're like little sisters to me."

Noah asked, "Did you have any reason to believe that Dina or Alison were having any serious problems in the last couple of weeks? Had you noticed anyone unusual hanging around? Did they seem to be acting differently?"

Felicia answered no to each question as he asked it.

Josie said, "Had Dina or Alison come to you with any problems in the last couple of weeks?"

Felicia gave a tight smile. "Well, Dina was upset about Max. He flirts with the girls."

"We're aware," said Josie. "She was upset because she saw him speaking with another girl named Gia, is that correct?"

Felicia nodded. "Yes. I talked with both of them about it. I told Dina it was never going to happen and that he was entirely too old for her anyway. I told him to stop leading the girls on and whatever he was doing with Gia, it needed to stop."

"Something was going on with Gia?" asked Josie.

She hugged the clipboard to her body. "I don't know. I wouldn't put it past Max. I didn't ask. I just told him to stop talking to her. Period. Unless it was work-related."

Noah asked, "What did he say to that?"

"He said I was overreacting. He said nothing ever happened with any of the girls. That they read too much into things and were being overly dramatic."

Josie said, "How about you? Are you or have you ever

been in a relationship with Max? Beyond a working relationship."

A scowl made its way across her face. Her nostrils flared. "Who told you?"

Noah raised a brow. "No one told us anything. We're asking you."

She looked around, as if looking for the culprit, and then returned her gaze to them. "It was that bitch, Sadie, from housekeeping, wasn't it? She's had it out for me since I started. All because I reported her for not returning cash she found at a guest's table. She just kept it for herself. Slipped it right into her pocket. I saw her when she was cleaning up. She did something wrong but somehow, I'm the bad one. She acts like her shit doesn't stink, but I bet she didn't tell you that her husband left her and took their kids after she had an affair, did she? That's why she came back here, alone, because she blew up her whole life."

Noah said, "Ms. Bacarra's personal life is not relevant to our investigation."

"But she was the one who told you, wasn't she? Old Miss Holier Than Thou." When neither of them answered, Felicia sighed and dragged her fingers through her hair. "No one is supposed to know about me and Max. It undermines my authority. Plus, so many of these girls get crushes on Max. If they think we're together, they'll either see me as a rival or they'll think they can't come to me with problems. I want them to trust me."

Josie said, "So you have had, or you do have, a relationship with Max? Of a sexual nature?"

Felicia looked around to see if any of the kitchen staff were listening, but they were all too busy to care what was happening in the small corner that she, Josie and Noah took up. Lowering her voice, she confessed, "When I first started here, we had a thing. It lasted six months, tops. I broke it off. I needed this job and the rumors were becoming a problem. The staff didn't respect me anymore. They didn't see me as a supervisor, they saw me as Max's girlfriend. They didn't think I was qualified for the job. I told him it was over and then tried to repair the damage to my reputation here. Luckily, the staff in catering and events turns over quickly so almost everyone who worked here then is gone. Still, there are a few people who have it out for me."

She craned her neck, looking around Josie and Noah, as if she might spot an ill-willed coworker lurking behind a pot of soup or the walk-in freezer.

Noah took out the photo of Elliott Calvert and showed it to Felicia. "Have you ever seen this man?"

"Sure, yeah. I've seen him in the bar. At Bastian's. He's there a lot."

Josie said, "Do you know his name?"

Felicia shook her head. "No. I've never talked to him. But I've seen him. I mean, he's cute, right? Hard not to notice him."

"Cute" was not a word Josie would have used. She could never look at Elliott as anything other than a killer and a man who had lied to everyone in his life. She kept her thoughts to herself. "Did you ever see him with anyone?"

"No. He drank alone. Sad, right? Who is he?"

Noah put his phone away. Instead of answering her question, he asked her to gather the staff for an announcement and to provide them with a space where they could speak with each person individually. Twenty minutes later, the kitchen was silent, all the workers gathered inside it. Josie panned the crowd for Gia and found her standing near the door, dark hair pulled into a bun, dressed in the same clothes she was wearing in the photo with Max. Her arms were folded across her chest as she listened to Felicia break the news of the tragedy and instruct them each to take time to speak with either Josie or Noah before the wedding and awards banquet began. Josie nudged Noah with her elbow and tilted her head in Gia's direction.

"I see her," he muttered under his breath.

In one of the smaller events rooms that were not being used that evening, Josie and Noah set up at tables across the room from one another. The catering and events staff filed in for interviews. Hushed conversations buzzed like an undercurrent throughout the space. Most of them were in shock and had more questions for the detectives than Josie or Noah had for them. Everyone was asked about their relationship with Dina and Alison. How well did they know them? When was the last time they were in contact with either of them? Had they noticed either girl acting differently in the last couple of weeks? Did either of them appear to be having trouble with anyone? Had they noticed anyone unusual hanging around the hotel recently? Although almost everyone knew Dina and Alison, few knew them well. Most had seen them both on Friday evening at work. The people who had more than a passing relationship with them had not noticed anything unusual about their behavior, nor had they noticed anyone new or different hanging around the hotel. Everyone was shown a photo of Elliott Calvert. Some said he looked familiar, but no one recognized him.

Dead ends.

Hours passed. Josie tried to mask the sound of her stomach growling by tapping her fingers on the table. From across the room, Noah's gaze met hers. He shook his head. No Max yet. Also, no Gia. They finished up several more interviews and still neither Max nor Gia had appeared.

Once they were finished, they met in the middle of the room. Josie said, "Max may not have come in yet but Gia was there. She heard what Felicia said. Where did she go? You didn't show anyone the photo of her and Max, did you?"

"No," replied Noah. "You?"

"I didn't," said Josie. "I was waiting to discuss it with her. Do you think she left?"

"Let's find out," Noah said.

CHAPTER 25

Gia wasn't in the staff areas or any of the events rooms. Josie and Noah were about to head back to the lobby to check for her there when they noticed that one of the doors to the outside had been propped open with a small metal trash bin in spite of the sign taped to the door that said:

DO NOT PROP OPEN.

On the other side of the door was a small walkway, hemmed in with a metal railing, that led to a loading dock. Halfway down the walkway, Gia leaned over the railing, puffing on a vape pen. She looked up when they walked through the door. Giving them a tight smile, she pushed away from the railing and tried to edge around them. "I have to get back to work," she said.

Josie stepped directly into her path. "It's Gia, right?"

She froze. Up close, Josie could see why Dina might have felt hopeless at the thought of Max turning his attention to Gia. She was both beautiful and striking with tanned skin, high cheekbones, full lips, a perfectly straight nose, and wide brown eyes beneath long, thick lashes. Her skin was smooth and unblemished. She wore some make-up but she didn't need it. Josie would guess her age to be mid-twenties, a much more age-appropriate match for Max Combs than Dina Hale.

Gia said, "How do you know my name?"

Noah held his phone out to her, showing her the picture of her and Max. Josie watched her face, noting a flash of fear behind her eyes before her expression went blank. "That's me and my boss," she said. "Did he tell you my name? Why are you looking for me?"

Josie didn't answer her questions, instead asking her own, "What's your last name, Gia?"

"Sorrento. Max didn't tell you that?"

"When is the last time you spoke with Max or saw him?" asked Noah.

"Friday night at the corporate party."

"How well did you know Dina Hale?" said Josie.

Gia rolled her eyes. "Well enough to know she had it out for me, okay?"

"She was jealous," Josie said. "She thought you and Max had some kind of relationship."

Gia laughed. "Me and Max? Oh my God. That's why? I should have known. Everyone knows—knew—she had it for him bad. It was kind of pathetic."

Noah said, "So you and Mr. Combs were not in a relationship?"

Gia pointed a finger at her chest. "I'm in high school!"

Josie did her best to keep the surprise from her face. "Which high school?"

"Saint Catherine of Siena Academy."

Josie knew the school. It was a private boarding school,

small and prestigious. The cost of tuition was comparable to most state colleges.

"Are you a senior?" asked Noah.

She nodded. "This is my last year."

"Where does your family live?" Josie asked.

"Philadelphia. My dad thought if he sent me here, it would keep me out of trouble. Boys and drugs, he says. That's what he thinks is trouble. He thinks I'm safer here, too."

"You're not?" asked Noah.

She shrugged. "I guess."

"How old are you?" asked Josie.

"I just turned eighteen."

Josie said, "From what we've gathered here today, someone being high school age wouldn't stop Max Combs from pursuing her. Plus, at eighteen, it would be legal for the two of you to be romantically or sexually involved. Actually, the age of consent in Pennsylvania is sixteen. Were you or were you not in a relationship with him?"

"I wasn't. Max likes to flirt, okay? That's all."

Noah said, "What were the two of you talking about the night this photo was taken?"

"I don't know. I don't remember. Sometimes I go out and sit at the bar during my breaks. I see him there. We talk."

"Dina took the photo," Josie told her. "She thought something was going on between the two of you."

Gia shook her head. "So? She's wrong."

"You said she had it out for you," Noah said. "What did you mean by that?"

"Just that lately, she's been doing stuff at work to mess with me. Like if I had to set up a room, she would come in after me and take out things like place settings or centerpieces. Remove chair covers. Then Felicia would be all over my ass about it."

"Did you confront her?" asked Josie.

"No. It's not worth it. I just figured she would turn her attention to someone else eventually if she didn't get any reaction from me."

"Did you tell Felicia about it?"

Gia laughed drily. "Felicia? You're kidding, right? She thinks this is some kind of sorority where we should all act like sisters or something. If I went to her we'd have to have a week's worth of team-building and conflict-resolution meetings that would only make things worse for me. So no, I didn't tell Felicia."

"How about Alison?" asked Noah. "Was she involved in this campaign to make your life difficult?"

"No. I never had a problem with Alison."

Josie asked, "How long have you worked here?"

"About a year," Gia answered. "I'm stuck here in Denton for the school year, so it's not like I've got big plans on the weekends. It's a good gig."

Noah pulled up a photo of Elliott Calvert and turned it toward Gia. Josie noted an immediate reaction—a sudden tension in her jaw. A slight widening of her eyes. "Do you know this man?" he asked.

She stared at the photo for a beat before answering. Josie watched the micro movements of her face as Gia tried to arrange her expression back into a blank stare. "No."

"Look closely," Josie said. "Are you absolutely certain?"

Immediately, Gia looked away from the photo. The vape pen went to her lips. Smoke that smelled of raspberries puffed from her mouth as she said, "Don't know him."

Noah glanced at Josie from the corner of his eye. He, too, knew that Gia was lying. "That's probably a good thing," he said. "That you don't know him. He's in police custody for murder. Well, he will be when he gets out of the hospital."

Josie and Noah went quiet, letting Noah's words hang in the air along with the cloud of vape smoke. Sometimes, not filling the silence was the best strategy. After several seconds, Gia said, "What happened to him?"

"Broke his arm," Noah answered. "Had to get surgery. But once he's discharged, he'll be headed straight to jail." He touched his phone screen again, pulling up the photo of Dina. Shaking his head, he muttered, "She never stood a chance."

More silence. Gia's fingers fidgeted with the vape pen. She sucked on it again but nothing happened. "Dammit," she whispered. Finally, she met Josie's eyes. "Fine. I've seen him here, okay? I don't know his name or anything, but I've seen him in the bar. He tried to talk to me a couple of times, but I wasn't having it."

Noah said, "Talk to you about what?"

She threw her hands into the air and let them fall to her sides. "I don't know! The weather. The drinks menu. The stupid sports playing on the TV. He was drunk. Clearly drunk. I told him I wasn't interested. Is that what you want to know?"

"Why did you lie just now?" asked Josie.

"I don't know. Because I don't really know him and it's just weird, you know? It's weird and it's gross. I know I look older but I'm still just a high school student. I'm eighteen! But these men, especially here at this hotel, they don't even care. If you're sitting alone at the bar or at a table, they think you're just there for their amusement or for them to proposi-tion you or something. Even working events in catering, especially at weddings and stuff, men don't even think twice about grabbing your ass or saying something lewd. Although that guy?" She pointed to Noah's phone even though Elliott's picture was no longer visible. "He was nicer than most. He seemed like he was probably a decent guy who just had too many drinks. As soon as I shut him down, he was fine with it. He backed right off. He even apologized. But it still made me uncomfortable, you know? I'm sorry I lied, but I don't like talking about it. And before you ask why I don't just quit, the truth is that I need this job."

Josie thought about the fact that her father could afford to send her to St. Catherine's, but she didn't bring it up. Perhaps he didn't provide her with much else. Perhaps Gia didn't want to depend on her father for complete financial support.

"You said he approached you a couple of times," Noah said. "How many exactly? Two? Three?"

Gia tapped her vape pen against her bottom lip. "Two. Don't ask me the dates because I don't remember. It was sometime in the last couple of months probably."

Josie said, "Did you ever see him in the bar other than those times?"

Gia shrugged. "I don't know. Maybe. I really don't remember."

Noah asked, "Did you ever see him with anyone else?"

"I don't think so, but I wasn't exactly keeping track of him. He was just one of many creepers in this place."

"Detectives?" Mr. Brown stood in the doorway to the loading dock, looking down and frowning at the trash bin.

Gia whirled to face him and froze in place.

Brown's eyes moved from the bin to Gia. Wordlessly, she sprinted up the walkway and bustled past him before he could speak to her. Brown gave a small shake of his head and then looked up at Josie and Noah, beckoning them back inside. As the door closed behind them, Brown said, "I'm afraid that all of the footage that you requested is... inaccessible."

Josie said, "What does that mean?"

"It means I cannot access it."

Noah said, "Why not?"

Brown folded his hands at his waist and looked down at them. "Because it's no longer there."

"Why is that?" Josie said.

"It appears to have been erased. At least, that is the only explanation I can offer."

"The entire hotel?" Josie asked. "Or just portions?"

"The entire hotel."

Noah said, "Who has access to the footage?"

Brown lifted his eyes. "The security team."

"We're going to need to question them," said Josie.

CHAPTER 26

Josie shuffled the stack of papers on her lap, riffling through the papers one by one for the fifth time since they'd gotten into the car and left the Eudora Hotel. From each page stared a different set of eyes. Brown had provided them with color photos of every member of the Eudora's security team along with their personal information. He had made every single one of them that weren't on shift at that moment come in for a special meeting so that Josie and Noah could interview them. They'd spent two hours with the head of security as he tried to figure out how footage from all the dates and times Elliott Calvert had been at the Eudora had been deleted. It remained a mystery.

"One of them has to be lying," Josie said. "Only a small group of people have access to the footage and every single one of them denied deleting it."

The dull glow of streetlights illuminated businesses and homes that had been shuttered for the night as Noah wended his way through the city toward the hospital.

Noah said, "Brown also has access."

"You think Brown deleted it?"

Noah shrugged. "I don't know. I'm saying we can't rule him out. He did log into the security system database a few times in the last month. He could have deleted the footage at any point. Hell, he could have deleted it today when he went to pull it."

Josie stopped fingering the pages in her lap and groaned. "You're right. You think Brown's covering for Calvert?"

"I think Brown's covering for Brown," said Noah. "Whether he knows Calvert or not, it's not good for the hotel to be associated with a murderer."

Noah turned onto the long hill leading up to Denton Memorial.

"Do you think he told the truth about Calvert never having rented a room there?"

Noah said, "He showed us the search results."

"Which means, regardless of whether or not Brown was the one who deleted the footage, Calvert did not rent a room there," Josie said. "But we know he was there because Gia saw him in the bar on at least two occasions."

"It's not that unusual for people to frequent Bastian's and not rent rooms."

Noah pulled into a parking spot near the hospital's front entrance. Josie abandoned the personnel files of the Eudora's security staff, tucking them safely inside the glove compartment, and they went inside. In the lobby, they showed their credentials at the reception desk, advising that they were there to see Elliott Calvert. As the receptionist wrote their names and Calvert's room number in her log, Josie watched the television on the wall to the left of the desk. It was tuned to their local station, WYEP. The news broadcast was in progress. Next to the anchor's head flashed a photo of Alison Mills. Posed awkwardly in front of a blue backdrop, she gave a subdued smile. It had to be a school photo. The chyron across the bottom of the screen read:

Police Looking for Tips in Case of Missing Teen.

Josie was too far away to hear any of the news anchor's words. Next, the screen cut away to footage of Chief Chitwood and Marlene Mills standing in front of a podium that had been set up in the police department's municipal parking lot. The Chief spoke at length, waving his hands as he did so. A breeze lifted strands of his white hair. Beside him, Marlene Mills looked straight ahead, her eyes wide with abject terror. She clutched the straps of her purse so hard, her knuckles were white. When the Chief stopped talking and stepped away from the podium, beckoning her to step up, she froze. Josie read his lips: *Mrs. Mills. Mrs. Mills. Please step up to the podium.*

But Marlene was paralyzed. Even her eyes failed to blink.

Finally, the Chief walked over and put a hand to one of her elbows, breaking the spell. Marlene's eyes, now shiny with tears, found his and she offered a tremulous smile. The Chief leaned in toward her ear. Again, Josie read his lips: *you got this.* Gently, he guided her to the podium. Still clutching her bag, Marlene looked toward the camera. Her fingers twisted the purse straps. She licked her lips and then began talking. After a few words, she stopped abruptly. The Chief stepped in, adjusting a microphone on the podium. He tapped it and Marlene leaned in and began speaking again.

Josie couldn't tell what she was saying but with trembling hands, she pulled out an eight-inch by ten-inch glossy photo of Alison. The same one they were using on the

WYEP report. She sensed Noah at her back. He said, "She's saying, 'Alison, just come home. Everything's fine. It's safe. Just come home or come to the police. You're not in trouble. Everyone just wants you home safe. Please, anyone out there, if you see my baby, tell her to come home or call the police.'"

One of Noah's ex-girlfriends had been deaf. He'd learned some sign language but mostly, he was very adept at reading lips. Far better than Josie.

Alison's photo shook so badly in Marlene's hands that it was impossible to see it any longer. The Chief stepped in, taking the photo from her hands and holding it up for the cameras to zoom in on, which they did. Alison's face filled the screen. A tip line appeared along the bottom of the screen. Then WYEP cut away, back to the anchor in the studio, who moved on to another story.

"This poor woman," Josie mumbled. "Jesus, Noah. Where is this kid?"

Stepping up beside her, he said, "I don't know, but Gretchen's out looking for her as we speak, and with this press conference, hopefully she'll be home soon. Let's go see if Calvert will talk to us."

They took an elevator to the fourth floor. Calvert was still on the surgical floor. His room was across from the nurse's station. Brennan sat in a chair beside the door, scrolling on his phone. "Detectives," he said as they approached. "He's up but he ain't talking."

Noah said, "Did you arrest him? For homicide?"

Brennan put his phone away and leaned back in the chair, stretching his legs out in front of him. "Sure did. He acknowledged his rights and then he said he wasn't talking to anyone. His wife is here. She's still in the surgical waiting room, I believe." He hooked a thumb to his right, indicating a long hallway. "I told her she can't see him. Not that he would anyway. She says she's not leaving until we let her talk to him. He is also pissed that we called her in the first place."

Josie said, "He must be on a lot of pain meds right now. Are you sure he understood what was going on?"

Brennan shrugged. "Seemed pretty lucid to me."

"Has he asked for an attorney?" Noah said.

"Nope. Not yet."

Josie sighed. "All right. Let's see if he'll talk to us."

"Good luck," Brennan said with a laugh as they entered Calvert's room.

He was propped up in his bed, his casted forearm in a sling across his torso. Fluid dripped from an IV bag into a vein in his good arm, at the crook of his elbow. His dark hair was greasy and uncombed. A patchy beard covered his jaw. The lights had been dimmed. He blinked several times as Josie and Noah took up position on either side of his bed. His shoulders rose up toward his ears, tense, until he took them in fully, then they dropped. A long breath escaped his lungs. "It's only you," he muttered.

Josie said, "Who did you think it would be?"

He didn't answer.

Noah said, "Mr. Calvert, are you aware that you've been placed under arrest for the homicide of Dina Hale? Do you recall Officer Brennan reading your Miranda rights to you?"

Elliott's expression darkened. Through gritted teeth, he said, "I'm aware. I recall."

Josie said, "We'd like to ask you some questions."

Elliott said nothing.

Noah said, "Mr. Calvert, we're aware that you've been frequenting Bastian's without your wife's knowledge for the past several months. We're aware that you've lied to her about working on the Locke Heights account at work. Your boss told us work on that account concluded three months ago. We're aware that you've been keeping photos of a woman who is not your wife on an app on your phone that is specifically for hiding photos."

Elliott looked straight ahead while Noah spoke. A vein in his right temple pulsed.

Josie added, "We know that you've gotten yourself into something. We know that when you attacked Dina Hale and Alison Mills, you were looking for something. We know that you're afraid."

Noah picked up the thread. "The best thing you can do for yourself and for your family right now is talk to us. Let us help you."

Elliott's voice was low and taut. "The best thing I can for myself and my family right now is nothing."

Josie said, "Will doing nothing ensure that your wife and daughter are safe?"

He didn't respond, but Josie could see the subtle change in his expression—from anger to fear. Still he didn't speak. Josie and Noah waited but unlike most people, he didn't attempt to fill the silence. Instead, he let it stretch on. The sounds in and outside of the room grew louder in his silence. The drip of his IV. The sounds of bells and alarms in the hall. Feet shuffling back and forth past his door. Muffled voices calling things out to one another.

Noah said, "What were you looking for when you attacked Miss Hale and Miss Mills?"

He didn't respond.

Josie asked, "Who was the woman in the photos on your phone?"

Nothing.

"You sure you don't want to talk about her?" asked Josie. "At least give us her name so we can warn her about... whatever is happening here."

Still, no response. He stared straight ahead as if they were not even in the room.

They peppered him with more questions, but he remained stoic, not answering, not saying a single word.

Noah said, "Mr. Calvert, should we instruct your wife to take your daughter and leave town?"

No response.

Josie leaned forward over the bed until he had no choice but to look into her eyes. "I don't know what you got yourself into, but I firmly believe your wife and child are innocent. You don't want to talk to us about what's going on? Fine. But Tori and Amalise?" She let their names hang in the air and watched as tears filled his eyes. "They deserve more from you. They deserve to be safe. It's the least you can do. So, one more time: are your wife and daughter safe?"

Josie counted off four seconds. Then Elliott swallowed and said, "I don't know. That's the truth. I really don't. I hope so, but I don't know."

They waited again, hoping he would add to his last statement, offer some explanation, but he didn't.

Finally, Noah said, "We'll tell her to take Amalise and leave town."

CHAPTER 27

She is thirteen when her father notices that she knows certain things. They're going to brunch together as a family and when they get to the diner, Pea tries to take the seat with the best view of the front doors and most of the establishment. "Always keep your back against the wall," Mug told her. "Never give people your back. If you're at a booth or a table, you want the seat that puts the fewest number of people behind you and gives you the best view of the doors and everyone else around you."

She's still not sure why this is important, but she listens closely to everything Mug tells her and tries to practice it. She has a feeling that one day she will need all of the skills Mug teaches her. She's just not sure in what way they'll be necessary.

"Hey," says her dad, interrupting both her thoughts and her view of the front door. "Get up. I'm sitting there."

Pea looks up at him, unsure how to respond. This was something Mug did not prepare her for. Her mother, sitting on the other side of the booth, pats the seat beside her and says, "Come on, honey. Sit over here with me."

"I—I can't," says Pea. "I have to sit here."

Her father raises a brow at her. "You have to sit there? Why do you have to sit there? I'm sitting there. That's my seat."

"Actually," Pea says. "It's not your seat. It's just a seat. I was here first."

Her mother rolls her eyes. "For the love of God, both of you sit down. Pea, move over. Your father can sit next to you."

He shoots her mother a look. Not anger but bewilderment, like, why should he have to share a seat with her? Pea knows from the things Mug told her that it's because you never want to be blocked in by someone else, and if you've got the outside seat of the booth, you better trust the person on the inside.

Pea slides across the bench and points to the seat next to her. "Come on, Dad. You can have the outside, and you can trust me."

He gives a little shake of his head, studying her, and then he half smiles and slides in next to her. They look at their menus. When her mother gets up to use the restroom, her dad says, "I can trust you, huh?"

Solemnly, Pea nods. "Yes, Dad. You can trust me."

He doesn't look up from his menu. "You been spending a lot of time with Mug, haven't you?"

She's not sure how to answer. She doesn't want to get Mug in trouble. Then again, he's her dad's best friend. They work together. He's at their house once or twice a week. He's like family.

Her dad says, "Do you know what you are?"

Pea doesn't know how to answer so she says nothing.

He looks over at her. "You're my princess."

She doesn't want to be a princess. Her mom says the

concept of a princess as society has come to define it in movies and literature is antiquated and sexist. "Women don't need men to save them," she always says. "You can damn well save yourself."

"You listening to me, Pea?" says her dad.

She nods.

"You're my princess. That means you shouldn't have to worry about anything. Nothing at all. Whatever you want? Whatever you need? I can make it happen."

If her mom wasn't in the bathroom, she'd be scoffing. Or outright laughing. Then her dad would tell her to shut up and Pea wouldn't know if he was serious or not.

He puts his menu down and turns toward her. Then he takes her menu from her hands and places it on the table. He locks gazes with her. The moment feels important. She's not sure her dad's ever looked at her this intently before. She gets the sense that this is the first time he's actually seen her.

"Mug's a good friend, but a princess doesn't need to know any of the stuff he's been teaching you. The only thing you need to worry about is your schoolwork, your friends, and not ganging up on me with your mother."

With that he gives a slight grin and Pea knows it's okay to chuckle.

"You'll be a good girl, right?" he says. "Stick to hair and clothes and make-up, would you?"

Pea didn't know she was being a bad girl. She doesn't really understand what her father is trying to say. She just knows the last thing she wants to be is a princess whose only concern is her appearance. But she knows better than to argue with him. Besides, he didn't explicitly say she can't talk to Mug anymore.

"Sure," she tells him.

CHAPTER 28

Tori Calvert lay across two vinyl chairs in the surgical waiting room, fast asleep. Her knees were tucked into her chest, only the bottoms of her khaki capris, white ankle socks, and gray sneakers peeking from under a thin sweater she'd pulled over her body. Her head rested on top of her purse. A stroller sat beside her, its hood pulled forward with a blanket draped over it. Amalise's small, chubby legs stuck out from under it. Even in sleep, Tori kept a hand wrapped around one of the stroller's legs. Josie peeked beneath the blanket to find Amalise snoozing, a pacifier hanging half in and half out of her mouth. A stuffed elephant lay next to her.

Josie put the drape back in place and then crouched down so that she was face-level with Tori and whispered her name. When that didn't work, Josie touched her shoulder. Tori blinked awake, her sleep-addled face morphing from blissful ignorance to painful realization. "Oh God," she said, sitting up. Quickly, she checked Amalise, letting out a relieved sigh when she saw her daughter was still asleep.

Josie took a seat beside her. Noah remained standing. They let her take a moment to wake up. She fiddled with her sweater, finally finding the sleeves and thrusting her arms into them. "Did you see him?" she asked, keeping her voice low so as not to wake Amalise. "Did he talk to you?"

Noah said, "We saw him. He was awake. He seems fine."

"But he wouldn't tell us anything," said Josie. "Except that he doesn't know if you and Amalise are safe."

Tori shook her head. Tears fell from her already red and puffy eyes. She ran her hands through her hair. "This is ridiculous. He's my husband. You won't even let me talk to him?"

"I'm sorry, Mrs. Calvert," said Noah. "It's Denton PD policy. Once he's been transferred to a holding facility, they may be able to arrange for you to visit him."

She kept shaking her head. "This is insane. I can't talk to him, and yet he thinks we might not be safe? What the hell does that even mean? Safe from what? From who? Are people going to come and attack us? Who? He's a damn architect. What has he gotten himself into? I don't understand this at all."

Josie nodded along with her words. "Mrs. Calvert—"

"Please," Tori snarled. "Do not call me that. I'm not his wife. I'm not his partner in life. I'm some woman who lives in his house and had his baby. I don't know who that man is —that is not the person I married!"

Josie tried again, "Tori, we don't know what's going on. Not yet. We're working on it, believe me, but right now, we think it might be best if you take Amalise and leave town. Can you go to New York? Stay with your parents?"

"Oh," said Tori. She unzipped her purse and started digging through it. Amalise began to stir. Deftly, one of

Tori's feet shot out and hooked onto the bar across the bottom of the stroller, just above the wheels. Using the ball of her foot, she moved the stroller back and forth a couple of inches. The rhythmic pattern lulled Amalise back to sleep. Tori continued, "I'm already ahead of you there. In fact, there's something you should know. I wasn't even sure if I was going to tell you this—I wanted to ask Elliott about it first. I hoped he would have some kind of reasonable explanation for it, but since I can't even talk to him, I'm just going to tell you."

A sheaf of dog-eared papers emerged from her purse. She waved them in the air. "I didn't plan on leaving town yesterday after you came to talk to me. I really didn't. I thought it was all some kind of horrible misunderstanding. But as the day went on, I couldn't stop thinking about it— like, what if it was real? What if my life here was about to blow up? I don't know anyone here. I mean, look at this—my husband is in the hospital, and I don't even have anyone to watch my daughter while I'm here. I've got no one. Which is why I thought maybe I should plan—just make a plan—to head to New York and stay with my parents if necessary. I thought, I'm going to need money. I logged into our online banking to see the balances in our checking and savings, and guess what?"

Josie was pretty sure she wasn't expecting them to answer, although she had a feeling she already knew where this was going. It made her sick to her stomach.

Tori looked at Noah and then at Josie. "There is one hundred seventy-two dollars in checking and fourteen dollars in savings."

Noah said, "How much did you think was in those accounts?"

"Well, I know that two weeks ago when I checked the

balances, there was over three thousand dollars in our checking account and ten thousand dollars in savings."

She handed Josie the pages. It took a moment for Josie to flip through them and figure out exactly what she was looking at, but she found the withdrawals. "He took out almost thirteen thousand dollars last week."

"Yes," said Tori. She tapped against the pages, indicating for Josie to keep looking at the bank statements. "He also drained his retirement account. Tens of thousands of dollars. Gone. He didn't even leave enough in there to pay the penalties!"

Josie found that statement, her heart dropping when she saw that Elliott had taken an early withdrawal of nearly two hundred thousand dollars. She passed the pages to Noah, who studied them.

Josie asked, "Do you have any idea what he intended to use this money for?"

Tori shook her head. "I checked everything I could—his email, his other accounts. I thought maybe he had some kind of gambling habit I didn't know about. Maybe he does, but I couldn't find anything. I don't know what he did with the money. I searched the house, hoping maybe he stashed it somewhere. It's gone." She flopped back in her seat, closing her eyes even as more tears spilled down her cheeks. Her entire body shook with sobs. "It's all gone."

CHAPTER 29

Josie stood at her open refrigerator and shoveled cold pasta into her mouth. The chilly air billowed all around her. At her feet, Trout whined, nudging her leg. Usually when Josie went to the refrigerator before bed, it was to give him a small carrot. Between bites, she said, "I know, I know, buddy. Just a minute."

Noah sailed into the kitchen, freshly showered, his wet hair tousled on his head. He wore only sweatpants, his bare chest distracting her from her rabid hunger. "Have a seat," he told her. "Stay awhile."

He walked over and put a hand on her hip, reaching past her into the fridge to find something edible. There wasn't much. Noah sighed. "I see why you let me shower first. It was so you could get the pasta. Guess I'm eating this possibly expired yogurt. Can't eat Trout's carrots, or I'll be in the doghouse for weeks. Maybe a few slices of cheese. My mom always said, 'Just scrape the mold right off.'"

Josie laughed and thrust the Tupperware container toward him, along with her fork. "I'm sorry. I was starving. You eat the rest."

Without moving, he took both from her and started eating. Trout whined again. Josie fished a few small carrot sticks from their special container and tossed them across the kitchen floor. As Trout gave chase, Josie's eyes were drawn to Noah again. Desire stirred inside her, in spite of the deeply disturbing day they'd had uncovering one strange thing after another in the Hale/Mills/Calvert case. Or maybe because of the disturbing things. There was no greater distraction from the stress of the job than losing herself in Noah.

Her fingers traced the gnarled circle of scar tissue on his right shoulder as he polished off the pasta. It had taken years for her to stop being overwhelmed with guilt whenever she saw it. Noah had forgiven her for shooting him practically the moment the bullet passed through his skin. She hadn't wanted to do it, but at the time she thought she had no choice. They'd merely been colleagues then. Josie had uncovered a staggering level of corruption across all ranks of the police department. Noah had been tasked with guarding a young girl placed in Denton's holding cells. Josie needed to get her out of the police station. Noah tried to stop her. Back then, she didn't know if Noah was simply doing his job or if he was part of the corruption.

So she shot him.

He never told anyone it was her, and in fact, he covered for her so that she and the girl could get away. That had been the beginning of their relationship. Now, seven years later, they were married and there was no one in the world Josie trusted—or wanted—more than Noah.

She looked up from the scar to find him staring at her, an easy smile on his face. They locked eyes. A silent burst of communication flashed between them. Noah tossed the empty Tupperware container and fork onto the floor and wrapped her in his arms. His mouth crashed down onto hers.

Josie lost track of time—of everything that was not Noah, that was not their bodies melting into one another. It was only later, when they lay breathless in bed, that she glanced at her bedside clock. An hour had passed since they met in the kitchen. She wondered lazily if they'd left the refrigerator door open. Sitting up, she saw that Trout was not in the room.

It was probably still open.

Josie flopped back onto her pillow. Noah's hand traced her bare arm from wrist to shoulder. "I think I need another shower."

Josie laughed. She turned and kissed him on the mouth before rolling the other way and out of bed. "It's my turn. You should go downstairs and make sure Trout hasn't eaten that moldy block of cheese." She looked over her shoulder and winked at him. "Also, clean up your dishes."

When she emerged from the shower, Noah and Trout were in the bed. Noah scrolled through his phone. "Gretchen did a background check on Felicia Koslow. She has two arrests for possession with intent to deliver in Philadelphia County."

"Interesting," Josie said, towel-drying her hair. "Narcotics?"

"Yep. Schedule one, so it could have been oxy."

"She lied," said Josie. "She wasn't just harassed by the police. She was arrested and charged. What happened?"

"The first time the charges were dismissed. The second time she pled down. Fines and probation for three years. That was five years ago."

She tossed her damp towel into the laundry bin. "So

she's been in the clear for some time now. Looks like Denton was her new start."

"Or a new place to deal drugs," said Noah. "You think the oxy that Dina found was Felicia's?"

"It's certainly possible," Josie said. "But if that's the case, Felicia is certainly not going to tell us."

Noah went back to scrolling. "You're right about that."

"Any news on Alison Mills?"

"They haven't found her yet," he said. "Gretchen said they've gotten a couple of tips—people who think they saw her near that little development by the road leading to the hospital—but nothing solid. She also said she still hasn't been able to trace the burner number that Calvert called all those times."

Josie found an old pair of sweatpants and a Denton PD T-shirt in her dresser and pulled them on. "We may never track the owner of that number. Noah, Alison Mills could blow this entire case wide open if we could just find her. Do you think she's dead?"

He looked up from his phone screen. "I don't know. I hope not. We've had sightings."

"None of them confirmed, though," Josie said.

"Maybe she's hiding. Whatever this is—whatever is going on—she must be terrified. Even if she saw her mom on the television, maybe she just doesn't believe that it's okay to come out."

Josie climbed into bed. Turning to face him, she ran a hand over Trout's silky fur. The dog rewarded her with a contented sigh. "Terrified," Josie said. "Like Calvert. Someone was blackmailing him. I've been thinking about it and there's no other explanation."

Noah put his phone on his nightstand and stretched out, facing her. "We don't know that that's the only explanation," he said. "But I agree, it's the most likely. If someone was blackmailing him, I'm thinking it has something to do with the photos of that woman that were on his phone."

"You think someone found out he was cheating on his wife and blackmailed him? Divorce seems like a much better option. Besides, that doesn't account for what he was looking for when he attacked Dina and Alison."

Noah yawned. "We know that Dina had found drugs worth almost four grand."

Josie shook her head. "I'm still not sure he would have killed over that. If it was just over drugs, then why would he drain his accounts of almost two hundred fifteen grand?"

Noah's hand bumped against hers as he, too, petted Trout's side. The dog made another noise of happiness. "Then maybe he was looking for the money. His money."

Josie gave that some thought. She rolled over and grabbed her phone, texting Gretchen to see if she'd asked Dr. Feist about whether or not Dina's midsection matched the midsection of the mystery woman in Calvert's photos. It was after midnight, but Josie knew she was still awake. To Noah, she said, "GPS does put them at Eudora at the same time on several occasions. That's not out of the question. Maybe there was a scenario in which he was there, had the money with him, and Dina or both girls took it. Although, if he had that much money in cash on him, it would have been no small thing. We'd be talking at least a duffel bag or backpack or something. A box. Something large enough to hold it."

Gretchen's reply came back within seconds:

The woman in the photos is not Dina.

Josie turned her phone so Noah could read the

exchange. He nodded. "We know that there was no money at the Hale home. We could ask Marlene to take a look around her home. Although in the text exchange between the girls on Thursday, it seemed obvious that they had not found whatever it was people—whether it was Calvert or whoever ransacked the Hales' place—were looking for. But Josie, even if we're right and Calvert was having an affair, someone found out, tried to blackmail him but these girls took his money, who was blackmailing him in the first place?"

"Right," said Josie. "Also, why would he allow himself to be blackmailed over an affair? It's not like he's a public figure. His marriage would end. Tori could make his life hell, maybe make it difficult for him financially or in terms of seeing his daughter, but otherwise, why pay someone to keep that a secret?"

"Unless it's the person he was having an affair with who is the issue," said Noah. "Maybe he doesn't want anyone finding out her identity."

A shiver enveloped Josie's body. "Oh God. You don't think it's one of the girls from catering and events, do you? An underage girl? Gia Sorrento? He flirted with her—she lied about having met him."

Noah shook his head. "I thought of that, but if we're operating under the assumption that Calvert's mistress rented the room they met in each time, it couldn't be an underage girl. You have to be eighteen to rent a room at The Eudora. Gia Sorrento said she just turned eighteen. She couldn't have been renting the rooms all these months."

"True," said Josie. "Okay, so why does Calvert think he's not safe from whoever is blackmailing him? Or that his family might not be safe?"

Trout let out a long, audible fart. The noise startled him

awake and he jumped up, looking around for the source of the racket.

Josie and Noah dissolved into laughter. After some convincing from them, Trout settled back into place between them and fell back to sleep.

Noah said, "On that note, I think we should get some sleep. It will be another long day tomorrow. All we've got are questions and no answers."

CHAPTER 30

Josie was struck by how quiet the Eudora Hotel was at eight in the morning. It was a Monday, but still, she'd never been there when the lobby wasn't bustling with incoming and outgoing guests. Now, as she and Noah waited at the front desk for John Brown to come for them, it was practically deserted except for someone from housekeeping pushing a cart around, laboring over the thick carpet, and stopping to dust tabletops, water the potted plants, and run a small handheld vacuum over the upholstered furniture.

Noah pointed up toward the ceiling. "Hear that?" he said.

For once, the sound being distributed across the lobby wasn't classical music but a local radio station. "In today's news," a radio broadcaster announced, "police are still searching for missing Denton teen, Alison Mills..."

He went on to read off the same information that WYEP had offered the day before. Then a pop song played.

"Detectives." John Brown appeared behind the counter, a strained smile on his face. "If you'll come to my office."

He had called them early that morning, saying he had

found some footage of Elliott Calvert at the hotel. He didn't say how or where, but had invited them to meet with him so they could review it. Then he'd still kept them waiting for fifteen minutes.

In his office, his laptop was open and turned toward the guest chairs. Josie and Noah sat while he tapped on the mouse pad, bringing the screen to life. Perching on the edge of the desk beside the computer, he said, "I told you that we keep footage of certain incidents."

"Incidents that you believe could result in the hotel being sued," Noah said.

Another drawn smile. "To put it bluntly, yes. On one of the nights that you advised Mr. Calvert was here, we had such an incident. A guest fell in the lobby. In fact, she has already retained a lawyer and initiated a claim. Whether it will turn into a lawsuit or not remains to be seen and is entirely in the hands of our insurance company. However, we're still required to preserve the footage. We did just that and turned it over to our insurance company."

"You made a copy," said Josie.

"Yes. That copy is wholly independent from our database here. Given that fact, I took the liberty of reaching out to them and asking if they could share that copy with us." He pointed to his laptop. "Here it is. There are several cameras in the lobby. We'd obviously always been focused on the ones that show the guest's fall most clearly. When I went back through to look for Mr. Calvert, I was able to find decent footage of him from a different camera. At least, I believe it is him. Perhaps you two can tell for certain."

He tapped the mouse pad again and an overhead view of the lobby filled the screen. The camera must have been positioned over the doors to the main entrance, given how much of the lobby it took in. To the left were the doors to

Bastian's. Brown tapped against the screen as a man emerged from them. "I think this is him."

The man was dressed in a light-colored suit but wore no tie, the top buttons of his white shirt undone. He stopped just outside the restaurant and looked around, giving them the opportunity to get a full view of his face.

"That's him," said Josie.

Elliott panned the lobby twice, slowly. Not looking for someone, Josie thought, but making sure no one he knew saw him. Then he walked across the lobby, past the settees and their perfectly polished coffee tables and past the front desk, which was crowded with guests. Just as he reached the other side of the front desk, there was some commotion that drew everyone's attention, including Calvert's. They all froze and turned toward the lobby doors. "That's the fall I told you about," said Brown. "From this angle you can't see it but that's what everyone is reacting to."

Some of the guests waiting at the counter drifted off toward the front doors to get a better look. Elliott turned around and kept walking to a set of elevators. He quickly tapped the *Up* button on the wall and then took his place among a throng of hotel guests standing before the doors. When one of the elevators opened, he moved with the crowd and got into it. No one noticed him. No one even gave him a second glance. Why would they? He was just a man in a hotel going up to his room.

Except Elliott Calvert had never rented a room at the Eudora.

Josie said, "Do you know which floor he went to?"

Brown closed his laptop. "I'm afraid not. The footage from the rest of the hotel is gone. Erased, it seems, like I told you yesterday. We only have this lobby footage because that's where the guest fell."

Noah said, "You have no other bars or food establishments on any other floors, correct?"

Brown nodded.

"What about other amenities?" Josie asked. "A business center? Somewhere clients can work? A gym? A pool?"

"Of course," said Brown. "We have all those things, but you need a room key to access them. Mr. Calvert—to my knowledge—did not have a room key."

Noah said, "May we have a copy of that?"

"Of course," said Brown. He scooped up his laptop and went to the other side of the desk. From one of his drawers he plucked a USB drive. "This will just take a few minutes."

Josie said, "We would also like a list of guests who had rented rooms on that date, if you wouldn't mind."

Frowning, Brown said, "For that, I will need a warrant, I'm afraid. Hotel policy."

"We'll have it to you later today," Josie replied.

Brown nodded and carried on with copying the footage. As they waited, Noah leaned in toward her and whispered, "Calvert's mistress rented the room. That's why he's not in the hotel records. Maybe she's from out of town. Someone from New York, possibly. It definitely fits."

"Yes," Josie agreed, keeping her voice low to match his. "She rents a room here when she's in town and he comes to see her. But there was no evidence on his phone of any calls or texts or ongoing communication with another woman."

"Except the disconnected cell number," Noah pointed out. "The owner of which Gretchen hasn't been able to track down yet."

"True," Josie agreed. "That could be the mystery woman's number. They avoid texting so as not to leave any tangible evidence. If they stick to phone calls, it makes the relationship a lot easier to hide. No one knows the contents of your phone calls. But that doesn't explain him flirting with Gia Sorrento, more than once, in the bar."

"Josie, we're talking about a guy who cheated on his wife pretty much immediately after she gave birth to their first child. A guy who strangled a defenseless teenager on the side of the road. You think Elliott Calvert has some kind of moral code? He doesn't."

He looked away from her, but she could already see that the case was getting to him just as much as it was getting to her.

"Here you are," said Mr. Brown, coming around his desk, proffering the USB drive.

Josie stood and took it, managing a smile for him. "Thank you," she said. "We appreciate this. Just one more thing before we go. Although we were able to speak extensively to your staff last night, we still haven't spoken with Max Combs. As Dina and Alison's boss, he may have something important to add to our investigation. Did he come in last night?"

Brown pursed his lips, staring at her as if he was hoping she'd forget all about her question and bid him good day.

Noah stood up as well. "He didn't show up for work, did he? He hasn't been to work for two days."

Brown shook his head.

"Did he call to let you know he wasn't coming in?" Josie asked. "Or give any explanation for why he failed to show up?"

"I'm afraid not," said Brown. "But he is due in this afternoon. Like I told you, punctuality is not Max's strong suit, but he is exceptional at his job—"

"So you let a lot of things slide," Noah finished for him. "Mr. Brown, we really do need to speak with him. Could you ask him to call us when he gets here, and if he doesn't show up for work again, we'd like to hear from you."

With a heavy sigh, Brown nodded. "Certainly," he said. "I'm sure he'll contact me today. I'll ask him to call."

He didn't sound at all convinced.

CHAPTER 31

In the car, Noah started the engine but made no move to leave the Eudora. They didn't need to talk about it. He waited while Josie called the stationhouse. Mettner answered, sounding far more refreshed after his mini vacation than either Josie or Noah was after their week-long honeymoon. He assured her that both he and their press liaison—and his girlfriend—Amber Watts had been brought up to speed on the case. No promising leads had come in concerning the whereabouts of Alison Mills, but Amber was going to contact all local media to ensure they kept pushing her photo for the foreseeable future. Marlene Mills had already called three times.

"This is a damn mess," said Mettner. "I'm reading all the reports. I talked to Gretchen and the Chief. How does a seventeen-year-old girl disappear into thin air?"

"She doesn't," said Josie. "She's there, probably right under our noses. We have to keep looking, keep asking the public for help. She may not want to come forward because of whatever it is that she and Dina have got caught up in, but hopefully some concerned citizen won't hesitate to call if they spot her. Have Amber keep it up. For now, I need you to write up a warrant for the Eudora." She explained that they needed a list of the names of guests renting rooms for the date of the footage that Brown had given them. She rattled off the date. He promised to prepare it, have it signed and serve it on the hotel within the next couple of hours.

"One more thing while you're in front of your computer," Josie said. "We're running down some stuff on the hotel end. In fact, I need you to get an address for me. Max Combs. He's the catering and events manager at the Eudora."

"Just a second," said Mettner.

Josie heard his fingers drill across his keyboard with machine-like precision. A few minutes later, he said, "I've got him." He rattled off the address. "Looks like it's a rental."

"Great," said Josie. "We're going to go over there now and see if we can talk to him."

As they hung up, Noah pulled out of their parking spot and headed toward a newer tract of townhomes that had been built in Southeast Denton in the last five years. Combs's residence was tall but narrow with tan siding, white trim, and three stories, the first of which was comprised of the garage. Black wrought-iron steps snaked around the side of the house and up to the second floor.

As they climbed the steps, Noah said, "A front door on the side of the house. Interesting choice."

The landing in front of the door was barely big enough to fit them both. A small awning extended from the wall, providing scant shade. A single light hung from inside the awning. In the daylight, Josie could just make out its dull glow. It was on. The door itself was black and windowless.

"It must have been a bitch to move furniture into this

place," Josie muttered. She rang the doorbell. They heard the chime from inside the house. No one answered it. Josie rang it twice more and then she shuffled backward so that Noah could stand closest to the door. He pounded on it, yelling out Max Combs's name in a loud, firm voice.

Nothing.

They looked around, but no neighbors peeked from their windows or strolled along the street. Josie said, "I have a bad feeling about this."

Noah nodded. "Me too, but unless we have reason to believe this guy is injured or dead, we can't do much about it but come back later."

Josie leaned in toward the door and caught a whiff of something familiar but stomach-churning. "Noah," she said, waving him closer. "Do you smell that?"

She moved aside so that he could put his face to the crack of the door. He sniffed several times. Then he grimaced.

"It's unmistakable," Josie said with a sigh.

He shook his head. "Better call everyone. The ERT, Dr. Feist, a couple of units to seal the perimeter. We'll need to get a hold of the landlord so we can get in. Ask Mett to draw up a warrant."

Josie was already dialing.

They waited almost two hours for Mettner to arrive with the warrant and Max Combs's landlord in tow. By that time, patrol units had already arrived and cordoned off the driveway. Dr. Feist and the ERT weren't far behind. A quick sweep of the house was done, clearing it to make sure that it was safe for the ERT to work. Then Officer Hummel took his team of evidence techs inside. Josie knew it would be a few hours until they finished. To kill some time, she called Mr. Brown from the Eudora to see if he had the list of guest names yet. Mettner had served that warrant before coming to the Combs scene. Brown told her it might be a day or two. Mettner canvassed the street, talking to neighbors to see if anyone had seen anything. Finally, Officer Hummel gave Josie and Noah the all-clear to enter the scene. They suited up and made their way back up the stairs and into Max Combs's townhouse.

As it had been earlier, the stench of decomposition was overpowering. Josie stepped through the front door first, and it hit her like a slap. Behind her, Noah said, "He's been here a while."

The first floor of Max's townhome was open-concept. The living room, dining area and kitchen all bled into one another with hardwood floors from wall to wall. The walls were a plain white with only sleek, black cylindrical updown wall sconces mounted every three to four feet apart, providing dim light for the entire room. Hummel had had to bring in portable halogen lights so that they could view the scene more easily.

The place was in ruins.

To one side was a living room set that had been turned over. The upholstery of the couch and loveseat had been shredded. Stuffing from the cushions lay in fluffy heaps all over the floor. A television lay face down, its back pried open to reveal its innards. A small console table was the lone piece of furniture still standing—empty. To the other side was a pool table. Josie couldn't imagine how Max had gotten it into the building, given its massive size. Its green cloth top had been torn away and the slate beneath it removed. Its hollow inside gaped open.

"Watch your step," came Hummel's voice from the kitchen area. He stood behind the island countertop, placing brown paper evidence bags into a box. "There are pool balls all over the floor. The eight ball almost took me out."

Noah walked over toward Hummel and Josie followed. The kitchen was the most in disarray, every cabinet and drawer opened, their contents emptied all over the floor. Utensils, dishes, pots, pans, dishtowels. Everything in Max's kitchen was now scattered across the floor.

"Someone was looking for something," said Noah.

"Think they found it?" asked Josie.

"No."

A low hum filled the room. Cool air caressed the back of Josie's neck. Looking up, she saw two vents side by side in the ceiling.

Hummel produced a thick black marker and scrawled something across the side of the box. "We turned the air conditioning on. It was not on when we arrived. Nothing was on. We opened all the windows, too. Tried to vent a lot of the decomp smell out, but it doesn't seem to have done much good."

No airflow for however long the body had been there and yet the horrific odor had carried all the way to the front door.

Hummel pointed to a set of steps off to the side of the kitchen. "You can go upstairs. Like I said, just watch your step. There's stuff everywhere. Dr. Feist is up there now in the main bedroom. We've already taken photos, dusted for prints, collected whatever DNA we could find, and a number of other items. Oddly, we haven't found a phone. Almost a thousand dollars in cash but no phone. We did, however, find a wide variety of illicit drugs in this guy's bedroom. Cocaine, Ecstasy, Xanax, OxyContin. Looks like he kept it in either his dresser or nightstand. Hard to tell with the way everything was dumped." He hefted the box from the kitchen countertop. "But we'll process everything we can, send the rest to the state police lab, and get you whatever we can as soon as we can."

They thanked him and climbed the steps to the top floor. They were narrow and unusually steep. At the top was a landing wide enough for two chairs and a small table. Max had chosen patio furniture so these, at least, were not overturned or destroyed. Three doors stood open, each one with detritus tumbling from its opening. They poked their heads into the bathroom, a bedroom that Max clearly kept as a home office, and finally, the largest room: his bedroom. There wasn't much to it besides a queen-sized bed, a nightstand, and a dresser. The contents of the nightstand and dresser had been dumped. The closet doors hung wide open, every item emptied from it. On one wall gaped a hole that held a small safe. Its lock had been smashed in. The mangled door hung from one hinge. Inside were what looked like some documents but nothing else. On the floor below the safe was a painting of a woman, seated naked on a stool, giving an alluring glance over her shoulder. It had been broken in two, its canvas ripped.

"They tore the mattress apart, too," said Dr. Feist.

Josie looked over to see her kneeling on the bed, her upper body bent over the head of a man Josie assumed was Max Combs. He lay in the center of the mattress, legs straight, arms spread wide, wearing only a pair of boxer shorts and black socks. Josie could tell by the discoloration of skin, the way his body appeared to shrink, and the fluid leaking into the mattress that he was in active decay, which usually began about three days after death. Beside him was a pillow with a hole blasted through its center and blood soaked into its white pillowcase. As Josie and Noah stepped closer, picking their way through clothes, shoes, a small shattered television, a few paperback books, packs of condoms, and a few pairs of women's panties held together with a hair tie, Josie saw that the mattress had been sliced open in several places. Its stuffing was scattered along the floor with the rest of Combs's personal items.

Noah said, "What've you got?"

Dr. Feist sighed and straightened her spine, rolling her shoulders back to loosen some of the tension. "I've got an adult male with a gunshot wound to the head. It appears as though someone put a pillow over his head and shot through it, but I won't know for sure until I get him on the table. If the shooter used hollow points, I'll be able to get the plug of fabric from the slug." She leaned back over, her gloved hands probing the man's jaw. "I should still be able to identify him using dental records. My God, this is ugly."

Josie said, "It sure is. Doc, the last time anyone saw this guy was Friday night. You have any thoughts on time of death?"

Dr. Feist climbed off the bed and looked at them. "Based on the stage of decomposition, body temperature, the temperature of this room, and the fact that the AC wasn't on when your team arrived, I'd say he was likely killed late Friday evening or early Saturday morning."

Again, the hum of the air conditioner clicked into gear. Josie looked up to see two vents, side by side, just as she had in the kitchen. She waited for the cold cascade of air on her face, but nothing came.

"That feels good," said Noah.

Josie turned her head to look at him. His face was lifted toward the ceiling. "You can feel the air?" she asked.

He looked over at her. "You can't?"

"No," she said.

"Vent must be broken," he told her.

Josie trod carefully back out to the landing. She checked the other rooms. Each one had two ceiling vents and both had good airflow. Even the landing had vents and both of them worked. Back in the bedroom, Dr. Feist was at the door. "I'm all done here. I'll let the guys know they can remove the body. I'll do the autopsy as soon as I can. Call you with the findings. ID might take a day or two depending on how long it takes me to find this guy's dentist. I'm assuming your team believes this is the resident, Max Combs."

"Yes," said Noah. "We can track down his dentist. Try to expedite things."

"You got it," said Dr. Feist.

Josie watched her go down the steps and then turned back into the room. Noah circled the bed, studying the disarray. "They didn't take his drugs or the cash that was here. Who wouldn't help themselves to a thousand bucks? I mean, you're already in for the murder rap. Who cares about some petty theft?"

"They were only looking for one thing," Josie said.

Noah sighed. "Whatever was on his phone?"

"It could be." She glanced at the vent again. No airflow for three days. Had the killer turned off the HVAC system or was it like that when they arrived? "But if you've got something that people are looking for, that people are willing to kill for, you'd hide it, right?"

"Yeah, of course."

She pointed to the vent over her head, the one not dispensing any air. "We're going to need a ladder and a screw gun."

Noah raised a brow. "Really?"

"Really."

It took a half hour for Hummel to retrieve a ladder and

screw gun from the impound lot, which also housed the building that Hummel and his team used to process evidence that could be analyzed in the city, without being sent to outside labs. Josie watched as he set it under the non-functioning vent, climbed up, unscrewed the panel and pulled it off. He handed it down to Noah and took another step up the ladder, poking his head into the opening. Josie heard him whistle. Then he said, "What do you know? The boss was right. Let me go get Chan and we'll get this stuff out." He climbed back down the ladder. "Don't touch anything. In fact, wait in the hall."

Josie and Noah seated themselves in the patio chairs while Hummel and his colleague Chan worked. Half an hour later, Hummel called them back in. He and Chan stood side by side at the foot of the ladder. At their feet were two backpacks, unzipped. In each one were stacks of hundred-dollar bills. "Jackpot," said Hummel. "Literally."

"How much?" asked Noah.

Chan said, "We'll have to count it out back at the lot, but we estimate about north of three hundred sixty thousand dollars."

CHAPTER 32

They stopped at home for a shower and change of clothes. They were sweaty and foul-smelling. Even after showering until the hot water ran out and using copious amounts of shampoo and body wash, Josie still felt like she smelled of death. They stopped at Komorrah's to get coffee and pastries for the team before returning to the stationhouse. In the great room, Gretchen and Mettner were at their desks, both of them on their phones.

Daisy was seated at Amber's desk, looking intently at her laptop while Amber leaned over her shoulder. They spoke in hushed tones. Daisy pointed to something on the screen. Amber said a few words and then Daisy began typing. Both of them looked up long enough to flash welcoming smiles when Josie and Noah entered.

Noah handed Amber a cup as he weaved his way between the desks. Looking down at Daisy, he said, "We didn't know you'd be here or we would have gotten you that tea you like. You're welcome to have my coffee, if you'd like."

A flush spread across Daisy's cheeks as Noah held out

the cup slashed with an N on its lid. "Thanks," said Daisy, taking it with both hands. "Amber's helping me with some homework."

Amber said, "The Chief is downstairs with some city council guy. Pierce something."

"Fuller," said Josie.

"Yeah. That's it. He had me print out some proposal he had come up with for training and implementing a K-9 unit. Anyway, they're down in the conference room going over that."

Noah distributed the other coffees. He riffled through the bag of pastries until he came up with an apple strudel which he finished in two bites. Josie downed more of her coffee and then handed it across the desk to Noah. "Finish mine," she told him.

Gretchen hung up and spun in her chair, holding a piece of paper over her head. "Got it! Max Combs's dentist!"

Mettner glanced at her and then told whoever he was speaking with, "Never mind," and hung up.

Gretchen put on her reading glasses and focused on her computer. "I'll write up the warrant and go get these. Drop them off to Dr. Feist."

Mettner said, "Hummel called. They've still got a lot of work to do, but Chan counted the money you found in Max Combs's ceiling. It was three hundred sixty-three thousand dollars. They're trying to get prints from the bags, but it doesn't look good. He said the texture is an issue. He can try printing some of the bills if he can't get anything from the bags, but that's going to be difficult and time-consuming. Plus, you've got the issue of how many people handle bills. Might be hard to get good prints from the cash."

"Maybe one of the sets of prints they took from the rest

of the house will pan out," Noah said. "That's a strange amount."

"Two hundred thirteen thousand dollars is what Elliott Calvert took from his and Tori's accounts," Josie said.

"Still a weird amount," said Noah.

"We talked about the blackmail angle before," said Josie. "We can't prove it, not without fingerprints or DNA evidence or Elliott Calvert talking, but it's possible that Max Combs got at least two hundred thirteen thousand dollars of that money from Calvert."

Without looking over, Gretchen said, "They could have made the exchange at the hotel. We know Calvert's been there several times."

"Where'd he get the rest of the money?" asked Mettner. "The hundred fifty thousand? What's he doing with all that money hidden in the ceiling?"

"The real question is, why was it worth dying for?" said Noah. "He obviously didn't give it up."

"Unless the shooter killed him before he tossed the house," Gretchen suggested.

Josie said, "I think Mett is right. We need to figure out why he had the money. Assuming that's what got him killed, we know Calvert didn't do it. We've got his GPS and he was nowhere near Max's house Friday or Saturday morning, which means even if he gave Max that money, he's not the killer. Plus, we still don't know how any of this fits with Calvert attacking Dina and Alison Mills."

Gretchen said, "When I'm done with this warrant for dental records, I'll write one up for Combs's financials and see if I can find anything there. Also, since his phone is missing, I'll send a warrant to his carrier and see if we can track it and get records from it for the last few weeks. We might be able to locate it, but the records could take longer. Mett, show them the surveillance."

"Oh yeah," Mettner said. "Although I'm not entirely sure it's connected to the homicide at Max Combs's home." He tapped on his keyboard and nudged his mouse around a few times. Then he pointed to his computer screen. "One of the neighbors who lives three doors down from Combs has a doorbell camera. It caught two men pulling up in a dark-colored SUV early Saturday morning. We can't tell the make or model from this video. The timestamp is 1:06 a.m."

Josie and Noah moved around the desks and stood behind Mettner, peering at the screen. It wasn't the best quality and had been taken at a distance, but they could see clearly enough a large SUV park at the curb. Two men got out. Both looked tall but one was far more muscular than the other. Unfortunately, they wore dark clothing and hoods pulled low over their heads. It was impossible to see any distinguishing features. Within seconds, they had walked out of frame.

Noah pointed to the screen. "Did they head in the direction of Combs's place?"

"Yeah. I mean, there is no proof that they went there. I can't get a plate number from this footage. I did talk to all the neighbors on the street to see if any of them recognized the vehicle or had visitors around one a.m. on Saturday, but they all said no."

Josie said, "Are there any traffic cameras in the area that might have picked up the vehicle?"

"I don't think so," Mettner said. "But I can check."

Noah asked, "Do you have them leaving?"

Mettner clicked his mouse a few more times and a new video came up showing the SUV parked just as it had been in the last video. The time stamp read 3:39 a.m. This time the men were jogging when they came into frame. They got back into the vehicle and pulled away.

Josie said, "They're not carrying anything."

"Not that we can see," Mettner agreed.

"They were there for two and a half hours. That's a long time to be at a crime scene."

"But not enough time to find whatever it is they were looking for," said Noah.

Mettner's desk phone rang, and he snatched it up. Josie and Noah returned to their seats.

Noah said, "Speaking of Alison Mills, if we're all here then who's looking for her?"

Gretchen looked away from her computer screen, eyeing Noah over the top of her glasses. "We're manning the tip line now. Chief's orders." She pointed toward Mettner. "Sounds like he's got one now."

With the receiver trapped between his ear and shoulder while he tapped away at his keyboard, Mettner said, "Right. You think you saw Alison Mills on Hopwood Street. When was that? Yesterday? Or today?"

To Gretchen, Josie said, "Have there been any tips?"

"A few. None that panned out."

Mettner hung up, the clatter of the receiver meeting the cradle startling them all. He clicked his computer mouse and the ancient inkjet printer across the room lurched to life. "I think this is another dead end," he told them. "But I have to check it out. Some lady thinks she saw Alison Mills near the city park this morning."

"The city park," said Josie. "That's nowhere near where she was last seen."

"Could still be her," said Noah. "She could be anywhere by now. Hell, for all we know, she's not even in Denton anymore."

"If someone has her," Mettner said. "If this kid is hiding somewhere, she's still in town. How far could she have gotten on foot?"

"It's not how far," Josie said, "it's where she's hiding. Clearly, it's somewhere no one has thought to look."

"If she really is hiding," said Noah, "she may have to come out soon, especially if she doesn't have food or drink. Where could she possibly hide that she'd have access to those things?"

Daisy's voice surprised them all. "What kind of teenager is she?"

All heads swiveled in her direction. Her pale face was earnest. Gretchen said, "What do you mean?"

Daisy gave a half-shrug. "My moth—well, the woman who—"

Amber said, "We know who you mean."

Daisy said, "Is Alison the kind of teenager who stays close to her family? Is she afraid of being away from them? I used to have to give teenagers the travel test."

Josie's stomach burned.

Mettner said, "What's the travel test?"

"You find out where they want to go more than any place in the world. Like, their dream vacation. Then you ask them, 'If you could go there tomorrow, all expenses paid, but you'd have to be out of contact with your family the entire week, would you go?' Their answer tells you a lot about them."

Josie glanced around the room, noticing how the posture of every adult had tensed. They all knew that Daisy had been taught such things so that she could manipulate teenage girls into situations that got them killed. However, Daisy hadn't realized what was happening until it was too late. She had truly believed she was making friends. She'd had no knowledge of what happened to them once they were whisked away. Her strange upbringing had robbed her of a more natural and organic way of seeing the world, instead instilling in her that people should be studied like insects or specimens of some kind. Josie wasn't even sure Daisy understood that yet.

Josie said, "What does their answer tell you about them?"

"If they say yes, they'd go in a heartbeat, then they're probably outgoing and not too worried about following rules. They're more independent and able to solve problems without help. They don't fear new experiences all that much."

Noah said, "If they say no?"

"Obviously they're very attached to their family and feel afraid to do anything without them. They need structure and authority. They're afraid to make decisions without their family's opinions and not confident they can do stuff by themselves."

Noah looked at Josie. She knew he was thinking the same thing she was: the travel test had been designed to figure out which teenagers could be most easily manipulated, pressured or even fooled into doing things they wouldn't normally. Still, in this instance, Daisy's insight might prove useful. Josie gave Noah a small nod.

He said, "Okay. I think I understand what you're getting at, and you want to know which one of these Alison Mills is because...?"

"Because knowing which one she is will tell you where she's hiding."

Josie stood up and went over to Amber's desk, looking down at Daisy intently. She thought about the text messages that Alison had exchanged with Dina. Alison was the one who wanted to go to her mom. Dina had said no. Next, Alison had suggested the police. Dina had said no. Josie said, "Alison is the second type. She wouldn't go on the trip."

Daisy picked up the coffee Noah gave her and sipped it. Then she said, "I know Bobby doesn't want me to know stuff you guys are working on—well, he doesn't want me paying any attention to it—but it's kind of hard not to hear things. Plus, I saw the news. I know what happened to her."

"It's okay," Amber said, resting a hand on Daisy's shoulder. "We know you overhear a lot of stuff. I think the most important thing is that you don't repeat anything you hear in this building or from any of us to anyone else."

Daisy rolled her eyes. "Duh. I know that. Bobby was very clear about it."

Josie said, "You've got all the facts. Based on your travel test, where do you think Alison is hiding?"

"Somewhere familiar to her. A place she's been many times, where she feels comfortable."

Mettner said, "We know she's not at home. Where else could she be? Her high school? The hotel?"

Noah said, "We can send units out to look."

Amber asked, "Wouldn't she have shown up on surveillance by now? Most schools have it, and the hotel definitely has it."

"Except someone is erasing footage at the hotel," Josie said. "But yes, we should send units to both places to search just in case. It's possible she has somehow blended in or, if she is familiar with the premises of either one, maybe she knows how to avoid the cameras."

"I'm not sure she's thinking that clearly," Noah said. "But I agree it's worth a look. I'm going to call the sheriff and see if we can get a K-9 unit back, at least for searching the hotel, since it's massive. Marlene will give us something of Alison's for the dog to scent."

"Great idea," said Josie.

Gretchen said, "Maybe we're thinking too big, though. What if she just went to a friend's house and they're hiding her?"

"Dina Hale was her best friend," said Noah. "She's dead."

"Gretchen's right, though," said Josie. "It won't hurt to send someone out to each friend's house and rattle some cages. As of right now, Marlene has called all of her friends. One of them could have simply lied. Sending units to houses might have a bigger impact."

"We're talking a lot of manpower here," said Mettner. "Maybe we should prioritize."

Daisy said, "She would be too recognizable at her school or the hotel where she worked."

Josie thought about their conversation with Marlene the day Alison went missing. She returned to her computer and pulled up a map of Denton. She pointed to the place on the map where Alison had last been seen. "Look," she said. She ran her finger upward and tapped against the symbol for Denton Memorial Hospital. "You think she's hiding, right? If she's really hiding, she'd go somewhere that she isn't too recognizable but somewhere she would have access to food, water, shelter and also comfort. Why not her second home?"

Everyone gathered around Josie. Noah said, "That's what Marlene called the hospital. Alison's second home."

Daisy said, "I bet that's it."

Gretchen said, "Put the hospital on the list."

As everyone else dispersed, Mettner stayed close to Josie. He leaned down, speaking in a lowered voice into her ear. "Boss, are you sure it's wise to take advice from a kid? One who was raised by psychopaths?"

Josie matched his tone. "She has a point, Mett. We did outdoor searches. We canvassed all the places we know she was seen. We've been following her trail. That trail is cold. What's next?"

"But she could have been taken by someone," Mettner argued.

"You're right," Josie said. "But if she was, we've got no leads there. Not even a place to start. There's a fifty-fifty chance that she's simply hiding, and we haven't looked in any of the places where she might take refuge if she is terrified and hurt—too terrified to contact her own mother. What's the alternative, Mett? Do nothing?"

He sighed, taking the words out of her mouth, "You're not built that way."

Josie looked up and grinned at him. "I'm glad we had this talk. Let's go."

CHAPTER 33

Josie turned in a slow circle, studying the hospital lobby. She'd been through it dozens of times in her life but she'd never taken a good look at it. Usually, in her capacity as a detective, she entered the hospital through the ER. Noah had taken the ER entrance while Josie started in the lobby. They planned to meet somewhere on the first floor, probably near the cafeteria. They had already had security personnel take them through the camera footage at both entrances since Saturday afternoon, but there was no clear evidence that Alison had entered the hospital. There were a few women who had come in via the lobby wearing hoodies, who hadn't turned their faces toward the cameras. They'd managed to get past the reception desk unnoticed and gotten into elevators. Security traced some of them to other floors but not all. Any one of them could have been Alison but without clear views of their facial features, Josie couldn't say for sure, which is why she was in the lobby now, trying to physically trace the steps of Alison Mills. That she was even considering another one of the hospital's scorched tar, sugarless coffees with expired creamer spoke to how exhausted she felt.

"Can I help you?" said a woman behind the reception desk. Her name tag read: *Pam Ramsey Corey*. "Are you lost?"

Josie took out her police credentials and offered them to Pam. "Just having a look around." She pocketed her credentials and took out her phone, pulling up a photo of Alison. "Have you seen this girl lately?"

Pam needed only a glance. "That's the girl they're looking for on television. I know that. If I had seen her, I would have called about it."

"Thank you," said Josie. Again, she scanned the lobby from right to left. There were hallways on each side accessible only if you walked past the reception desk. One side led to the emergency department and cafeteria. The other side led to a range of departments, including the lab, radiology, medical records, and other administrative offices. Josie returned her gaze to Pam. "Is everyone required to stop here when they enter?"

Pam pulled a face. "I wouldn't say required. We try to flag as many people down as possible. There are also times this desk isn't manned, particularly at night."

Which meant Alison could have come into the hospital this way without being noticed if she timed it right, especially if she'd gotten her hands on a hoodie and kept her face away from the cameras—just like the mystery women they'd seen on the security footage. But which way would she go? Where in the hospital would she hide? Denton Memorial didn't have a pediatric ward, but Alison had been fifteen years old when she'd been admitted. Old enough for Denton to treat a broken hip and subsequent bacterial infection. However, that meant she could have been on almost any floor—or multiple floors, depending on the hospital's census. Josie could eliminate the surgical floor and the geropsyche floor. She could very likely eliminate this ground floor as well. It was far too busy to hide anywhere for any length of time, particularly with people moving back and forth from the ER to radiology for testing.

Josie walked over to the nearest bank of elevators on the emergency department side of the first floor. She might as well start from the bottom and work her way up. She reached out to punch the up arrow when she realized the bottom was actually the basement—the same floor that housed the morgue. Opposite that was the kitchen that supplied food to the floors, which was different from the first-floor kitchen that served the cafeteria. Between the morgue and the kitchen were dozens of empty rooms. Perfect for anyone who wished not to be disturbed. Josie and Noah had once spent some time in one of them. The ambience wasn't great, but they hadn't cared about anything but each other at the time.

Shaking off the memory, Josie pushed the downward arrow and was immediately rewarded with a *ding*. A moment later, she was walking the dingy halls of the basement. She passed Dr. Feist's suite of rooms, the smells from inside just as pungent as ever. Leaving them behind, she circled around to the kitchen side of the building, checking each room as she went. Some were completely empty. Some were crammed with old, broken-down medical equipment. Others remained as they had been decades ago when the hospital still used them: windowless patient rooms complete with vinyl beds and tray tables. If there had been a television in any of them, they'd been removed long ago.

The smell of food reached Josie's nostrils: chicken and various other smells mingling together until she couldn't identify each one. Next came the sounds of dishes clanking, water running, and muffled voices. The door to the kitchen lay ahead at the end of the hall, on the other side of the elevators that came down from the radiology and administrative departments. Josie counted out the rooms left to search. There were six in all, but two of them were restrooms.

Food and a bathroom. It was the perfect place to hide.

Josie went one by one, opening each door, flipping on the lights and searching the room. All of them were former patient rooms but the third one had sheets and blankets stacked high on the bed and a collection of food wrappers and beverage bottles cluttering the tray table. Josie stepped across the threshold, noting the pile of discarded clothes in the far corner of the room. She could smell dried blood, dirt, and sweat. No Alison.

But she had been here. Someone had been staying here.

Josie turned back toward the hallway and that was when she saw her. Alison Mills emerged from the restroom wearing hospital scrubs. Her dark curly hair fell across the sides of her face. She kept her head down but paused as the door swung closed behind her. She looked toward the kitchen and then turned back toward the room. An audible gasp escaped her when she spotted Josie standing just outside of her safe haven.

She threw her hands up. Her eyes searched all around, wide and blind with panic. Josie saw the extent of her injuries. Noah had been right. Calvert had broken her nose. It was red and swollen with a laceration on the bridge. The skin around both of her eyes was black and bruised.

"Alison," Josie said. "Stop. It's okay."

She didn't listen. Instead, she ran toward the kitchen doors, slamming into them and pushing with both hands.

They didn't budge. She was too panicked to realize they opened outward. Josie took a few tentative steps toward her and stopped. There was nowhere for her to go.

"Alison, my name is Detective Josie Quinn. You're not in trouble. I'm here to help you."

The girl turned, pressing her back into the doors. Tears gathered in her eyes. Her voice was throaty. "Dina's dead."

"I'm so sorry, Alison."

Alison squeezed her eyes closed and nodded.

Josie came within a few feet of her and lowered her voice. "Alison, your mom is worried about you. The whole city is looking for you. Your dad is on his way home from Hong Kong."

At this, Alison's eyes snapped open. "My dad? He's coming home?"

"Yes. He's been having trouble getting a flight, but he'll be here as soon as he can. He's doing everything he can to get back to you."

"Is he mad?"

Josie smiled. "No. Of course not, Alison. No one is mad at you. We all just want you to come home. Everyone just wants you to be safe."

"Is my dad going to lose his job?"

"That I don't know. You'll have to ask him, but Alison, it's not your job to worry about that. I can tell you with one hundred percent confidence that all your parents care about is that you come home and that you're safe."

Alison nodded along with Josie's words. Tears streamed down her face. A sob shook her. Josie took another step forward and held out a hand. "Why don't you come with me? We'll get you checked out and call your mom. She'll be so happy to see you."

Alison ignored Josie's hand, instead throwing herself at

Josie and wrapping her arms around her waist. She sobbed hard into Josie's shoulder, wetting her shirt through to her skin. Josie's arms circled her, holding her trembling body as she wept. A man emerged from the kitchen and pulled up short, eyes going wide with surprise. Over the top of Alison's head, Josie managed a wan smile. "It's okay," she mouthed to him. "I've got it."

"You sure?" he mouthed back.

Josie nodded.

He walked past them quickly and quietly and got into one of the elevators. When Alison's sobs began to subside, Josie pulled away from her. "The elevators there go up to the ER. Let's go there now, okay? I want someone to look at your nose before we do anything else."

"I think it's broken," Alison said, stepping back from Josie and wiping her tears. "I guess you want to know what happened. I—"

Josie touched her shoulder. "Let's take this one step at a time, okay? Emergency room, your mom, and we'll go from there."

CHAPTER 34

She is fourteen when her world shatters. Standing in the hall of the hospital's emergency department, she hears her father cry for the first time. It is the worst sound she's ever heard. Far worse than the things she heard in the garage when she was eight—the memory of which she's spent six years trying to vanquish. Now it seems not to matter at all. She turns around in a slow circle. Nurses, doctors, and other patients all stride about, not even glancing her way. The moment is appallingly ordinary and yet, she knows that from this moment on, her life will never be the same. She understands that everything has changed irrevocably.

She sees that she is utterly alone with this knowledge.

There should be tears. She knows there should be many, many tears. Her father, who hasn't shed a tear in the fourteen years Pea has been alive, has tears. Pea squeezes her eyes shut, counts to three, and opens them again, blinking rapidly. Nothing comes. A doctor emerges from the room where her father is wailing and stops to touch her shoulder. "I'm so sorry for your loss," he tells her.

Still, no tears come.

Pea doesn't know what to do, so she finds a chair down the hall and sits in it, making her back very straight like she does in church. Maybe she should pray. But she can't remember any prayers in that moment. Her mind is blank.

It is not until she sees her father, staggering down the hall, the front of his suit soaked in blood that something breaks inside her, unleashing a torrent of emotion. Pea looks down at her hands and sees they are shaking. Every part of her trembles. Her fingers touch her cheek and come away wet with tears.

"Pea," says her father. "What are you doing here?"

She looks at him like he is a stranger. Something thick and heavy is working its way up from her diaphragm to her throat and she is afraid of it. "The police came to the house to—to tell you. But you weren't home. They told me what hospital. I—I got a ride from a friend," she whispers, feeling stupid. Her lower lip quivers. The sensation inside her chest gets bigger. She wonders if she'll actually explode, which is absurd. Then again, her mother always said emotional stress takes a physical toll. Can it kill you? Pea wonders.

Her father gathers her up into his arms, holding her tightly. His hand strokes the back of her head over and over. "I'm sorry, Pea. I'm so sorry."

She starts to feel dizzy. Her legs grow weak. Soon, her father is holding her upright, sagging under the weight of her. "Pea?" he says. "Are you okay? Pea?"

But he's far away now. The whole world is far away and she's so tired.

She is aware of him guiding her back to the chair, placing her in it, kneeling before her. "My princess," he says. "My princess, look at me."

She tries to focus on his face but all she can see are the

police standing outside their front door. How long was it? An hour? Two hours? Their arrival along with them delivering the news replays again and again, in slow motion and at double speed. The outcome is always the same. The complete unmaking of Pea's life.

"I'm going to make this right, Princess. You hear me? I'll make it right."

But not even her father can make this right.

CHAPTER 35

Josie thought Marlene Mills was going to break one of her ribs. The woman arrived at the hospital in record time and left a wake of commotion behind her as she stormed through the emergency department calling out, "Where's my daughter? Alison? Where's my Alison?" She spotted Josie standing outside of Alison's room and barreled right into her, hugging her with the might of a dozen people. "Thank you," she muttered into Josie's hair. "Thank you so much."

Then she released Josie, not bothering to ask where Alison was, instead tearing back the curtain and rushing in. A split-second wave of panic washed over Alison's bruised and battered face, but Marlene didn't even register it. Instead, she gathered her daughter into her arms and squeezed her—Josie hoped not as tightly as she'd just been hugged. Marlene crowded onto the bed with Alison, holding her daughter close with one arm and smoothing her hair back from her face with the other.

"Oh sweetheart, look at your beautiful face. Does it hurt?"

"A little," Alison said. "Mom, are you mad at me?"

Marlene laughed even as tears of relief spilled from her eyes. "Mad? Honey, no. I'm just relieved that you're okay. I was worried sick."

"Where's Dad?"

"He's been having some trouble getting a flight back, but he's trying his best to get here as soon as possible."

Josie said, "I'm going to leave you two alone for a bit. The doctors will be in soon to talk with you."

Alison looked up. "Don't you need to, like, talk to me or whatever?"

Josie smiled. "We do, but first we want to make sure you're okay. Later, if you're up to it, your mom can bring you by the police station and we can sit down and talk."

She left the two of them huddled in the bed together and went down the hall to find Noah. He was standing at the nurse's station, cell phone pressed to his ear. From his end of the conversation, she gathered he was talking with the Chief, and that it was going to be a while. Josie went in search of coffee, managing to find some sugar this time, and when she returned, Noah was finished.

"The Chief is having Amber do a press conference to let the public know that Alison's been found safe. Mett called off the K-9 unit and the rest of the searchers. We'll need a statement from Alison, of course, but the Chief agreed that we need to give her some time. He said since it's so late, we should go home and get some rest."

"I'm not going to argue with that."

By noon the next day, Josie's lower back ached from sitting so long at her desk doing paperwork. Two empty Komorrah's cups sat before her. Across from her, Noah worked in silence. Using traffic cameras as well as exterior surveillance footage from local homes and businesses, Mettner had managed to track the black SUV from Max Combs's neighborhood to a development near the interstate before losing it. He'd also managed to capture a partial license plate number, but a search had turned up far too many results for them to sift through in this decade. He'd left his report with Josie and gone to the Eudora to see if the manager had the guest list compiled yet. Josie had called Mr. Brown when she arrived at work, and he'd said it wasn't ready yet. Mettner thought having a police presence there waiting for it might speed up the process. Gretchen was due back any moment. She still hadn't been able to track the burner phone that Elliott Calvert had called so many times. However, she had gotten her warrants for Max Combs's financial and dental x-rays signed and delivered. She had also drawn up a warrant for Max's phone records which she had served on his carrier by email. Unfortunately, those records could take up to two weeks. She had also texted Josie and Noah that she planned to stop and speak with Tori Calvert to again encourage the woman to take Amalise and go to New York for a few weeks, at least until the Denton PD had a handle on what had led up to the events of the last few days.

Josie could not quell her nagging feeling of unease that there was so much more to the case. Who were the men in the SUV near Combs's house? If they were the ones who had ransacked Combs's house, what were they looking for? What was Calvert looking for? Were all three looking for the same thing? Was it money? Drugs? Something else that wasn't yet on their radar? Why was Max Combs blackmailing Calvert? The mystery woman in the photos hidden on Calvert's phone? What about the other hundred fifty thousand dollars? Where had Combs gotten that? Was he blackmailing someone else? Where did Dina and Alison fit into things? If Calvert wasn't the one who ransacked Dina Hale's home, was it the same men who had torn apart Max's house? What did the drugs that Dina had given to Needle have to do with any of it? Were they dealing with some sort of gang? The mob?

The thought sent a shudder down Josie's spine. Before she could think too deeply about a potential mafia connection, the stairwell doors whooshed open, admitting Gretchen, who carried a large manila envelope tucked beneath one arm and a fresh round of coffees and a bag of Komorrah's pastries in her hands. A pecan croissant hung from her mouth, raining flakes down onto her chest. Noah jumped up to take the cup-holder and bag from her. "Hungry?" he said.

Gretchen tossed the envelope onto her desk and used one hand to tear at the croissant, chewing the portion she'd bitten off. Once she had finished, she said, "These things are so good. Fresh out of the oven! They're never fresh out of the oven. It was actually warm when they put it in the bag. I couldn't wait."

Noah laughed. "I think you have a problem."

Gretchen stuffed the rest of the croissant into her mouth, letting her eyes roll to the back of her head for a moment, feigning ecstasy. Then she returned her gaze to the two of them. Pinching a roll of skin above her waist, she said, "My problem is this. Is it too much to ask to live in a world where you can eat as many pastries as you want and not gain a pound?"

"Apparently, it is," Noah laughed.

Once seated at their desks, Gretchen said, "The dental records are a match. Dr. Feist made a positive ID on Max

Combs. He's got family—a dad and a brother—but one lives in Oklahoma and the other in California. Dr. Feist called the medical examiner's office in the county where his father lives. They're giving the death notification within the next hour."

Noah asked, "Is the autopsy complete?"

Gretchen nodded. "Yeah. No report yet, but I talked to her about it. Time of death is early Saturday morning. Cause of death is exactly what we presumed: gunshot wound to the face at close range through the pillow. Looks like a .38 caliber bullet. Hummel managed to find the shell casing in all the mess. That'll go to the lab for analysis. There is one small detail that you'll find interesting."

"What's that?" asked Noah.

"All of Max Combs's fingernails were torn off."

Josie's stomach churned at the thought. "Just like Dina Hale."

"Just like Dina Hale," Gretchen echoed.

Noah said, "Are we looking at mafia involvement here?"

Gretchen shrugged. "If we are, they're a little out of their area. I mean, Denton has some gang activity, and we get some stuff passing through here from time to time. We've definitely got a drug issue, but there isn't really a mafia presence. Not like they've got in larger cities like Philadelphia and New York."

Josie said, "Philadelphia isn't that far away. Neither is New York, come to think of it. Calvert's got ties to New York City."

Noah said, "If we're looking at the hotel connection, Felicia Koslow, the manager directly under Max, has ties to Philadelphia and she's got a prior drug conviction."

"It's possible Max had ties to one of those cities," Josie added. "We really don't know much about his past."

"True," said Gretchen. "It's possible that something having to do with any one of those people brought a mafia presence to Denton. Also, there's more than just one mobster, so if these two guys are with the mafia, we'd need to figure out who they answer to."

"How do we do that?" asked Noah.

"We need more information."

"So, easy stuff then," Noah laughed.

Josie said, "Did you talk with Tori Calvert?"

"I stopped at the Calverts' house, and no one answered. I tried calling her, but it rang and rang until it went to voicemail."

"Hopefully that means she's left town," said Josie.

Gretchen tapped her fingers against the manila envelope on her desk. "You'll want to know about this. I still have some requests out to various institutions, but I was able to get financial records for Max Combs from his bank and three of his creditors."

She pulled a sheaf of papers from the envelope and handed them across the desk to Josie. Noah stood and walked around the desks so he, too, could read them. Josie scanned each page before handing it to him. "Jeez," she said. "He wasn't just broke."

"He was in a ton of debt," added Noah.

"Yep," said Gretchen. "All three of those credit cards are maxed out. Mostly cash advances. Some random charges for gas and food but a lot of charges from three different casinos. One in the Poconos, one in Philadelphia, and one in Atlantic City. He was busy."

"He was running up gambling debts," Josie said. "He needed cash to pay them off."

Gretchen nodded.

The phone on her desk rang. Snatching it up, she said, "Quinn."

Their desk sergeant, Dan Lamay, said, "I've got Marlene and Alison Mills down here to see you. What do you want me to do?"

"Put them in the conference room. We'll be right down."

Josie hung up, slugged down her coffee, and stood. "Alison and her mom are here."

In the conference room, Alison sat at the head of the table, still wearing the scrubs she'd worn in the hospital, but now with a hoodie over them. Her hair had been combed and tied back in a ponytail. Her face looked dreadful, mottled with bruises of various shades and intensity. Marlene paced the length of the table, stopping when Josie and Noah entered.

"Alison just wanted to get this over with," Marlene blurted out. "I told her it could wait, but she didn't want to go home until she talked with you."

"That's fine," Josie said. She looked at Alison. "But if at any point you want to stop or you get tired, we can call it a day and talk another time. How are you feeling?"

Marlene said, "The doctors said her nose is broken but it won't need surgery. I think she's more shaken and exhausted than anything else."

Noah gestured toward one of the chairs around the table near Alison. "Mrs. Mills, why don't you have a seat? Can we get either of you anything?"

"Nothing for us," said Marlene.

"Coffee," said Alison. "Please."

The two looked at one another, Alison's expression filled with uncertainty.

Marlene gave her daughter a sad smile and patted her hand. "You're almost eighteen now. There's no reason you shouldn't ask for exactly what you want. Coffee it is."

Alison looked relieved.

Noah said, "I'll be right back."

Once the door closed behind him, Josie took a seat next to Alison, across from Marlene. "Thank you for coming in," she said. "I know you've been through a lot. We don't want to keep you any longer than we have to, so let's just jump right in. Why don't you tell me about Saturday morning."

Alison pulled the hoodie more tightly around her body and looked at the table. "We, uh, we were driving to work. I mean, we were going to get breakfast first at the Denton diner. Then going to work. We were coming from Dina's house. I slept over. We work at the Eudora."

"I told them," said Marlene.

Josie said, "Dina's car was found not too far from her house. Did you pull over because of the fog?"

Alison nodded. "Oh yeah. It was so bad. She found a place to pull over, and we thought we'd just sit there and listen to music for a few minutes until the fog lifted or whatever. But then all of a sudden my door swung open and this guy just pushed himself inside the car, like half inside and half out. I didn't even know what was happening. He started pulling on me—my arms, my hair—and I guess he was trying to get me out of the car. Dina was screaming so loud. Just screaming. I wouldn't get out. I was too afraid. Then he—" She lifted a hand and touched the back of her skull. "He put his hand here and just smashed my face into the dashboard. I don't even remember the pain, to be honest. I just saw the blood pouring down on me, all splattered across the dash, and I got so scared. Dina was still screaming."

Beneath her bruises, her skin paled as she recalled the events of that morning. Beside her, Marlene closed her eyes, her lips moving in some kind of silent prayer. Alison went on, "He got me out of the car then and kind of just, like, tossed me onto the ground. I was so scared. Oh my God. He was just terrifying. All in a rage. His face, when he was standing over me, it was so red. That's when I got a good look at him. I'll never forget that face." Her entire body shuddered.

Marlene opened her eyes and took one of Alison's hands, squeezing it tightly.

Josie said, "Alison, would you mind looking at a photo line-up to see if you can identify the man who attacked you?"

Alison looked to Marlene, who nodded. "Sure," she said.

Josie excused herself and went to find Noah so that they could pull together a suitable photo line-up. Twenty minutes later, they returned. Once seated at the table, Noah gave Alison the coffee she had requested while Josie laid out eight photos on the table. Seven were of men who looked similar to Elliott. The eighth photo was Calvert himself.

Alison stared at the photos, wide-eyed. After a long moment, she pointed to Elliott Calvert's picture. "That's him. God, he looks so normal."

Marlene gave her daughter's shoulder a reassuring squeeze.

"Thank you," Josie said while Noah pushed the photos into a stack and moved them to the other end of the table. "You're doing great, Alison. Let's go back to Saturday morning. What happened after he pulled you out of the car?"

"He kept yelling at me, 'Where is it? Where is it?' and I told him I didn't know what he was talking about. He grabbed my purse and dumped it all over the ground. He was searching inside it, but I guess he didn't find what he was looking for because he kind of kicked at my leg and said, 'Tell me where it is. Give it to me or I'll kill you both.' I told him I didn't know what he was talking about. That's when he turned around and saw Dina. She was still in the driver's seat. I don't remember if she was still screaming or not at that point. To be honest, all of it is a blur. It was like I couldn't hear anything anymore. Like my ears were filling with this buzz that was so loud I thought it would crack my head open."

She used her free hand to hold the side of her head.

Noah said, "It's called auditory exclusion. It happens when your fight or flight response is provoked. You get a huge adrenaline dump, and then your senses feel like they're shutting down."

"Yes! That's exactly it!" Alison said. "It was like all of a sudden I couldn't hear, could barely see, couldn't even feel my body. I just thought I was going to die. I mean, where did this guy even come from? It was just sheer terror." She looked at her mother. "Kind of like when Dad and Billy and I were in that accident."

Sadness shrouded Marlene's features. "I'm so sorry, honey," she whispered to her daughter.

Alison looked back at Josie. "That man, he went around to Dina's side of the car and all I could think was, 'Run.' That was it. So I did."

"The man who attacked you," Josie said. "Do you know his name?"

Alison shook her head. "No. I never even saw him before, and like I said, I couldn't even figure out where he came from. It was so foggy, and we were up there on that deserted road. I guess he must have driven there, but I don't remember hearing or seeing another car."

Noah said, "His name is Elliott Calvert. Does that sound familiar to you?"

"No. I'm sorry, it doesn't."

Josie said, "Did Dina ever talk about him?"

"No."

Alison's hands trembled as she touched her coffee for the first time, pouring two sugars and two creamers into her cup and stirring. Josie let her take a few sips before returning to the questions. "Alison, you ran before Calvert forced Dina out of the car, is that your recollection?"

"Yeah. Like I said, there wasn't much thought behind it. Now I really wish I had stayed. I left her there, and she's dead."

More tears rolled down her cheeks. Snot leaked from her battered nostrils. Noah found a box of tissues at the other end of the table and slid them to her. She thanked him and dabbed at her face, wincing as she did so. Marlene's face was frozen in a look of utter horror.

Turning her attention back to her mother, Alison whispered, "Do you think this is how Dad feels? When he thinks about Billy?"

Marlene's face crumpled. She held her arms open, and Alison fit herself into them, sobbing into her mother's neck. The two of them cried together. After several minutes, they pulled apart, and tried to compose themselves. Alison used a tissue to dab carefully at her swollen face.

Josie waited until the girl's attention was focused on them once more and said, "Alison, this is very important. What happened on that road was not your fault. Do you understand?"

Alison gave a weak nod.

"What happened to Dina is not your fault," Josie repeated. "She's not dead because of anything you did or did not do. She's dead because Elliott Calvert chose to murder her."

Marlene reached over and patted Alison's shoulder. "She's right, honey. I know this is hard. I know you and Dina were great friends, but you did the right thing by running away. He would have killed you, too."

Alison looked as though she wanted to retract her entire body inside her hoodie.

Josie said, "How did you know Dina was dead? When I found you yesterday, you already knew."

"The hospital," Alison said. "While I was hiding there, I went to the morgue. I didn't, like, look at her body or whatever. I don't even know where they keep them there. But I went into the exam room and saw her name on the whiteboard there. Well, it said, 'Hale, D.' Wasn't hard to figure out."

Josie said, "We're very sorry for your loss, Alison."

Marlene said, "Thank you."

Alison stared straight ahead, curling her hands around her coffee.

Noah said, "You said you went to hide at the hospital. How did you get there?"

"I ran and walked, mostly. But then I ran into this kid I go to school with. He's a big-time stoner. I asked him to give me a ride to the hospital. He wouldn't take me up to it, but he dropped me off at the bottom of the hill that goes up to it."

Josie gestured toward Alison's bruised face. "He didn't ask any questions?"

Alison glanced down at her coffee. "Well, yeah, he did

but I just told him I needed him to be discreet. You know, the way I would be discreet and not tell anyone about all the pot he drives around with."

"Alison!" Marlene said, her tone incredulous.

"What?" Alison said, eyes flitting briefly toward her mother. "He was cool. He even gave me his hoodie."

Before Marlene could say anything more, Noah continued, "Can you tell us why you chose to hide instead of calling your mom or the police?"

Alison's bottom lip quivered. "Because from what Dina told me, that Calvert guy was probably not the only one looking for us."

CHAPTER 36

Josie watched as Marlene's face morphed through a number of expressions. She withdrew her comforting hand from Alison's shoulder and looked at her daughter as if she had never seen her before. "Alison Louise Mills, what are you talking about? What did you—what did you do?"

Alison looked at Josie and Noah as if asking for help. When none was forthcoming, she turned back to Marlene. "Mom, it's not what you think. I didn't do anything. Dina— she made a mistake. She didn't mean it. She didn't mean anything by it. But she told me about it and then I knew and, like, we're together all the time, so it was like I was guilty by association. I think. I'm not really sure. Maybe it's fine now that she's dead. Maybe they'll think that's it, like whatever they were looking for is gone."

Alison's voice grew squeakier with each word. Her breath came in short gasps.

"Wait, wait," said Josie, holding up a hand. "Slow down. Let's take this one step at a time."

Noah added, "Alison, take a couple of deep breaths for me, okay? Look at me." He used the index and middle finger of his right hand to point to his eyes. "Right here, Alison. Deep breaths."

Noah breathed with her, whispering, "In... and out... in... and out."

Josie noticed that Marlene had joined Alison in taking the calming breaths. When the tension in the room had decreased somewhat, she said, "Why don't you start at the beginning? With Dina. You said she made a mistake. What happened?"

Alison took a sip of her coffee and then licked her lips. "It started like, two weeks ago? Maybe a little longer? There's this girl we work with, Gia."

"Gia Sorrento," Josie said. "We talked with her."

Alison nodded. "Okay, so you know who I'm talking about. It actually all started with Gia. One night Dina saw our boss, Max, in the bar with Gia. They looked like they were in some deep conversation. Dina took a secret picture and texted me. I guess she thought they looked... I don't know... close or whatever. Dina has the biggest crush on Max. I mean, she's like, in love with him."

Marlene interjected, "Isn't Max in his thirties?"

"Yes," said Alison, adding, "I know, it's gross, right? But Dina was like, 'When I turn eighteen, our ages won't matter.'"

Noah said, "Were they having some kind of relationship?"

Alison rolled her eyes. "God, no. Max flirts. That's what he does. That's all he does. Unless you seem like you're not into it, then he ignores you. He tried flirting hard with me when I started, and I just blew him off so he lost interest. But Dina always flirted back. It became this whole thing. Then he would say stuff to her like, 'Too bad you're under-age, 'cause I could really fall in love with a girl like you.'"

Josie tried to suppress her eye-roll. Alison made a gagging face, like she was going to vomit. "So corny, right? Like, who says that kind of stuff?"

The question was rhetorical, but Marlene answered it anyway. "Perverted men who are trying to sleep with underage girls, that's who! Alison, I can't believe you never told me any of this. That man should be fired. He shouldn't be able to work with minors at all, ever again!"

"Mom!" Alison said. "It's not like he was doing it against her will or whatever. I told you, if you weren't into it, he stopped. And if he made you really uncomfortable, you could go to Felicia."

Josie said, "Did any of the girls ever go to Felicia about Max's behavior?"

Alison nodded. "Yeah, a couple of them. She talked with him and it was fine."

Marlene bristled. "I doubt it was fine. He's still employed. That is not appropriate at all. Felicia should have gone above his head the first time she had a complaint."

Felicia had covered for him, Josie thought. So much for being a "big sister."

"Mom," Alison protested. "I'm just telling you what happened. Besides, Dina liked it when Max came on to her." She made another face of disgust. "I don't know why but she did. I mean, she fell for all his cheesy lines. She thought that once she actually turned eighteen, they'd start dating—except that they didn't. Just like I warned her, Max really wasn't interested in her at all. He totally blew her off. I tried to tell her he didn't mean any of the stuff he said. He said things to *everyone*." She drew out the word "everyone" and rolled her eyes.

Marlene bristled. "Still. It's inappropriate. I'm going to have a word with the hotel manager."

"Please don't, Mom," said Alison. "That would be mortifying." Again, she looked to Josie and Noah for help.

Josie and Noah exchanged a glance. Although they had a positive ID on Max Combs's body and they knew he'd been murdered, until his next of kin had been notified of his death, they weren't in a position to tell people about it.

Josie said, "Let's get back on track. Dina sees Max and Gia in the bar. She thinks something is going on between them. She gets upset. Then what?"

"At first, she just like messed with Gia, trying to get her in trouble with Felicia or with Max by making it look like she forgot things or hadn't done them or messed things up. Nothing happened. Gia just ignored her. She didn't even report her to Felicia or Max. I told Dina that first of all, Gia and Max were probably not seeing each other to begin with, but second of all, if the person she was really upset with was Max, then she needed to take it out on Max. She went to his office to confront him, I guess. I don't know, except he wasn't there. *But—*" She said the word "but" emphatically, eyes widening as she extended her chin. "Dina found this bag inside Max's office. It was behind his desk. Just sitting there. So she took it. She thought it was his and she wanted to mess with him."

"Good God," said Marlene. "She stole someone's bag? Alison—"

"Mom! Please. I didn't know she stole it until later. I didn't know anything. The night that she found the bag, she didn't even tell me about it. I asked her if she talked to Max and she said no, he wasn't in his office, but it didn't matter because she was done with him. It wasn't until a week later when she started acting super weird that I found out about the bag."

"What kind of bag?" asked Noah.

Alison shrugged. "I don't know. Like a messenger bag. You know, about the size of a laptop—long shoulder strap."

Josie said, "Was it Max's bag?"

"I have no idea. I mean, obviously Dina thought it was but now I'm not sure she was right. We had never seen him with one before but he's always at the hotel when we get there and we leave before him, so if it was his bag, we wouldn't know. It's not like we're ever in his office. I think the last time either of us was in there was when we were hired. Plus, Felicia discourages him from speaking to female employees alone in his office."

Noah asked, "Could it have been Felicia's bag? She's also a supervisor. Does she share office space with Max?"

"No," said Alison. "She wants to but he says she doesn't need an office. But I do see her in there plenty of times. He usually leaves the door unlocked so I don't really know. Maybe it was hers."

"Anything distinguishing about the bag?" asked Josie.

"It was black, if that helps."

Noah took out his phone and started texting. Josie knew he was contacting Mettner, who was still at the Eudora. It wouldn't be difficult for him to ask around to some of the staff and find out if anyone had ever noticed Max carrying a black messenger bag.

"Let's go back to Dina for a moment," Noah said. "She was acting weird in what way?"

"She seemed... I don't know... like, not herself. Extra quiet. Subdued. I noticed she was always looking around wherever we were, like she thought someone was watching her or something. I asked her what was going on, and she said that someone had been in her house. I was like, 'What do you mean?' and she said her dad came home and the whole house had been torn apart. Stuff everywhere. She said it was like someone was looking for something. They didn't call the police 'cause nothing was missing. I said maybe it was a case of mistaken identity, and she said she didn't think so and the way she looked—like guilty and also scared—I knew something was going on. I promised she could tell me whatever it was, and I wouldn't tell anyone. She made me promise: no parents, no police."

Marlene said, "Alison! You can't make a promise like that!"

Alison gave her mother a pleading look. "I'm sorry, Mom. I didn't really think it was that serious. I mean, Dina can be overdramatic sometimes!"

Josie said, "What did Dina tell you?"

Alison turned her attention back to Josie. "She told me she took the bag from Max's office. It had a tablet in it, and he used a tablet a lot at work. She thought she was really screwing him over. She wanted to get back at him because she thought he was seeing Gia. She tried to get into the tablet, but it required a passcode and she didn't know it. She tried so many times, it locked her out."

Josie said, "Was there anything else in the bag?"

Alison took another sip of her coffee and drew in a deep breath. "Um, a few things. Hand sanitizer, some pens, a pack of tissues. Oh, and drugs."

Marlene's head reared back. "Drugs? What kind of drugs?"

"I don't know, Mom!" Alison said irritably. "I don't do drugs!"

"Dina knew what they were," said Josie. "Didn't she?"

"Yes," said Alison. "She said it was oxy. She thought that's what the person who came to her house was looking for. I told her, 'Just talk to Max and tell him what you did.' Like, if she thought it was Max's bag, and she took it from

Max's office, she should just go to him and confess. Tell him he didn't need to be skulking around breaking into her house and stuff. But she said she didn't think Max was the one who came looking for it 'cause Max never said anything to anyone at the hotel about a bag or his tablet being missing. Dina said if it was Max and he knew she took it, why wouldn't he just come to her and ask her for it back? Then I said she should just put the bag back into Max's office. Or talk to him and explain that she took it from there, ask him for help. But she was too freaked out. She didn't want him to know that she took it. She was embarrassed. And scared."

"But someone already knew that Dina had taken the bag," said Noah.

"Yeah. I don't know how they knew, but someone knew."

"The cameras," said Noah. "The hotel has cameras everywhere. It would have been easy for Max to ask security to pull the footage from outside his office and see Dina walk out with the bag."

Which meant that Max Combs had definitely been involved in whatever was happening.

"You think Max knew?" Alison hugged herself. "I didn't even think of that."

"Felicia could just as easily have asked for security footage to be pulled," Josie pointed out. "She's already on high alert, she's got a prior drug conviction—she wouldn't want anyone knowing about the drugs in the bag. She'd try to keep it quiet."

Alison's voice went up an octave. "Felicia? You think the drugs were hers? That she ransacked Dina's house?"

"We're really not sure at this point," said Josie. What she was sure of was that they'd need to have another talk with Felicia.

Noah said, "So Dina comes clean to you about the bag, shows it to you, and tells you about the drugs. Then what?"

"She said she knew people from back when she used to do drugs and she'd get rid of them. She thought that would be the end of it."

Josie knew from talking to Needle how Dina had gotten rid of the drugs. "What about the bag? What did she do with that?"

"I threw it in the dumpsters out back. At the back of the hotel," said Alison.

"Alison Louise!" Marlene exclaimed.

"What was I supposed to do?"

Before Marlene could speak again, Josie said, "That wasn't the end of it though, was it? Something else happened after that, didn't it?"

Alison shivered again. "Yeah," she said, swallowing. "Something bad."

CHAPTER 37

The rest of the story spilled out in fits and starts, Alison talking over her mother whenever she interrupted. A few days later, Dina had called Alison and asked to meet at Starbucks. Dina looked terrible. Alison thought she had the flu. "But then she showed me her fingers. Her nails were all messed up. Bleeding and so red. It looked so painful. She said that someone—some guy—had come up to her while she was jogging outside her development—along Widow's Ridge Road. He grabbed her right off the side of the road. It was like something out of a bad movie, like when you see a black van pull up and snatch a person off the street, except this guy had some big SUV. He stuffed her into the back, and she was going to keep going right out the other side, but there was another guy in there and he made sure she didn't go anywhere the whole ride."

Just like the two men who had parked near Max Combs's house the night of the homicide.

"Where did they take her?" asked Noah.

"She wasn't sure," said Alison. "They made her put her head between her legs for the drive. She wasn't sure even how long they drove. They went into some place deserted but outside. Like in the woods or something. But they never got out of the car. The driver just turned around and started asking her all these questions while his friend tied her up and started pulling off her nails and sticking needles under them and stuff."

She closed her eyes, her entire body shuddering.

For once, Marlene had nothing to add.

"What did they look like?" asked Josie.

"She said one was big and muscular and tattooed with a shaved head. He just had on black jeans and a black T-shirt."

"What kinds of tattoos?" asked Noah.

"I don't know," said Alison. "I didn't ask, and she didn't tell me."

"What about the other guy?" asked Josie.

Alison lifted a hand to her head. "Thick black hair. Black clothes. Long sleeves, though. He was skinnier than the other guy, she said. Oh, and he wore latex gloves."

With each revelation, Josie felt more and more uneasy.

"Is that it?" asked Noah.

"I'm sorry. That's all she told me. I wasn't like, focused on what they looked like. I was freaking out that she got kidnapped and basically tortured."

"What did they want?" asked Josie.

"They didn't say. They were just like, 'You took something from us. You know what it is. We want it back or we're going to kill you.' She thought it was the drugs and she told them they were gone. They said there was something else they were looking for so she told them about the tablet. She gave it to them. Well, she said they drove her to her house. Her mom and dad were at work—they both work most of the evening—and one of the men went inside with her and got it."

"That was it?" said Noah.

Alison shook her head. "I wish. They came back for her Wednesday night when her parents were working. They did more stuff to her nails. She said she tried to scream so the neighbors would hear her, but one of them kept his hand over her mouth. They said she lied to them. No matter what she said, they insisted she lied. They told her she knew what they wanted and if she didn't give it back, they were going to kill her and her family."

"Oh my God," Marlene blurted out. "What kind of people—Alison—what on earth did Dina get herself into?"

"I don't know! I really don't, okay?"

Before they could argue or Alison dissolved into tears, Noah asked, "They didn't give her any instructions as to how to get them whatever it was they were searching for when she came up with it?"

"I think they said that they would find her and that she better have it by the next time they found her. Then they left."

Josie wondered at how the two men could have moved in and out of Dina's small housing development without raising any eyebrows. Then again, Denton police hadn't canvassed the area because they were focused solely on Elliott Calvert, whose presence there they could prove via GPS records. It was possible some neighbors had seen the SUV or the men although, as Guy Hale had pointed out, no one had home surveillance cameras. Still, someone might remember the make and model of the car or something distinguishing about the men that they weren't yet aware of. Josie took her phone out and texted the Chief, asking him to dispatch units there to canvass the neighbors.

"What do you think they were looking for?" asked Noah.

Alison tugged at her ponytail and pulled her hoodie tighter. "I don't know. I wish I did! Dina said it had to be something in the bag that she had overlooked. The hotel trash hadn't been picked up yet, so I said I'd go dumpster-diving and get the bag back."

"Alison!" Marlene said, incredulous.

"What was I supposed to do? Mom, her fingers were so messed up. I couldn't let her do it. She'd get, like, an infection or something. Anyway, I found the bag pretty quickly. First dumpster I looked in. There was nothing in it. Dina told me to cut open the liner to make sure nothing was sewn into it, so I did. There was nothing. It was just a bag."

Josie recalled their last text exchange.

Dina: *Did you check on that thing I asked about?*

Alison: *Yes. There is nothing there. Nothing. Are you sure that's what all this is about?*

Dina: *I don't know. They never said for sure. But if I don't find whatever it is they want, they're going to kill me. I'm really scared.*

The bag was the thing that Dina had asked Alison to check on. It hadn't panned out. Two days later, Dina was dead.

"Where is the bag now?" asked Noah.

Looking sheepish, Alison said, "I was supposed to throw it back into the dumpster but instead I put it in Max's office. I know it's stupid, but I thought maybe if I put the bag back where it was originally found, I could make all of this stop. I did it at the end of the night. Dina doesn't—didn't—know I did it. I was just hoping—I don't know." She looked down at her lap. "I guess I thought if we gave it back, maybe it would be okay."

Josie made eye contact with Noah who gave her a nod and then left the room. She knew within seconds he would be on the phone with the hotel manager, John W. Brown, asking him to check Max's office for the bag. It hadn't been found in Max's home.

Turning back to Alison, Josie said, "Dina wasn't entirely sure whether or not the bag was what those men were after. When you two spoke on Friday night, while you were sleeping over at her house, did she have any ideas as to what else those men might be looking for, if not the bag?"

"No," said Alison. "But what else could it be? I mean, Dina didn't take anything else. I know her dad thought she was using drugs again, but she wasn't. Even if she was, she wouldn't be dumb enough to steal someone's stash. She wasn't into anything else. I'm telling you, it all comes down to that stupid bag. She swore to me that there was nothing else that would have gotten her into so much trouble."

Josie said, "Unless there was something inside the bag that Dina never told you about. Is that possible?"

Alison considered it for a moment. "I mean, I guess so. But we're—we were—best friends. Why wouldn't she tell me if there was something else? Something dangerous?"

Marlene took Alison's hand. "To protect you, honey."

Alison gave a frustrated sigh. "Protect me from what? Look at my face! Why would she lie?"

Josie said, "It's our job to find out. Alison, you've been a tremendous help. I think right now you two should get some rest. If there's anything else we need from you, we can get in touch."

Alison said, "That's it?"

Josie smiled. "Yes. For now, that's all we need from you. I'd like to make a suggestion though, and that is that maybe the two of you stay at a hotel for a few days or with a friend or family member."

Marlene smiled uncertainly. "What? Why?"

Alison said, "Because, Mom! People were trying to kill Dina and now they might try to kill me."

"But you didn't take the bag," said Marlene. "No one put you into a black van and pulled your fingernails off. This is absurd."

Josie said, "It's possible that we're being overly cautious. Dina was clearly involved in something illegal, whether she meant to be or not, and it appears as though she was their main focus. It's likely that Alison isn't even on anyone's radar other than Elliott Calvert's, and he is in custody, but it's a guilt by association type of situation. Since they were best friends, the men who were after Dina might assume that Alison knows something or even that Dina gave her whatever it is that everyone's looking for. Really, it's just a precaution. In a few days our investigation will hopefully be much further along, and we can assess the risk to you and your family much more realistically."

Marlene picked up her purse and hugged it to her chest. "A hotel is expensive. If you want us to be in protective custody, shouldn't you pay for it?"

"This isn't protective custody," Josie clarified. "You won't be in our custody at all. There's no need for that. We're simply suggesting that you don't go home for a few days. The press has been made aware that Alison was found safely. If the same people who thought Dina had something that belonged to them think Alison now has it, the first place they'll look is your home. You don't have to stay at a hotel. You could stay with family or friends."

"I really don't want to involve anyone else in all of this... chaos," Marlene said.

"As I said," Josie repeated. "It's just a suggestion." She handed each of them one of her cards. "My cell phone number is on there. If you need anything or you have any questions, call me immediately."

Alison said, "I don't have my phone."

"Right," Josie said. "We've got it. We can release that to you before you leave. I'll go get it."

Josie left to retrieve Alison's phone. She returned with it several minutes later to find Alison staring at her card. Her lips moved although no sound came from them. She was memorizing the numbers, Josie realized. When she finished, she slipped the card into one of her hoodie pockets. Noticing Josie's gaze, she said, "My dad told me, always memorize numbers. You know, in case of an emergency? Everyone puts them into their phones now so they don't actually know them."

Josie smiled. "Very smart."

"Detective Quinn?" said Alison. "What do we do if those people come for me?"

"Alison!" exclaimed Marlene.

"What? Even if we go to a hotel, they could still find us."

"Call 911," said Josie.

CHAPTER 38

The great room was empty except for Gretchen, still seated at her computer, tapping away, and Chief Chitwood, who stood over the detectives' desks, surveying what was left of the coffees and pastries. Daisy and Amber had gone. Mettner was still at the Eudora. Josie checked her phone and saw that Noah had left her a text. He had decided to go to the Eudora in person so he could see for himself whether or not the messenger bag was still in Max's office. He and Mettner would also speak with Felicia Koslow. The Chief picked through the Komorrah's bags until he came up with a bear claw. Josie said, "You get your K-9 unit approved yet?"

He grunted. "Not yet. This Fuller guy wants a damn college course on K-9 units before he'll agree to back it. Pain right in my ass. You get anything from this kid?"

Gretchen stopped typing and turned her chair in Josie's direction.

Josie plopped into her seat. "It seems this entire thing started over a messenger bag."

The Chief raised a bushy brow. "A bag?"

Josie brought him and Gretchen up to speed on everything she and Noah had learned from Alison Mills. Dina Hale had stolen a bag from Max Combs's office at the Eudora. The bag's owner was a mystery—or so it seemed. She had found a tablet inside which she could not access; and drugs, which she'd gotten rid of at the East Bridge. Someone had come to her house and ransacked it, searching for something. Then she'd been taken by two men, tortured, and instructed to return whatever it was that she had taken, at which point she had relinquished the tablet. The men returned and tortured her some more, accusing her of lying and giving them the wrong thing—whether that was the wrong tablet or something else altogether was anyone's guess. Dina had told Alison she didn't know what they were after. Alison had found the bag in a hotel dumpster and searched it. Finding nothing, she'd returned it to Max's empty office on Friday evening. Max, too, had been tortured in the same way as Dina although they weren't able to say definitively when—whether it was the same night he was killed or prior to that. He was then murdered in his home which had also been ransacked. Two men in an SUV had taken and tortured Dina. Two men in an SUV were also seen parking a few doors down from Max's house the night he was murdered. There was no messenger bag in his house, but there was three hundred sixty-three thousand dollars hidden in his ceiling.

The morning after Max was killed, Dina and Alison were attacked by Elliott Calvert. The only connection they had found between him and Max Combs was tenuous at best—they were sometimes at the hotel at the same time. Calvert had depleted his bank accounts of two hundred thirteen thousand dollars. Max had that amount plus an additional one hundred fifty thousand dollars.

The Chief said, "You can put Max Combs and Elliott

Calvert at the Eudora at the same time, but you can't prove they ever came into contact?"

Josie said, "Not unless Hummel finds Calvert's prints on something in Max's possession, like the bag of money. We're waiting on Hummel to process all the prints."

"Torture, ransacking, Combs shot in the head? Two guys driving around here in an SUV? Palmer, this sound like some mob shit to you?"

Gretchen nodded. "A little bit, yeah."

"You got this hotel guy, Combs, blackmailing a regular guy, Calvert. Probably over his affair, given the photos we found. If this really all did start over a bag, then Dina Hale lied about what was in it."

"Unless there was something in it that she threw out because she didn't realize its importance," said Josie.

"Like what?" said the Chief.

"Like a phone, maybe? Max Combs's phone is missing, too."

"Speaking of that," said the Chief. "Did any of you try to ping it? Get its location?"

"I did," said Gretchen. "It last pinged near his house. Wherever it is now, the battery is dead. We can't get its location."

"You think the two guys in the SUV took it with them?" asked the Chief.

Gretchen shrugged.

Josie said, "Maybe the bag did belong to him, and his phone was in it and there is something on the phone that all these people are looking for."

"But what?" Gretchen said. "What could be that valuable to both the mob—assuming we're right about our friends in the SUV—and a regular guy like Calvert?"

"Photos?" Josie suggested. "Videos? Documents? All

three? That could explain why they took the tablet when Dina offered it. They clearly thought what they were searching for was on it. When they didn't find it there, they came back."

Gretchen said, "The question is: photos or videos of what? Documents pertaining to what? In my experience, there's not much the mob is afraid of. It's always been a challenge for law enforcement to get charges to stick, much less for prosecutors to get convictions."

The stairwell door swooshed open, and Hummel strode through with a sheaf of papers in hand. "Hey," he said. "I've got the fingerprint reports from Max Combs's house."

Josie stood up and took the reports from him. As she scanned them, Hummel recited the findings. "We got one partial print from the larger backpack that matches Elliott Calvert."Gretchen walked over to where Josie stood. She slid her reading glasses onto her nose and peered over Josie's shoulder at the fingerprint reports. "That confirms that Calvert gave Max Combs the money he took from his accounts. What else?"

Hummel said, "We found a lot of prints in the place. Pretty much all of them are unidentifiable. We did get one hit that might be of interest. You know the drugs we found? They were stored in small plastic baggies. Four of them had prints from Felicia Koslow."

Josie's eyes snapped toward Hummel. "Really?"

He gestured to the pages in her hands. "It's all there."

"Well," said the Chief. "Looks like you need to join Fraley and Mett at the Eudora. Fraley's got your car, so I'll drop you off there. If Koslow won't talk to you there, bring her here."

CHAPTER 39

Felicia Koslow stood before Josie, hands on her hips. Today she wore a black pencil skirt and white sleeveless silk blouse. A red-tailed hawk wrapped its wings around her right bicep. Its head rested on the outside of her shoulder, one eye staring fiercely—much the way Felicia glared at them now. For all her posturing, her voice shook when she said, "I cannot believe you are doing this to me." Gesturing around them, she said, "The manager's office? Are you trying to get me fired?"

Josie perched along the edge of Mr. Brown's desk. "Speaking in here was Mr. Brown's idea. It ensures privacy."

The door to the office opened and Noah walked in, a stack of papers in his hands. Over his shoulder, he called, "Thanks, Mett."

Felicia stared at him as he closed the door behind him and crossed the room to stand beside Josie. Shooting Felicia one of his charming smiles, he handed Josie the papers, tapping his thumb against a line that had been highlighted.

Josie felt her pulse tick upward. From the corner of her mouth, she whispered, "Every time?"

"Yes," he replied. Turning back to Felicia, he gestured for her to have a seat in one of the guest chairs, but she remained standing in the middle of the room.

Noah said, "If you'd be more comfortable, we could go to the police station."

A long, manicured finger stabbed the air, pointing accusingly at him. "I am not going to the police station."

Smile still in place, he said, "Then we'll talk here."

Felicia folded her arms over her chest. Narrowing her eyes, she said, "I want to call my lawyer."

Josie looked back down at the report, turning pages to find more highlighted lines. "You should."

"What?"

Noah said, "I think maybe Detective Quinn is being premature. You can call your attorney anytime. You know that. You've got your cell phone on you. Right?"

"Uh, yeah, I—"

He went on. "You don't even have to talk to us. You know that as well, don't you?"

"Is this some kind of trick?" asked Felicia.

Josie looked up to see Noah shake his head. "No tricks. I'm just saying you're a smart woman. In addition to that, you've had some experience with police. Enough to give you a healthy distrust for us."

Josie raised a brow. Meeting Felicia's eyes, she said, "Speaking of distrust, you lied to us about that 'experience.' It wasn't just your boyfriend who was dealing drugs. You were arrested twice for possession with intent to deliver."

"That's none of your business," Felicia shot back. "I was under no obligation to disclose that to you—especially not at my place of employment. That was a mistake. I was young and stupid. That's in the past."

"You're right," said Noah. "I don't want to talk about that. I want to talk about the here and now. Before she died, Dina Hale found almost four thousand dollars' worth of OxyContin. Do you know anything about that?"

Felicia's eyes widened in shock. "What? No. I don't know anything about that."

Josie said, "Max Combs was murdered in his home in the early hours of Saturday morning. Drugs were found at the scene. Your prints were found on the bags in which those drugs were kept. Can you tell us why?"

A yelp of surprise issued from Felicia's throat. Stumbling backward, she fell into one of the guest chairs. Her knees knocked together. She covered her mouth with one hand. From behind it came a muffled, "Oh my God. Oh, poor Max."

Noah walked over to the other guest chair, spinning it to face Felicia and sitting down in front of her. "I know you and Max were... close. At least at one time. I'm sorry for your loss."

Felicia kept her eyes locked on Noah. "I can't believe it. What—what happened?"

"He was murdered," Noah responded gently. "We're trying to figure out why and who did it. I hate to have to ask you questions after you've had a shock, but it's important to the investigation. Detective Quinn is right. Your prints were found on the packaging of several illicit drugs in Max's home. Now, you have every right to end this conversation right now. To call an attorney. I don't need to tell you that."

Her gaze flitted to Josie and back to Noah. She took several seconds to prepare what she said next. Josie could see her assembling her lies inside her head, making sure there were no weak points in her story. "I found those in Max's office," she said. "I'm in and out of there sometimes. I was looking for something in his desk, and they were there. I didn't even realize at first, I was just digging through a drawer. So yeah, I touched them. But that's it. I confronted him and told him I was going to report him to management. He took them home after that. That's all I know."

Noah let the story slide, moving on. "The times you've been in and out of Max's office, did you ever notice a black messenger bag?"

Felicia gave a small, swift shake of her head, as if to reorient herself to the change in questioning. "A messenger bag? I don't know. I mean, I guess so."

"Did Max own one?" Noah asked.

"I don't know. Maybe. I never really paid that much attention."

"You were lovers," Josie said. "You didn't notice?"

Felicia rolled her eyes. "That was ages ago. I'm just saying that I am pretty sure I've seen him with one, but I don't really remember for sure."

Noah asked, "Did he have a tablet?"

"Everyone in management has one. The hotel purchases them for us."

"Do you know if his went missing in the last few weeks?" Noah said.

"No. He had it. I saw him using it. What is this about?"

Josie asked, "Do you own a black messenger bag?"

Felicia said, "No." Scowling at Josie, she said, "Are you going to accuse me of transporting drugs in this mysterious bag?"

Ignoring her, Josie stepped forward and handed Felicia the sheaf of pages. Felicia stared at the top page, uncomprehending. "What is this? Am I supposed to know what this is?"

Softly, Noah said, "The man we've arrested for the murder of Dina Hale is called Elliott Calvert. In the last five months, he's come to Bastian's on sixteen occasions. After a few drinks at the bar, he gets in an elevator. We believe he was going to a room, except that he has never rented a room in his own name. We know he has a mistress. It makes sense that she would rent the room instead of him. We know the dates that he was here because the GPS on his phone places him here. So we looked at the guest list for the hotel for all sixteen times he was here."

Felicia continued to stare at the page in front of her, face utterly blank.

Noah continued, "There is only one name that came up all sixteen times that Mr. Calvert was here. It's yours."

Her gaze snapped to Noah's face. "What?"

"Employees in management are comped rooms when business is slow. Mr. Brown told us. All you have to do is log into the hotel's internal database, jump through some electronic hoops, and you've got yourself a room."

Felicia shuffled through the pages frantically. Some of them fluttered to the floor. Noah reached down to gather them.

Josie stepped forward. "Were you having an affair with Elliott Calvert?"

Stricken, Felicia looked up at her, hands frozen, clutched around the two pages that remained in her grip. "What? I didn't even know that man! I'm not having an affair with anyone! I did not rent those rooms."

Josie said, "These records suggest otherwise."

Felicia shot to her feet. "I did not reserve those rooms. Listen, I've done some shitty things, okay? I slept with my boss—with Max. I let some... things slide. Girls came to me and said Max was making them really uncomfortable. Suggesting things. Disgusting things. I talked to him, but I didn't report him. Because Brown loves Max and I need this job, and I didn't want to rock the boat. And yeah, I've got a drug conviction. I did some things I'm not proud of—to make money. To keep a roof over my head. But I'm not having an affair with some... murdering psychopath, and I did not rent those rooms."

Josie said, "Felicia, you've lied to us at least once that we know of. Why should we believe you?"

Felicia looked down at Noah, her eyes beseeching, but he offered only a sympathetic smile. Returning her gaze to Josie, she took a few rapid breaths. "Because. Because this time I'm telling the truth. Besides, you can't prove that was me. Anyone can rent a room in anyone's name. In management, I mean. I could sign in right now and rent a room under Max's name or Mr. Brown's name or any of the other supervisors. I'm telling you, it wasn't me."

CHAPTER 40

"What do you think?" asked Noah.

Josie sighed and stared out the window, watching the Eudora recede from view as Noah drove them home. "I think Felicia Koslow is lying, but I'm not sure about which parts."

"Definitely the drugs," Noah said. "She's got contacts. She could be getting her supply from her ex-boyfriend and selling it to Max. Then he sold to God knows who. The staff, maybe? Clients? We'll probably never know. He may have been doing it to pay down his gambling debt until he realized blackmail was more lucrative."

Josie took out her phone and logged into Instagram. "I don't think Felicia Koslow is the woman in Calvert's photos." It took her only a moment to locate Felicia's account, which was not private. A few seconds of scrolling and she found what she was looking for: Felicia posing beside the ocean in a bikini. She held it up for Noah to see. "In fact, we can rule her out based on this photo."

"You think someone else rented the rooms in her name, like she said? But who? And why?"

"So that their name wouldn't be attached to it," Josie said. "So that if the shit hit the fan in whatever the hell is going on in this city, we'd go looking for Felicia instead of the person who actually rented the room."

Noah nodded. "Sure, but the list isn't that long. We only need to look at hotel management. My money is on Max, though. He's already connected to Calvert by way of the blackmail."

"But we need the rest of the pieces," Josie said. "We're still missing so much."

"We'll get there," said Noah. "Maybe some sleep or other activities will clear your head."

At the mention of other activities, Josie felt a wave of desire surge through her. She reached over, snaking a hand behind his head, and tangled a hand in his thick hair. "It's other activities," she told him. "That's what would clear my head."

As they pulled up to their house, Noah frowned. "I'll have to give you a raincheck."

Josie spied a vehicle sitting in their driveway with New York plates. Noah parked behind it. "Shit," said Josie. "I forgot."

Noah laughed as he turned off the engine. "You forgot that your sister was coming in from New York City for your birthday?"

Her twin sister, Trinity Payne, was a famous television journalist who now had her own show called *Unsolved Crimes with Trinity Payne*. If it was possible, Trinity was even busier than Josie, and yet she made sure to carve time out of her schedule to see Josie whenever possible, usually several times a year and always around their birthday.

Josie said, "Because it wasn't always my birthday. For

thirty years I thought my birthday was a completely different date. I'm still getting used to the real date."

"Fair enough," said Noah as they walked up the path to the front stoop and let themselves in.

Josie and Trinity had spent a lifetime apart. Trinity was raised by their parents while Josie was raised by the woman who abducted her and her former boyfriend, Eli Matson. When Josie was six, Eli died. His mother Lisette spent years locked in an expensive and protracted custody battle with Lila in her attempt to get full legal and physical custody of Josie, which she finally did when Josie was fourteen. The years living with Lisette had been the best years of Josie's childhood. They'd always been close. Lisette had been everything to Josie: her North Star, her anchor, her guide, her stability in a life of chaos.

So it had come as a complete shock when, at thirty years old, Josie found out that they were not related. But Lisette had encouraged Josie to forge relationships with her biological family. Now they felt like her real family, and Josie's bond with Trinity was unlike anything she had ever experienced. Although it didn't help her remember their birthday plans.

Josie and Noah waited in the foyer for Trout to come running, but a glance into their living room revealed that he was heavily invested in a game of fetch with Drake Nally, Trinity's boyfriend, who also happened to be an FBI agent.

Trinity appeared in the kitchen doorway with a bowl of popcorn in hand. She was dressed down in gray sweatpants and an oversized FBI T-shirt, no doubt Drake's. Her glossy black hair was tossed up into a loose ponytail. Still, she looked shiny, glamorous, and a hundred times more put-together than Josie on her best day. Josie always wondered how she did it. Was it just from years of being on television

—being forced to dress stylishly and have her make up just so? Or was Josie just not doing something right?

"You're home!" Trinity exclaimed. She strode across the foyer and gave them each a one-armed hug, managing not to spill any popcorn. With a devilish smile, she added, "I told Drake you forgot we were coming. You did forget, right?"

Drake hopped up from the living room floor and jogged in to greet them. Trout finally noticed them and followed, his Kong toy forgotten. He cried until Josie and Noah knelt to pet him. Josie said, "I'm really sorry."

Drake reached into his jeans pocket and pulled out a twenty-dollar bill, handing it to Trinity. She slipped it into her sweatpants.

Noah laughed. "You guys bet on it?"

Trinity winked. "I know my sister. It was a sure thing."

Drake said, "We were going to watch a movie. You guys want to join, or are you on some big case?"

As Josie stood back up, Trinity studied her face. "A case."

Josie smiled. "We are in the middle of a case but we're home for the night, so yeah, a movie sounds great."

Noah said, "I'll let Trout out."

Drake pulled a face. "Uh, yeah, about that. Did you know there's a bouncy house in your backyard?"

Josie and Noah looked at one another. He said, "I thought that wasn't happening for a week or two."

She laughed. "Call Misty."

The four of them walked through the kitchen and out the back door. Sure enough, a huge inflatable bounce house complete with a slide took up the majority of their yard. Josie laughed. Trout squirmed out from between their legs and started sniffing every inch of its base.

Drake said, "You think it's rated for adults?"

Noah had his phone pressed to one ear but he said, "I requested that." Then, "Hey Misty, question for you..."

He walked back into the house while Josie explained the presence of the bounce house. Her phone buzzed in her back pocket. She reached for it just as Noah came back out. "It was a mistake on the part of the company," he said. "She'll call about it tomorrow."

Drake said, "You should see if you can keep it for two more weeks. How fun would that be?"

Josie looked at her phone. It was a text message from a number she didn't recognize.

D Quinn its me A need help asap someone in house.

Her heart did a double tap as she took in the words, her mind trying to process their meaning. "Noah," she said.

Another message appeared.

Mom in trouble can't call 911 they will hear me help come soon.

She turned her phone screen toward Noah and watched the tension that had left his face when they walked into their home gather once more. "Shit," he said.

"A is for Alison Mills," said Josie. "Noah, we have to go right now."

CHAPTER 41

Noah's knuckles turned white as they tightened around the steering wheel. Racing through the darkened streets of Denton, he used the hands-free feature in the vehicle to call dispatch and request all units to respond to the Mills' address while Josie tried to get more information from Alison. He instructed all units to go in quiet, with no lights or sirens and to park along the road rather than pulling into the Mills' driveway. The police would need the element of surprise.

"We need to know how many assailants," Noah said. "And whether or not they're armed."

"Already asked," Josie said, holding the phone so tightly her hands ached. She stared at the screen, willing Alison to respond. A gasp escaped her throat when a message popped up.

2 *I think not sure only saw 2 and both have guns*

"Two men, armed," she said loudly for dispatch to hear. "Copy that," said the dispatcher.

Josie typed back: *Where are you in the house?*

A few seconds later, Alison responded:

upstairs hall closet pls hurry

On our way, Josie texted back. *Stay in the closet until I come to get you. Where is your mom?*

Several seconds went by, each one feeling like an hour to Josie. Finally, Alison wrote:

in kitchen men r saying they will shoot her they r beating her pls come help

We're on our way, Josie wrote. *I need you to tell me the layout of the house from top to bottom. Is there a basement? I saw the first floor when we were there the other day but how is the second floor laid out? Are any doors open?*

More seconds ticked by. Then came answers:

Both front and back doors open never locked. Yes basement. The door is in kitchen. Upstairs top steps bathroom then left my room spare room parents room. Pls hurry they r hurting mom

Josie read out the locations of Alison and Marlene as well as the other information Alison provided and then Noah hung up with dispatch. "Why did they stay in the damn house?" he muttered. "You told them to go somewhere else, right?"

"Yes. I suggested it. Marlene was resistant to it. Didn't want to pay for a hotel or involve anyone else. Should I call the state police?" asked Josie. "Request SERT?"

SERT was the state police's Special Emergency

Response Team—the equivalent of a SWAT team. It was made up of two units: tactical and negotiation. Each one was supervised by a full-time commander. The rest of each unit, which included twenty-four members, was made up of troopers throughout the state who worked part-time on the team.

"SERT will take too long," said Noah. "They have to call in all the guys, get here, and be briefed. It could be over an hour. The nearest Denton units are closer. There will be enough of us to cover the perimeter. You've got contact with Alison, who is in the house. We should do this with our own people."

The road that the Mills lived on was dark. There were no streetlights out here on the edges of the city. Noah slowed when he saw the red mailbox, passing it and then pulling over onto the shoulder. He called dispatch to advise of their location and then turned off the vehicle's engine. There were some trees between the house and the road, but headlights would be visible from any window at the front of the house. They got out, moving quietly to the back of their vehicle, and popped open the hatch. The dim bulb from inside was enough for them to find what they needed. As they fitted their tactical vests over their torsos, Josie said, "How far away are the other units?"

"Ten minutes," Noah replied.

Josie stepped away from the car, letting her eyes adjust to the night. A bright half-moon hung in the sky, casting a silver glow over their surroundings. "There's no vehicle," she said. "Where did these guys park?"

"The driveway?" suggested Noah, turning his phone to vibrate. He took his radio out of his vest and clicked it on, testing it. Josie did the same.

"That would be monumentally stupid," she said.

"There's only one way for a car to get off the property, and it's this driveway."

Noah quietly gave instructions over the radio for all units to switch over to a tactical channel. Then he closed the hatch to the car and gestured around them. "Maybe they don't expect any other visitors. It's pretty remote—or at least, it seems that way."

Josie opened her mouth to respond when a gunshot cracked the air. They froze, staring at one another. In Josie's back pocket, her phone buzzed.

Noah clicked his radio. "Shots fired. Shots fired."

Another gunshot rang out. Josie's fingers fumbled to lift her phone from her pocket. Alison had texted:

theyre shooting her pls help pls

Josie swallowed and tapped in:

Stay where you are. We're coming.

Noah said, "It's your call."

Conventional wisdom dictated that they wait for the rest of the units to arrive; form a plan; set a perimeter; choose a single point of entry; ready a tactical shield and go in with a shield officer, a cover officer and at least two others who would act as the hands team, clearing rooms; but since the rise of mass shootings the country over, that thinking had changed. Waiting only risked more lives, and in this situation, they'd already been inside the house once. Josie knew the layout of the first floor—she had been the one to get Marlene a glass of water from the kitchen—and they had Alison acting as their eyes from inside the house.

"If we wait, they'll die," she said.

Noah unholstered his pistol. "Let's go."

CHAPTER 42

Cloaked in darkness, they ran soundlessly up the long driveway, keeping to the edge. They switched their radios to silent and held their pistols at the ready. At the top of the driveway, both garage doors were shut. There were no vehicles in sight. The front door was also closed but light glowed from behind the living room curtains. Noah looked at Josie and she motioned toward the front door. They had to choose their point of entry. They also had to go toward the sounds of the gunshots. If Alison's information was correct, the men and Marlene Mills were in the kitchen. The closest point of entry and the fastest way into the house was the front door. Entering from there would also give them a chance to get inside unnoticed, whereas if they tried to make entry through the kitchen they'd lose the element of surprise.

They took up position on opposite sides of the door. Noah used a hand signal to indicate that Josie should take the lead. Then he reached over and quietly turned the doorknob. They didn't announce themselves. Without back-up and with the possibility that Marlene or Alison or both could be gravely injured and still in danger, their focus was to neutralize the threat. Giving themselves away too soon would only put their own lives in greater danger.

A roar began in Josie's ears. Her heartbeat galloped so hard she was certain it was jarring her tactical vest. Keeping her pistol up, aimed in front of her as if it were an extension of her arms, she swept the barrel across the right side of the room. She sensed Noah behind her and knew he was panning the other side of the room. Some hyper-alert part of Josie's mind registered the mess. The entire room had been torn apart. Couch cushions stabbed, tables and lamps over-turned, even part of the wall-to-wall carpet had been pulled up.

The men were searching for something.

They moved past the steps that led to the second floor, pausing to listen for any sounds, but there were none. Next was the dining room, also in disarray. Only the heavy table in the center of the room still stood. All the chairs were on their sides, cushions ripped off. The drawers of a pine side-board lay scattered across the floor, contents everywhere. Josie and Noah slowed down, not wanting to step on something that would send their legs flying out from under them or that would make enough noise to alert the intruders.

Approaching the kitchen, Josie tried to quiet the thunder in her head. Adrenaline surged through her body until it felt like she was trying to contain an entire ocean wave within her average human-sized frame. There were no sounds. Had the men gone? Escaped through the back door? Or were they upstairs, searching for Alison or for whatever it was they were looking for? Wouldn't she have heard their footsteps overhead? The intruders wouldn't be taking care to be quiet. As far as they knew, they were alone with Marlene and Alison Mills.

Josie shot a quick glance at Noah, who had taken up position on the other side of the kitchen doorway. His face was lined with tension, a muscle in his jaw pulsing. Her gaze returned to the threshold that led from the dining room into the kitchen. All she could see from where she stood was a slice of tile and the edge of a large white island counter. Josie was about to step into the room when a sound came. It took her brain a second to process what she was hearing. A gurgling breath and something being dragged over tile.

Heart in her throat, Josie moved swiftly into the kitchen, pistol sweeping her designated side of the room. Noah followed. More destruction. Every cabinet open. Every drawer pulled from its home. Broken dishes, discarded utensils, food items, towels, potholders, cleaning products. Even the appliances had been thrown from the countertops. It was impossible not to step on the debris. Glass crunched under their feet. The toes of their sneakers bumped against utensils and ceramic shards. As they rounded the island, Josie almost missed the sight of a bloody hand clawing its way toward them. She pulled up short, bobbing her head at Noah. He circled to the other side of the island. There, on the floor, was Marlene Mills. She lay on her stomach, a pool of blood spreading beneath her.

A jumble of sounds became audible. Marlene's labored breathing and her legs kicking weakly at the detritus all around her, trying to propel her body forward. Then, from somewhere else in the house, thuds and thumps, and a muffled clatter. Josie couldn't tell if it was coming from above or below them. Without lowering her pistol, she clocked the doors in the kitchen. One that led out back. A second door to Josie's left was partially open, revealing a pantry. Every last bit of foodstuff had been yanked from the shelves. Boxes of dried food had been dumped, making a mish-mash of powder, uncooked pasta, and cereal across the tile floor. The third door, which was to Josie's left, was closed.

Josie caught Noah's eye, took one hand off the pistol grip, and pointed toward the closed door. She mouthed, "Cover me." He took up position in a corner of the room so that he would easily be able to respond to any threats that might come from either the first or third door. Josie kept her pistol up and ready but squatted down so that Marlene would be able to hear her. Keeping her voice low, she said, "Mrs. Mills, it's Detective Quinn and Lieutenant Fraley from the Denton PD. Where are the men?"

Marlene looked up at Josie and then her face collapsed onto her outstretched arm. Josie heard what sounded very much like a sigh of relief.

"Mrs. Mills, where are the men who hurt you?"

Marlene's body tremored. A cough erupted from her, spasming her entire frame. This close to her, Josie could taste the coppery tang of blood in the back of her throat. Marlene whispered, "I have to get to Alison."

"Is Alison still upstairs?" Josie said.

"Upstairs."

"Where are the men?"

More noises came. Items being shuffled. Something thrown or maybe dropped. Again, Josie couldn't get a bead on precisely where the noises originated from.

Marlene struggled to push out her words. They came slowly. "I sent them to the basement. They want... something. Don't... know what. But I told them it was there so I could go get Alison and get out. I said... red bin, fifth row from the—from the back."

Again, she tried to move, to crawl, one of her knees moving up, trying to gain purchase in the pool of blood.

Josie put one hand on Marlene's shoulder. "Is that the basement door there? Across from the pantry?"

"Y—yes."

"Mrs. Mills, listen to me very carefully. I need you to stay right here where you are. Do not move."

"Alison. My—my Alison."

She could not lift her head, but Josie saw a tear slide from one of her eyes. Josie felt everything at once for one wild, unmanageable second. Sadness at seeing Marlene fighting for her life on her kitchen floor. Fear that she might not make it; that all of them might not make it. They were here in this house alone with two men who thought nothing of shooting a woman who was in no way a threat. But most of all she felt rage, fractious and bucking against her professional restraint. Here was a mother who worried over her daughter at every turn, who even now, shot and bleeding, was trying with her last ounce of strength to get to her daughter, to get her out of the house, away from harm.

Stowing her feelings, Josie said, "We'll get Alison. Your job is to stay here and stay still. We're going to get you both out of here as soon as possible."

"Wa—wait," Marlene croaked.

It tore Josie's heart out to leave her there, but their training dictated that they neutralize the threat before they tended to the wounded. Standing and stepping over more debris, Josie made her way to the basement door. Noah followed her lead, moving along with her. She readied herself to go first. He pulled the door open, and Josie stepped through, onto a small landing. At the bottom of a small staircase hung a single dull yellow light bulb.

Beyond it was only darkness and two killers.

CHAPTER 43

Josie's heart squeezed in her chest. When Noah closed the door behind them, her breath came faster. She tried to will her body to calm down. They were at a tactical disadvantage, having no idea how the basement was laid out or what was in it. Their feet would be visible before they made it to the bottom. Josie drew in a deep breath as she stepped down the wooden staircase and sent up a prayer to anyone who would listen that the men weren't right near the base of the steps watching the two of them descend.

Even though Noah's descent was silent, she could sense him just a few steps behind her. From below came more sounds of items being dropped, dragged, and thrown. Taking another step down, she heard muffled voices and tried to gauge how far away the men were from the steps. The next step creaked loudly and Josie froze, holding her breath. Noah, on the one above her, went still. Relief flooded her when the sounds continued unabated and she realized the men were still fully engaged in their search. Part of her wanted to plunge down the rest of the staircase and get it over with, but she held fast.

Please don't creak, she begged with each step.

Almost to the bottom, the basement came into full view. Most of it was lit by only the small hanging bulb. In a far-off corner was a fluorescent light that blinked on and off rapidly, on its last legs. The floor was concrete. Boxes and plastic bins were stacked all around, forming a maze. Some stacks were at eye-level. Others at waist-level. A row of shelves along one wall held more bins marked in a hand-written scrawl that Josie couldn't make out from where she stood. The dome of a man's bald head gleamed in the shuddering light of the fluorescent tube. Over the pounding of her heart, she heard him speaking to another man although she could not see him.

"It's not down here."

"She said it was. She said the red bin. Fifth row from the back. That's the back, right? One, two, three, four, five. It should be right here, somewhere."

Josie took one hand off her pistol grip and signaled to Noah. He looked in the direction of the men and then nodded. He saw what she saw.

"I don't even see any damn red bins. She lied. Why did you shoot her? We should have made her come down here with us and show us. This is going to take all night."

"I'll shoot her again. Maybe it will draw the kid out."

"She said the kid's not here."

A dry laugh. "You believe anything she said? She probably sent us down here to look for it so the kid can get away. I got an idea. We go back up and make it known we're gonna shoot her again if that kid doesn't come out."

Josie reached the bottom step. It creaked under her foot.

"Shhh—did you hear that?"

"Hear what? It's probably that bitch upstairs trying to get up. Come on, we'll take care of her."

Josie kept going, feet now firmly on the concrete. Noah followed, skipping the final step so it didn't creak, and landing soundlessly beside her. The bald man's companion stepped from behind the boxes into the open, a shadow figure. "Hey!" he said.

Josie shouted, "Police. Put your hands up!"

The man raised his hand. The strobing of the fluorescent light backlit him. It was difficult to tell whether or not he had a gun in his hand. Until the concussive boom of a gunshot filled the cellar. Everything moved at warp speed. Beside her, Noah stumbled and fell, crumpling to the floor. Josie returned fire. Directly above them, the light bulb shattered, raining down glass on them. More booms. A bullet whizzed past her head, and she dropped down to her knees, firing more rounds. She aimed for the man's center mass but in the mayhem, her shots were off. She swore under her breath when the fluorescent light exploded, plunging them into darkness.

Josie's ears rang, the echo of the gunshots going off in an enclosed space blotting out all sound.

In the dark, the smell of cordite burned Josie's nostrils. She was aware that she was breathing rapidly. She willed herself to stay calm, to focus, but it wasn't easy. She had never done well in dark, enclosed spaces. Not since she was a child and the woman claiming to be her mother regularly locked her in a stinking hole of a closet, sometimes for days on end.

Chest tight, her breath came in short gasps.

Josie swore she could smell cigarettes and the stale scent of the scratchy, threadbare carpet she'd spent her most terrifying hours crying into. In her chest there was a thundering so powerful she worried it might lift her off the ground.

It's not real, she reminded herself.

"Josie," Noah said, jerking her back to reality. His voice somehow pierced the ringing in her ears, muffled and weak.

She kept her pistol pointed toward where she had last seen the men but with her other hand she reached back, feeling for his body. Her fingers brushed something. Her mouth formed words although she couldn't hear herself speak. "Jesus, Noah. Are you okay?"

She thought she heard him say, "Took one to the vest."

Josie moved her hand away from him and brought it back to the pistol. She staggered upright and aimed straight ahead into the blackness. The wheeze was still there. A tremble worked its way up her legs. Beside her, she sensed Noah moving, climbing to his feet. He clamped a hand down on her shoulder. His touch felt like a shot of Wild Turkey. Warm and calming.

Noah's instructions seemed to come from very far away. "Get your flashlight out."

The present moment slammed back into focus. She found the pocket on her tactical vest that held her flashlight and unsheathed it. Positioning it out and up away from her body, she flicked it on, its cone of light illuminating part of the basement in front of her. Next to her, Noah did the same.

Ahead, boxes toppled and crashed. Josie's paralysis broke and she started across the cellar, her flashlight sweeping in tandem with Noah's.

"Denton Police," she called out. "Come out and put your hands up."

The circle of light brushed across a man's crumpled form. Face down, dark hair, black clothes. A .38 caliber pistol loose in his right hand. Josie kicked it away from his body and leaned down, pressing two fingers against his throat. She felt a thready pulse. She looked to Noah to make sure he was keeping his focus on the darkness ahead, and then she quickly zip-tied the man's hands together. As long as he was alive, he could still pose a threat, especially since they didn't know the full extent of his injuries. Once he was secured, she stepped past him, continuing their search for the bald man. As they moved deeper into the basement, more boxes and bins shifted, some falling over. Using their torches, Josie and Noah followed the movement. Where was the man going? Was he circling back to the steps?

They moved through the maze of bins and boxes, approaching the corridors the same way they would any hallway in a house, continuing to move toward any movement the remaining intruder inadvertently made.

Josie's hearing still had not returned to normal, but she heard Noah beside her. "There's nowhere for you to go. Just come out into the open with your hands up."

Seconds later, a wall of boxes to their right crashed down on them. Josie fell onto her back, her flashlight tumbling out of her hand and away from her. She managed to keep a grip on her pistol. Noah half fell on top of her, blocking her from the impact of most of the boxes. She felt his breath against her neck, the weight of him across her, boxes pinning them both to the floor.

"Noah," she said.

He struggled to roll off her, bucking the boxes off, grunting in pain. Josie didn't know where his flashlight had gone. The only light now in the entire basement was from her flashlight which had rolled away from her, somewhere among the mess of boxes, bins, and their spilled contents. It didn't give off much illumination.

But enough for Josie to see the hulking silhouette of a man approaching. The deep shadows made it impossible to tell just how close he was, but her skin went cold with the knowledge that she and Noah were both flat on their backs, sandwiched among fallen bins and boxes, the light enabling him to see them probably better than they could see him.

"Stop!" she ordered, swinging her pistol upward toward his center mass.

Noah was on his knees, turning toward the man, pistol aimed at him. "Stop right there," he said.

Josie noticed the twitch of the man's shoulder too late. There was a muzzle flash, a deafening boom, and Noah fell again. Without hesitation, Josie fired off another shot. The shadow man ducked down and retreated. Josie stumbled to her feet and climbed over a small mountain of boxes and plastic bins. Corners of boxes poked her legs. The lids of plastic bins scraped against her. Her feet hit a patch of cleared concrete and she stopped, trying to listen over the sound of her labored breath. The light from her dropped torch didn't reach this part of the cellar.

Again, her mind snapped back to that time in her childhood when the dark was endless, and her only companion was unadulterated terror. Her throat began to close. She felt a wheeze in her lungs. She tried to talk over it, mumble-whispering, "It's not real."

Fighting her way through even more fallen bins, she tried to get her bearings, turning a full circle, pistol held outward. She could make out the vague shape of the basement steps from the weak light of the flashlight she'd dropped. Had he gone back upstairs? Without thought, her body moved in that direction, like a moth to light. She was almost there when a scream ripped through the air, reverberating through the entire house. Josie swore she felt its vibration in her bones.

Alison.

"Mom! Oh my God, Mom!"

Josie's feet moved faster, toward the sound. In spite of Josie's instructions, Alison had not stayed put. Her screams were coming from the kitchen overhead. As Josie neared the bottom of the steps, a hulking shape resolved. The second man. He was just a wall of shadow, and from the sound of wood creaking, he was starting up the steps.

"Stop!" Josie yelled.

He swung his gun wildly in her direction, firing a shot wide of her and then kept going, climbing the stairs in a jog, his feet thudding against the wood, each step protesting under his weight. Josie charged after him, scrambling up the steps at his heels. Her mind made several split-second calculations. He had a gun. He had already fired on both Josie and Noah more than once. He was clearly a danger and within seconds, he would be in the same room as Alison and Marlene. Aiming at his center mass, her finger depressed the trigger. Dry click.

She had used up all the rounds in her magazine. She had another in her vest but in the time it would take to get it out and load it into her gun, the man could be in the room with Alison and Marlene. Josie couldn't risk it. She holstered her pistol and surged upward, using both hands to grab for some part of him. She snagged what felt like his ankle as he reached the landing and swung the door open into the kitchen. Light blinded her momentarily, but she held tightly to his leg and yanked as hard as she could, sending him flat on his face. Alison's screams intensified. Josie clambered into the kitchen after him, hoping to subdue him while he was on his stomach, but he was too fast. He rolled onto his back and pointed his gun directly at her face. Without thought, Josie swung a roundhouse kick at his wrists, knocking the gun away from him. Another shot rang out, again wide of her. Josie jumped on top of him, straddling him and attempting to restrain him, but he was massive. With an arm easily the size of a small tree trunk, he batted her aside, knocking a meaty fist into her temple.

Josie had no time to register the pain. She landed on her side, something sharp poking into her shoulder. The man started to stand up. Josie followed, her feet slipping and sliding in something powdery—flour, maybe? As he rose, the man's eyes searched the kitchen, looking for his gun, no doubt. Before he could get fully to his feet, Alison stepped over her mother's body and picked something up from the mess on the floor. Josie opened her mouth to tell Alison to fall back but it was too late. The girl's hands were wrapped tightly around the handle of a large frying pan, choking up like she was batting in a major league baseball game. She swung so hard at the man's head, her entire body spun.

The sound of metal against bone stopped Josie in her tracks. Stunned, the man froze as well, swaying on his feet. He stared down at Alison for what felt like a full minute, although in reality it was only a few seconds. His large hand reached up to touch the blood pouring from a laceration over his ear.

Josie tackled him from the side, her head tucked under his armpit, arms trying to wrap around his thick waist. Together they flew into the countertop next to the back door. His hip cracked against the edge of the counter, and he grunted. Josie clung to him like a barnacle, staying close to his body, moving around behind him and trying to bring his arms behind his back, but he stood up straight and flexed his shoulders, one arm swatting her away from him like she was a gnat. She was on her back again, half her body landing on a large toaster. Ignoring the pain, she picked it up as she scrabbled back to her feet, aiming it at his head.

Their eyes met for a fraction of a second.

He turned toward the back door, hands fumbling at the doorknob. Josie leaped at him, toaster in one hand like she was about to dunk on a basketball net. The toaster glanced off the uninjured side of his head. With all her weight behind it, Josie crashed into him, knocking him off balance. One of his elbows smashed into the glass in the upper half of the back door, shattering it. Again, Josie tried to hang onto him, grabbing onto one of his shoulders. His shirt was wet with the blood that dripped from the wound Alison had given him. Josie's hand slid off, slick, and again, he flicked her away. Before she could get back to her feet again, he was through the back door.

With one last glance at Alison, now kneeling over Marlene's prone body, Josie went after him, plunging into the night.

CHAPTER 44

As Josie sprinted into the woods behind the Mills' house, she used her radio to call in all the information she could: the house was secure. Marlene Mills had been shot and needed immediate medical attention. One intruder down. Noah down. Panic clenched her stomach as her mouth formed the words. She didn't know if he was dead or grievously injured or if he'd sustained some minor injury that had slowed him down. She knew he'd taken at least one round to the vest upon entering the basement, possibly two. He very likely had a broken rib. She hoped that was all. Tears pricked her eyes as she thought about it. She had wanted nothing more than to stop and check on Noah, make sure he was breathing, render any aid necessary, but Josie had a job to do, and they would not have been safe with the other intruder in the cellar with them.

She steadied her voice as she called in the last bit of information. She was in pursuit of the second intruder.

Dispatch promised units to follow. Using her mental map of the area, Josie requested additional units on the other side of the wooded area. There was a road there. She

rattled off the name of it. By feel, she found another magazine in her vest and reloaded her pistol. Then she used the
flashlight app on her phone to light her way, holding her
pistol at the ready. Branches snatched at her arms and legs.
Even with the light from her phone, twice she tripped over
something. First, a rock. Then a tree root. She kept going,
marching forward through the trees, trying to keep her mind
on the task at hand and not on Noah.

But he kept climbing inside her head. Her mind kept
replaying everything that had unfolded in the basement,
again and again.

Voices sounded from ahead and Josie ran toward them.
Their flashlights announced them as Denton Police officers.
"Over here," Josie called. "It's Detective Quinn!"

Zigzagging around a few maple trees, she found two
uniformed officers, Brennan and Daugherty.

"Hey," Brennan said. "You got us back out in these
woods."

"You're going the wrong way," said Josie.

The two looked at one another. Daugherty said, "No,
we're not. We were following you."

Josie looked behind her even though all she could see
was blackness. "You came from the house? The Mills
house?"

Brennan hooked a thumb over his shoulder. "Yeah, it's
right there. About thirty paces, and you'll see the lights from
the kitchen. What happened? You didn't find him?"

"No," Josie said. "I—I got... turned around."

Daugherty must have seen something in her face. "It's
fine. Really. It's dark, and these forested areas, they can be
really tough to navigate at night."

Not for me, Josie almost blurted out. Her focus had

split. Her mind was with her husband even while her body chased after a killer.

Brennan said, "We've got units coming at him from the other side, too. Searching for a dark-colored SUV on the road where these woods come out. We'll get him, I'm sure."

Josie swallowed over a growing lump in her throat. "Is— is Lieutenant Fraley—"

She couldn't bring herself to finish the question.

Daugherty said, "Last I saw him, he was in the kitchen, tending to Mrs. Mills."

Brennan added, "Looks like she took two GSWs to the abdomen. He was trying to keep pressure until the EMTs could move her."

Josie swayed on her feet, her relief so profound that it loosened every muscle in her body.

"Thank you," she muttered.

The two men started walking into the forest. Over his shoulder, Daugherty said, "The kid's still in there, though. Said she wasn't going anywhere without you."

CHAPTER 45

A buzz of energy spread through Denton Memorial's emergency department. Josie sensed it the moment she walked through the double doors of its main entrance with Alison clinging to her side. The security guard, who was usually seated calmly behind the desk, stood at the door to the triage area, one hand on his radio, his chin canted to the side slightly, as if he was ready to bark instructions into it at any second. When he spotted Josie and Alison, he waved them over. Once he and the triage nurse were satisfied that neither Josie nor Alison needed care, they let them into the back.

Josie heard the sounds of doctors and nurses desperately trying to save the lives of Marlene Mills and the intruder Josie had shot before the two trauma rooms came into view. These rooms were larger than the curtained cubicles, with glass walls and far more equipment. In one, the man lay on a gurney, perfectly still. The tattered sides of his shirt hung loose where the medical team had cut it open. A nurse held two panels of an emergency defibrillator in her hands and hollered, "Clear!"

Everyone around the bed stopped what they were doing, lifted their hands up, as if in surrender, and stepped away. The nurse shocked the man. His chest jumped and one of his arms slid off the edge of the bed, dangling. Josie noticed a tattoo on his forearm—a snake twisted into an odd shape, its red tongue flicking outward. It took Josie a second to process the shape. Was it an oval? A box? A square? Rectangle? Or maybe, she thought, peering more closely at it while the nurse shocked the man once more, the letter D?

Pressed against Josie's side, Alison made a tortured squeaking noise. Turning her attention to the second trauma room, Josie first saw blood everywhere—splattered across the floor, soaking discarded pads, drenching crumpled linens. Next she saw Marlene Mills being wheeled out on a stretcher. Her pale face was slack, eyes closed. A doctor and three nurses ran alongside the stretcher, propelling it toward a set of open elevator doors at the end of the hallway. She was being rushed into surgery.

Josie had a sudden flashback of standing in this spot a year and a half ago, watching the medical team work on her grandmother—who had also had a gunshot wound—before rushing her to surgery as well. A surgery that ultimately had not saved her life. Josie gripped Alison's arms and turned her away. "You shouldn't see this."

Alison craned her neck over Josie's shoulder, twisting away from her, trying to see. "But that's my mom! Is she dead? I need to know what's happening!"

"You will," Josie said, pushing her into an empty curtained area and pulling the curtain shut behind them. She turned Alison to face her, gripping both her arms again and looking into her eyes. "If they're running like that, they're taking her to the OR. But trust me. You do not want to see that room."

Alison thrust her chin forward. With her bruised and battered face, defiance made her look like some kind of battle-scarred warrior rather than a terrified seventeen-year-old girl. "I've seen things like this before. I was in the accident with my dad and Uncle Billy. I watched them try to save my Uncle Billy. There was blood everywhere. I can take it, you know."

Josie felt everything in her soften. She squeezed Alison's shoulders and lowered her voice. "I know you can, Alison, but you shouldn't have to." *None of us should have to*, a voice in her brain added silently.

She guided Alison to a chair beside the empty gurney and then gestured for her to sit. Reluctantly, Alison did. Josie took in a deep breath. "Give them some time to work. There's nothing we can do right now except wait. Why don't you tell me what happened?"

Alison's upper body rocked back and forth. She wrapped her arms around her middle and glanced past Josie, as if she might be able to see Marlene. "We were just home. I talked to my dad on the phone. He was happy I was okay. He's still coming home, but now he's stuck in France trying to get a flight to Philadelphia or New York City on short notice. Anyway, my mom didn't want to go to a hotel because it would cost too much. She said that because this whole thing was on the news and so public, if there were men out there who thought I might have whatever it is everyone is looking for, they wouldn't come to our house. Too brazen, she said. Her friend Sadie came over for a while to see how we were. She tried to get us to stay with her, but Mom didn't want her involved. We had dinner with Sadie and then after she left, I went up to bed. My mom was downstairs. She fell asleep on the couch watching TV. I came down to get something to eat and woke her up, told her to go to bed. She said she would. I was going back up the steps when I heard all this noise. Like some kind of smashing—glass breaking, or something. I think it was coming from the back of the house. My mom jumped off the couch. She didn't actually speak. She just kind of looked at me and mouthed 'hide.' I went to the top of the steps. I listened. I know I was taking a risk of them coming up to find me, but I had to know what was happening. I needed to know because I knew I had to do something. Anything. I heard two male voices. They were telling her to sit down and shut up. She kept talking, though—you know how she is. Well, maybe you don't—"

Josie smiled. "I do."

"Right, so she wouldn't stop, and they were getting frustrated. She was saying, like, 'Don't hurt me. Just take whatever you want and go, but leave me alone.' They asked where I was, and she lied and said that I wasn't home. Then one of them said to the other that they didn't really need me, they could just search the house. My mom kept arguing, saying, like, she didn't have anything they could possibly want. It sounded like one of them might come up the steps —the floor in the living room near the landing creaked—and I ran. I went to my room and got my phone and then I thought, if they come up to search, the first place they'll look is my room! So I took the phone to the hall closet and I was going to call 911, but then I knew they'd hear me so I texted you. I had to do something. I had to try to save my mom. Maybe I should have just gone down there and talked to them. Maybe if I had, my mom would be okay. I mean, I keep thinking about Dina and how I left her behind and she's dead now."

Josie said, "Alison, that wasn't your fault."

Alison's body stopped rocking. She met Josie's eyes.

"But it was! I left her alone! I ran and ran and I didn't even go for help. I just ran and I hid like a coward."

"Alison—"

"But what if I *could* have saved her? Like, I'm not Supergirl or whatever, but I didn't even try. What if I could have stopped him or something? Or at least gone for help right away. Maybe then she would be alive. This is all my fault!"

As she spoke, her eyes grew glassy with moisture. A single tear fell from her right eye, spilling down her bruised cheek.

Josie moved over and perched on the edge of the empty gurney. She looked at the girl, so young, and saddled with something so heavy. Josie knew a thing or two about survivor's guilt. Over a year after Lisette's murder, she still replayed the scene, cataloguing all the things she could have done differently that might not have led to Lisette's death. No matter how many scenarios she concocted in which Lisette did not put herself in front of that shotgun to shield Josie from the blast, Lisette was still dead, and Josie was alive.

"Alison," said Josie. "Even if you had stayed, even if you'd tried to stop Elliott Calvert from attacking Dina, even if you had gone for help directly, Dina might still be dead."

Alison's eyes widened in surprise. "Is that supposed to make me feel better?"

Josie smiled wanly. "Do you think there is anything I can say to you—that anyone could say to you—that is going to make you feel better about Dina's death?"

Slowly, Alison shook her head.

"Sometimes," Josie said, "in the best-case scenario of a tragic event, the person you love still dies."

Alison stared at her for a long moment. Then, in a scratchy voice, she said, "Like with Uncle Billy."

It wasn't a question. Josie gave her a minute to think it through. She continued, "My dad said that in that accident, the response couldn't have been any better than it was—the 911 call went right through, my dad knew what to do to keep Uncle Billy alive until the ambulance arrived, I was there to help my dad so he didn't have to stop CPR to call 911, and they got there in under four minutes. They had all the equipment they needed to try to keep him alive, and they did. All the way to the hospital. Even then, there was a trauma surgeon at the hospital, ready and waiting for when the ambulance brought him in. He still died."

Josie nodded. "But I bet your dad still blames himself, doesn't he?"

"Yes, he does. He was still distracted while he was driving. That's how it happened in the first place. I still blame myself for Dina. Are you saying... are you saying this never goes away?"

"I don't know."

Alison considered this. "What if it doesn't? What if it never goes away?"

"You live with it," Josie said.

Alison lifted a hand and pressed it to her chest. "Live with it? That's it? That's your answer? What kind of adult are you, anyway?"

Josie said, "The kind who believes that lying to you and giving you some kind of bullshit platitude about death and grief and guilt is not going to serve you at all. It's never served me. The truth, Alison, is that these things you're feeling? They're here. They're tough. They can be crippling. But no matter how much pain you're in, how much guilt you feel, it changes nothing. Absolutely nothing. Not one tiny thing."

Alison stared at her, rapt, eyes wide.

Josie went on. "So why not look those feelings right in the face? Eyes wide open. Tell that overwhelming guilt and that pain, 'I see you.' Stop fighting it so hard. All of it. You can't change it. Life moves forward, and whether you like it or not, so do you. So yes, the pain? The guilt? You find ways to live with it. I don't know what those ways are for you, but I don't recommend drugs or alcohol."

Alison laughed. "Well, now you sound like a real adult."

Josie gave a dry chuckle. "Maybe one of those ways is that you react differently in future situations. Like with your mom."

Another tear streaked down Alison's face. "But I didn't do it differently with Mom. She's in there fighting for her life."

Josie said, "That's right. She's fighting for it, Alison. She has a chance because you got in touch with me right away. Because you hit that guy over the head with a frying pan when he came out of the basement. That was pretty badass, you know."

Alison blushed, a tiny smile flitting across her lips.

Josie continued, "What if you had waited to contact me? To call the police? Your mom could have bled out. What if you hadn't hit that guy? He could have hurt her even more—he could have hurt all of us."

Alison raised a brow. "I don't think so. You were like, feral with that guy. Tackling him... and what you did with that toaster. Then you just kept coming at him. You ran him right out of the kitchen."

"Because you helped me," Josie said. "You helped me

fight him off. Just like you helped your mom. Right now, she has a chance. You gave her that chance."

Sneakers squeaked over tiles. Voices drew closer. A male voice said, "We need a clean-up in Trauma One."

Josie pulled the curtain back and saw Dr. Ahmed Nashat, one of the ER doctors—the one who had worked on Josie's grandmother—standing outside of the empty trauma room.

"Detective Quinn," he said.

"The woman who was in that room, her name is Marlene Mills," Josie said, bobbing her head in Alison's direction. "Her mother."

Dr. Nashat smiled grimly at Alison. "Your mother is strong. She's holding on, but she needed surgery immediately. There were two bullets. One nicked her liver. The other damaged her small bowel. Those injuries need to be repaired. The trauma surgeon is with her now." He looked back at Josie. "Your other GSW was DOA. Dr. Feist will be up for him shortly. I imagine you'll have to conduct some sort of investigation."

"Thank you," said Josie. "Will you call me when you hear anything on Mrs. Mills?"

"Of course," he said before walking away.

Josie said, "Alison, you need to call your dad right away. He should know what's happening. We need to make arrangements for you to stay with someone. We'll need his input and his permission. For now, you'll stay with me. I've got to check on someone and then get back to the stationhouse for a little while."

Dr. Nashat left them standing outside the trauma rooms. Josie slipped into the first one and used her phone to take a quick photo of the man's unusual snake tattoo. Back in the hallway, Alison was still staring down the hall after Dr. Nashat. "GSW is DOA? What's that mean?"

"Gunshot wound—one of the men who attacked your mom was shot while trying to evade us. He was dead on arrival."

"What about the other guy?" Alison asked. "Did you guys get him?"

Josie looked at her phone, scrolling for any updates. There were none. "No," she said. "Not yet."

CHAPTER 46

Josie left Alison at the nurse's station under the watchful eye of the unit clerk with instructions to try to get in touch with her father. Then she found Noah resting comfortably on a gurney behind another curtain. The medical staff had given him a hospital gown, but he still wore his jeans and boots. The knees of his pants were stained dark with blood. It crusted along the soles of his boots. He smiled at her, lifting a hand. "Hey."

It took everything in her not to run across the room and leap onto the bed with him.

Instead, she walked over and perched on the side, staring at his face. He looked tired but alert, his hazel eyes twinkling. Tears stung the backs of her eyes. Her voice was husky when she said, "Don't 'hey' me. You got shot."

He lifted the gown, revealing two dark areas of bruising that had already started to spread, labyrinthine, along one side of his torso. "I took two in the vest."

"You got shot, Noah."

He tried to sit up but couldn't, instead hissing air between gritted teeth.

"How many broken ribs?" she asked.

He held up three fingers.

Josie stood up and moved closer, leaning into him until their foreheads touched. To her chagrin, some of the tears slipped down her cheeks. Gingerly, Noah reached up and snaked a hand around her neck. "I'm fine," he whispered. Tilting his chin upward, he brushed his lips over hers.

Her voice quaked. "You got shot."

"The vest saved me, Josie. I'm fine. I promised to always run toward the danger with you, remember?"

She sighed into his face, felt the pads of his thumbs brush her tears away. Another gasp of pain. "That was a really stupid vow," she said.

He started to laugh but then abruptly stopped. Taking another slow, careful breath, he said, "It was the only one that made sense."

They kissed softly and Josie stepped back. "Will they keep you?"

He shook his head. That small interaction had caused him quite a bit of pain. Josie could tell by the pallor taking over his face. "I'll call Drake and Trinity," she said. "To come get you. I've got to get Alison settled somewhere."

"Go ahead," Noah said. "I'll see you at home."

At the nurse's station, Alison was leaving a voicemail for her father. Josie texted Trinity while she waited for Alison to finish. Her sister readily agreed to come get Noah and provide any care he needed at home. Once Alison was through leaving a rambling, teary message for her father, Josie drove them to Denton's police headquarters. The municipal lot was almost completely empty, which was no surprise, since most units were either at the Mills scene processing and canvassing, hunting for the other intruder, or searching the city for the dark-colored SUV that he had likely gotten away in. Josie parked in the spot closest to the door. Clint Mills called Alison's phone just as Josie put the gearshift into park.

"It's my dad!" Alison said with one part nervousness, one part excitement.

The moment she heard his voice, she broke down. Josie was grateful they were still in the car. Sobs wracked the girl's body. The phone tumbled from her grip. Leaning over, Josie fished it from the floor between Alison's feet and pressed it to her ear. "Mr. Mills?"

His voice shook. "Who—who is this and what's going on? Is something wrong? Where's Marlene? Is my daughter okay?"

Josie identified herself and as clearly and calmly as possible, explained the situation to him. A rustling sound came from the receiver. Josie heard the sound of muffled crying and she waited patiently, keeping the phone pressed to her ear with one hand while she stroked Alison's back with the other. Clint Mills calmed down before his daughter. There was more rustling, then a loud sniffle, and finally, he said, "I'm sorry. I just needed a minute. I'm trying to get back to them as fast as I can. I—oh my God. Alison. What is she going to do? She can't go back to the house. You can't send her back there. Where is she? Where are you?"

Josie said, "We're at the police station and Alison will stay with me until we can figure out suitable arrangements."

"Suitable arrangements? Oh, you need a place for her to stay until I get back."

"I need her to be safe, but yes, she needs a place to stay. She's exhausted. Is there anyone here we can call?"

"My wife's best friend. Sadie."

Alison sat up straight and said, "Mom didn't want to get her involved."

In Josie's ear, Clint scoffed. "Please. Those two are as thick as thieves. Tell Alison I'll call her, okay? I'll call her right now. If Sadie doesn't think she's safe, then I'll pay for them to stay somewhere else. A hotel or someplace. I'll tell Sadie to just come to the police station and get her, okay?"

"That would be fine," said Josie.

"Can you put my daughter back on?"

Josie handed the phone back and waited for the conversation to conclude. Alison seemed much calmer when she hung up. Wiping her nose with the sleeve of her sweatshirt, she said, "We should have just gone to Sadie's in the first place."

Josie said, "Come on. We'll go inside and wait for her there. I've got some calls to make."

Ten minutes later, Alison was seated at the conference room table, her cheek resting on her folded arms. Within moments, her eyes drifted closed. Her nose whistled with each breath. After dimming the lights, Josie left her there and went down the hall, letting their desk sergeant, Dan Lamay, know that Alison was dozing in the conference room and she was going up to the second floor to make some calls.

"If she comes out looking for me," Josie told him. "Send her up."

"You got it, boss," he said.

Upstairs, Josie plopped down at her desk. She pulled up the photo she had taken of the dead intruder's tattoo and studied it. There was little doubt in her mind that the men who had invaded the Mills' home and shot Marlene were also the men who tortured Dina Hale and who were seen near Max Combs's house before and after his murder. Josie was convinced that they were affiliated with some sort of gang or more likely, some arm of the mafia. Everything about them—their looks, their presence, the things they'd done—smacked of organized crime. The question was, who did they work for?

Josie hoped once the scene and the man's body had been processed, they might find an ID or a phone that would give them at least some of that information, but for now, all she had was a tattoo. It might not tell her who he was but it was possible it might reveal his employer. Unfortunately, there wasn't a database she could just run the photo through. The Commonwealth of Pennsylvania tracked tattoos via their prison database and some county prisons took photos of tattoos when they booked prisoners, but both of those limited databases required more information than simply a photo of a tattoo. The state prison database, for example, would only be useful if the owner of the tattoo was currently an inmate. Since their John Doe was on a slab in the morgue, that wasn't going to help. For years now, the FBI had been trying to develop a national database where law enforcement could search tattoos using photographs, but it wasn't in service yet, which left Josie with few options.

There was, of course, one resource she could use, unofficially.

She tapped out a text to Drake.

You've worked some gang cases, right? Cases involving the mafia?

His reply came back a moment later.

Very limited but yes. What've you got?

She sent him the photo.

Trying to figure out if this means anything or if the guy who had it just liked weirdly positioned snakes.

Another minute ticked past. Then came Drake's reply.

I can ask around for you. Unofficially.

Thanks, Josie typed.

She closed out her text messages and called the hospital. Marlene was still in surgery. There was no news. Her next call was to Noah. He was home, propped up in their bed with Trout at his side, and a lot of pain medication on board. They talked for several minutes until he started to sound drowsy. She hung up and called Gretchen who reported that the Mills' house was still being processed and that neither the second intruder nor the dark-colored SUV had been located but that the Chief had authorized the search to continue throughout the night.

"Gretchen, we know these guys have been driving around Denton in this SUV wreaking havoc for at least a week. When they kidnapped Dina, they didn't take her to a building. They parked in a secluded outdoor area."

"Which means they don't have a base of operations here," Gretchen supplied.

"Right. What if they're not from here? What if they're from out of town?"

"You think they're staying at a hotel? Here in the city?" Gretchen asked.

"I don't know. Maybe outside of the city. We should send units to all the local hotels to ask about the men and the SUV. Did you get anything on the guy in the morgue?"

"No ID. A phone, but it's a burner and he's only called

one other number. We tried it but it says it's no longer in service."

"It's probably the other guy's," said Josie. "He's likely dumped it now."

"Yep," Gretchen said. "I'm sure he has. Look, I'll get units out to local hotels, okay? See if we can kick up any leads that way."

Josie thanked her and hung up. She stood and stretched, only now registering the various pains in her body. Lower back, shoulder, legs, hip. She riffled through one of her desk drawers until she came up with a half-filled bottle of ibuprofen. She swallowed two pills dry and went back downstairs. The conference room door was closed. She looked up and down the hall. The inside of the building was just as dead as the outside, with all available units still out searching for the second intruder. Josie turned the doorknob and pushed but the door wouldn't open all the way. Only a sliver of the room was visible. Josie peered through the crack in the door. "Alison?" she called.

All she could see was one half of the long table. All the chairs were in place but one. The one closest to the door. The one wedged beneath the door handle, she realized.

"Alison!"

Josie heard a gasp, then a strangled cry, grunting, and finally, a loud bang. Her heart thundered into overdrive. It took a split second for her to turn her head and gauge the distance from the door to the lobby and back. Was it worth the lost seconds to enlist Sergeant Lamay for help? Josie shouted his name as loudly as she could and then she stepped back and threw her body at the door. It shuddered in its frame but didn't swing open.

Alison's voice became audible. "Hel—" and was cut off abruptly.

As Josie stepped back again, she heard the sounds of chairs toppling on the other side of the door. She brought her booted foot up and kicked hard against the door, focusing her force just to the side of the door handle.

"Police!" she shouted. "Open the door!"

Again, the door juddered but didn't open. Josie kept kicking, screaming all the while, alternating between calling for Sergeant Lamay and telling whoever was on the other side of the door to open up.

"Boss?" Dan came running down the hall as quickly as he could, which wasn't that fast given his age and bum knee.

At that moment, Josie's kicks dislodged the chair on the other side and the door opened a couple of feet. She muscled her way through it. In the half of the room she hadn't been able to see, chairs were upended and a dark-haired man loomed over Alison, pinning her to the wall. Both his hands were wrapped around her throat. Alison's feet dangled beneath her, flailing, trying to kick him, but he was too tall. He angled his lower body away from her even as he held her in place. Her fingers curled over his hands, trying to drag them away from her neck. Her eyes bulged.

"Where is it?" the man snarled.

It took only a second for Josie to register the scene. Behind her, Dan barked orders at the man. For Josie, time slowed. Her brain registered the maze of overturned chairs and sent her body up onto the table. Her feet scrambled over its glossy surface. She flew toward him, hammering an elbow into his side, under his raised arms. His ribs gave a satisfying crack. Stunned, he floundered, his grip on Alison broken, and staggered backward. Josie snagged one of his wrists and spun him toward the table. Her other hand found the back of his head, pressing his face onto its surface. He cried out as she yanked his arms behind his back, pinning his wrists in place. She held him there until Dan made it through the tangle of chairs and cuffed him.

"You're under arrest," said Dan.

Josie turned toward Alison, who had slid to the floor, both hands rubbing her throat. When she took her hands away, Josie could see angry red marks. Josie knelt in front of her. "Are you okay?"

Alison nodded. "I'm, I'm—oh. I... hurts to talk."

"Then don't," said Josie. "We'll get you back to the hospital and have them examine you. Can you stand up?"

Alison nodded again and stumbled to her feet, grabbing onto Josie's arms for support. Her eyes searched over Josie's shoulder for the man. Now that Alison was safe, Josie took a moment to get a good look at Alison's attacker. The first thing she noticed was the full head of hair. Not the fugitive home invader then.

"Let's go," Dan said, pulling the man upright.

"Oh shit," said Josie under her breath.

Alison squeezed her arm. "What is it?" she croaked.

Dan pushed the man around to the other side of the table to avoid coming close to them as they walked out. Josie waited until they were out of the room, and she could hear their footsteps recede down the hall before she said, "That's Pierce Fuller. He's a city council member."

CHAPTER 47

Josie dozed in the vinyl chair next to Alison's bed in the emergency department. One of the nurses had turned off the lights directly overhead and pulled the curtain so that they could have some peace. The sounds of the busy ER still reached them: nurses and doctors shouting instructions to one another; patients clamoring for help or more medication or just because they were in pain; the shrill beeps and shrieks of empty IV machines, call bells, and vital signs gone awry. In spite of all the noise, Alison had fallen asleep almost instantly. Josie fought it, closing her eyes but promising herself she wouldn't drift into a deep sleep.

The curtain rustled, and from her half-sleep, Josie jumped out of the chair, ready for a fight. But then a short, stout woman stepped through, clutching her purse to her side, her face drawn with worry.

"Sadie," Josie said.

Sadie looked at Alison and kept her voice to a whisper. "Is she okay? I went to the police station after my shift, like Clint asked me to, but they said something happened and she was here. I was so worried. And Marlene! Clint told me about her. Have you heard anything?"

Josie motioned for her to take the chair she herself had just vacated. Sadie sat down but kept her eyes on Alison.

"Marlene is out of surgery. It went well, they say, but she's still in a critical condition and she'll be in the ICU for at least the next day or two. She's not out of the woods yet. Alison's injuries are not serious, just bruising."

Sadie reached over and touched Alison's hand. Even in her sleep, she flinched and pulled back. Sadie looked crestfallen.

"She's been through a lot in the last few days," Josie said. "She's going to be on edge for a while."

"Of course," said Sadie. "Will they discharge her tonight?"

"Yes," Josie said. "They should have the paperwork any minute."

The curtain rippled and slid open. Chief Chitwood stood before them, bathed in the harsh fluorescent lights of the hall. "Quinn," he said. "I came as soon as I could. Sergeant Lamay told me everything." He looked over, noting Sadie's presence and clamping his mouth shut.

Josie made the introductions. Sadie said, "I've just come to take her home. Or maybe we should go to a hotel."

"I'm glad you're here, Mrs. Bacarra," said the Chief. "It's admirable that you'd take Alison in after everything that's happened, but I think for your safety and hers, we'd like to bring Alison into protective custody, especially given what happened tonight."

Sadie stood up, her fingers twining in the straps of her purse. "Protective custody? What? Like the witness protection program?"

The Chief smiled. "No, nothing like that. I just want

Alison to have the benefit of a police presence for the time being. I'd also like to ensure that you and your family are not put at risk. Just until we get a handle on this case."

Sadie looked at Alison and back at the Chief. "I promised her father."

"I think her father would agree that keeping you both safe is the best course of action." He pressed a business card into her hand. "You can call me anytime if you have questions or concerns, but what I'd like you to do now is go home. Make sure you lock your house up real good, and you call 911 if you have even the slightest notion that something's off. Okay?"

Sadie looked at the card, at Alison and then at the Chief again. "You think I'm in danger?"

"No," said the Chief. "But Alison is and we don't want you to be put at risk by association. Like I said, just until we put this case to rest."

"Where will you take her?" Sadie asked.

The Chief smiled, walked over and put a hand at her elbow, guiding her out of the curtained area. "Just you let us worry about that, okay? We'll be in close touch with her father."

Josie watched the Chief walk Sadie to the exit. When he returned, she said, "Protective custody?"

The Chief beckoned her out into the hall, out of earshot of Alison even though Josie could tell by the wheezing noise of her nose that she was deeply asleep. "A sitting city councilman came into our department and tried to kill a seventeen-year-old kid. Quinn, until we figure out exactly what the hell is going on in this town, Alison Mills doesn't leave our sight. You got that?"

Josie nodded. With one hand, she smoothed down the back of her hair. "How do you want to do this?"

"You two stay at my place for now."

"Chief," Josie said.

"Daisy's already at Gretchen's. Paula's there with her. Noah told me you two have guests who will take good care of him. Besides, I'm the Chief. All of you are my responsibility. You bring her to my place. At least for tonight. We'll see what tomorrow brings."

"Not a hotel?" asked Josie.

He shook his head. "Too risky. Too visible. Too many people who can be persuaded to give away a room number for a few bucks. I don't know what the hell is going on here with architects and city councilmen attacking kids and mob guys going around town shooting people, but we need to keep this kid alive. You with me on this, Quinn?"

Josie was too exhausted to think of anything but a soft bed and a few hours of sleep. The Chief's house was remote and on several acres of old farmland. She felt confident that Alison would be safe there for the next several hours. "Yeah," she said. "I'm with you."

CHAPTER 48

She is almost fifteen when her father shows his true colors. It is the garage again. This time she is looking for empty plastic soda bottles for a school project. The recycling bin will have plenty. It is mid-afternoon on a weekday. Her school dismissed early due to a bomb threat that turned out to be nothing more than rumors. All of her friends went out to lunch, but Pea is home. She hasn't felt like doing much of anything since The Day Her World Shattered. Her father is up her ass about school on a daily basis though, so she decides to get an early start on her project.

This time, it's not a gaggle of men that she sees. Instead it is only her father. He stands over his handiwork, chest heaving, a look of bloodlust and absolute satiation on his face that sends Pea's stomach plummeting.

Before she can turn away, he sees her. He smiles.

A voice in her mind tells her to run but where would she go? This is it. This is what she has in life. This is her life. She can run, but this man will always be her father.

She hears something dripping, sees her father turn toward her, hands at his sides. He says, "I had to, Pea."

She wants to tear her eyes from the carnage before her, but she can't. From the recesses of her mind, Mug's words return. *Sweetheart, no one wants to fight, but sometimes you have to handle your business.*

Did she always know? Did a muted part of her psyche always know that her father was a monster? Or was she just a dumb kid living a fantasy life under the watchful eyes of her mother and Mug?

"Pea," her father says. His voice is husky but not with sadness or regret or any human emotion that Pea would understand in this moment. No, this is exhilaration and it makes her want to vomit.

He steps closer. "My princess."

"Don't." Her voice squeaks out, clawing past the lump in her throat. "Stay away from me. Don't come near me. Not ever again."

CHAPTER 49

A light touch across her cheek brought Josie out of sleep. Familiar fingers smoothed the hair away from her skin. She floated back up to consciousness, her entire body filling with warmth at Noah's touch. A smile spread across her face before she even opened her eyes. When she did, he was there, face hovering above hers, concern in his hazel eyes. "Hey," he whispered.

Josie sat up and looked around at unfamiliar surroundings, the night before rushing back at her like a slap. Alison and Marlene Mills. The home invasion. Marlene's injuries. Alison being attacked by Pierce Fuller, a city council member. The Chief insisting that they stay with him for the night. Alison had barely been conscious when Josie and the Chief herded her out of the hospital and into the Chief's car. She hadn't asked any questions, and once they got to his house and he showed her the bed she could sleep in, she had collapsed face down. Within seconds, her nose was whistling with each breath. Josie had insisted on sleeping in the same room with her.

"In our sight at all times means just that," she had told the Chief.

He had promptly provided her with a camping cot, blanket and pillow. Under normal circumstances, she wouldn't have found it at all comfortable, but nothing about the last day—or this bizarre case—had been normal. Josie was too tired to register any discomfort. She turned her head and saw that Alison's bed was empty. "Where is she?"

Noah shifted from kneeling on the floor to a seated position beside her on the narrow cot. He moved stiffly, still grimacing with pain. "She's downstairs with the Chief. He made her something to eat."

"He cooks?"

Noah smiled uncertainly. "I'm not sure I would call it cooking but Alison doesn't seem to care."

"What are you doing here?" Josie asked. "You should be home, resting. You must be in pain."

"It's not that bad," he assured her. "I wanted to see you."

Josie leaned forward and kissed him. "I'm glad you're here. Has there been any news? Did they get the other guy? What about the SUV?"

"We found the SUV abandoned near the interstate. It's a rental. Gretchen's trying to run down the details of who rented it and when. Gretchen said no leads turned up at any of the hotels, but she's pretty sure someone is lying. Probably someone at one of the seedier hotels—or motels—where it's cash only, no questions asked."

"Yeah," Josie said. "That makes sense."

"No sign of the guy, although we caught the SUV on a few traffic cameras and we think you were right—they parked on the road behind the Mills property and trekked through the woods to the house."

"Which means he found his way back to the SUV after

he fled into the woods. If I hadn't lost his trail, gotten disoriented, we could have him in custody."

"Josie," Noah said.

Before he could say anything else, Josie asked, "What about the guy who was killed? Still no ID on him?"

Noah shook his head. "No."

"What about Pierce Fuller?" Josie asked.

Noah looked away. Josie could tell by his body language, rigid though it was, that she wasn't going to like what he was about to say. "He lawyered up about five seconds after he was put into holding. You broke one of his ribs, so he had to be taken to the hospital for care. Lawyer met him there. He was treated and released into the custody of the Alcott County sheriff for processing."

Although Denton Police had their own holding cells, anyone who was charged with something went to the county sheriff's much larger and better-equipped holding facility where they were processed and held for arraignment.

"He's already out, isn't he?" Josie said, heart sinking.

"I'm afraid so."

"He tried to kill a seventeen-year-old girl. A defenseless girl. In a police station. What is more brazen and out of control than that? How could a judge allow it?"

Noah sighed. "You know how these things work, Josie. He's a city councilman. A fine, upstanding citizen with no prior history of violence or a criminal record. Not so much as a parking ticket." His words dripped with sarcasm, and she knew he was quoting Pierce Fuller's attorney. "He's a devoted husband with deep ties to the community. Not a flight risk at all. The judge gave him bail and his wife posted it."

Josie stood up and smoothed down her polo shirt and

jeans from the night before. Powder and what looked like oatmeal from the Mills' kitchen still clung to her pantlegs. "Unbelievable. Not even an ankle bracelet to ensure he doesn't come near Alison again?"

"I'm afraid not."

Josie thought about how this would make Alison feel— knowing this man was still out there, free, after he had walked into a police station and tried to kill her. She thought about Alison's parents and how they would feel. "What about Marlene Mills?" Josie asked. "Has there been any news?"

"She's still in the ICU. There's been no change. The Chief talked with Clint Mills. He's still in France. He said we should do whatever it takes to keep Alison safe until he gets home. Although honestly, I don't know much about Clint Mills but I'm not sure he's a match for whatever the hell is going on in this city."

The sound of tires over gravel sent Josie to the window. Pushing the curtain aside, she was relieved to see Trinity's tiny red Fiat Spider bouncing the length of Chief Chit-wood's driveway. It stopped next to Noah's car. The driver's side door opened, and Drake unfolded himself from the vehicle.

"Drake's here," Josie said.

Noah went to the door and picked up an overnight bag. Holding it out to her, he said, "Why don't you get changed? Brush your teeth. I'll see you downstairs."

Josie hadn't realized how much of a train wreck she was until she got into the Chief's bathroom and saw herself in the mirror. One side of her hair was matted to her head. The other side stuck up in some shape she couldn't discern. She did her best to freshen up, dragging a brush through her uncooperative hair, washing her face and hands, brushing her teeth and changing into fresh clothes before heading downstairs.

Alison was at the kitchen table with the Chief, shoveling food into her mouth. A large platter of scrambled eggs and bacon sat in the center of the table. Across from Alison, the Chief had only a half-empty coffee mug in front of him. Noah and Drake remained standing, each of them leaning against a part of the countertop that formed an L around the room.

The Chief gestured for Josie to sit. "Have something to eat," he told her.

She didn't think she was hungry, but the smell of food sent her appetite into overdrive. She knew where the Chief kept all of his dishes after having helped him recover from an injury several months ago, so she found a plate and fork and joined him and Alison at the table. Between bites of scrambled egg, she said to Drake, "Did you find anything on that tattoo?"

He folded his long arms across his chest and nodded. "Boy, did I."

The Chief said, "What tattoo?"

Josie explained.

Drake said, "The snake in the shape of the letter D, usually found on the forearm, is a mark of the Discala crime organization."

"Discala?" said the Chief. "You mean Johnny Discala?"

"Out of Philadelphia, yes," said Drake. "His organization operates from New York City down to Baltimore with Philadelphia as his hub. Drugs, money laundering, human trafficking, gambling... you name it. He's got his hands in everything. He came up through the Lugo organization, served as the underboss for years until he took out Lugo, established himself as the boss. He's known for his brutality."

"Aren't all mobsters?" said Noah.

Drake bobbed his head in agreement. "I guess so, yeah."

The Chief said, "These two guys running around my city, you think they're Discala's men?"

Drake held up his hands. "I don't think anything. Quinn asked me to look into a tattoo. If you've got a couple of guys running around Denton with that tattoo then yeah, they're Discala's guys. Soldiers get those once they're initiated into the organization."

Alison, who had not yet said a word, instead listening with rapt attention, said, "Soldiers?"

Drake said, "Italian mafia organizations have a certain structure: the boss is the big guy, the one in charge of everyone. Then you've got his second-in-command, the underboss. There's a consigliere, who is a sort of advisor and go-between for the boss and underboss. Below them are capos, guys who run their own crews and have their own gigs or areas they're in charge of. Every capo has soldiers who report to them. They're low-level guys, there to follow orders."

Alison swallowed hard. "You think the mob is involved in..." She pointed to her face, still sporting an assortment of unsightly bruises, and then her throat, covered in finger-marks. "This? What happened to me?" She looked at Josie. "I thought you said Calvert was an architect and the guy from last night was a city council member. What's the mafia got to do with this?"

Noah said, "That's what we're trying to figure out. Your old boss, Max Combs, had some serious gambling debts. He could be the connection to Discala. Combs blackmailed

Elliott Calvert and maybe someone else, given the amount of money he had in his possession."

The Chief said, "Someone should look into Pierce Fuller's financials. See if he frequented the Eudora or ever came into contact with Max Combs. What could Fuller be blackmailed for? Get Mett and Palmer on it. See what they can dig up."

Noah took out his phone and fired off some text messages.

Josie said, "Okay, let's say Max Combs was blackmailing Calvert and maybe even Fuller so that he could pay off his gambling debts. If some or all of those debts were held by Discala, why wouldn't Max have given Discala's men the money when they showed up at his house to torture and kill him?"

"Max is dead?" Alison blurted.

All heads turned toward her.

"Shit," said Noah.

"I'm sorry," said Josie. "We couldn't tell you—or anyone —until his next of kin had been notified. I'm not sure that's happened yet, so you'll have to keep that to yourself."

Alison waved a hand around the room. "Who would I tell?"

Noah said, "We're back to the question that started all of this: what the hell are all these people looking for?"

Josie looked at Drake. "What would Johnny Discala be so desperate to keep from getting into the wrong hands that he'd send a crew out here to find it?"

Drake took a moment to think about it and then shook his head. "I don't know. Nothing sticks to this guy. A lot of people think he's got some judges and prosecutors in his pocket since whenever charges do come down, they get dropped. Evidence has a tendency to disappear when it comes to Discala and most of his capos."

Josie said, "So even if there was, say, a video of Discala himself murdering someone in cold blood, you're saying it wouldn't really be a threat?"

"Murder? That might be a tougher rap to beat but it wouldn't surprise me if the charges got dropped. Of course, the video would have to disappear pretty early in proceedings. Then again, nothing ever makes it to the press where Discala is concerned. A few years ago, another syndicate had a beef with Discala. They targeted his family. Gunned his wife down while she was at church. Discala went nuts. Wiped out almost the entire syndicate and their families. It was a bloodbath. The prosecutors thought they had one of the shooters but then some key evidence went missing and the district attorney had to drop the charges. Next thing anyone knows, that guy vanishes off the planet. Discala wiped out dozens of people and walked away like it was nothing."

The Chief said, "His men wiped out dozens. He gave orders."

Drake shrugged. "Word is he killed some of them himself—and their families. Of course, there's no way to prove it."

"How long ago was that?" asked Josie.

"Two or three years ago," said Drake. "Maybe four. It wasn't covered in the press much. I think one newspaper might have done a piece on it but that was it. You can look up the wife's murder for the exact date. Her name was Renatta Discala. Anyway, look, I've got to run." He looked from Josie to Noah and back. "Since you guys are neck-deep in what seems like a pretty complicated case, Trin and I are going to drive down to see your parents for a couple of days."

Josie stood and walked over to hug him. "Thank you," she said.

He wished her luck and left. Josie looked around for her phone, realizing that she didn't know where she had left it. Or if she had even charged it. The Chief said, "Your phone? It's in the living room. I hooked it up to my charger."

Josie flashed him a smile and went into the living room to retrieve it. Back in the kitchen, she used her internet browser to search for Johnny Discala. There were several news articles throughout the years having to do with him being charged with crimes: racketeering, bribery, and extortion but just as Drake had said: he always walked away a free man, either because the charges were dropped or because he was acquitted. One article from seven years earlier showed a photo of him exiting a federal building in Philadelphia. Press surrounded him but he towered over them, tall and wiry but imposing in a crisp three-piece suit. He had thick black hair swept back from his forehead and a severe jaw. Hawk-like eyes punished the camera, at odds with the smug curl of his lips.

Federal Jury Acquits Discala in Extortion Case read the headline. She scrolled through the entire article, shock rippling through her as she came to another photo. This one showed Johnny and another man getting into a black sedan. The other man was behind the open driver's side door, looking at the camera, a scowl on his face. He was tall and thick, his massive frame dwarfing the door. Sunlight gleamed off his bald head.

Josie quickly scanned the caption.

Reputed mob boss, Johnny Discala and his associate, Matteo "Mug" Marrone leave the federal courthouse after Discala's surprising acquittal.

She turned her phone toward Noah and the Chief and jabbed a finger at Marrone. "This is him! This is the guy I fought in the Mills' kitchen."

The Chief slid on a pair of reading glasses and peered at the phone. "Well, shit."

A long, silent moment passed. Then Noah said, "How do you want to handle this?"

The Chief took off his reading glasses and looked around the kitchen, as if the answers might be on the table or countertop.

"Chief?" said Josie.

"I don't want this in the press. Not yet. I'll put it out to our people that this is who we're looking for, but that's all. For now. I'll get my phone."

He walked into the living room and Noah followed.

Josie closed out that tab and opened a new one, searching for information about the death of Renatta Discala. It didn't take long. There was an obituary and then an article from a small local news outlet in Philadelphia. The headline read: *Wife of Alleged Mob Boss, Johnny Discala, Gunned Down Inside Church.*

Josie noted the murder had happened four years earlier. As she scanned the article, her heart jumped into overdrive.

"I'll be damned," she muttered.

"Quinn?" said the Chief, walking back into the kitchen.

She looked up from her phone and met his eyes. "Can you stay here with Alison?"

He eyed her for a long moment then decided to trust

her. "Yes," he said. "If I need to leave, she'll either come with me or I'll have someone with her."

Josie felt Alison's hand on her arm. "I don't want to stay with anyone else. I want to go with you."

"No," Josie told her. "You can't. You're safer here."

Alison's voice rose an octave. "I'm safer with you."

Josie put her own hand over Alison's and smiled. "I'll be back in a few hours, okay? It's important."

"Where are you going that's so important?" she demanded, withdrawing her hand.

"To talk to Johnny Discala's daughter."

CHAPTER 50

The campus of St. Catherine of Siena Academy was situated on thirty acres of rolling green hills in South Denton. It included the church, two academic buildings, a library, a small structure marked "Maintenance" and a single dormitory that had been converted from an old elementary school into a full-time residence for students. The double doors to the dormitory were locked. Affixed to the wall beside them was a black box that had a slot for swiping what Josie assumed were dorm keys; a camera; a speaker, and a button. She pressed the button and waited.

Noah said, "You sure you want to do this?"

"It's not a coincidence that Johnny Discala's only daughter is attending school here and his henchmen are going around shooting people," Josie said.

"I know, but Johnny Discala's daughter is here for a reason. A private, exclusive school with what? Maybe fifty students in total that costs tens of thousands of dollars a year in the middle of Central Pennsylvania? She's here to keep a low profile. We have no reason to think that she's involved in whatever is happening here."

"She worked for a man who was most likely murdered by Discala's men."

Noah held up his hands. "Lots of people work at the Eudora. Discala might not take too kindly to police questioning his daughter."

"We questioned her at the hotel," Josie pointed out.

The speaker squawked to life. "Can I help you?"

Josie took out her credentials and shoved them toward the camera. "Detective Josie Quinn, Lieutenant Noah Fraley. Denton PD. We're here to speak with Gianna Sorrento."

Noah muttered, "Showing up at her private school to question her alone is different than questioning her as part of interviews with every employee at the hotel."

"Just a moment please," said the man's voice on the other end of the speaker.

Josie put her hands on her hips and glared at Noah. "I don't take too kindly to this guy setting his goons loose on my city, and I don't give a rat's ass if he's the biggest mafia guy in the world. Right now we've got one dead teenage girl, a dead man, a woman in the hospital fighting for her life, and another teenage girl we can't let out of our sight because apparently there is some contingent of men in this city who are willing to kill her for what they think she has. I'm doing my job, and that means talking to Gia Sorrento."

The speaker said, "Buzzing you in now."

As promised, a buzz sounded, followed by the click of the door's lock disengaging. Quickly, Noah pulled one of the doors open, waving Josie ahead of him into the cool, brightly lit cubicle that stood between the doors and the lobby.

As they approached a desk manned by a security guard,

Noah sidled close to her and whispered, "The fact that no one intimidates you is turning me on a little bit."

She flashed him a quick grin. "We'll talk later."

The security guard spent several minutes studying their credentials. Then he called the Denton police station to confirm that they were who they said they were before signing them both in on a clipboard labeled "Visitors." Finally, he scanned both their photo IDs into his computer system. Josie could see what Johnny Discala's money bought at St. Catherine of Siena private school.

The security guard pointed to Josie. "Room 306. She can go up." His index finger bobbed in Noah's direction. "You can't."

Noah opened his mouth to protest but Josie cut him off. "It's fine." Turning to Noah, she said, "Keep an eye out for any of our 'friends.'"

The guard buzzed her through to the lobby, an open-concept area with lots of couches, chairs, and coffee tables clustered together, likely to encourage socialization. Arrayed along one wall was a series of high tables with stools tucked beneath them. Charging stations jutted up from their surfaces at two-foot intervals. Across from those tables were vending machines. A female student, far younger than Gia, fed a dollar into one of them. She didn't spare a glance as Josie walked past her to a wide set of stairs.

On the third floor, Josie searched out Room 306. Its heavy wooden door was ajar when she arrived. She rapped her knuckles against the door anyway and waited until Gia answered. Dressed in a pink tracksuit with her hair cascading down over her shoulders, she looked like a completely different person than the one Josie and Noah had interviewed at the Eudora. She poked her head into the hall, scanning in each direction. "Come in," she said.

The room was sizable, larger than some studio apartments that Josie had been in. Although Josie didn't see a bathroom or any kitchen area, the space was big enough to fit a full-sized bed, desk, and even a small couch. Sunlight streamed through the large windows that lined one entire wall. Clothes, shoes, and purses burst from a closet near the bed. More clothes were strewn over the top of the couch. A half-open bookbag sat on the floor next to the desk, the surface of which was littered with cosmetics and a small mirror. A thick area rug covered hardwood floors. Almost everything was pink. The rug, the couch, the bedclothes.

Gia stood between the couch and the desk, hands on her hips. "What do you want?"

Josie said, "You're Johnny Discala's daughter."

Gia said nothing.

"Your father's men have been spotted in several places in this city as of late, and we believe they're responsible for at least one murder, potentially two."

"You're talking to the wrong Discala. Actually, I'm not even a Discala anymore. My dad let me change it to my mom's maiden name when I moved here. After what happened to my mom, he agreed that carrying on his name might be too dangerous."

"Is that why you're here? For your own safety?"

Gia rolled her eyes and flopped down onto the couch. She did not invite Josie to sit. "I'm here because I wanted to get away from my father. It's not far enough, but he pays the bills, so here I am."

"How much do you know about your father's activities?" Josie asked.

Gia turned her head and sneered in Josie's direction. "Do you think you're the first cop to try to get information from me about my dad? Do you think I'm an idiot? That I don't know who he is or who everyone says he is?" She raised both hands and used air quotes. "'Alleged mob boss. Reputed mafia don.' If you have questions about my dad, you need to ask my dad."

"Fair enough," Josie said. "Let me ask you this. Do you have your own personal security detail? Does your father provide that?"

Gia laughed. "Here? No. He wanted to but I convinced him it wasn't necessary. It's bad enough I'm stuck out here in the middle of nowhere. No life. No friends, even. But at least I'm away from him. I can handle being in this boring old boarding school in this boring city if it means no contact with my father. I couldn't deal if I had to have his body-guards following me around, reporting my every move back to him."

Josie said, "You don't know anyone in Denton who has ties to your father, then?"

Gia rolled her eyes. "I told you. If you have questions about him, ask him."

"Did he get you the job at the Eudora?"

"No. He doesn't want me working at all. I saw online they were looking for catering staff so I applied."

Josie asked, "Were you seeing Max Combs?"

Laughter erupted from Gia's throat. "Max? Oh God, no."

"Did you have a black messenger bag stolen or go missing from work in the last couple of weeks?"

Gia stared at her with an expression that was almost blank. Almost. The slightest flicker of her eyelid, lashes twitching, showed that she knew something about the bag. Whether it had been hers or not, Josie couldn't be certain. She licked her lips before answering. "No."

Josie took a step in the direction of the closet and

motioned toward the mess of clothing, shoes, and purses tumbling out. "Do you own a messenger bag?"

"Probably," said Gia, twisting to see over the back of the couch. "I have a lot of different bags. Messenger, clutch, tote. Regular purses. Backpacks. You name it, I'm sure it's there. Gifts from Daddy. He can afford this place, can't he? I've even got some Gucci stuff, too. You want to borrow something?"

Josie laughed. "Do I look like the kind of person who owns Gucci bags? Or even Coach?"

"I guess not."

"Your dad buys you things, but you still work at the hotel. Why?"

Her eyes flickered back to Gia in time to see a sliver of exposed flesh at her midsection. With one arm draped over the back of the couch, her body angled so she could view the closet, her sweatshirt had come up. There, to the left of her navel, was a spray of freckles configured in the shape of an S which stretched down to her waistband. Josie's heart stuttered.

Gia said, "I wanted something for myself, you know? My own money. My own thing. I'm tired of being under his thumb. I don't want to be dependent on him forever. I'd be happy if I never saw him again. As if he'd allow that—"

Cutting her off, Josie said, "Why did you lie about knowing Elliott Calvert?"

Gia's mouth clamped shut. Her eyes widened, gaze flitting toward the door, as if calculating whether or not she could make a run for it. When she didn't answer, Josie added, "He didn't just flirt with you, did he? You two had a physical relationship. A married man having an affair with an underage girl—with the underage daughter of Johnny

Discala? I can't imagine that would go over well with your dad."

Gia stood up, folding her arms across her middle. "How do you know about that?"

Josie stepped closer to her. "Elliott Calvert had photos on his phone, Gia."

"No," she said.

"Yes," said Josie.

"You can't prove it's me. He promised he would never get my face."

"How did it start, Gia?"

She looked down at her bare feet. "How do you think? I told you how it started."

"Flirting in the hotel bar," Josie supplied. "How long was it going on?"

"Does it matter?" asked Gia.

Josie thought about Elliott Calvert grooming an underage girl, having an affair with her, using the hotel. "How did Calvert get the rooms?"

"What?"

"At the Eudora. You saw each other there. He had to have rented a room. But he isn't listed as a guest."

"How the hell should I know?" Gia asked. She pushed past Josie and began to pace the room. "I don't want to talk about this. You can't tell anyone. It doesn't matter. It's over."

Max Combs had known about Elliott and Gia and blackmailed Elliott, which meant that Max had photos or even video of the two of them together—something that proved the two of them had been together. That would be something that Johnny Discala would kill to hide.

"But it's not over, Gia," said Josie. "Your dad's men are out there looking for something. Something that was in a messenger bag in Max's office. Dina Hale took it and she paid with her life. She didn't even know what she had. There were drugs in that bag. She thought they would get her into trouble so she sold them under the East Bridge. But it wasn't ever about drugs. I'm guessing your dad's men are looking for proof of your relationship with Elliott Calvert. Maybe you don't care about Dina Hale—I know there's no love lost between you two—but last night your dad's men broke into Alison Mills' home. Shot her mother. She's in the hospital right now, fighting for her life. Her mother, Gia."

Gia stopped in place, hands trembling at her sides. Her eyes looked in Josie's direction but remained unfocused and glassy. It was as if she was somewhere else. After a few beats, she blinked, and Josie sensed she was back in the present. She said, "What do you want from me?"

"I need to know what you know, Gia. Everything you know."

"I told you what I know. What else do you want from me? What else do you want me to say?"

Josie's mind cycled through the case. She was close to unraveling it, but there were still pieces that didn't fit. If Max was the one with the blackmail material all along, then why had the stolen bag set everything off? How had Discala's men found out about it? How had Calvert known? Where did Fuller fit into all of it? Would Max have kept something that sensitive in a messenger bag and then just left it lying around his office at the hotel? He'd gone to the trouble of hiding his money in a heating vent. Why be so careless with something that could get him killed? That probably *had* gotten him killed? Or had he meant to pass the bag on to someone else but Dina had intercepted it? Was that how Discala's men knew about it? Max had meant to give it to them or even to Elliott Calvert but then Dina took it? But Dina had given Discala's men the contents of the bag when they first came to her. Alison had said that she gave them the tablet and they'd taken it, leaving her alive. It was only when they realized it did not contain what they were searching for that they returned to torture her some more.

Another thought occurred to Josie. What if Dina had lied about the bag entirely? All of the information they'd received about the contents of the bag and what Elliott Calvert, Discala's men, and Pierce Fuller were looking for had come to them secondhand, via Alison. What if Dina hadn't told her friend the truth about what she had taken? Or what if she had, and Alison was the one lying? Elliott Calvert had gone after both girls but Discala's men and Pierce Fuller had sought out Alison, even after Dina's death. Josie had assumed it was because they believed that Dina had either told Alison something or passed along the all-important item to Alison.

Dina had had something. Her home had been ransacked. Josie had independent confirmation of that from Guy Hale. Dina had been tortured. There was physical evidence in that regard.

But the things they couldn't see, couldn't know, couldn't prove in any measurable, tangible or quantifiable way they were extrapolating using information Alison had provided.

"I think you should leave," Gia said, drawing Josie out of her thoughts. "Unless you're going to arrest me for something. I haven't done anything. I won't, like, testify against Elliott, so don't even go there. He never forced me to do anything."

Josie said, "Do you know Pierce Fuller?"

"Who?" Gia looked genuinely confused.

"He's a city councilman." Josie took out her phone and

used her internet browser to search for a photo of Fuller on the city website. She showed it to Gia.

"I don't know him." She walked toward the door and opened it. "Now, please. I think you should go."

Josie followed her to the door and stopped at the threshold. She stared hard into Gia's eyes. Her eyelashes fluttered again, the motion so minuscule that Josie was only able to see it because they were so close. "Gia," she said, "I don't think you've told me everything you know. Is that because you're afraid of your father? Of what he might do if you tell the truth about the things you know?"

Gia's lower lip quivered. "My father won't hurt me. You have to understand that. He would never harm me. But Detective, you must understand this. He would burn this entire city to the ground if he knew anything we talked about, if he knew you were even here right now talking to me. I'm not afraid of him, but you should be."

CHAPTER 51

Josie dropped her freshly restocked overnight bag onto the Chief's living room floor. Behind her, Noah closed and locked the door, leaning his back against it, arms folded loosely across his chest. Josie could tell by his pallor that he was in a lot of pain but she knew he would ignore any entreaties for him to go home and rest. Alison's battered face peered up at them from a small opening in the blanket she'd wrapped around her. The Chief sat in his recliner, eyes focused on his phone. He didn't look up until Josie snatched the television remote from the coffee table and pressed the power button, plunging the room into silence.

Alison said, "What took you so long?"

"I needed a shower, a change of clothes. I had to stop home for a couple of hours. I called the hospital about your mom. She's hanging on."

"I heard," Alison said. "The Chief told me. Did you talk to that guy's daughter? The mobster's daughter?"

Josie ignored her question, circling the coffee table and perching on the edge of the couch beside Alison. "What did Dina take from Max's office?"

"What?" Alison looked from Josie to Noah and then to the Chief.

"Look at me," Josie told her. "I'm not angry with you. You're not in trouble. I just need the truth. What did Dina take from Max's office? It wasn't a bag, was it?"

"Yes, it was. I told you that."

"Alison, don't lie to us."

She pulled her knees to her chest and again, her eyes panned the room, pleading. Her voice rose an octave. "I'm not lying. I'm not. Dina took a bag. There was a bag in Max's office. It was exactly what I said."

Noah took a few steps forward until his shins were inches from the edge of the coffee table. His voice was gentle. "Then tell us what was really inside the bag, Alison."

"I did. I told you. Well, I mean, I didn't see it. I just know what Dina said. It was, like, drugs and a tablet—"

Josie said, "Max Combs was shot in the head over what was in that bag."

Alison froze. "But I'm telling you the truth."

Noah said, "Max was tortured because of what was in that bag. No. Let me rephrase that. He was tortured because he didn't have what was in that bag. He wasn't tortured over drugs or money or the tablet you say that Dina found inside. What was really in that bag?"

"Kid," said the Chief. "You don't have to lie to us, you got that?"

Alison's gaze flitted to him and then back to Josie. Silence filled the room while they waited. In Josie's experience, especially with kids, waiting worked. They couldn't stand the silence. They had to fill it. But Alison was either very scared or very stubborn. Or both. She said nothing.

Josie tried again. "Alison, we will keep you safe, but you

need to tell us the truth. We need to know what we're dealing with here. Your best friend is dead. Your boss is dead. Your mom is in the intensive care unit with two gunshot wounds. Whatever you're not telling us? There are men trying to kill you for whatever it is that you're hiding. I can tell you with one hundred percent certainty, it's not worth your life."

Her voice was so low, Josie strained to hear it. "I didn't think things would get this... bad."

From the recliner, the Chief let out a long sigh. In it, Josie heard both disappointment and relief. Noah said, "Tell us, Alison."

She cowered, pressing her back against the couch and gripping the blanket tightly around her body. With her knees pressed to her chest, she was no bigger than one of the Chief's oversized couch pillows. "I'm so sorry. I really am."

Josie put up a hand. "Right now we just want to know the truth. That's all."

"We're not mad, kid," said the Chief.

"No, but you're disappointed. I can tell. That's worse than if you were mad. My parents are going to be disappointed, too, when they find out how badly I screwed up. Oh my God."

Noah said, "Your parents will be relieved that you're safe, Alison. That's all that matters. We can only continue to keep you safe if you're completely honest with us. Was there really a messenger bag in Max's office?"

Alison's head bobbed up and down. "Yes. I didn't lie about that. All of that was true. Dina saw Max in the bar with Gia. She got jealous. She went to confront him but he wasn't there. She saw a bag on the floor behind his desk. She thought she would royally get back at him for seeing Gia by stealing it."

"You said you didn't think Max was seeing Gia," said Josie.

"Right, but Dina did. That's why she took the bag. She was mad at Max."

Noah said, "Was there really no identification inside it? No way to tell if it really belonged to Max or not?"

"That's what Dina told me. I told you the truth about that, and about what she said was inside it. Oxy and this tablet. She got rid of the drugs, kept the tablet, and threw the messenger bag in the dumpster."

"When those men came for her, she gave them the tablet," said Noah. "But it wasn't what they were looking for because they came back. Is that part true?"

Alison nodded emphatically. "Yes! That was true. But when they came back, she didn't have anything else to give them."

Josie said, "You found what they were looking for, didn't you? When you retrieved it from the dumpster."

Alison nodded. "There was a small compartment sewn into the bottom of the bag. It looked like another seam but actually it was Velcroed together. I still didn't notice it until I started looking at the liner. I was supposed to cut it open like Dina said, but I didn't. Not once I found the compartment."

"What was in it?" asked the Chief.

Alison let out a sigh. "It was some stupid book, okay? I don't know why everyone is going so nuts over it."

Noah said, "What kind of book?"

"I don't know. Like a small journal or something. It had a plain blue cover. About the size of an index card, maybe a little bigger. It just had names and numbers written in it."

"Whose names?" Josie asked.

"I don't know, okay? I didn't look. I just flipped through

it quickly. I still wasn't even sure if that's what everyone was going nuts over or not."

"There was nothing else with it? Nothing in the compartment? A flash drive? An SD card?"

Puzzled, Alison said, "No. Just some stupid book."

"Did you recognize the handwriting?" asked Noah.

"No."

The Chief said, "You told Quinn that you put the bag back in Max Combs's office. The book, too?"

Looking sheepish, Alison pulled back deeper into the blanket, like a turtle retreating into its shell. "I put the bag back, but I kept the book."

Noah said, "You knew that your best friend had been tortured, her life threatened, and you didn't tell her about the book?"

"I was going to, I swear I was!"

Josie touched one of Alison's knees. "Why didn't you?"

Alison shrank deeper into the blanket. "Because it was worth something."

"What are you talking about?" asked the Chief.

Alison kept her eyes on Josie. "It had to be worth something if people were willing to do terrible things to get it back, right? If those men were willing to kidnap a teenage girl in broad daylight and stick needles into her nails, then they'd probably pay to get it back, right?"

Noah raised a brow. "You thought you could use it to... blackmail the men who took Dina?"

She didn't answer.

Josie said, "Why would you put your best friend—and yourself—at risk to try to blackmail these people? What were you going to do with the money?"

"I was going to help my family. We're broke. My mom would never tell anyone but ever since the accident, we've been broke. That's why my dad is in Hong Kong. He had no choice. He had to take that job. We were going to lose our house. Probably everything, and he's going to be over there for months, maybe even a couple of years. We might not see him for a year and a half! All because of me! He wasn't hurt in the accident. I was. It was one thing for him to lose the business—he told my mom he still owes people money from that—but then on top of that there were all my medical bills."

Noah said, "You thought you would blackmail mobsters so that you could repay your medical bills?"

Alison rolled her eyes. "I didn't know they were mobsters! I didn't even know if I'd go through with it. I wasn't, like, planning things out. I just thought... I don't know what I thought. The problem was that once I told Dina that I hadn't found anything, I couldn't think of a way to tell her I lied. I mean, that would have been a complete deal-breaker. I just thought she didn't know about the book, she never knew about the book, and if the trash had already been picked up, then I wouldn't have known about it either. If she didn't have it, they couldn't, like, kill her for it. They wouldn't get it."

Josie closed her eyes briefly. After opening them, she glanced at Noah. She could tell he was barely holding his frustration in check. Teenage naivety had gotten them all here, leaving a trail of destruction in its path. Josie knew he wanted to rail at Alison every bit as much as she did about how monumentally stupid and completely illogical her behavior had been, but that wouldn't help them now. They still needed Alison to cooperate. Berating her wasn't going to achieve that.

Seeing the look pass between them, Alison pushed her face out of the blanket opening and said, "I know it was stupid, okay? I know that now. I knew it pretty much right after I took the stupid book and lied to Dina about it. I mean, how would I even get in touch with the guys who were looking for it? How much would I even ask for? How would I do, like, an exchange? And once they knew I had the book, what would stop them from just killing me and taking it? And even if, by some miracle, I could pull it off, what was I going to do? Bring home a bag of cash to my parents, like, 'Ta-da! Here's enough money to keep Dad from having to stay in the job in Hong Kong.' Like they weren't going to ask any questions? I know how stupid it all sounds now. But at the time, I just... I had this idea that I could help my family. That was all. Once I realized I'd never be able to work up the nerve to tell Dina the truth, I figured I'd just get rid of the book, and it would be like it never happened. Any of it."

Josie said, "What did you do with the book?"

Noah and the Chief looked at her expectantly.

"I hid it," said Alison.

"Where?" asked Josie. "Where is it now?"

"Dina's house."

Noah said, "You hid the book in Dina's house?"

Alison looked at him as though he was stupid. "Well, yeah. Her house had already been ransacked. It's not like they would come back. They already knew it wasn't there. I hid it in her bedroom."

The Chief stood up and pointed at Alison. "Get your ass up. We're going to get that book."

CHAPTER 52

At the stationhouse, Alison sat at Josie's desk, head tipped back. Her eyes were closed, her mouth open. Josie knew from her wheezy nose that she was fast asleep. She had gone into a panic when the Chief suggested visiting the Hales, so they had sent Mettner to their home to retrieve the book with detailed instructions from Alison as to where to find it. Now, Josie, Noah, Gretchen and the Chief stood around Mettner's desk.

In his hands was a paper bag on his desk marked as evidence. "It was easy to find," Mettner told them. "I took Hummel with me. He thinks he can get prints, but I know you guys need to see it. You have gloves?"

A pair of latex gloves appeared in front of Josie. She looked over to see Noah holding them. "Thanks," she said, snapping them on.

Mettner cleared a space on his desk and Gretchen got out her phone, ready to snap photos. Josie removed the small book from the evidence bag and placed it on the desk. The first few pages were blank. After that the pages were filled with lists. First, a man's name. Under that, a phone number, presumably belonging to the man. Beneath that were initials followed by dates. Each date had an X beside it.

Mettner said, "I don't get it."

Josie flipped the pages until she came to Elliott Calvert's name. The entries started almost six months earlier. All of the initials under his name were the same:

G.S. 4/13 X

G.S. 4/27 X

G.S. 5/1 X

G.S. 5/20 X

On it went. There were some gaps in the dates but no gap greater than three weeks.

Next, she found Pierce Fuller's name. His list was quite a bit longer and went back almost a year. Josie counted at least four different sets of initials beneath his name: A.P., G.M., R.C. and G.S. All of Pierce Fuller's entries were marked with Xs.

Josie was relieved not to see the initials A.M. in the book.

Gretchen said, "Is this what I think it is?"

"What?" said Noah.

The Chief nudged Gretchen out of the way, and studied the pages as Josie turned them. Some of the names she recognized, most she did not. Nausea swirled in her stomach. "Oh my God."

Mettner looked more closely. "Wait a minute. It can't be. Can it?"

The Chief said, "Make a list of all the names that have G.S. under them. We need to know how many more there are. And I want a list of every girl who works in the catering and events department—or has worked there—however far back these dates go. We match them up and bring them in to talk."

"What are you guys doing?" Alison said on the end of a yawn. She stretched her arms over her head and spun in a half-circle in Josie's chair. Her eyes landed on the book in Josie's hands. "Oh," she said.

Josie looked into her face, now a swirl of yellows and greens to go with the black and blue from her neck to her eyes. "You don't know what any of this means?"

Alison shook her head. "You think I'm lying again?"

"This is very important," Josie said. "You're not in trouble. Do you know anything about this?"

Alison lifted both hands and slapped her thighs. "I'm telling you the truth now. Yes, I lied before but I'm not anymore. Like you said, it's not worth it."

Noah said, "You really don't know what any of this means?"

Alison rolled her eyes. "No. I don't. Should I?"

Gretchen said, "Alison, you didn't notice that Max was running a—"

"Palmer," the Chief said. He gave a swift shake of his head and Gretchen quieted. They were still dealing with an active investigation and although Alison was in their care, she didn't need to know everything about it. Certainly not things they did not yet intend to make public.

Josie said, "Alison, when you first told us about this book, you said that you didn't recognize the handwriting. Did you mean that you don't know whose handwriting it is, or that it doesn't look like Max's handwriting?"

She shrugged. "Both? I didn't recognize it because it didn't look like anyone I know."

Josie held the book up, pages spread so Alison could see them. "Are you saying this isn't Max's handwriting?"

Alison looked around the room, as if searching for help. When none came, she said, "Well, I can't, like, say for sure but it doesn't look like his writing."

Josie turned the book over and shook it. Then she opened the front cover and felt inside it, looking for a seam or some kind of slit. She did the same with the back cover.

"What are you doing?" asked Mettner.

"Looking for an SD card," Josie said. "It's the only thing small enough and slim enough to hold video footage but also fit into this book."

She closed the book and examined it from the outside. There, at the top of the spine was a small opening. Josie nudged Mettner over and held it beneath his desk lamp.

She sighed. "Nothing."

"No video?" said Noah.

Lowering his voice so that Alison wouldn't hear, the Chief said, "That book is damning enough if we can gather enough information to prove our case. There are men's names in it. We drag every one of them in here. If Max had a partner, one of them might know about it."

Josie's mind was racing, puzzling through the new information. She matched the Chief's tone. "But this isn't damning," she said.

"What do you mean?" asked Mettner in a low voice. "It's pretty sick what this guy was doing at that hotel."

Josie slid the book back into its evidence bag. "But alone, it doesn't mean anything. Not to Gia Sorrento. Not to Johnny Discala. If there was video of footage of her with these men, that would be a different story."

"True," said Gretchen quietly. "I could see him going to pretty extreme lengths to make sure video footage was destroyed."

The Chief said, "Unless he wasn't looking for footage. Maybe he was just looking for the list of men."

"So he could kill them," Noah said. "If what Drake said is true—about how he handled the rival gang after his wife's death—we know he would want to wipe the men who saw Gia off the planet."

The Chief said, "Which would explain why Calvert and Fuller went out of their damn minds trying to get the book back. Max must have told them it was stolen. Then he tried to blackmail them. He knew Dina took the bag. All he had to do was sweet-talk her to get it back, but in the meantime, he got hundreds of thousands of dollars out of Calvert and Fuller. He probably threatened to give them up to Discala. But then Dina threw the bag away and everything went to shit. Max probably put them on to her."

Gretchen said, "Or maybe he told them both he would reveal who had the book if they paid him off and once they paid, Max put them on to Dina. He didn't care what happened to her."

Josie said, "But where do Discala's men come in? Someone did tell them. They were looking for it, too."

The Chief said, "We're still missing pieces."

Josie's mind worked back through the case, trying to fit the pieces they had together into different configurations, hoping something they hadn't considered yet would reveal itself. "When I talked to Gia, she said her dad would burn this entire city to the ground if he even knew that I was talking to her. Just talking to her. Not even that I was talking to her about what was going on with Elliott Calvert. Just my presence there at her dorm she believed would enrage him that much. When his wife was killed, he executed dozens of people."

"So?" said Mettner.

Noah said, "So if he knew about this book, he would decimate this entire city. He wouldn't just send two guys to quietly retrieve it."

The Chief said, "He didn't just send 'two guys.' One of them is Mug Marrone, who, from the research I've done since Quinn showed us his photo, is basically Discala's underboss."

Josie said, "For something this sensitive, he would have sent more than just a couple of guys. Discala didn't order these guys to come out here and handle this thing with Gia. Discala might not even know about it."

Mettner said, "Are you serious?"

"If Discala didn't send them, who the hell did?" said Gretchen.

"Gia."

They all stared at her. Noah said, "We need to talk to her again."

Josie said, "I'll go. Gretchen can come with me this time. You stay here and guard Alison. Run down the list of names in the book."

CHAPTER 53

In the lobby of the residence hall of St. Catherine of Siena, the security guard frowned at Josie and Gretchen. "Miss Sorrento is not here."

"How do you know that?" asked Gretchen, pointing at his computer. "Did you check?"

"I don't need to check. She left here about a half hour ago with her mother."

Josie and Gretchen exchanged a glance. "How do you know it was her mother?" asked Josie.

"She said she was Miss Sorrento's mother," he explained as if it was the most obvious thing in the world.

Josie leaned across the desk, drawing face to face with him. "Earlier, when my colleague and I were here, you examined our IDs at least three times. You scanned them into your damn computer. You called our stationhouse to make sure that we were who we said we were, but today some woman waltzes in here and says she's Gia's mother and you're totally fine with that?"

"She didn't want to go up," the guard explained, a flicker of doubt in his eyes. "She only asked me to buzz Miss

Sorrento and tell her that her mother was here, so I did. Miss Sorrento came down about five minutes later and they left together."

Gretchen tapped his monitor. "Video. We need video of the woman standing in this lobby."

He spread his hands apart. "I can't. You need a warrant."

Anger sent a flush from Josie's collar to the roots of her hair. "Do you understand that Gia Sorrento may be in trouble? Her life could be in danger. Are you going to waste our time with this warrant nonsense? Do you want to tell her mobster father that you slowed us down in finding her over a warrant?"

"Boss," Gretchen said quietly.

The guard shrank in his chair. "I'm sorry. I have to follow the rules. If I don't, I get fired."

Gretchen clasped one of Josie's arms and tried to pull her away from the desk. "Fine," she told the guard. "We'll be back with a warrant."

Josie stayed put. "What did she look like? You don't need a warrant to describe the woman you saw."

He shrugged. "I don't know. Average height, average build. Blonde hair."

"Shaved on one side?" Josie asked, thinking about Felicia Koslow.

Another shrug. "I don't know. I didn't notice."

Gretchen said, "Did you even notice if she looked old enough to be Gia's mother?"

"I mean, I don't know. I guess she did."

Josie took out her phone and found Felicia Koslow's Instagram feed. She found a selfie Felicia had snapped in the city park. "This her?"

He studied it for a few seconds. "No. Not her."

Gretchen tugged at Josie's arm again. "Let's go get that warrant, boss."

In the car, Josie stewed.

Gretchen said, "Who do you think this woman is that's posing as her mother?"

"I don't know," said Josie. "Who else does Gia know in Denton who might be old enough to pass for her mother?"

"I don't know," said Gretchen. "Do you think Gia's in trouble?"

"I don't know."

Josie's mind was working back through the case, now with a new lens—with Gia pulling the strings. How would she have known about the book? Max? Max's silent partner? Was the silent partner the same person posing as Gia's mother? Why bother posing as her mother? Was she hoping to retrieve the book as well?

Again, something about the book nagged at Josie. Its existence wouldn't have been a surprise to Gia. Josie questioned whether it would have even been concerning to her. To begin with, it was a low-tech way to keep track of his operation. No digital footprint, which meant that there weren't multiple copies floating around in the world or across the internet. In addition, taken out of context, it proved nothing. Her name wasn't even in it, only her initials. They could be anyone's initials.

What else was Josie missing?

Gretchen said, "Mett says he'll get the warrant drawn up, signed and served."

Josie hadn't even realized Gretchen was talking on her phone. "Okay," she said.

"That might take a while. What do you want to do now?"

"Go to the hospital," Josie said. "I want to talk with Elliott Calvert."

CHAPTER 54

A new officer waited outside Elliott Calvert's room, sitting in a vinyl chair, scrolling on his phone. He nodded at Josie as she swept past him and into the room. Calvert was sitting up in bed, his broken arm slung across his stomach, eyes fixed on the television on the wall across from his bed. The tinny sound of the show he was watching came from a small handheld device attached to his bed. His eyes widened when he saw her. His good hand fumbled for the television remote, pressing buttons until the sound stopped.

"Get out," he said.

"This is not about Dina Hale or Alison Mills," Josie said.

"I don't care. Get out."

Josie ignored him, advancing toward the bed until her shirt brushed the rail. She recited his Miranda rights. When she asked him if he understood them as she had stated them, he said, "It doesn't matter. I'm not talking to you."

"I didn't ask if you were going to talk to me," said Josie. "I asked if you understand your rights as I just told them to you."

"Jesus," he muttered, looking at the muted television screen. "You're relentless. Fine. Whatever. I understand them. Are you done?"

"I know what happened, Elliott."

Ignoring her, he turned the volume back up. The canned laughter of a game show filled the room.

"You were going to the Eudora to see a girl. Gia Sorrento. Except that it wasn't... a consensual thing."

His finger found the mute button once more. Now, he met her eyes. His lips twitched. For a fleeting moment, he looked as though he was struggling with whether or not to respond. Finally, grudgingly, he said, "It was entirely consensual. Entirely."

"Because you were paying for Gia's company," Josie said.

He went silent and still, his gaze turning back to the television.

Josie continued, "Max Combs hires teenage girls onto the catering and events staff. He flirts with them, sees how far he can go, what they'll tolerate and what they won't. Some of them are receptive—maybe not to his advances but to the idea he puts into their heads that they can earn a lot of extra money. He lines up the clients—like you—vets them, rents the room—under a colleague's name so he is never connected to it—and... the girl is already there, isn't she? Or she's nearby."

He said nothing.

"Gia Sorrento was an escort. You were her client."

Still, he didn't utter a word. His finger hovered over the mute button but he didn't turn the sound back on.

"Max groomed the girls and vetted clients, but he didn't run the business, did he? That fell to someone else. A woman. A madam. She kept a book with names and dates and crosses to mark that each encounter had been properly paid for. She didn't keep electronic records because she didn't want anything coming back to her. A book can be burned, no trace of it left at all. No electronic imprint. No way to firmly establish ownership."

His gaze drifted away from the television, toward the window. A slight tremor started in his free hand, and he clenched a fistful of sheets in it.

"She called you, didn't she?" Josie said. "Or did you call her to make an appointment and that's how you found out? Or was it Max who told you?"

He bit his lower lip, scraping his teeth across chapped skin.

"It was Max," said Josie. "He was the one who told you. Someone took the book and oh, by the way, the escort you'd been meeting with for the last five months was the underage daughter of a serious mobster. Maybe Max told you his name. Maybe you googled him. That must have been a good time."

His eyes briefly landed on her, and she could see the flash of panic in them before they found the television again. "I'm not—I'm not a horrible person," he said through gritted teeth.

Josie had to stop herself from reminding him that he'd cheated on his wife, who had just given birth to their daughter, with an underage escort before strangling another teenage girl in an effort to cover up his first crime. She didn't care what he thought. She needed information.

Ignoring his proclamation, she went on. "Max told you he could get the book back and that no one would ever find out. He knew who took it. Some girl who worked in catering and events. This dark-haired girl who was always around, hanging on his every word. She didn't know what it was, she just took it because she was mad at him. All he had to do was turn on the charm and he'd have it back, no problem. But he wasn't doing it for free. He blackmailed you. You gave him whatever you could quickly clear out of your accounts—two hundred thirteen thousand dollars—and he'd get the book back. But if you didn't give him the money, he would go directly to Johnny Discala and tell him everything you did to his one and only daughter."

A blush stained Elliott's cheeks. "You make it sound so... tawdry. It wasn't like that. I liked Gia. A lot."

Josie was sure he believed that. Of course he "liked" a teenage girl who was being paid to make him feel good. It was a fantasy, but Elliott was too stupid to realize that. Still, Josie didn't call him on the utter nonsense coming out of his mouth.

"Regardless," she said. "Maybe you weren't afraid of Max. Maybe you weren't afraid of your wife finding out and leaving you. Maybe you weren't even afraid of being brought up on criminal charges. Because all of that seemed like a vacation compared to what Johnny Discala would do to you."

Elliott looked at her again. "I did read about him, okay? I did. I looked him up to make sure Max wasn't bullshitting me. Do you know what he does to people? Well, none of it can be proven but you can connect the dots. Did you know that the guys who were believed to have killed his wife were found partially skinned with their... with parts of them cut off? He tortured them before he shot them. In one article I read, the medical examiner said he thought that one of them died even before being shot—from the torture. Yes, I'm afraid of Johnny Discala. Yes, I wanted that book back but more importantly, I didn't want Discala to ever find it and see my name in it."

"But you didn't get the book," said Josie. "You gave Max the money, but he didn't have it yet. You went to the hotel a couple of times to find out what the hell was going on and he asked you for more money. But you didn't have it, so you decided to take matters into your own hands. He left everything in the possession of a teenage girl as insurance for himself. What was to stop you—or the other men he blackmailed—from beating the hell out of him or even killing him and taking the book back? Nothing. But if some nameless girl had it, he was protected. It never occurred to him in a million years that you or anyone else he was blackmailing would become desperate enough to approach her, much less harm her. It wasn't hard to figure out which girl Max had been talking about—it was the one following his every move, looking at him with stars in her eyes, flirting with him. He'd already described her to you. All you had to do was follow her."

And once Dina Hale was out of the picture, it wasn't hard for any of the other men Max had played his dangerous little game with to figure out that her best friend, Alison Mills, was either in possession of the incriminating book or that she knew where it was. They were just as desperate as Max had been. Pierce Fuller, in particular, had been so desperate he'd risked attacking Alison in the police station.

Elliott's voice was low. "I would take a prison term over what Discala would do to me."

"You're going to get your wish," said Josie.

"No," said Elliott. "He can still get to me in there. If he finds out about me and Gia and he knows what happened, he'll send someone to kill me. Probably torture me first, too. I was just trying to get the book. If I could stop that from getting out, from getting to Discala, then even prison wouldn't be so bad."

Josie didn't need to agree with him. They both knew that was true. It was probably the exact same reasoning that had driven Pierce Fuller to the police station to attack Alison.

Elliott loosened his fist, letting go of the sheet and shaking the tension from his hand. He ran his fingers through greasy hair. "I'm screwed," he said.

Josie didn't disagree.

"You didn't come here to tell me what I already know. What do you want?"

"Who was the madam?"

"I really don't think I should—I mean, she didn't really do anything wrong. This was Max. It was all Max."

Josie was no longer surprised by how badly his moral compass was skewed. "You contacted her by cell phone when you wanted to make an appointment, didn't you?" She rattled off the number of the defunct burner phone they'd found in his phone records. "You tried to call her after you found out that her client book had gone missing, but the phone was disconnected. You would have wanted to make sure that she wasn't going to rat you out to Discala like Max planned to. What did you do?"

"If I tell you who she is, it only puts her in danger."

Josie gripped the bedrail and leaned in toward him. "If you don't tell me who she is, Gia might be in danger."

He looked stricken. Josie struggled to figure out if it was real emotion or not. As distasteful as it was, it appeared he had developed some kind of feeling for Gia Sorrento.

"I don't know her name," he said. "She never told me. I didn't ask. She never wore a name tag. She works at the hotel. In housekeeping."

CHAPTER 55

Gia is seventeen when she becomes her father's daughter. She doesn't mean for anyone to get hurt but she can't risk him—or anyone else—finding out what she's done. The first time she knows something is wrong is when work slows down. "We have to keep a low profile," she is told. "We're getting a lot of heat."

But the other employees, she notices, are carrying on as usual.

She pushes back. She can't lose this job. She is going to be eighteen soon and then she's going to graduate high school. Her father is going to make her return home and she's afraid of what awaits her there. Since her mom died, he's been fixated on her being his perfect, untouchable princess. Like she's some kind of exotic animal he has to keep glassed in and separate from the rest of the world. The standard he's constructed in his mind of what she should be has deviated so far from reality by now that Gia is afraid of what will happen when she inevitably disappoints him. He won't hurt her, not physically. Of that she is confident. But there are other things he can do to her. Other ways he can hurt her. Freedoms he can steal.

Since the day she walked in on him in the garage and saw what he did to the men suspected of killing her mother, she's thought of little else besides getting out of her father's sphere of influence. She could go to the police and tell them what she saw, what she knew. Hope to get into witness protection. Start a new life elsewhere. But that would be on the government's terms. She would only be moving from one invisible prison to another.

Gia wanted autonomy. Agency, her mother used to call it. She was going to disappear because that was the only way to truly escape her father. Even from prison, he would have a tight hold on her. But she was going to do it on her own terms. For that, she needed every cent that the job provided.

When she points out that the others are still working, she is finally told the truth: Max found out who her father is and now he's nervous. Because of that, they have to let her go. Angry, she goes to Max and pleads with him to let her keep working. It doesn't matter that her father is Johnny Discala. In Denton, only he and Sadie know the truth about her identity. Sadie has known all along and it was never an issue for her. In fact, she was the one who offered Gia the job. Gia needs this job. She needs the money. Because Max has the hots for her, he says to give him some time and he'll bring her back. At least, that's what she thinks. She doesn't realize until much later that Max had his own agenda.

They all have their own agenda.

The next time she realizes that something is very wrong is when she finds out about the book going missing. That she's not the only person who knows about the book. Somewhere out there is proof of what she's done. What Johnny Discala's perfect princess, his Sweet Pea, did. At the same time, she finds out that more than just the book went missing. Something else was stolen. Something Gia cares far more about than the book. Something that was promised to her. She spent months manipulating, coaxing, and needling to get it. She had given up a cut of her earnings to ensure that it was delivered to her. She was so close. Then it was gone, along with the book. Decisions were made about these items, about Gia, without any thought to her, without her knowledge, even.

She needs agency.

She calls Mug. He's always been more of a father to her than her own dad. Throughout her entire life, he's always been the only person she trusts completely. When she gives him orders—retrieve the book and the precious item; don't tell my father—he doesn't ask questions. He doesn't judge. He doesn't hesitate.

CHAPTER 56

Josie stood at the elevators, punching the down arrow while she filled Gretchen in on what she'd learned from Elliott Calvert. The elevator dinged. Doors slid open. Josie and Gretchen waited for everyone to exit before getting on. Alone inside, Gretchen said, "Well, we know who Gia's 'mother' is now. I'm going to call the stationhouse and fill in the rest of the team. Mett can look up her registered vehicles and have someone swing by her house, although I doubt she'll be there. We can put out a BOLO for her."

Gretchen made the call as they exited the elevator on the first floor and walked out to the parking lot. In the car, Josie sat with her hands on the steering wheel, unmoving.

Gretchen said, "Boss?"

Josie's mind kept buzzing, picking up each piece of the case, discarding it, and picking it up again. "What am I missing?" she mumbled.

"What do you mean?" said Gretchen. "We've got this. We've got it figured out. Sadie and Max were running an escort service out of the hotel using underage girls from the catering and events staff. Felicia was Max's cover. A closer look into her wouldn't stick but if we came looking into the escort service, she would show up as the person who rented the rooms pretty much immediately, and that would give Max time to come up with some lies or, who knows, maybe even flee. I do think Felicia was supplying Max with drugs, though. Unrelated to the escort service."

"Yeah," said Josie. "I think you're right."

"But you're not satisfied that we've worked everything out," Gretchen said. "I can tell by that look on your face."

Josie flashed her a smile.

Gretchen took out her notebook and paged backward through her copious notes on the case. "Dina took the messenger bag, which we now know had Sadie's book in it, and that set this whole thing off. I think the way you've pieced it together is probably exactly what happened: Max blackmailed Elliott Calvert over the book, threatening to go to Discala with it if he didn't pay. Then once Calvert paid, he still didn't return the book. Calvert probably did some recon at the hotel, figured out Dina was the one with the book and then he attacked her and Alison. Fuller was probably in the same situation: he paid Max off with the understanding that Max would get the book back but then Max didn't. He had no way of knowing who had the book until Dina was killed—"

"And Alison went missing," Josie filled in. "It was on the news. That's when he started buttering up the Chief about the K-9 unit. He didn't care about that—he was trying to get inside information on the investigation."

Gretchen flipped two pages in her notebook, eyes scanning the scrawled notes. "Right. In the meantime, Gia decides to take things into her own hands. She calls her father's goons and tasks them with getting the book back. She had an inside track, though."

"With Sadie," Josie said.

Gretchen looked up from the notebook. "Yes. Gia probably found out from Sadie that it had gone missing in the first place. I'm sure Sadie confronted Max when she realized the book was missing."

"It was Sadie's bag then," said Josie.

"Maybe," said Gretchen.

"No, not maybe," said Josie. "That book was in a secret compartment. It was not casually thrown inside. It had to be Sadie's bag. The oxy were probably hers as well. Felicia may have been supplying both Max and Sadie with drugs. Maybe Sadie has her own oxy habit."

Gretchen nodded along with Josie's words. "That would make sense. She could have even been getting the oxy from Max who got it from Felicia. That might explain why the bag was in his office."

Josie stared at a family walking toward their car across the parking lot. Mother, father, daughter. "That makes sense. Sadie and Felicia hated one another. It's way more likely Sadie bought drugs from Max. They were already running the escort business together. She leaves her bag in his office, he deposits the drugs, she picks it up after. No one is the wiser."

"Until the bag goes missing," Gretchen said. "Which would have been just as catastrophic for Sadie as it was for Calvert or Fuller. It was certainly not in her best interests for that book to be floating around in parts unknown."

The mother and father flanked their little girl, each of them taking a hand. Together, they swung her into the air. She giggled convulsively. Josie could just make out her saying, "Again, again."

"But Gia didn't send her father's goons after Sadie," Josie pointed out.

"Because Sadie obviously didn't have the book."

"But she sent them after Max. Why? Max was a partner in the whole escort thing. Why would she need to get the book back from him? What leverage would he have? If he told her father about the whole thing, it would have been a death sentence. He had to have known that. Why would Gia send them to ransack his home, torture, and kill him?"

Gretchen let out a long breath. "It wasn't about the book."

"For Calvert and Fuller, it was about the book. But not for Max," Josie said.

"There's something else," Gretchen said.

The mother and father swung the girl in the air once more, higher this time, eliciting a high-pitched shriek. They all laughed. "There is something besides the book," Josie agreed. "Something very, very important."

"But the goons—and even Gia—don't know what it is," Gretchen said. "Otherwise, they would have specifically asked Dina for it." Rapidly, she turned more pages in her notebook, going backward. "Dina gave them the tablet and they accepted it but they were back days later insisting that she lied to them. They don't know exactly what they're looking for. Jesus. What the hell could it be? Do you think Alison wasn't entirely honest with you when she told you about the book?"

Josie shook her head. "No. I think that's all that was in the bag when she got her hands on it. Whatever it was— Dina had it."

"But didn't give it up even after being tortured twice?"

The mother, father, and daughter reached their car. The mother opened the back passenger's side door and leaned inside. She put a knee onto the seat and fidgeted with the seatbelt. "Because she had already gotten rid of it. She didn't even know it was important."

"The drugs?" asked Gretchen.

"No. Something else. Something that she did not want to have in her possession."

"Okay," Gretchen said. "What did she do with it?"

Father and daughter stood near the back of the car, talking, while mother got the seatbelt into working order. After a few seconds, she stood up straight and motioned for the daughter to get in. The father looked down at the girl, smiling, and ruffled her hair.

"Son of a bitch," Josie said as the realization hit.

"What?"

Rage coursed through her. Firing up the engine, she said, "That son of a bitch."

Her foot slammed into the gas pedal, and the car lurched out of the parking spot. Soon they were heading down the long hill away from the hospital.

Gretchen gripped the door handle on her side. "Who?"

"Needle," Josie said.

CHAPTER 57

The late-afternoon sun had sunk low to the horizon, leaving a cool breeze in its wake. On the shore under the East Bridge, even more cold air whipped off the surface of the churning river. Gretchen fought to keep up with Josie as she stomped from one makeshift dwelling to another calling out Needle's real name. "Zeke! Zeke! It's JoJo. I know you're down here. Come out right now."

After several minutes, a woman stepped out of her tent and told them, "Zeke ain't here. He don't stay in this part. You wanna talk to him, you go that way." She pointed in the direction of the flat rock that Josie and Noah had found him sunbathing on the other day. "He's got a little shack in them woods over there, not far from the water. You might have to wait though, 'cause he's already got some visitors." She looked Josie and Gretchen up and down. "Couple of women like you. He sure is popular."

Josie thanked her and switched direction, Gretchen huffing as she drew up beside Josie. "Paula's right," she breathed. "I really need to take up running."

"Two women," Josie said as she picked her way over mud-crusted rocks. "Sadie and Gia."

Gretchen said, "How would they know to come here?"

Josie sighed. "I told her that Dina had come to the East Bridge to get rid of the drugs. She is probably taking a shot in the dark. The two of them likely asked around until someone pointed them in Zeke's direction."

Gretchen took out her cell phone. "I'm calling this in. You didn't see any other vehicles up at the top of the bridge, did you?"

They passed the flat rock. Beyond it, the ground turned to mud. "No," said Josie. "But there are other places to park —back this way, actually, along the bank. Anyone could come from that way. Better ask for units to come in from both directions."

The riverbank narrowed until there was only a foot or two of dirt between the river and the trees. Gretchen made the call and the two of them started threading their way through the trees. The air was crisp but Josie picked up on the smell of fire, rotting food, and body odor. They were close.

"That's hardly a shack," Gretchen whispered as they found a small clearing.

In the center of it was a dilapidated wooden structure no larger than a small garden shed. Its planks had warped and peeled, now barely holding together. The hinges of the door had rotted off and so now what was left of it sat crookedly over the dark opening. Half of the roof had caved in. The odors here were even worse.

Josie put her hand on her holster, unsnapped it, and took a step forward. "Nee—Zeke!" she called. "It's JoJo."

Gretchen unsnapped her holster and glanced at Josie. "Denton PD. Mr. Fox, come on out, please."

No answer. Josie made a motion with her hand, urging Gretchen forward. They stayed clear of the doorway, moving to either side of it. Josie knocked the remnants of the door aside. "Come on, Zeke. We need to talk."

Josie heard a rustling inside and some hushed voices. Gretchen took out her pistol, and Josie did the same. They kept them trained on the doorway. A moment later, Zeke, barefoot, his threadbare clothes hanging on him, walked out. His steps were slow and careful. He held his hands up in the air. At first, Josie thought he was doing it for her and Gretchen's benefit but then, as he crossed the threshold, she saw a gun barrel pressed to the back of his head.

In spite of his predicament, he smiled at Josie as if they were old friends. "Little JoJo," he said. "Come to my rescue. How about that?"

The gun nudged his head forward, sending him off balance. He almost fell, arms flailing, feet skittering. When he regained his footing, he chanced a glance back. Sadie Bacarra put her gun right between his eyes.

Josie said, "Miss Bacarra, put the gun down."

Sadie didn't respond. She kept her eyes on Zeke, who now turned to face her. Hands still up, he smirked. "You heard her. Put that gun down."

Gia emerged from behind Sadie, blinking in the daylight. Briefly, she met Josie's eyes before looking down at her feet.

"What a shitshow," Sadie muttered.

Gretchen said, "Miss Bacarra, put your weapon down right now. Weapon down, hands up. Now."

Gia's voice was small. "You're outgunned, Sadie. Just—just let it go."

Sadie's eyes narrowed. Her hands tightened around the pistol. "Easy for you to say, you privileged little bitch. I put this gun down and I'm the one going to prison. It's your fault I'm even here. All of this is your fault."

Gia stepped forward, circling around Sadie so she could look her in the face. She stood three feet to the side of Needle. Sadie would only need to move her pistol forty-five degrees to the right in order to shoot Gia. Josie and Gretchen remained in their positions on either side of the trio, angled so that they wouldn't shoot one another if they fired, weapons trained on Sadie.

Josie said, "Put the gun down now."

Gia stepped closer to Sadie, eyes flashing with anger. "My fault? You think this is my fault? You're the one who left the damn bag laying around. None of this would be happening if you weren't so careless. You knew what was inside. You knew how important it was to me."

"You think I wanted that to get stolen? You have no idea what I had to do to get that. No idea!"

"Bacarra!" Gretchen said, voice louder now. "Put your gun down and your hands up."

"I'm gettin' tired here, lady," said Needle. "Listen, I told you I'd show you where I hid it, but you need to relax. Now you got JoJo to deal with." He chuckled. "You ain't gonna like that."

Sadie said, "Shut up."

Gia said, "Where is it?"

Before he could answer, another voice came from behind them. Male, calm and almost amused. "Well, look at this mess."

Johnny Discala and Mug Marrone stepped into the clearing. They both wore jeans, black boots, and plain black T-shirts. Each of them held a gun, one-handed, in an almost casual pose. Josie tore her eyes away long enough to meet Gretchen's gaze. They'd worked together for so long now and in so many frightening and unpredictable situations that they didn't even need words to communicate. Josie gave a tiny nod and returned her attention to Discala while Gretchen eyed Sadie, who had gone stark white, her eyes wide with shock. Still, she kept her gun on Needle.

"Daddy," Gia said. The crack in her voice made Josie look at her for a split second. Her face lost all color. She looked half terrified and half crestfallen. Josie wondered how confident Gia really was that her father would never harm her.

Josie looked back to Discala. A humorless smile curved his lips. "Princess, did you really think you could use my men, my resources, to clean up your little mess here and I wouldn't find out about it?"

Gia stepped past Josie, careful to go around her so that she didn't pass in front of the barrel of Josie's gun. She walked up to Mug. A tear slid down her cheek. "How could you?"

Mug didn't look at her.

Johnny grabbed Gia's arm roughly and spun her around, shaking her. "Look at this mess. Look what you got us into. These are cops, Gianna! Cops! How stupid could you be?"

Gia's nostrils flared. Angrily, she said, "Like you care about killing cops."

Mug said, "Johnny."

"Gettin' real tired here, folks," Needle reminded all of them. "I don't really care what you all do among yourselves, but I'll give you what I got and you can all be on your way."

Johnny used his gun to motion toward Josie and then Gretchen. "You two pigs are outgunned three to one."

From the corner of her eye, Josie sensed Sadie's shoulders slump a little with relief.

Mug said, "Put your weapons down and kick them over."

Josie and Gretchen had already decided what they would do. They only needed to stay alive long enough for the back-up units to respond. Getting in a shoot-out in which they were outnumbered, in a small clearing with two innocent and unarmed people, was not a scenario either of them wanted to engage in. Silently, they each squatted, laid their pistols in the dirt, and kicked them toward Mug and Johnny. Using his gun like he was some kind of airline runway agent directing traffic, he herded them together and made them stand with their backs against Needle's shack, to the side of the doorway.

"Good," Johnny said with a satisfied smile. He squeezed Gia's upper arm until she squeaked in pain and then he said, "Here are two ladies who are smart enough to know what's good for them. Unlike you." He tossed Gia aside and moved closer to Sadie.

Josie could see Sadie beginning to tremble. "And you. Meddling bitch. You had one job. To look after my daughter. My princess. I let you live after that shit you pulled with Antony's wife. I let you move here so you could keep an eye on my Gianna. This is how you repay me?"

Sadie's arms shook and she squeezed her pistol grip until her knuckles went white. "She came to me, Johnny. It was her idea."

He spared a glance at Gia, who stood frozen in horror, her mouth forming a small O. "I can believe that my princess asked you to use your affair with Antony to look into her mother's murder. She's been obsessed with it since it happened." Again, he looked at Gia. She flinched beneath his gaze. "Apparently, my efforts in that regard went unappreciated."

Josie's mind worked to fit these new pieces of information into the puzzle. Sadie had told them herself that she had lived in Philadelphia and recently moved back to Denton. Felicia had told them that Sadie's marriage ended because of an affair.

An affair with one of Johnny Discala's men.

Gia's mouth worked for a few seconds before any words came out. Then, "You killed indiscriminately and for no reason. You used Mom's death as an excuse to kill your... enemies. You never cared about the evidence. You murdered all those people whether they had a hand in Mom's murder or not. So many people. For what?"

Johnny glared at her.

She thrust her chin up at him, defiant.

He said, "You think I didn't gather evidence? I sent every man I had to find out who killed your mother."

"You didn't gather evidence," Gia said. "You stole it. You had it stolen from the prosecution so that the shooter had to be released. And then... then you didn't even treat him the way you treated the others. I saw what you did to the men you thought killed her." She balled up a fist and banged it against the side of her head. "It's burned into my brain. Every time I close my eyes, I see it. Nothing I do gets rid of it. Then the supposed real shooter was released and he just disappeared. That was it. Why? What are you hiding?"

Mug said, "Sweetheart."

She ignored him.

Johnny's sharp look stopped him from uttering any more words.

"It's not your job to question me, Gianna."

She gritted her teeth, making a sound that was half

groan and half growl. "I know. I'm just supposed to be your princess. Shut up. Look pretty."

He turned his attention back to Sadie. "Did Antony tell you what it was? The evidence you asked him to steal from me?"

She shook her head. "No. I didn't ask questions. Gia knew you had someone steal evidence in Renatta's case from the prosecutor's office. She asked me to look into it."

Gia said, "Asked you? I begged you, and when that didn't work, I paid you out of my earnings."

Johnny ignored Gia's outburst, maintaining focus on Sadie. She continued, "I talked to Antony. Convinced him to get it. He brought it to me in a box. I was going to give it to Gia. That's all. I never looked inside."

Johnny shook his head. With a sigh, he said, "How can I believe you, Sadie? You went behind my back. Used one of my men to betray my trust. Then what you did to my princess. Turning her out like she was some street hooker."

"She asked for it," Sadie cried. "She wanted to get away from you. She was saving up to leave you forever."

With lightning speed, he raised his gun, pressed the barrel to Sadie's head and fired.

CHAPTER 58

Sadie's body crumpled to the ground. Everyone but Gretchen and Mug startled. Needle jumped back, falling onto his rear. Gia pressed her hands to her ears and screamed.

Mug sidled over and gently touched Gia's shoulder, but she shrugged him off. "Don't touch me!" she screamed.

Josie felt Gretchen's hand touch hers. With her finger, she tapped five times against the inside of Josie's wrist. Five minutes until units arrived. That meant possibly ten to fifteen minutes until those units located them. Could they stay alive that long?

Johnny kicked at Needle's bare feet. "Get up, junkie. You have something of mine. I want it back."

Silently, Needle scrambled to his feet. He walked over to the other side of the doorway, where his sorry excuse for a door had fallen. Tossing it aside, he dropped to his knees and used his hands to clear dirt, rocks, and moss away from where the ground met the shack. A shoebox-sized hole gaped beneath the shack. Needle laid down, rolled onto his side, and stuck his arm into the hole up to his shoulder. Josie glanced over at Mug to see that he was still watching her and Gretchen. Gia stood frozen in the center of the clearing, Sadie's body between her and the shack. She watched as Johnny nudged Needle's other shoulder with the barrel of the gun. "No tricks, junkie. You got it?"

Unconcerned, Needle waved Johnny away. With a grunt, he pulled out a small metal lockbox. Once he stood and handed it off to Johnny, Mug gestured for him to stand next to Josie. As he took his place, his shoulder brushed hers. The smell of body odor was overpowering.

Johnny tucked the box under one arm and waved his pistol toward Josie, Gretchen and Needle. "Come on, Mug. Let's take care of these three and get the hell out of here." To Gia, he said, "You're coming home with me today. We'll discuss what happens to you later."

Gia raised a shaking finger and pointed to the box. "I want to see what's in there."

"You're in no position to give me orders, Gianna."

He took a step away from the shack. Gia unleashed a shriek from deep in her lungs, primal and rage-filled. Rushing forward, she slapped the box out from under his arm and pushed him away. She dropped to her knees, hands prying the lid open. Mug took a step forward, but Johnny held up a hand to stop him. With a resigned look on his face, he watched Gia lift something out of the box.

"No." The single word held a universe of pain. It went right through Josie like a knife slicing her gut. Gia held the item out like an offering of some kind, staring at it as though it was a severed head. Silent tears streamed down her face.

Josie craned her neck to see what she held. A handgun with a custom-engraved pistol grip. From where Josie stood, the engraving looked like a female grim reaper.

Gia turned it over in her hands and ran her finger over

the other side of the pistol grip. She dug a nail into a groove where one of the lady reaper's teeth used to be.

Gretchen tapped against Josie's wrist. One beat. Back-up would find them soon. They were probably already under the bridge, questioning people, and along the other side of the bank where Discala and Marrone likely parked.

Gia looked up at her father, trying to rearrange her broken expression. "Your gun?" she gasped. "You killed Mom?"

Johnny smiled and Josie had to fight not to physically recoil. He seemed to take great pleasure in his next words. "Not me, Princess." He looked meaningfully toward Mug, who hung his head, unable to meet Gia's eyes.

For the first time, neither Johnny nor Mug were looking at them. Josie tried to calculate the distance from where she stood to her discarded pistol several feet away. She'd never make it in time. Mug or Johnny—or both—would shoot her before she could even pick it up.

"No," Gia said. "I don't believe you."

"Tell her," Johnny said.

Mug looked up, a grimace stretched across his face. "It was me. I'm sorry, sweetheart. You have to understand—"

"Shut up, Mug," Johnny said. "You see, Princess, Mug is loyal to me. Not you."

"Why?" Gia cried. "Why? My mother! She was your wife!"

"She was talking to the Feds, Gianna," Johnny told her. "She was going to destroy us all. I wanted her to know the weight of her betrayal. I wanted the job done right. That's why I sent Mug. That's why I gave him my gun. So your mother would know. For all the things that Mug taught you, he never got the most important thing into your head, did he?"

Gia didn't ask what. With trembling hands, she dropped the gun back into the box and slowly closed the lid.

Johnny answered the unspoken question anyway. "Nothing happens unless I say it does."

His words hung in the air.

Barely audible, Josie heard Needle say, "They're gonna kill us, JoJo. Better do something."

Josie resisted the urge to elbow him in the ribs. He was right. As soon as this father—daughter reunion was over, they were all dead. Before Josie could come up with any sort of plan, Gia clambered forward, past her father, over to Sadie's body. She snatched up Sadie's discarded pistol and spun to face Johnny, aiming it at his chest.

Josie didn't know if he did it out of instinct or if he truly intended to harm his daughter, but he raised his pistol in response.

"Gia!" Josie shouted.

Time slowed down. With perfect clarity, Josie saw Gia's finger curled around the trigger. Johnny's face registered surprise and confusion. He, too, seated his index finger against his trigger. Josie surged forward, moving toward Johnny. He was closest. She could knock him off balance, screw up his aim. In her periphery, she saw Mug raise his own gun, aiming at her. Gia's finger tapped against the trigger. Once, twice, three times. From the corner of Josie's eye, she saw a form fill in the space between her and Mug. A fourth shot rang out. Needle and Johnny Discala collapsed at the same time.

Josie blinked back into real time, the sounds and smells of the present moment coming back to her. Somehow, Gretchen had crossed the space between them and their pistols, edging around Mug while he took the shot at Josie. Now she stood next to him, threatening him with her service weapon. She was shouting something, but Josie still couldn't hear over the echo of gunshots reverberating in her ears. But she was acutely aware that his pistol was still pointed at her chest. Her heart galloped, rattling her rib cage.

Gia stood with Sadie's gun aimed at the space that Johnny used to inhabit. Her chest heaved. When she turned toward Mug, Josie said, "Gia, no. Put it down. This is over."

Gia sniffled. "It's not over until he dies."

"Don't do it, Gia," said Josie, moving closer to her. The barrel of Mug's pistol followed her. "It's not worth it."

Mug said, "It's okay, sweetheart."

"Shut up," Gretchen told him. "Put your weapon down and your hands up. Now."

"Why?" Gia asked, as if she and Mug were the only two people there. "Why? I trusted you. More than anyone."

Mug shook his head, lips pursed. Josie knew there was no answer that would ever satisfy Gia, especially the obvious one, which was that he was a cold-blooded psychopath. Instead of answering her question, he said, "I'm sorry, Pea."

Josie stood between Gia and the barrel of Mug's gun, waiting. At her feet, Needle lay curled on his side, gasping for breath. Blood seeped from under him into the dirt. The sight evoked an unexpected feeling of fear in the depths of her heart. She hated herself for it. "Gia," she said. "Please. Just put the gun down. Don't make things worse for yourself than they already are."

Gia didn't back down.

Josie turned to Mug. "Marrone, you can shoot me, but then you'll have two guns pointed at you. Even if Gia puts hers down, you've still got my colleague to deal with and you're not fast enough to turn, aim, and fire at her before she can shoot you. We've got back-up arriving any second. As long as you're armed, there's no possible way out of this without you getting shot. You can take me with you, but you're still getting shot. Then you'll just be the guy who killed an unarmed woman before he got shot."

"An unarmed woman like my mother," Gia said.

All the energy seemed to go out of Mug. His shoulders slumped. Hanging his head, he tossed the gun aside. As if he'd done it a hundred times, he got down on his knees and laced his fingers behind his head. Gia dropped her weapon as well. She sat down right where she was and pulled her knees to her chest, rocking and sobbing. Josie helped Gretchen get zip ties around Mug's meaty wrists. Then she got down on the ground and checked on Needle. His skin was cold and clammy. She turned him onto his back. His eyes were open. She pressed two fingers to his throat and found herself relieved to find a pulse.

"JoJo," he croaked.

"I'm here, Zeke," she said. "Just hang on, okay?"

"You just go on out and play, JoJo," he whispered before falling into unconsciousness. "Go on out and play."

CHAPTER 59

ONE WEEK LATER

Josie knocked on the door to Room 407. When she didn't get a response, she knocked again. A voice called for her to come in. Inside the hospital room, Needle lay on top of his covers, wearing only a hospital gown. His arms and legs were thinner than Josie realized but for the first time maybe ever, he looked clean. One of the nurses had even trimmed his beard. The antiseptic smell of hospital soap was an absolute delight.

He grinned at her and tapped a finger on the tray table next to his bed. "JoJo, what'd you bring me?"

Josie hefted the backpack she had purchased that morning onto the table and unzipped it. She catalogued the items for him as she took them out and placed them on the tabletop. "Two new shirts, two new pairs of pants, socks, briefs, deodorant—and really, Zeke, if you only use one thing in this bag, let it be the deodorant—toothbrush, toothpaste. A comb—novel idea, I know."

He raised a bushy brow. "No one likes a smart-ass, JoJo."

Josie paused with one hand still in the bag. "Now that's just not true. I like smart-asses. They're hilarious."

He shook his head. "What else you got?"

She resumed the inventory. "A new pair of boots."

"Nothing good then."

"And a carton of cigarettes."

"Now you're talking." He grabbed the carton out of her hands, his grin as wide as a toddler's on Christmas Day.

"You can't smoke those in here," Josie reminded him.

"Nah," he agreed, tearing open the box and lifting a pack of cigarettes from it. He inhaled deeply. "But I can later today when they spring me loose."

Josie stepped back from the table. She looked at the chair next to the bed but decided not to sit in it. "Today, huh?"

"Yeah. I gotta stay at some shelter and get this wound dressed a few more times at the outpatient clinic till I'm all better. They said if I agreed to that, I could leave today."

Josie knew beyond the shadow of a doubt that he would do none of those things.

He took out a cigarette and rubbed it beneath his nostrils. Josie was beginning to think she should leave him alone with it when he said, "JoJo, what happened with that pretty girl? The one who shot her daddy?"

"Gia Sorrento? She's in a heap of legal trouble right now, but her dad left her a lot of money and her lawyer thinks that he can argue self-defense and that if she helps put away the johns in the escort case, she can get off with probation."

He nodded. "That's good, that's good."

It was certainly a good outcome for Gia, but Josie was filled with sadness whenever she thought of the widespread and deep damage the case left in its wake. The police had located the other girls who had worked as escorts for Sadie and Max. Most of them were willing to testify against the johns, but their lives would never be the same. Clint Mills had finally made it home. Marlene had been released from the hospital into his care. They had more medical bills than ever, and Alison had to live with her betrayal of Dina as well as everything else that had happened, but they were all alive. Still a family unit. The Hales were forever destroyed by the loss of their child. Even Tori Calvert and her precious Amalise were left to deal with the aftermath of Elliott's betrayal and his crimes.

"Stop looking so sad, JoJo," said Needle, drawing Josie's attention back to the present. "You done good. Solved another big case!"

Josie said, "Zeke, why didn't you tell me that Dina Hale brought you a gun when she gave you those drugs to sell?"

He grinned and winked at her. "You didn't ask."

She opened her mouth to castigate him. The entire case could have been solved much sooner if he'd just told her the truth. But her phone chirped in her pocket. She took it out to find a text from Trinity.

Where are you? The food is almost ready. Everyone's here. 12 seven-year-olds and two grown men on a bouncy slide. You don't want to miss this.

Josie smiled and tapped back, *On my way.*

When she looked up, Needle was staring at her, a look of resignation on his face. "I know you gotta go, JoJo. It's okay. You been real kind to me since I been in here, and I sure do appreciate that."

Josie felt acid burning her throat. He was giving her an out. Every cell in her body wanted to take it. Turn around, head for the door, leave, and hope she didn't see him again for years, if she saw him at all.

But her feet wouldn't move. Her mouth opened and the words spilled out. "You saved my life, Zeke."

Three times now, she added silently.

He seemed surprised by this information even though he had thrown himself in front of a bullet for her. "Guess I did, JoJo."

The words didn't hurt nearly as bad as she thought they would. "Thank you."

A LETTER FROM LISA

Thank you so much for choosing to read *Local Girl Missing*. If you enjoyed the book and want to keep up to date with all my latest releases, just sign up at the following link. Your email address will never be shared, and you can unsubscribe at any time.

www.bookouture.com/lisa-regan

As always, it has been my great pleasure and absolute privilege to bring you another Josie Quinn book. I love writing these stories for you. As with all of my books, in *Local Girl Missing* I did my best to make the police procedural elements as authentic as possible. There are usually things that I must sacrifice, change or overlook for the sake of entertainment since this is, ultimately, fiction. Do keep in mind that any errors or inaccuracies in the book are my own.

It's no secret how much I adore my lovely, loyal readers. I love hearing from you. You can get in touch with me through my website or any of the social media outlets below, or through my Goodreads page. Also, I'd really appreciate it if you'd leave a review and perhaps recommend *Local Girl Missing*, or any of the Josie Quinn titles you've enjoyed, to other readers. Reviews and word-of-mouth recommendations go a long way in helping readers discover my books for the first time. Thank you so much for your passion for this series. It means the world to me! I am so grateful for you and to you! I hope to see you next time!

Thanks,

Lisa Regan

www.lisaregan.com

facebook.com/LisaReganCrimeAuthor
twitter.com/LisaReganCrimeAuthor

ACKNOWLEDGMENTS

Incredible readers: I must always thank you first because without your relentless enthusiasm for this series, we wouldn't be here together on the page. I want to scream it from every mountaintop that you are the best readers in the world! I mean that, and I hope you know it and remember it. Thank you for being here with Josie (and me) through every adventure.

I have to give special thanks to my husband, Fred. This was the first book I turned in on time since my dad died, and almost all of that is owing to my devoted husband who kept me on track; kept me motivated; and kept me writing. He brought a lot of creativity to this book, not just in figuring out what was going to keep me focused, but to the story itself. He had amazing ideas for the plot that I've incorporated, and he was by my side for the entire process, helping me work out difficult story issues throughout. I always tell him that he missed his calling. He should be in a writer's room somewhere, creating captivating stories. I stand by that.

Thank you, as always, to my very patient and supportive daughter, Morgan, who always knows when to leave me alone and when to interrupt, and who always says the exact right thing at the exact right time to buoy me. Thank you to my first readers: Katie Mettner, Dana Mason, Nancy S. Thompson, and Torese Hummel. Thank you to Matty Dalrymple and Jane Kelly. Thank you to my wonderful friend and fabulous assistant, Maureen Downey, for doing all the things; knowing what I think and what I want before I even have to say it out loud; for helping keep me on track; for putting up with my anxiety; for making me laugh; and for being a critical early reader. Thank you to my grandmothers: Helen Conlen and Marilyn House; my parents: Donna House, Joyce Regan, the late Billy Regan, Rusty House, and Julie House; my brothers and sisters-in-law: Sean and Cassie House, Kevin and Christine Brock and Andy Brock; as well as my lovely sisters: Ava McKittrick and Melissia McKittrick. Thank you as well to all of the usual suspects for your ongoing support and for always spreading the word—Debbie Tralies, Jean and Dennis Regan, Tracy Dauphin, Claire Pacell, Jeanne Cassidy, Susan Sole, the Regans, the Conlens, the Houses, the McDowells, the Kays, the Funks, the Bowmans, and the Bottingers! As always, thank you to all the fantastic bloggers and reviewers who return to Denton again and again for each of Josie's cases and are so generous with their support!

Thank you, as always, to Lt. Jason Jay for answering all of my questions which really, truly are endless. You are so patient and supportive and I am so incredibly grateful to you. Thank you to Lee Lofland for answering all the strange and obscure law enforcement-related questions I throw his way as well as for always getting me in touch with experts whenever needed. Thank you to Stephanie Kelley, my wonderful law enforcement consultant, who so kindly and thoroughly answered all of my questions and then read the entire book, providing me with detailed notes and thoughts. I learn so much from you, and I'm so grateful to have your help. Thank you to architect Jaime Kelly who helped me to get the Stamoran Firm right. Thank you to Kisber Mettner and Sylvia Knorr for medical expertise in emergency nursing! Thank you to Dana Conlen for the name of the hotel bar/restaurant, Bastian's! Thank you to Michelle Mordan for her wonderful help with all things related to EMTs! Thank you to the following lovely readers for offering names of establishments in Denton: Candice Gold for Cadeau; Michele Taylor for the Lotus Lounge; and Amanda Schmeltzer for the Locke Heights account!

Thank you to Jenny Geras, Noelle Holten, Kim Nash, and the entire team at Bookouture, including my lovely copy editor, Jennie, as well as my proofreader, Jenny, who are, as always, brilliant. Last but never least, thank you to the greatest editor in the entire world, Jessie Botterill. What else can I say that I haven't already? You save the day with each book, always getting the very best out of me, somehow. Thank you for never losing faith in me and always being so patient. I would be completely lost without you, and I am so grateful every single day that we get to work together!

Made in the USA
Las Vegas, NV
22 August 2023

76450322R00239